T0159291

IDENTITY: LOST

IDENTITY: LOST

A Novel

PASCAL MARCO

Oceanview Publishing

Longboat Key, Florida

Published in the United States of America by
Oceanview Publishing,
Longboat Key, Florida
www.oceanviewpub.com

2 4 6 8 10 9 7 5 3 1

PRINTED IN THE UNITED STATES OF AMERICA

To my grandparents
Giuseppe Rossi and Maria Mazzocco
and
Pasquale Marcovecchio and Merceda Carlomagno.
This book is a celebration of your
enduring legacy and selfless efforts.

To my parents
Genevieve Rossi and Dominic Marco,
who challenged me to never quit.

In the dry places, men begin to dream. Where the rivers run sand, there is something in a man that begins to flow.
　　—WRIGHT MORRIS, *The Loneliness of the Long Distance Writer*

Regardless, he finished the book, a triumph of the spirit. Why must the greatest successes come in the midst of adversity? he asked himself. Or is it the adversity that forces us into greatness?
　　　　—KARL ALEXANDER, *Papa and Fidel*

Baseball, it is said, is only a game. True. And the Grand Canyon is only a hole in Arizona.
　　　　　　—GEORGE F. WILL

IDENTITY: LOST

PROLOGUE

When the judge said, "It saddens me, but as the law requires, I have no other choice but to find the defendants not guilty of murder," the victors' side of the gallery erupted into howls, followed by high-five hand slaps amongst the freed youths and their families. On the other side of the aisle, the prosecution's twelve-year-old eyewitness didn't move a muscle. Rather, he sat silent, a stunned look of confusion dominating his face. His parents, who had accompanied their son each day of the long trial, sitting like obsidian bookends beside him on the gallery's hardwood benches, however, sprang to their feet.

"They'll kill my boy!" the mother screamed. "They'll kill my sweet baby!"

"They'll hunt my son down!" her spouse cried over her pained voice.

But their fruitless pleas went unheard, overshadowed by the raucous voices that filled the cavernous courtroom from followers of the acquitted defendants. "Rangers rule! Rangers rule! Rangers rule!" supportive gang members chanted.

The judge's gaveling for the assembly to come to order was no match for the shouts from both sides—one in gleeful disrespect, the other filled with spiteful epithets for the obvious failing of the county's criminal justice system.

Through all of this mayhem, thoughts spun through the boy's head: they told me it would be an open-and-closed case; a "slam-dunker" they called it. They told me not to worry, to just tell the judge what I saw. I saw these boys kill him with my own eyes. But they didn't listen to me. They didn't listen!

The most terrible thought dominating his thinking, though, was that he knew he'd never be safe in his neighborhood again. How will I get to school without them jumping me? The police told me they'd go to jail for a long, long time. Now they're going to pay me back! *The fear engulfing his small frame prompted him to begin cracking his knuckles, panic setting into his trembling body.*

The county sheriff, who had watched him and protected him since the first threat against his life, interrupted his despair, pulling him up from under his elbow. "We need to get you out of here. Right now."

PART ONE

MARICOPA COUNTY'S
MOST RUTHLESS PROSECUTOR

CHAPTER 1

Stan Kobe escorted his wife, Maxine, and their six-year-old twins through the backyard's iron gate entrance. Smoke billowed from three Weber charcoal grills, tended by a man wearing a white apron, which had handwritten on it in black marker: CHICAGO WHITE SOX—2005 WORLD CHAMPIONS. "Can you believe this guy?" Stan chided as the family walked toward the boisterous crowd, drinking and laughing on the huge, Spanish-style patio.

What Stan had been thinking prior to arriving at Kaitlin Hanley's birthday party was the fact that just like the other three hundred days a year there wasn't a cloud in the sky as he sauntered into the festive Glendale, Arizona, gathering.

The Hanley's backyard events were always over-the-top affairs. Even at birthday parties for his kids, Brian Hanley put his best effort into making sure the adults had the most fun, and today was no exception. Beer and liquor flowed, and tiki torches rimmed the Pebble Tec pool, standing like soldiers waiting to be ignited for their winless battle against the approaching cool desert night.

"There he is, Stan the Man," Brian called, looking up, beer in one hand and meat tongs in the other. "Hey, nice pants."

Stan evil-eyed his pal. Brian had always teased Stan about the way he dressed off the job— "Early Sears, Roebuck" Brian called it—because when Stan was in the courtroom, standing before judge and jury, he never wore anything less than a cuff-linked, starched white shirt, adorned with an Armani silk tie, and topped off with a three-piece tailored suit.

"Maxine, what's it feel like to sleep with Arizona's *most ruthless prosecutor*? The man who's never lost a case."

"Well, I don't kiss and tell." Maxine pulled Stan close to her and fussed at his peach-colored polo shirt collar, tugging at the corners, flattening each one out. "Anyway, Brian, I think that's an awful nickname the press has given him. Stan's not ruthless. He's honest and truthful. As a matter of fact, he's the most decent man I've ever met. He feels for his victims, and I don't think there's anything ruthless about that."

Stan smiled at her as she gave her soulful answer to their host. He loved her so deeply. In fact, he believed marrying Maxine Marcy was the best thing he had ever done in his life. After they had met at Chaparral High School in Scottsdale, it was the only thing that kept Stan in the Phoenix area. Once he had turned eighteen, he could have left anytime and no one—not one solitary person—could have stopped him. But once he'd been smitten by her, he decided, for better or worse, to stay in the so-called Valley of the Sun.

After delivering her heartfelt defense of her husband's demanding job, Maxine smiled wide as she leaned in toward Brian, giving him a quick peck *hello*. The big Irishman lingered with his lips puckered, then made a clumsy effort to inch toward her in a futile attempt to make the kiss last longer.

"All right, you two. Knock it off. This is supposed to be a kid's party, remember?" Stan said. At nearly five foot ten, just an inch shy of his height, Maxine was a gorgeous woman with beautiful olive skin and long flowing, dark hair. Looking into her deep green eyes usually took a man's breath away. But Stan didn't mind that Brian lit up when he saw Maxine or even flirted with her. Brian was his best friend and not part of the "Pussy Posse," Brian's name for his fellow cops; macho guys always on the make.

"Louisa. Lewis. Go find Kaitlin and wish her happy birthday. I think she's in the jumping jack," Brian instructed the Kobe's twins.

Maxine urged the twins on with a gentle nudge, and they ran off to join the screaming mass of kids scattered throughout the huge yard.

"Hi, Stan. Hi, Max." Claire Hanley's high-pitched, nasal voice was a perfect match to the petite blonde's frame. She walked toward the group, holding an empty tray in her outstretched arms. Brian took the tray from his dainty wife as Claire gave a hello kiss to Maxine and then to Stan. "Good to see you guys. You're just in time to eat. Can I get you two a drink? Pop? Wine?" She looked over at her husband as he fumbled with the food on the grill. "I'd offer you a beer but I see by the way my husband's handling those tongs that Mister Weber here may have drunk us dry already." Claire playfully squeezed Brian's cheek with a thumb and forefinger.

"Hey, Stan. How 'bout one of Claire's special margaritas?" Brian suggested, continuing his fight with the uncooperative hot dogs.

"Nothin' for me," Stan said. "I'm driving."

"Well I'm not!" Maxine jumped in. "A margarita sounds great!"

Brian looked up at Stan. "Hey, buddy. I gotta show you what I did with all my dad's baseball memorabilia stuff after he died. I wanna—"

"Uh, oh. Here we go," Claire interrupted. "Let's go fix you that drink, Max, 'cause Stan's gonna be a while if he goes into my husband's new shrine."

"Just a few minutes, Claire, that's all, darlin'," Brian said. "No long stories. Scout's honor." The detective lifted two fingers in a Boy Scout salute.

"Yeah, let's see it, Bri."

Stan's attempt to throw his buddy a life preserver didn't save Brian from Claire's scowl.

He and the City of Chandler, Arizona's top homicide detective had become friends since the first case they closed together, the Tisdale murders, almost thirteen years earlier. Both discovered they had originally hailed from the Midwest—Brian growing up in Chicago before his father moved the clan to the southwestern state; Stan from Gary, Indiana—and that both loved sports, especially baseball. But they became inseparable buddies the day when, over beers, each had described themselves a "diehard" Chicago White Sox fan.

"This-a-way," Brian said, waving for Stan to follow him toward the house as he handed a tray full of cooked hotdogs to his wife.

Claire and Maxine trailed off toward the kitchen while Brian led Stan down the hallway to one of the rear bedrooms. When he walked through the doorway, Stan was overwhelmed by the collection, which crammed the modest-sized room floor to ceiling with framed photos, news clippings, and trophies of all shapes and sizes. Worn baseball bats and gloves along with dozens of baseballs, faint signatures dotting most of them, occupied every open space. Stan smiled in sheer delight and began a reverent scrutiny of the scores of items. There wasn't an inch of the room's walls that wasn't covered with some type of baseball memorabilia. "Holy cow," he murmured. To say he looked like a kid in a candy store would have been an understatement.

Brian pointed to an old black-and-white picture on the wall. "Hey, Mister World's Number One White Sox fan. Do you know what this is?"

Stan stepped over to take a closer look at the photo. "That's good old number nine, Al Smith, getting beer dumped on him during the fifty-nine World Series. Any real Sox fan knows that."

As he answered his friend, Stan felt an unexpected twinge of unease. He struggled to push away the uncomfortable sensation that popped into his head. Entering the room began as an exhilarating feeling, but the sudden confrontation with these images, all seeming to stare back at him, began to unnerve him. Stan wasn't sure he could handle the unwanted sensation rushing through him. A sense of dread began to grip his mind and his body. This powerful emotion always crept over him whenever he encountered memories from his past. He needed to shove them aside.

As a child he had honed the ability to deftly cover up his painful feelings, keeping them tightly locked up inside, not revealing them to anyone. In this room he felt different, sensing something he hadn't felt in years—a desire to just pour it all out, freeing him from his horrendous pain once and for all. He paused a moment and regained his self-control again, continuing his conversation, reminiscing about the White Sox as if his unanticipated panic attack had never happened.

"They lost the Series in six games to the Dodgers. The papers reported the next day how crushed Sox fans were. My daddy said it was one of the best Sox teams ever assembled. He knew a lot of those guys."

Now I've done it! Why did I have to mention my father? He's never asked me about my dad. Why bring him up now?

On the other side of the room, his back to Stan, Brian mumbled as he took a deep swig of his beer, "What you say, pardner?"

"Nothing. Never mind," Stan said, wanting to change the subject. He turned to another photo on the wall. "Hey, this looks like a rare one." He stepped forward to take a closer look at the oversized photograph. It hung in an oval, antique-looking wood frame. Without thinking twice, he asked Brian, "Do you know what this picture is?"

"My guess is it's one of the turn-of-the century Sox teams," Brian shrugged, walking over to him. "My dad never labeled the darn thing. I have no idea what year it was taken. Do you?"

"Yeah, I do. At least, I'm pretty certain, that is. This looks like the World Series photograph of the entire nineteen-nineteen Black Sox team. Look." Stan began pointing to the faded images, tapping with a finger on the clouded glass as he recognized the players in the picture. His voice rose with each identification. "Here's Shoeless Joe Jackson and this is Eddie Cicotte. And here's Eddie Collins. This guy here is their catcher, Ray Schalk." He grabbed the frame by its edges and pulled it closer to him. "This is an extraordinary photo, Bri. There're only three copies known to exist. There's one in Cooperstown, one at the Smithsonian, and one in the National Archives." He looked right at Brian, confused. "Where did your dad get this?"

"No idea. Like I told ya, my old man was a Chicago cop. Back in the seventies." Brian took another gulp of beer then wiped his mouth. "In those days lots of things just kinda ended up on your desk, if ya know what I mean."

Stan's facial expression matched the tinge of anger in his voice. He told himself to go no further, to drop the subject before he was in too deep, but he was too excited to stop.

"Brian, you don't understand, do you? This was the *Black Sox.* Eight guys from this team conspired to throw the nineteen-

nineteen World Series. Then they conspired to cover up their crime. They not only ruined one of the greatest teams of all time but the lives of almost every player on it. Every one of these guys you see in this picture, their lives were never the same again. Every one of them. Especially—"

Stan's voice trailed off. *Okay, that's it. Do not go any further. Get yourself out of this while you still can.*

"Especially what?"

He's my best friend. If I can't tell him, who can I tell?

"Especially a guy who played for them my father knew," Stan replied, voice quavering.

"Hey, pardner! You mean to tell me your old man knew a guy who was on the Black Sox? That is so cool. So cool!" Brian took another swig of beer. When he finished swallowing, he asked, "Did your dad ever get his autograph?"

Brian's childlike question made Stan chuckle despite his growing panic. *Only a true baseball fan would ask such a question.*

"Hey, what's so funny? I mean that is really cool that your dad actually knew someone from the Black Sox. So did *you* ever meet the old guy?"

Should I tell him? Should I finally trust someone with the story?

"Huh? What? Meet him? No. No. I never met him."

"Hold on there, pardner." Brian brushed Stan aside and moved in, pushing his nose inches from the milky-looking glass that protected the historic picture. "If this guy was on the Black Sox, he must have been like a hundred years old when your dad knew him, right?" Brian took another deep swig from his bottle of beer.

"Try eighty-five. Dad met him in nineteen seventy-five. I remember because I was twelve years old. The guy only played one year in the big leagues, nineteen-nineteen. He was twenty-nine years old at the time."

"Too wild, man. That is too, too, wild." Brian gulped again from his nearly empty bottle. "So, what was the old codger's name?"

"Hey. What are those?" Stan moved over to another wall, holding a grouping of baseball bats, ignoring Brian's last question.

"Oh, you're gonna love those," Brian said, diversion accomplished as he followed behind Stan, right in step.

A dozen or so antiquated bats covered the wall. In the center of the display, however, rested a modern-day Louisville Slugger. The pine-tarred lumber caught Stan's eye, drawing him closer. It was as if some urgent force propelled him toward the signature bat whose enormous size dwarfed all the others. Alarm bells sounded in his head, but he couldn't stop himself. Stan yanked the massive ash splinter from its bracket on the wall. He turned it in his hands a few times.

No! It can't be! He has the bat?

He shoved the bat in front of Brian's face, glaring at him. "Where did you get this?"

"Whoa! Careful there, buddy." Brian held his hands up in defense. "Dad said he got that baby right from the Bard's Room at old Comiskey Park. He said that's the bat Dick Allen hit his thirty-seventh home run with the year he led the American League in homers. I found it in one of his storage lockers the other day when I was cleaning out after he passed away. I just put it up there yesterday."

Stan's heart hammered in his chest. Even though he knew his next words might antagonize or at the very least bewilder his inebriated friend, Stan couldn't stop himself.

I've never come this close before. Do I really want to do this? Can I do this? Should I push this further?

"I know this is Dick Allen's bat and I know about Dick Allen's home run record, but your father didn't get *this* bat from no Bard's Room. No matter what he told you."

"What the heck you talkin' about?" The tone of Brian's reply sounded like that of the guy who throws the first punch in a barroom brawl. "You callin' my dad a liar?"

You're damn right he's a liar!

Stan knew he'd be entering into treacherous territory if he pushed this further. He dug down to take control of his emotions then took a deep breath before continuing.

"No. I'm not calling your dad a liar. I just know that this isn't the bat Dick Allen hit his thirty-seventh home run with. That's all I'm saying."

"How do you know that?" Brian slurred.

Oh my God! He doesn't know! His father must have never told him the story!

"Because—because I just do." *Just tell him what he wants to hear and maybe you can still get yourself out of this.* "Look. I'm sorry, man. Maybe your dad was right. Maybe this really is the Dick Allen home run record bat. I could be wrong." Still holding the bat in his hands, Stan rubbed the barrel several times, following its circular shape with the palm of his hand. He fondled the wood as if he were caressing a woman. When he got to the tip of the barrel he made an abrupt stop, closed his eyes, and dropped his chin to his chest.

"What's up, pardner? You all right? Listen, I'm the one who should be droppin' his noggin' after all the brewskies I've had today," Brian said. "So, tell me some more about your old man. How come you've never talked about him?"

Stan knew if he didn't leave now, he'd wind up telling Brian the whole story. *He's got the bat! How can I ever get around this?* He knew the moment wasn't far off from when he would have to face reality and confront the truth, not only with Brian, but also with everyone else important to him in his life, including Maxine. *Especially with Maxine.* Now wasn't the time, though. Not at a party for kids.

Like all the other times Stan had received a jolt that connected him to his hidden past, he felt the need to get out of there now, as fast as he could, before he divulged too much—before he let anyone into his protected past. He would catch hell from Maxine— *I'll be sleeping on that damn couch again!*—but that was something he was willing to accept.

Claire's chirping voice announced her return as she entered the trophy room, Maxine a step behind. "Are you boys about done in here. The food's getting cold. Those kids are hungry."

Stan opened his eyes, lifted his head, and turned to her. *Well, what are you going to do? You better get it over with.*

"Thanks, Claire, but I don't think we'll be staying to eat."

Stan was fully aware that he, Maxine, and the twins had been at the Hanley's for less than an hour. Leaving now would be difficult to explain to his friends, let alone to his wife. But his heart palpitations gave him a clear sign an imminent, full-blown panic attack was in the making after seeing and holding the Louisville. He was helpless, losing the battle that brewed inside him. Unable to control himself any longer, he pivoted. "Max, get the kids." Stan saw the stunned look on his wife's face but didn't cave in to her piercing eyes. "We need to go. Now."

Maxine felt like the rug had been pulled out from under her. Again. She watched her husband hand the bat back to Brian and walk out of the room. His demand to leave the party so suddenly didn't come as a complete shock. Married for almost two decades, this was not the first time Stan had done this to her, insisting they leave a gathering without warning and often without a reasonable explanation. And each time he had done this he acted as if someone or something had threatened him, propelling him to get out fast.

His abrupt order caused her to flashback to the time a few years earlier when her husband had insisted they leave a reception welcoming Michael Crow, the new president of Arizona State University. Maxine, a tenured history professor, was embarrassed beyond belief when, again without warning, Stan left a receiving line in which they had waited over an hour to personally greet the new university chief.

But the ASU reception was just one of the scores of times—going back as far as when they had first dated in high school—where Stan's bizarre mannerisms challenged her understanding of the man she loved. She had tried to talk with him about his odd behavior many times, but he'd always dismiss her claims with statements like, "You're imagining things, Max" or "I was just tired and wanted to go home" along with dozens of other feeble excuses.

She had even thought for a time that he might suffer from some sort of social disorder. Yet when she suggested he speak to a psychologist, he flew off the handle, berating her to "mind her own business" and that nothing was "wrong" with him.

It wasn't as if she hadn't tried to help him in other ways, either.

But she had her own pressing concerns with the pursuit of her career at the university and the demands of a tenure-track position. And once she became a mother to fraternal twins, her focus shifted almost entirely on balancing her children and her career, both of which took eventual precedence over her husband's troublesome behavioral oddities.

But even with the diversionary tactics Stan used to deal with his social conduct, Maxine remained convinced that his hurtful actions were the results of a deep-seated childhood fear. She often wondered what could have happened to cause him to bolt from social situations. Though she could never put her finger on exactly what it was or get to the heart of the matter by talking about it with him, she had always sensed her husband was hiding something from her.

Bringing her thoughts back to the present, she asked herself what could have *possibly* motivated his action today. Brian and Claire were their closest friends. Why would he want to get away from them? But this was Stan's M.O., wasn't it? His modus operandi as his fellow prosecutors called it. His habit was to discuss all his cases with her. She had heard him use this term a thousand times. She knew this was neither the time nor the place to challenge him, but now he had gone too far. He'd stepped over the line—dysfunctional as that line might be.

What will his excuse be now?

She knew by the tone in Stan's voice and the disturbing look in his eyes that the party was over for Maxine Kobe. She was embarrassed at the way Stan had just spoken to her in front of their best friends. She was torn between fighting with him right there versus following him out of the party like the supportive and understanding wife she had always been. All she had wanted to do was to have a little fun at her girlfriend's daughter's birthday party and no sooner had she arrived than her husband was demanding to leave.

She decided right then and there his habit of putting an end to her fun without any warning or even the courtesy of an explanation was a behavior that was about to come to a screeching halt. She would not stand for it any longer.

Alone now in the room with the Hanleys, Maxine glanced at Brian, standing there with a dumbfounded look on his face. Brian shrugged a "beats me" look back at her, his glazed eyes unclear as to whether he was more confused from the beer drinking or by Stan's inexplicable action. Maxine wondered how many times Brian may have experienced the same thing she had just witnessed when he was with her husband, perhaps while they had a drink at a bar, or were at an Arizona Diamondbacks baseball game, or even when they worked together at a crime scene. In all the years they had known the Hanleys, Stan had never acted this way when the four of them were together. But Maxine knew that even if Brian or Claire had begged him to stay, her husband's answer would have still been no. She knew he had made up his mind.

Maxine handed her still-full margarita glass over to Claire. "Sorry. But I guess the party's over for me and the kids." She felt guilty as she walked out, stealing one last look at the host couple as they stood in their trophy room in silence: Claire holding the pink concoction and Brian the enormous bat.

CHAPTER 2

The only discernible noise Stan heard on the drive back to their Scottsdale home came from the drone of the car's tires on the rubberized asphalt pavement. The twins had fallen asleep almost as soon as he steered the vehicle onto the entrance ramp to the eastbound lanes of the Loop 101 expressway. Another beautiful Arizona sunset faded below the horizon, unnoticed behind the silent passengers.

After nearly thirty minutes, Maxine spoke and broke the tense silence. "Why do you always do that?"

Stan was well aware that these early exits from parties without warning triggered terrible arguments with his wife. *Will I ever tell her why I have to do this?* He focused his eyes on the cars ahead of him, occasionally glancing in his rearview mirror, not looking at his wife nor answering her.

Raising her voice, she pressed on. "Why does it always seem that when I'm just getting settled in and ready to start having some fun, you suddenly want to leave?"

Sensing her hurt but more her seething anger, he desperately wanted to give his wife a truthful explanation, but his lie was now his life. So, he continued with his modus operandi and gave her his pat answer. "I don't know."

"Don't give me that 'I don't know' answer ever again!"

It was obvious that she knew his answer was another lie. A cover-up of the truth. Hadn't he seen defendants do this without flinching, lie a thousand times to protect themselves from revealing their guilt? Like his adversaries in the Maricopa County courtroom experienced him, Maxine would be relentless in her questioning until he gave her a better explanation, let alone the truth. If he didn't, they would end up fighting again and he'd more than likely be spending the night on the sofa in his home office.

"It's just that Brian thinks he knows a lot about baseball. Ah—ah—about that bat of his? He's so gullible. He doesn't even know what he's got there."

"You mean to tell me you had me gather up my family and leave a party that I was thoroughly enjoying just because you and Brian got into some sports-trivia pissing match over a goddamn baseball bat?"

I didn't think I'd get that excuse by her. She's really pissed this time.

Her voice rose. "Don't give me any bullshit that this is about some stupid baseball bat!"

Now what do I say?

"Well, I'm really not supposed to talk about it but if you really must know, you're right, it's not about the bat. It's about a case we're working on. And please, watch your language." He looked back to see if the twins were still sleeping.

"Don't you dare tell me to watch my goddamn language," Maxine exploded. "You must think I'm some kind of fool!"

"I don't know what you're talking about. What?"

"Don't '*what*' me! I have a goddamn Ph.D. I do research with some of the finest scholars in the country. I've written three books and lectured across the world. I've got six-year-old twins who try to bamboozle me every minute of the day. And now you think you're going to tell me that bolting from the Hanleys was about one of your cases you can't talk about?"

Everything was unfolding in slow motion for Stan, but he knew the best thing for him to do was to clam up and not respond to her verbal barrage. Doing so would only fuel her fire, so he remained silent. As he pulled the SUV up their driveway, he pressed the button for the garage door opener. It seemed like an eternity as he waited for the oversize steel door to completely rise. As it rose ever so slowly, he felt her glare burn a hole in the side of his head. He maneuvered the vehicle into its spot. All he wanted to do was get out of the car and run away as fast as he could from further questioning.

"Okay, Stanford. If that's how you want to play it, giving me the silent treatment, then fine with me. I'm going upstairs to my room. Why don't you just sleep in your office tonight? I'm sure you'll be up late working on that 'case I can't talk about.' Right?"

"C'mon, Max. Please. Don't—"

She slammed the car door closed. "Feed the twins and put them to bed," she shouted before heading into the house through the utility room. She slammed that door behind her, too.

Waking up sore and still contorted after a night of restless sleep on the couch in his office, Stan wished he could tell Maxine the truth. He loved her more than anything in the world, but he had kept the secret from everyone in his life, including her, for more than thirty years. He had no other choice. Lying was just something he always did. He had to. It was all he ever knew.

What good would it do now to let her know? What good could it possibly bring?

He convinced himself that explaining to her the real reason he acted the way he did, telling her about his fears, about his past, would only make her angrier that he had not told her in all these years. And her knowing the truth might make her worry about the safety of their children, too. But he knew the real reason he had held the truth from her was because he wasn't sure she'd stay with him once she knew.

There was a knock on the closed door to his den.

"Stan?"

It was Sunday morning. Sunday was their day to spend at home. The day would start with tea on the patio, then both of them futzing around the house the rest of the day with the kids. Usually, Stan would have been back from his morning jog by now; he would've already brewed a pot of tea and had it steeping, waiting for Maxine when she awoke. He knew it made her feel special when he had everything waiting for her on the patio outside their kitchen door. She had purchased a small, rattan bistro set just for that reason, so they could sit and have intimate conversations or read the newspaper over their morning brew.

He had always loved pleasing Maxine in this small way and would anticipate her walking over to him, still sleepy-eyed in her terry cloth robe, thanking him with a soft smile. It was the same feeling he had as a schoolboy when he would place an apple on the teacher's desk, hoping to please his favorite teacher.

"Stan? Can I come in?" Her sweet voice barely penetrated the heavy wooden door.

He knew whenever she asked permission to come in like this after one of their fights, like the one they had last night, she would be in an apologetic mood. He knew she still loved him, but he knew, too, that she had a right to be upset about being forced to leave a party early again due to another one of his lame excuses.

He opened the door. She stood there in her bare feet with only her nightshirt on, eyes slightly crusted in the corners. *Probably cried herself to sleep last night.* He wanted to hug her so badly.

"The kids are both at the zoo. My sister picked them up earlier this morning. We're alone."

"That's nice," he sighed.

"Will you forgive me?" she asked, giving him a hug, squeezing him tightly around the waist.

Her breasts always seemed so full in the morning but the opaque flannel garment she wore didn't allow him to see her erect, brown nipples she pressed against his chest, arousing him, too.

"You don't have to apologize, Max. I'm the one who ought to do that. I acted childish yesterday at the party. It was my fault, not yours."

"No, Stan. I understand. If you have a special case that's affecting you and Brian, then it's none of my business. I understand. I do."

He felt even guiltier as she said this, letting her believe this lie. *Why don't you just tell her the whole truth and nothing but the truth?*

"It wasn't a case, Max. It was the bat. It was about that Louisville."

Stan froze as Maxine pulled away from him. He watched the perturbed look from yesterday return to her face. It looked to him as if a switch had been thrown inside her head, rereleasing within her the emotional tide from the fiasco he caused yesterday.

"What about that goddamn bat?"

"I can't talk about it. I just can't. You don't understand. It's for your own good—"

"For my own good? Just what is that supposed to mean? If it's for my own good, then what about the nightmares you always have, waking me up screaming in the middle of the night. And what about all the other times you've demanded to leave places early, always without warning, ruining it for me so many times? And how about the constant suspicion you have of people, embarrassing me whenever I'm with you? Looking over your shoulder wherever we go? I used to think it was just the pressure of your job. Sending people to prison for life, putting some to death. But this is the last straw. Either you tell me what the hell is going on, or else—"

Stan's chest heaved with anxiety as she stopped short of completing her threat. He nervously began cracking his knuckles. He didn't want to lose one of the very few things in his life that still belonged only to him. He had suffered too much loss in his life of people he loved and never wanted to experience that feeling again. But telling Maxine what she wanted to know—what she deserved to know—was sure to be too painful for her to hear and possibly even more painful for him to share. Without thinking further, hoping all the memories of his past would go away forever, he blurted a reply to her implied threat.

"If you want to leave, then go. I won't stop you."

Stan couldn't believe those words came from his mouth.

I won't stop you? Did I actually say that?

He waited for a response. None came, but tears welled in her deep green eyes. She wiped them with the soft sleeve of her nightshirt, then turned away and ran out of his office and up the stairs.

As she did, she yelled down to him, sobbing, "You know what? Maybe it's you who should think about leaving!"

Regretting his words, Stan chased after her. When he got to the second floor, she was in their bedroom, already pulling clothes from her closet, throwing them on top of the unmade bed. He stood in the bedroom doorway, motionless. He wanted to hold her and tell her everything would be okay; wanted to tell her everything about his life and who he really was. But he remained frozen in silence.

"If you're not going to speak to me, then please leave the room—and shut the door behind you!" she said, not looking up at him.

CHAPTER 3

Maxine Kobe had scheduled an afternoon meeting with her graduate research assistant, Barbara Reyes, at her Arizona State University office. She and Barbara had decided to work on Maxine's latest book, knowing there'd be no pestering students, no ringing phones, and no annoying interruptions from other professors. Although she always spent Sundays at home with Stan and the kids, the six-hundred-page manuscript was overdue for her publisher's final edit and needed to go to print by the end of the semester. She needed to confirm a critical piece of Barbara's research work, and since she wasn't speaking to Stan, she was glad to have an excuse to go into the office.

As she aimlessly went through some papers on her desk, she couldn't help but think of Stan's reaction to her threat of leaving. After their last bitter argument two weeks earlier when he had gotten up and walked out in the middle the twins' music recital, she had threatened to take the kids and go to her parents. But this time, she had wanted to tell him to get out.

Confused as to how she really felt, she sifted through the unopened mail on her desk while waiting for her assistant to arrive. Maxine had expected Barbara forty-five minutes ago and was beginning to worry. Barbara was usually super punctual. She put the mail down and dialed Barbara's home number but got a recorded message: *"The number you have reached has been disconnected or is no longer in service."*

Thinking she had dialed the number wrong, she tried again and got the same message. A bit panicked, she thought her cell phone might be the cause of the problem since cellular service was oftentimes iffy in her cinder-block campus office. She picked up her desk phone. About to enter Barbara's number, she heard three stutter tones in the receiver, indicating she had a voice mail. She punched in her access code. The recording told her she had one new message, left at six a.m.:

Maxine. Hi. It's Barbara. I'm sorry to say I won't be able to meet with you today. I can't explain over the phone, but there is a letter waiting for you at the bottom of your mail pile. Thank you. Goodbye.

Hanging up, Maxine searched through her stack of mail on the desk. At the bottom lay a sealed, plain white business envelope with PROFESSOR KOBE typed on it.

Professor Kobe? She never calls me that.

Maxine ripped it open. Inside was an unsigned, typed letter. It read:

Dear Professor Kobe,
I am so sorry to do this to you right in the middle of all the research, but I had to leave town unexpectedly. Unfortunately, I can't explain the circumstances, but please know that if I could have stayed, I would have. I really did enjoy working with you.
                    Regretfully,
                    Barbara Reyes

Maxine's hands dropped to the desk, the letter still clutched tightly in them.

Stan jumped from his chair at the kitchen table, happy to hear the whir from the garage door opener, signaling Maxine's return. He hoped the time apart had calmed her down, as it usually did when they had this recurring argument. He couldn't recall how many times they had fought over his erratic behavior, and each time it happened, he felt more and more guilty. As she walked through the door to the garage and into the kitchen, Stan stood there, hoping for reconciliation.

"You're back early. How'd your meeting go?"

"We didn't have a meeting," Maxine said. "Barbara never showed up. She's gone."

"Whadya mean 'she's gone'?"

"Just what I said. She's gone. Left town. Vamoosed. What part don't you understand?"

"What are you talking about?"

"Here. She left me this. Read it for yourself."

She pulled the letter from her purse and handed it over to Stan. He skimmed the brief note and shook his head, saying, "Well, there must be some explanation. People don't just up and leave for no reason." He paused. "Barbara's not like that."

"I know. That's what was so great about her. She was the one person I was sure would never go MIA on me."

In the past, Stan had always chuckled when his wife used her sarcastic MIA acronym, which to her stood for: Missing in Arizona, a term she used for people who left town with no warning, something she had experienced numerous times since moving to the state. This time, though, he knew better than to laugh.

He handed her the letter back. "Well, I'm really sorry to hear that, Max. I know how much you counted on her."

"Stan?"

He could tell by the inflection in her voice she was going to ask him to do her a favor.

"Yes, Max."

"Stan?" she sheepishly repeated.

"What is it, honey? Just spit it out."

"Would you do me a huge favor and ask Brian to do a little snooping for me?"

Glad she asked him, he hoped he could use a domestic version of quid pro quo to get him out of her doghouse. "And if I do?" He grabbed her around the waist and pulled her close. "Will you let me stay?"

She forced a smile. "First, find out what happened to Barbara. This just doesn't make sense."

"I'll see what I can do."

"You will?" She put her arms around his neck. "I'm sorry about that silly argument this morning."

"You don't need to apologize. I'm the horse's ass. We've both been under a lot of pressure lately. Me with my caseload. You with your book. We need a little break."

"You're right." She pushed herself up on her tiptoes and whispered in his ear. "I got an idea of how we can take the edge off. Are the kids still at the zoo with my sister?"

When Brian Hanley arrived at work Monday morning, his telephone rang as soon as he entered his office.

"Homicide. Hanley."

"Hey, Brian, it's me."

"Hey, Stan."

"Buddy, I wanted to say how sorry I am for acting like a moron at your party Saturday."

"Yeah. Well, you did act a little strange. What happened? I mean, you took one look at dad's Dick Allen bat and—"

"No. You're wrong there. It wasn't the bat. It's just that I got sentimental there for a moment. Lots of feelings came rushing back of when I was a kid. I don't really handle feelings too well. What guy does, right?"

"You got that right, pardner."

"And I sure hope I didn't offend you, you know, in what I said about your dad."

Relieved, Brian could hear the sincerity of his friend's apology. "Hey. You're my buddy. You can't hurt my feelings. It's over. No need to mention it ever again. As far as I'm concerned, it's like it never happened."

"Thanks. I did call for another reason besides apologizing, though. I, well I should say, Maxine, needs a favor."

"You're in luck. Mondays are my do a favor for my buddy with the gorgeous wife who's too beautiful and too good for him day. What does she need? I mean besides a big strong Irishman who's not afraid of his shadow like someone I know who shall remain nameless."

"Okay, okay. I deserved that. But seriously, I need you to trace someone. Got a pencil ready?"

"Yep," Brian replied.

"Name's Barbara Reyes, 705 West Balboa, Unit A. It's a Tempe address. Phone is 480-555-9656. Find out what you can about her, wouldja?"

"You got it. I'll call you when I get a hit."

About an hour later, Brian called Stan in his downtown Phoenix office. "Hey, pardner. It's me. I ran that name for you."

"That was quick. What you got?"

"What do I got? I'll tell you what I got. I got a big fat zero is what I got. Zilch. Nada."

"What do you mean nothing? That can't be. She's got a husband and a kid. Did you cross-reference her social? Did you spell her name right? It's R-E-Y—"

"Hey, I know how to do my job. Barbara Reyes, just like you told me. I ran it with multiple spellings, first *and* last, and there's nothing on her. No SSN match. No credit history. No medical records. This babe doesn't even have a friggin' library card. It's like she was never even born."

Brian rattled off the details of his search. When finished, he told Stan, "You know, champ, if I didn't know better, I'd say she smells WP. She's got all the red flags. And if she is WP, then you can bet someone's wiped out her old ID and given her a new one already. Feds are real good at that stuff. Maybe she got flushed out?"

Brian waited for Stan's reply, but none came.

"I know one thing for sure. That's one ugly way to live, being in witness protection," Brian added. "Everyone we've ever put into it, well, let's just say, it fucks up your whole life."

Stan didn't respond to Brian's wry summation of one of the key programs used by lawyers in his office to get witnesses to talk: the promise of protection from whatever bad guys they needed to be protected from. Since he started working as a prosecuting attorney, Stan had never used Maricopa County's Witness Protection Program.

Brian had believed Stan didn't like the program since Stan had always avoided using witness protection whenever the police or the County Attorney's Office had recommended it for one of Stan's witnesses whose life might be in jeopardy. He even went so far as to ask Stan about his seeming aversion to using witness protection. He recollected now how his buddy had blown him off saying, "I'd rather guarantee my witnesses a guilty verdict and maximum sentencing, assuring them the perp will never get to them in their lifetime. And if they don't like that then I'll try the case without their testimony."

For that matter, Brian didn't like the program much himself. In his heart, he knew witness protection was a last resort. He was fully aware of the terrible consequences not only suffered by the individuals but by their entire families, prompting a very good chance of bringing about its eventual destruction. But the veteran detective also knew that in many times it was unavoidable.

"Thanks for looking into it, Brian. Maxine will appreciate it."

When Stan arrived home that night, he reported Brian's results to Maxine.

"I had Brian do a search on Barbara today like you asked," he said, sitting down at the kitchen table.

She settled the twins in their chairs and pushed them up to the table. Then she grabbed a hot Pyrex dish, placing it on the table. "So, what did he find out?" she asked, wiping her hands on the cotton dishtowel she had used to hold the hot dish.

"Nothing. He found out absolutely nothing. It's as if she never existed."

"What are you saying? How could that be?"

"I'm saying there's no trace of her. No records, like a bank account or utility bill. He even checked for a student record at ASU. Zero there, too. And not only that, there's no Social Security number with her name tied to it either."

"That's impossible! I've worked side by side with this woman for six months. I've met her husband and child. I suppose they don't exist either, huh?" She paused and stared at her husband for a moment. "Is there something you're not telling me?"

"Max, please don't shoot the messenger. I'm just telling you what Brian told me. The only thing—"

He stopped himself before he went any further. He realized all he could offer her was speculative at best.

"What *only thing*?" she asked. "You are holding something back, aren't you?"

"Well . . . Brian thought . . ." He hesitated, not wanting to broach the subject.

"What, Stan? Thought what?"

"Well, he thought she had all the signs of being in witness protection."

"Witness protection? Barbara in witness protection? You're kidding me. Right?"

He chose his next words carefully and restarted his explanation.

"I'm not saying she is. I'm just saying that Brian thinks that's what it sounds like. That's all."

"Why on God's earth would she be in witness protection? What could she have done? Or what could she have possibly witnessed that would have put her and her family in witness protection. Do you think that's why she got whisked away in the middle of the night?"

"I don't know, Max. People go into witness protection for lots of different reasons. There's no pat answer."

"Well, that's just not a good enough answer. If she is in witness protection like Brian seems to think, then how can she ever live a normal life? Do they expect her to just pull her child out of school? What about the family?"

"Hey, slow down. We don't even know if she's in witness protection. You're getting yourself all riled up for nothing."

"For nothing? You think her sending me that letter, disappearing like this, is nothing?"

"Well, that's not what I meant to say." Too late to retract his statement, he readied himself for her verbal onslaught.

"Well, then what *did* you mean when you said I'm getting all riled up for nothing? What if this was your family, Stan? What if I was in witness protection, and one night they knocked on our door and said, 'Oh, sorry to disturb you Mr. and Mrs. Kobe, but we need to move you and your family to another secret location immediately. You've been compromised.'" Maxine paused and caught her breath as tears welled in her eyes. "How about it? What if it happened to us? How would you feel?" She paused again, deepening her stare. " 'Course, how would I know? You never share your feelings! Sometimes, it's as if I don't even know you!"

Her accusation bothered him not because she was wrong, but because he couldn't deny that he believed she was right—he really wasn't sure he knew himself either.

CHAPTER 4

"I don't believe in defendants having a right to plea out their crime, Gabe."

Stan Kobe had uttered this proclamation almost two decades ago on his very first day on the job in Arizona's Maricopa County Attorney's Office.

"You may have graduated at the top of your class, Kobe, but you're living in a dream world, my friend. Pleading out cases is ninety percent of what we do here in this office. I suppose you just want a defendant to say, 'I did it,' then lock him up and be done with it?"

Stan's new office partner, veteran Assistant County Attorney Gabriel Lowen, didn't hold back on the rookie. Stan thought for a moment about Lowen's comment.

"Hey, call me crazy," Stan replied, "but I just don't believe criminals should have a right to a plea bargain. You probably think that just because I'm new I can't be old school. But I don't care. That's my belief. That's who I am." Stan pointed his pen in a jabbing motion at his new colleague. "I say, once we have them behind bars we keep them there and don't give them a chance to get back out on the streets."

From the very first day he entered law school Stan had always been a contrarian on this philosophy of how criminals were maneuvered through the judicial system. Indeed, Stan was contrary to all who had come before him. In 1988, he had become the first African-American to graduate magna cum laude from Arizona State University's School of Law. He married a girl completing her Ph.D. at the same Tempe school, and when he was offered a job as a county prosecuting attorney, it sealed the deal on deciding once and for all to remain in Phoenix's "Valley of the Sun." Although he had dreamt of leaving this "godforsaken place"—his own words for how he felt about where he lived since moving there with his family more than a dozen years before—Arizona was now home.

During his first year on the job at the County Attorney's Office, the most frequent cases assigned to Stan dealt with minor crimes like burglary, parole violation, unlawful use of a weapon, DUI, and the like. He relished these mundane prosecutions as they helped him hone his legal skills. He performed most of his own research, not relying upon law clerks to miss something and screw up his chance to win. He doggedly handled every case. If his case involved a victim, especially one harmed in the commission of the crime, he relentlessly pursued a full conviction. The overused and status quo approach of plea bargaining had no place in this rookie prosecutor's legal approach.

Stan Kobe was a rising star and he let nothing or no one stop his historic flight.

As the years progressed, so did Stan Kobe. He challenged and often circumvented the rules in his position as an officer of the court, becoming the most successful prosecuting attorney in the nation's forty-eighth state. And, as the lone black man in the lily-white office, he had much to prove. To say that Arizona was a little behind the times in terms of affirmative action was an understatement. Arizona wouldn't recognize the national holiday for Martin Luther King until 1993, ten years after it was passed as the law of the land, and was the second to last state to acknowledge the federal holiday. Stan personally led the challenge to successfully impeach then-Governor Evan Mecham, an open bigot, who had cancelled recognition of the federal holiday on the state level.

To prove his competency to those who believed a person of his color was inherently inferior, he prosecuted every criminal so they got the harshest penalty available by law. Neither the circumstance of their case nor the color of their skin mattered in Stan's approach.

"Someone must have done you wrong, Kobe," defense attorney John Barclay had accused him once after losing to Stan in a benchmark case. Stan had won the litigation on the state's behalf and put the defendant behind bars for twenty years in a second-degree deadly DUI case.

"Nobody's ever done me any wrong, John. I just believe in doing what's right. Upholding the truth. Protecting the innocent. I wish you could do the same thing, but it will never happen when all you do is represent scum. I sleep at night."

By the early nineties Stan Kobe would come to be known not only as Maricopa County's most successful prosecutor, but its toughest. He welcomed the state legislature's passing that decade of Arizona's mandatory sentencing laws, which became some of the toughest in the nation. Defense attorneys and public defenders cringed when they found out Stan Kobe had been assigned to prosecute their case.

"Stan, you're the most unreasonable prosecutor I've ever met." His opponent again was his old nemesis, John Barclay. The stodgy defense attorney had uttered those words in the hallway outside the county courthouse the umpteenth time the two faced each other. Barclay had tangled with Stan many times during their careers, always ending up on the short end of the stick.

Barclay's whining this time had been the result of his losing a pretrial hearing to Stan. For weeks prior to that hearing, the tenacious black prosecutor deprived his now full-time law clerk staff of sleep as they tirelessly researched the case. Acting like the proverbial slave driver—his clerks teasingly called him "Massa Kobe," at which he beamed when chided with the name—Stan drove them until they found a legal loophole in their favor.

"Do your homework better next time, John, when you come up against me. Especially when you're trying to put filth back on the street," Stan told Barclay.

Stan's determination to win every case gave reason for his meteoric rise in the Maricopa County Attorney's Office and would pave the way for his biggest accomplishment. The year was 1992 and the Arizona legislature had reinstated the state's death penalty. The Maricopa County Attorney's Office had changed its stance since Stan Kobe had been hired. Plea bargains for life sentences with the possibility of parole were no longer on the table as a bargaining chip. Stan Kobe had made this a thing of the past for those perpetrating the most heinous crimes.

"Stan, you're my go-to guy, aren't you?" Rick Romley, the chief county attorney at the time, had asked one day as Stan sat in his boss's pristine, corner office in downtown Phoenix. "I want a conviction on the first case we get with the death penalty on the table. You up to it?"

Without flinching, Stan replied, "I'm your man, sir."

"Good, because I want to send a message that on my watch anyone who commits a felony crime in Maricopa County and kills someone while doing it will get the maximum sentence allowable by law. Even if it is the death penalty. You make sure that message gets delivered, Stan, and the first animal to get our little telegram is Tisdale."

Romley referred to one Jon Patrick Tisdale, the man who had set fire to his own home in an attempt to cover up his crime after bludgeoning to death his wife and three small children. The forty-four-year-old chemical engineer at a Chandler, Arizona, Intel plant had piled up huge gambling debts at an Indian gaming resort. Despondent over his inability to pay his bills, Tisdale became an abusive and drunken husband and father. His wife had the court issue a restraining order against him to stay away from their Chandler home and five hundred yards away from her and their children.

Enraged over the ruling and after again losing large sums of money at another local casino, on the night of November 16, 1992, Tisdale drove his Chevy Tahoe through the garage door of his adobe-style home and proceeded to massacre his family as they attempted to flee the house. He then torched the structure with his children inside and took his wife's blood-drenched, lifeless body with him. From there he proceeded to butcher her corpse and painstakingly dispose of the woman's body parts in Dumpsters all across the City of Chandler. When authorities sighted him, Tisdale fled. A two-hour car chase ensued, involving five police agencies, until he was finally apprehended in the desolate outskirts of southern Maricopa County.

The case seemed to weigh particularly heavy on Stan. For

weeks he barely ate and would bicker with Maxine over the smallest things. He refused to leave the house for nearly the entire trial, hiding, he had told his wife, from the press. For six months, he stayed holed up in his home office, and only once left the house with Maxine when they attended a late-night movie.

The Tisdale jury had needed only four hours of deliberation to reach their unanimous verdict. Stan's prosecutorial effort—afterward described as "flawless" and "with testimony beyond reproach from his superbly prepared witnesses" by reporters' coverage in the *Arizona Republic* newspaper—came from reams upon reams of evidence garnered by Chandler Homicide Detective Brian Hanley. Tisdale was found guilty on three counts of first-degree murder and one count of second-degree murder.

During the subsequent sentencing hearing, the judge would hand down the death penalty to a sobbing Tisdale. Just after he did, the Maricopa County prosecutor rose and asked the bench for permission to address the court in the matter of setting the execution date. Stan's statement to the judge, jury, and family members of both the victims and the convicted would be displayed on the front page of the next day's *Arizona Republic* newspaper. A portion of it read:

> . . . and what more fitting day, your honor, could be chosen than this day I am requesting, sir, as the very day to put to death such a heinous felon as sits before you here today. It is on this very same day we celebrate our freedom, our freedom to rid ourselves of scum such as him from society. A day we must cherish without fear just like the 364 other days of the year. We cannot—we will not—allow a vicious murderer, a man who callously and selfishly slaughtered his entire family, to dare think that he can take away from us our God given right to be free from fear by his brutal acts or to attempt to shatter our dream to live our lives peacefully upon God's earth in the greatest country in the world.

The judge agreed with the Maricopa County Attorney's Office unique request—death by lethal injection on the Fourth of July.

On that day in attendance at Tisdale's Independence Day execution—a first in the history of the United States—besides the required state penitentiary personnel in Florence, Arizona: Stan Kobe, Rick Romley, and lead homicide detective on the case from the City of Chandler Police Department, Brian Hanley. An editorial in another edition of the *Arizona Republic* would herald the event, in part, thusly—

> . . . in a return, finally, to how justice should be done in one of the last remaining places of our true, Western tradition—THE GREAT STATE OF ARIZONA. Every Arizonan, we believe, owes their respect, admiration, and thanks, as we do, to Stan Kobe. This man has rightfully earned the title we give him here today as Maricopa County's Most Ruthless Prosecutor.

As they walked together out of the prison that day after Tisdale's execution through a secure back gate away from the media's view, Stan spoke to the detective. "Great police work, Hanley. Without your work I could have never gotten this result. County Attorney's office needs more cops like you."

"I was just doing my job. And, by the way, after all we've been through I think you can call me Brian."

Stan nodded to him.

"Just the same, I admire you. Makes a prosecutor's job easy." Stan held the gate for him to walk through.

"I can't take all the credit. I had a great teacher. My old man was a cop."

"So, your father was police, too, huh?"

"Yep. Ed Hanley. He was one of the last of the old school. A cop's cop. Worked homicide on the South Side of Chicago. I'm fifth generation blue. Love my job. I want to put the bad guys behind bars just as much as you do and put them to death, if necessary. I do it the only way I know how. Just like my old man."

Stan stopped dead in his tracks. Brian looked at him. They stared at each other for a moment.

"Something wrong?" Brian asked him. "You okay?"

Stan gave his head a few quick nods. "Me? Oh, yeah. Sure. Fine. Just thinking about what you said."

"What part? The part about me loving to put bad guys in jail or about my dad?"

"Yeah. I mean, no." Stan stumbled over his words. "I mean, the part about you loving to put the bad guys behind bars. That part. It's rare to meet law enforcement people who truly love to do that. Who relish those three little words from the jury foreman—'guilty as charged.'"

"Hey. Why don't me and you get together for a beer?" Brian suggested. "I'm sure we have a lot more in common."

"Oh, we do have a lot more in common. More than you know. Especially when it comes to good police work. In that regard, you and I are like two peas in a pod, my friend. Two peas in a pod. But I gotta run. I'd love to have that beer, though. Give me a call sometime." Stan rushed off, but before he got too far away, he turned back to Brian and asked, "You like baseball by any chance?"

CHAPTER 5

It had been nearly five days since Stan had spoken to Maxine. He wasn't sure what had kept him from apologizing to her. More than likely it was his bruised ego: she had accused him of having no feelings. Still unsure of how to deal with the situation, he had decided to keep his distance during the past week. This was his method of handling these stalemates.

Her biting words that he never shared his feelings were nothing new to him. But it still hurt him deeply, mostly because he knew she was right. He had kept his feelings hidden and bottled up inside since he was a boy, never sharing them with anyone— not even with his momma and daddy—since that day his life changed forever.

Who would listen anyway? And what would I tell them? What good could it possibly do to be honest with Maxine now? What she doesn't know won't hurt her.

But obviously, it had and still did hurt, since he felt her anger permeate their home, invoking an uncomfortable silence the entire week.

When Stan arrived at work Friday morning, Brian had already called and left a voice mail message for him. He listened to it.

> Stan. Hey, it's me, pardner. Call me pronto, would-ja? I need to talk to you about a big bust we made last night. We collared some pretty bad hombres and we want to bring charges against them right

away. And, hey, this one might make some more headlines for you, buddy.

Stan immediately tapped the switch hook down on his phone, got a dial tone, and called Brian at Chandler PD.

"Homicide. Hanley."

"Hey, it's me. I got your message. What's up? What you got?"

"Hey, pardner. We got a big one, that's what we got. The multiagency task force I've been working on the last three months may have hit the mother lode last night. We caught a couple of desperados from up north, Chicago way. Seems like scum from that part of the world's moved down to a warmer climate."

"That's all this county needs," Stan scoffed.

"Ain't that the truth. Well, anyway, we think these guys are working for a major connection up there, doing their bidding for them down here. You know, the usual happy shit—drugs, guns, money, and blowing the other guy's brains out over one or the other."

"So what do you have on them? Anything that will stick?"

"We ran a system-wide check and it seems they both have outstanding warrants back in Chi-town. Before our task force leader from the U.S. marshal's office contacts the local Chicago PD, Department of Homeland Security wants them kept under wraps here. Some political thing from what I've heard. But DHS wants to stay in the background, out of sight on this one, 'cause the feds are investigating some type of organized activity that could be tied in to some politicians up north. Word is they're looking at some people pretty high up. Scuttlebutt going around the unit here says even Chicago PD may be dirty on this."

"Infiltrated the police, too, huh? Let's hope for everyone's sake that's not true," Stan replied.

"You got that right. Last thing we need in this fucked-up world right now is finding more dirty cops. Anyway, that's why they want your boss, Andy Thomas, to step in. Our task force chief says he wants Thomas to charge them under the pretense of how the governor wants to make an example of them, show the voters how much her office is doing to protect our borders, spin it so the governor can use it for her next election. You know, like, 'Don't think you can come to Arizona and fuck up our state like the snowbirds,' that kind of PR bullshit.

"Personally, I don't care which way they slice it. These two we arrested were planning to do some very bad stuff. We're pretty sure they're running machine guns down to the Sinaloan cartel. We need to lock these two pieces of shit up and throw away the key."

Stan had been around the block and knew how to read between the lines of Brian's story, namely, if the feds were involved, somebody's political ass was being greased for some future election. But he also knew if they wanted to send this one to the county attorney's charging unit, then Stan would need to have something solid from Brian to charge them with. "Well, what are we holding them for right now besides the warrants. Did they break any laws here or not?"

"We don't have a local crime to hold them on, but I talked to some of the feds I'm working with and they're looking into the possibility of having them brought up on conspiracy charges," Brian replied.

"Federal conspiracy charges?"

"You got it. Besides what I just mentioned, we also busted them on tribal land last night. Since it was on a reservation, any bust made there gets the feds involved. But that's a plus. There's a lot more leeway since nine-eleven in bringing charges against these mothers, especially federal conspiracy charges of any kind. The feds can even treat the fuckers like terrorists if they want, especially since they suspect them of planning on bringing heavy weapons down and moving them across the border. They can make their life a waking nightmare. Hell, if these two Chicago ass wipes are Cubs fans, that would be even sweeter," Brian snorted.

"That would be too lucky. Where are you holding these guys now?"

"They're over at the Fourth Avenue Jail," Brian said.

"Have they lawyered-up yet?" Stan asked.

"Not yet. We're keeping a tight lid on this, but you better get on this right away before some bleeding-heart federal PD gets wind of it 'cause they'll have to start defending these suckers the moment they find out they got arrested on the rez."

"Send the paperwork over STAT, and I'll get on it right away. I might have to call someone over at the federal DA's office for some direction on this conspiracy stuff though. I don't want to tread on any of those thin toes over there, and besides, conspiracy law isn't my forte."

"Hey, the Stan Kobe I know has no weaknesses," Brian poked at him. "Do whatever it is you need to do to do that thing you do best—bringing the hammer down on these cocksuckers."

"You don't have to worry about that," Stan boasted.

"And another thing," Brian added. "Just make sure when the *Arizona Republic* interviews you this time, you get my name in there somehow, wouldja?"

"Don't worry, Bri. I'll make sure you're mentioned. I'll even give them your home address."

Not one to be outdone, Brian replied, "You do that, my friend, and I'll give *The Phoenix New Times* the address to that little fishing cabin of yours up in Payson, your personal cell phone number, and the titles of the DVDs you rented for that rookie Ramirez's bachelor party last week!"

CHAPTER 6

After Brian explained more details on the particulars of last night's arrest, Stan called an old ASU law school classmate working in the U.S. District Attorney's office in Phoenix. The two graduates had parted ways after law school but had reconnected a few years ago at a state bar association dinner where Stan had received an award.

"U.S Attorney's Office. Zadnik."

"Jake. Stan Kobe."

"Hey, Stan. Good to hear from you. How's that beautiful wife of yours and the—twins — right?"

"They're fine, Jake. Just fine. I'll make sure to tell Maxine you asked about them."

"Great. So, what can I do for you?"

"Jake, I need some help. Seems a local multiagency task force rounded up some guys last night on the Gila Indian Reservation. We're holding them right now at Fourth Avenue."

"Yes. I heard about that when I got in this morning. Anytime there's an arrest on the rez we get a ping. How are you involved?"

"Well, I don't know yet. Depends on what we can charge them with. A sting went down last night at the Comfort Inn off Interstate Ten in Ahwatukee. The perps fled the scene, ended up on the rez, and got in a smashup out there with their rental car. They also got some outstanding warrants from Chicago, so we really should notify the local PD there and start extradition proceedings. But the scuttlebutt here is that you feds want to keep these jokers in our local jurisdiction. Try them here and make an example of them. You got any inside info on that?"

"None that I've heard yet. But you probably know our office has been doing a press release a week about how serious we are about vigorous prosecution of gunrunners."

"Got any idea how we can hold them and stall the federal defender's office until I can take a look at their files and get over there and see them? I'm worried a federal P.D. could be appointed before we get to these two. I'm sure he'll advise them to clam up. "

"I could take a look at the Patriot Act. That thing gives us a lot of leeway now," Zadnik replied. "Also, if you had any federal officers, like Border Patrol, in your task force during the pursuit, we could probably talk to the folks over at Homeland Security. If we can get them onboard, we can bring them in on your behalf."

"I just spoke to a cop buddy who was there last night, and he mentioned a U.S. marshal is heading up their group. My buddy tells me these two Chicago bad guys were in town to meet with a Mexican drug cartel connection coming up from Sinaloa in Sonora. They have them on tape, discussing their plan to smuggle in some illegals and cash as well as move a large shipment of crystal meth north to their base of ops in Chicago. In return, they were planning to send some pretty heavy firepower back down across the border."

"If that information is solid and it will hold, then I'd say you got probable cause to charge them with trafficking the methamphetamines, the aliens, the cash, and the guns and, of course, probably a conspiracy charge to commit all of the above."

"I'll have to brush up on my understanding of federal conspiracy law."

"Don't worry about that. We'll help you on that from here. Anyway, you should be able to hold them for a little while without any problem on a state level in regard to their flight from pursuit. If you can do that, I can find out more about these guys and exactly what is going on around here with them. That would give me time to check it all out and see how high up this goes."

"Whatever you can do I'd appreciate it, Jake."

"No, problem. I'll be in touch. Oh, and Stan?"

"Yeah?"

"Make sure you say hello to that wife of yours."

As he hung up the phone, one of Stan's assistants came into his office and handed him the files on the two men arrested last night. Stan read their names, which were neatly typed on the tabs of the crisp, new manila folders: TURNER, P. and DeSADIER, R.

This can't be right!

Stan bolted from his chair, files still clutched in his hand, and headed for the hallway. As he ran past his secretary he shouted to her, "Yvonne, call me on my cell phone, but only if absolutely necessary!"

When he reached the bank of elevators, he pressed the down button repeatedly as if the more times he pressed it the quicker it might come. While he waited, he frantically flipped through their folders, reading their rap sheets.

What in the hell are these two doing down here?

Once on the ground floor, he made a beeline for the Fourth Avenue Jail, two blocks away. When he arrived, the guard at the door recognized him and immediately buzzed him in.

"Mornin', Mister Kobe."

Stan didn't reply. He made his way toward the intake holding cells in the basement of the building. Once there, he flashed his ID and shoved the two manila folders up against the gate, showing them to the guard and pointing to the names on the tabs.

"Turner and DeSadier. Where are you holding them?"

The guard behind the wire mesh squinted and cocked his head as he tried to focus on the folders pressed against the gate's screen.

"Those two? Holding Tank B."

Tank B? These two need to be in maximum security. The county sheriff's people have no clue who they're dealing with.

"I need to see them now!" Stan shouted.

The guard buzzed the gate's lock. Stan threw it open. He scurried to reach the Holding B wing. When he got there a guard Stan had known for years lounged outside the cell. He greeted Stan.

"Hey, Mister Kobe. You must be here to see those desperados Detective Hanley brought in last night. It was pretty late. But ol'

Jackson here is watchin' 'em good now. Hey? You and Detective Hanley workin' together again? If so, these two got no chance. No chance in hell is what they got o' gettin' outta here."

Stan acted as if he didn't hear the old-timer while the guard continued his banter.

"You sending these guys somewhere? I heard scuttlebutt they're being moved," the guard said, walking toward the gate."

To hell is where I'd send them if I could.

Stan still offered no reply, waiting impatiently as the guard fumbled his ring of keys, looking for the correct one to open the next gate to the hallway that led to the Holding Tank B observation rooms. Stan felt the adrenaline rushing through his body as his heart pumped wildly. He was sweating profusely now and wiped his brow and upper lip with his handkerchief. He loosened his tie and opened the collar to his starched white shirt.

"You okay, Mister Kobe, sir? You look like you seen a ghost."

"Jackson, please. Will you please just stop asking so many goddamn questions and open up this goddamn thing?"

"Yessir, Mister Kobe," the old guard said as he lowered his head. "Yessir. Sorry, sir. Jackson's just makin' small talk, that's all, Mister Kobe, sir."

Once opened, Stan rushed past him and went down the hallway to one of the observation rooms. The windows in the room were one-way, enabling him to see the prisoners without them seeing him. As he entered the darkened room, he tiptoed up to the glass. When he looked through it, he observed two men, each wearing the ubiquitous orange jumpsuits issued to those incarcerated in the Maricopa County jail. One of the men wore a patch over his eye.

"I can't believe this," he mumbled to himself. "These two motherfuckers are still alive. They're still fucking alive!"

"Who's still alive?" Brian Hanley flipped on the light switch for the bank of fluorescent lights recessed in the ceiling. Stan hadn't noticed him sitting in the back of the dimly lit room.

Startled, Stan turned to him and shouted, "Turn those lights off! And keep your voice down. I don't want them to know we're here." He wondered why Brian was already in the room. *He must have called me from here.*

"Stan? You okay? You've been in this Tank B observation room a hundred times. You know they can't see or hear us. Do you know these two, pardner? You seen them before or something?"

Stan paused, taking deep breaths, wiping his face again. Then he started cracking his knuckles and answered Brian without looking at him. "What? Know them? No. Of course not. How would I know them?"

"Well, then, what is it? 'Cause you're acting like a rookie prosecutor facing his first murder perp. I can feel your ass puckering from here."

"Sorry, Bri. I don't know what got into me." He stopped cracking his fingers and turned, looking directly at his buddy cop, then motioned back to the window. "I read their sheets. These fucks are worthless shits. I checked out your arrest like I promised with a friend over at the federal prosecutor's office. From what he tells me, I don't think the County Attorney's Office can hold and charge these guys with anything that will stick. So Chicago PD can have them. As a matter of fact, I'll phone the county attorney right now to get the extradition paperwork started right away." Stan reached into his pocket and pulled out his cell.

"Hold on there, pardner. What did you say? Extradition? You're going to extradite them on some petty theft warrants back in Chicago? That's not part of the plan. Were you not listening to what I told you earlier? We got these fuckers on tape conspiring to transport a truckload of meth, five hundred thousand in cash, human cargo, and guns across the border. What the hell you talking about extradition? What the fuck is going on here?"

Stan put his cell on the table and took his handkerchief back out of his breast pocket. He wiped his face and neck and then folded it and put it in the back pocket of his pants. He resnapped his collar and straightened his tie. "Just what I said. I'm turning them over to Chicago PD. And if they don't want them, then the feds can have the fuckers. Anyway, the feds have priority over this, so the county wouldn't be part of it anyway. And even if we did, my plate's full. I've got two cop murder trials pending and the Bee-line Highway serial killer case. I got no time for prosecuting ant-piss gangbangers from Chicago."

As his own rage subsided, Stan could see Brian's Irish temper boil as the detective picked up the two manila folders Stan had thrown on the table when he first entered the room.

"What the hell's going on with you, man? I don't give a shit if the feds have supremacy here. The Stan Kobe I know would do whatever he could to get a chance to prosecute this case and throw the book at filth like this. For crissakes, they were planning on tak-ing these drugs to Chicago and would probably end up selling the shit in school yards up there!"

Stan turned his back on Brian and didn't answer his accusa-tions, remaining silent as his mind stayed focused on the prison-ers—men he had believed he would never see again. He made a final adjustment to his tie in the window's reflection, wheeled around and grabbed his cell phone off the table. Without looking up, he walked out of the room.

Outside the building, Stan stopped and sat down on the nearest street bench, nearly collapsing. He once again loosened his tie and spread open the collar of his shirt. He struggled to breathe, chest tightening, trying not to look as desperate as he felt.

This isn't real. This isn't happening.

He fought to take deep breaths, wondering how he could keep his past hidden any longer after laying eyes on Pokie Turner and Bobby DeSadier. He cracked his knuckles nonstop. If he prose-cuted these two, there'd be no way to keep his lost identity hidden any longer and he couldn't allow that to happen. His life was un-raveling right before him; his past had caught up with him at light speed.

A nearby construction crew was hammering structural steel py-lons into the ground with a steam-powered pile driver, working to anchor the foundation of a new building's parking structure. The deafening noise rattled inside Stan's head with the repetitive bang-bang-bang of the incessant machine's pounding.

Wham! Wham! Wham!

Please stop! Make them stop! Get me outta here! Make them stop!

Maxine. The twins. How will I protect them?

He pulled out his cell and dialed a number.

"Jimmy? Yeah. It's me. I need a big favor."

PART TWO

MURDER IN MR. BURNHAM'S PARK

CHAPTER 7

FRIDAY, MAY 16, 1975
2:30 P.M.

No one enjoyed traveling to Chicago's Burnham Park more than twelve-year-old James Overstreet. Located on the city's near South Side just east of bustling Lake Shore Drive along the great lake called Michigan, he liked to go there everyday, either by foot or bicycle.

On school days, especially spring ones like today, James would travel up and down the park well before the bell rang, a time he would most likely be alone, save for the occasional angler. He'd return after school for another visit, as this was his regular routine. With the weekend looming, the precocious boy would spend extra time exploring the park's least used spaces. One of his favorite places was a desolate area where huge, pointed rocks jutted out all along the shoreline. Except on the calmest days, enormous waves from this majestic lake crashed against these limestone ramparts that protected the park's fragile shore from the relentless barrage.

A bit of a daredevil, James liked to leap back and forth across these sharp, white boulders, playing his own treacherous version of hopscotch. One false move, or an overzealous slip, would send him tumbling into the lake's unforgiving embrace. In testament to the danger, an unsuspecting lake admirer, venturing out too far on these lonesome jagged monoliths, would find himself swept into the water's deadly cobalt depths by a merciless wave. Back in the 1930s WPA workers had removed most but not all of these tempting yet dangerous rocks, replacing them with smoother, friendlier versions in an effort to make the area safer. Workers sculpted massive stones and placed them in neat rows, creating huge steps that cascaded from the grass twenty or so feet above, to the shoreline below.

Sometimes, as an adventurous change, an impulse took hold of James and he would tiptoe along the last row of these rock steps, the ever cold, uncaring, deep blue water only a few feet below him. One time, he ran as fast as he could along the edge of this bottom row, just out of reach of an immense wave that chased him, challenging the frothy opponent.

"Crazy little nigger!" someone on the grass above shouted at him. The yell caught James by surprise as he played his one-sided game of tag. But James paid no attention to the unseen voice, knowing danger would not come to him if he kept his cool. Though often unpredictable, he had nothing but respect for the mighty power of this massive body of water.

He felt no animosity toward the unknown voice's derogatory shout. James Overstreet held no deep-seated anger most boys his age already exhibited, an outcome of being raised in broken homes. Boys starved for love and attention in a poverty-stricken environment. James was fortunate in that regard, though. Parents who cared for him, brothers and sisters who loved him, teachers who welcomed him into their classroom, and classmates who admired him, fostered his warm demeanor.

He knew one of his greatest gifts, however, was living just a few short city blocks from the magnificent, indigo-colored lake and being so close to its expansive presence. Visiting her gave James the ultimate feeling of freedom, especially from the cramped basement apartment where he lived with his family near 39th and Ellis Avenue. Now a seventh grader, he attended the new Jackie Robinson Writing and Literature Academy, an experimental magnet school for gifted students, one of Chicago's very first. His mother, a short but stoic woman, had stood in line for hours on a cold, damp March day when applications initially became available, assuring her bright baby boy was among the first to be enrolled.

James Overstreet wasn't like most boys from his neighborhood.

For one, he never cursed—both his momma and daddy forbade it. The child loved learning new things and always participated in class discussions, rarely missing school. This was most unusual for a child his age. Boys from his neighborhood often dropped out of school by the time they were ten. But not James. He was a model student, a teacher's dream. The boy showed promise.

He did love to daydream, though. In school today, his teacher had demanded to know where the boy's reverie had taken him.

"Mister James Overstreet, what are you dreaming about now?" she asked.

Intended to snap the miles-away James to attention, her shrill voice jarred the entire class from the final period geography lesson she was giving on Arizona and the Grand Canyon.

"Nothin', Miss Burns," a sheepish James replied.

"That's noth-*eeng*, James. There is some-*theeng* at the end of noth-*eeng*, James, and it's called a '*g*.' Got that?"

Miss Burns always emphasized her *g*'s each time she repeated this precise phonics lecture. She did it exactly the same way every time she dispersed it, which seemed much too often to him. However, it did amuse him the way her tongue darted out between her large, white teeth, surrounded by her dark, pinkish-brown lips, emphasizing the *th* sound before the *eengs*. A frog catching flies, he imagined. James pictured Miss Burns on a huge, green lily pad— her hair tightly pulled back, making her eyes bug out so she could see all around her—catching flies as they buzzed in front of her, like the toads that lived along the crags of the lakeshore rocks he jumped about every day.

"Do you want your poor mother who worked so hard to get you into this school to think you're not learning some-*theeng* in my classroom, young man?"

James shook his head, keeping it low, hoping Miss Burns didn't see him roll his eyes. The month of May had arrived and he and his best friend, Clayton Thomas, couldn't wait for school to let out for the summer. It was the boys' daily job now to use the long, wooden poles needed to open the tops of the classroom's floor-to-ceiling, double-hung windows, facing the lake just a half mile away. Once opened, the smell of the nearby lake would waft through the huge openings: part air, part sky, and part fish. With spring now in full bloom, the scent of freshly mowed grass added to this sweet bouquet, teasing the children as the cool air washed across their bare arms, legs, and faces. No more boots, no more jackets, no more gloves and earmuffs were needed now. All these cumbersome items had been left at home, freeing the children to have their daily recess in the basking warmth of a Midwestern sun.

The biology of spring in Chicago meant everything came alive again, including the schoolchildren, and all of them, even Miss Burns, could feel the electricity of the changing season in the air. As each day advanced and the memory of winter's dreariness lapsed further and further behind them, Miss Burns would find it difficult to keep the children's attention focused on their lessons.

Like the burgeoning new season, James, too, had no control over his own metamorphosis. Every cell in his body screamed to be outside, to be in "that air," as he liked to call it, to cruise the lakeshore paths of Burnham Park as its legendary namesake designer, Daniel Burnham, had intended. James could not concentrate on school no matter what point Miss Burns tried to make. Soon summer break would be here and he would no longer have to worry about Miss Burns catching him daydreaming and snapping him from imagined pleasures of travels up and down Lake Michigan.

Crazed, he could barely contain himself as he watched the big hand on the classroom's clock twitch closer and closer, minute-by-minute, toward the magic time of three o'clock: dismissal. He kept his eyes glued on the timepiece until the final bell rang, giving him his freedom. Then he'd bolt for the door.

Today, James had ridden his bike to school and would use it on his after-school jaunt to Burnham Park. The bike, a black and silver Ted Williams model, had a decal of the Sears brand prominently emblazoned on the front of the bike's neck. These cherished wheels provided him with the means to cruise uninhibited along the park's smooth, asphalt paths. Since most kids his age didn't own a bike, the twenty-six incher—a birthday present from the previous year—had become one of his prized possessions. He never let it out of his sight, not even when he stopped for a quick sip at one of the park's drinking fountains, or for an impromptu ride on one of the dozens of playground swings.

Another bike James Overstreet greatly admired belonged to an old man who rode through the park on a candy-apple red, mint-condition, Huffy. James thought the man dressed funny, always wearing a blue, one-piece jumpsuit similar to what Evel Knievel wore in his death defying jumps on TV. The man also wore a rather odd, floppy gray cap. It looked to James like those he'd seen in photographs of old-time baseball players in sports books he borrowed from the Chicago Public Library.

James had seen the old man many times before, but until today, he had never found the nerve to talk to him. The boy pulled up to a fountain where the man sat on his bike, one foot on the ground, the other propped on a bench next to the short granite water station. Gray hair stuck out from under his cap, which looked small on the man's somewhat large head. James wasn't sure if he should speak to the silver-haired gentleman, but his curiosity to know more about him and more about his cool bike with the built-in radio prompted the boy to finally talk to him.

"You got one sweet ride there, mister," James said, coming to a stop and then straddling his Ted Williams. He leaned over the waterspout for a drink.

"Why thank you, young fella. She's a beauty, all right. Bought her back in 1960." The old man turned off the bike's radio, which had blared an AM talk show. "Yours is a mighty fine bike, though, too." He pointed to the decal on James's bicycle. "Ted Williams was one of the greatest I ever saw."

Coming up from his drink, James gulped. "You *seen* Ted Williams play?"

"I sure did—The Splendid Splinter."

"Splendid splinter?"

The old man dismounted his radio bicycle and dropped the kickstand, resting the bike. "Ballplayers give each other nicknames. That was Williams's—The Splendid Splinter. You see, ol' Teddy, well, he had one of the finest swings in the game." The old man had taken a step now onto the freshly manicured grass bordering the path. He started to take big, looping swings with an imaginary bat as he continued to speak to the boy. "Great hands with the splinter. The wood. The bat."

James watched in fascination as the elderly gentleman took one deliberate swing after another at an imaginary ball, thrown by an equally imaginary pitcher. The man squinted his eyes, focusing, pretending to wait for the next pitch. Then he swung through with a graceful motion, watching the "ball" sail off into the air. He had a sweet, smooth motion, like a big leaguer.

"Oh, I get it. Like Dick Allen, huh? He's great with the bat, too. Uses the biggest bat in the majors. Didjoo' know that, mister?"

"Dick Allen. Rookie of the Year, 1964, Philadelphia Phillies. American League Most Valuable Player, 1972, Chicago White Sox. Seven-time All-Star," the old man replied, still swinging away, yet not looking at the boy.

James raised his eyebrows, impressed with the man's knowledge of Allen's big league awards. The boy pushed his cap back on his head and bent down for another drink. If not in school or church, the only other time the tattered Chicago White Sox cap left his head was when he went to bed.

The old man kept swinging away. "You're a big White Sox fan huh, young fella?"

Coming up again from his drink, James said. "Oh, yeah. For sure. Dick Allen's still my favorite, even though he's not on our team anymore." James paused for a moment, looking directly at the old man. "Mister, sounds like you know a lot about baseball."

"Oh, I've seen a game or two in my day."

"I notice you ride through Burnham here a lot. Just about every day, seems to me." James pointed up and down the lakefront with an outstretched finger. "Always headin' south in the morning, comin' back this way now in the afternoon." He moved his head back toward the man, and quizzed him. "Where you go when you ride?"

The old man stopped his swings and looked at the boy.

"Well, you're quite the observant young man, aren't you? And inquisitive, too. But since you asked, I work part-time, south of here, down at Hyde Park Foods." The old man placed both hands on his hips and stretched his wiry frame, thrusting his chest forward. "Helps me keep in shape, riding my bike."

James eyeballed him, bent down for another sip of water, and said, "Just watch out. There's a big, tall dude called Pick who hangs out right around here with his gang. He doesn't like nobody ridin' through his park too much, 'specially white folks. You dig?"

"What do you mean *his* park? This park belongs to everyone." The man's voice rose to a high pitch.

James hadn't meant to upset the old guy but he also knew to speak the truth. His daddy had preached to him as long as he could remember, *You'll never go wrong, James, if you always tell the truth.*

James nervously began cracking his knuckles and stammered on, barely coming up for air. "Well, that may be, but they's Rangers and they're pretty bad dudes. Most of 'em come from over there." James stopped his knuckle cracking and pointed across Lake Shore Drive to a housing project about two blocks away. "But they usually hang out here all day, mostly jumpin' people comin' through, protectin' their turf, stealin' their stuff. They'd like nothin' more than that cherry Huffy of yours." James motioned his head to the man's bike. "Me and my best friend, Clayton, we just stay as far away from them as we can."

The old man pulled a crisp, white handkerchief from his back pocket and began wiping the chrome fenders of his immaculate bicycle. "Well, thank you for your concern, young man. But I can take care of myself. I've handled quite a few pretty bad dudes in my day."

James shrugged his shoulders and mumbled, "Whatever." He wondered if the man even listened to his warning. About to hop back on his bike, the old man stopped the boy.

"Hey. I didn't get your name, young man."

"James. James Overstreet."

"Well, my name is Manny. Manny Fleischman." He stuck out his hand and made a quick shake. "Nice to meet you, James Overstreet."

James then took off his baseball cap and scratched the top of his head. "Manny, huh? Don't know no Mannys. Matter of fact, don't know no Fleischmans, neither."

Manny smiled. "Actually, my full name is Emanuel. It was my grandfather's name. He was from Russia. And Fleischman, well, that's a Jewish name."

James scratched his head again. "I don't think I know nobody Jewish, neither."

Fleischman chuckled. "Well, now you do!"

"That's really cool. Miss Burns, my teacher, she said that's why we had World War II, to help the Jewish people." The boy paused. "I think you're the first Jew-man I ever met."

Manny nodded. "I'll consider that something special then."

James thought Manny Fleischman was something special, too.

"Maybe I'll see you tomorrow then, huh?" asked James.

"You bet," the old man replied. "I'll be coming through here tomorrow morning 'bout nine-thirty. But you already know that, don't you?" The old man winked at the boy.

James nodded in his typical sheepish manner, the same way he did to his teacher, Miss Burns. He realized he was beginning to feel the same way about the old man as he did her.

The next morning, James and Manny met at the same drinking fountain, as they had surmised they would. This time James was waiting at the fountain as the old man came whirring down the path. He stopped his Huffy and pulled up next to the boy.

"Hi there, James. So, no school today. Got any big plans? Are you headed anyplace special?"

"Nowhere particular. Just travlin', Mister Fleischman."

"Travlin', huh? I like that word."

"That's what my momma calls it. She always asks me, 'James, where you going travlin' today?' She says she thinks I'm goin' to be an explorer someday when I grow up, ya' know, travlin' to all kinds of different places. I wanna' be a geologist. Study rocks and stuff. Like in the Grand Canyon." James adjusted the grips of his handlebars and then the angle of his bike's seat. "But today, I'm just thinkin' about travlin' down to fifty-fifth street. Maybe go look at the Del Prado."

"Ahh, the Del Prado Hotel. That's some special place," Manny said. "Did you know that lots of big league baseball players used to stay in the Del Prado and other Hyde Park hotels til those fancy Loop ones came along?"

"Sure did. My daddy told me." They began to ride their bikes together down the path. "My daddy says Babe Ruth stayed at the Del Prado. So did Mickey Mantle and the Splendid Splinter." James smiled over at Manny. "Even Hank Aaron. Hey, Mister Fleischman. Do you know who Bill Monbouquette is?"

"Pitcher. Boston Red Sox. If I recall correctly, he tossed a no-hitter against the White Sox back in the early sixties."

"That's right! You knew *that*, too?" James shook his head. "He no-hit them the same day I was born—August first, nineteen sixty-two. Him and my daddy were best friends."

Manny stopped his bike with a jolt to his break pedal. When he did, James stopped, too. "Your father played big league ball?"

"Well, almost. He was a minor leaguer with the Red Sox. Says he woulda' been Boston's first black ballplayer in the big leagues, but he hurt his knee. He got replaced by Pumpsie Green."

"You don't say. So your dad's injury opened the door for Pumpsie. Well I'll be. You know, Pumpsie went on to become Boston's first black player. Did you know they were the last big league team to have a black ballplayer?"

James shook his head.

"That's too bad, James. Sounds like you're still very proud of your daddy, though."

"Yes, sir. Best daddy a boy could have. I'm just glad to have a daddy. My best friend, Clayton, he doesn't."

They walked their bikes down a side path that ended at the limestone rock steps just above the water. Manny pushed down the kickstand on his bike and the Huffy rested at a gentle angle. James did the same with his Ted Williams. Manny took a seat on the top rock step and James sat beside him. They both looked out at the glistening morning water to the east.

"You sure do know a lot about baseball, Mister Fleischman."

"I guess you can say that," Manny replied, cracking a wry smile. "But, it's really more like I know a little bit about a lot of things."

James shrugged, wondering what other things the old Jew, Manny Fleischman, might know. Before he could finish his thought, Manny spoke.

"You know, I've known a lot of black folks who have been the first at something very important. A lot of them became very famous."

"Really? What did you do when you were young, Mister Fleischman? I mean, what kinda job you have?"

"I was a high school teacher right here in Bronzeville. Forty-seven years. Taught over at DuSable, not far from here. Used to be called Phillips. Did you know that Phillips was the first high school in the United States to have a one hundred percent black student body?"

James raised his eyebrows and shook his head.

"I had a student there way back when by the name of Nathaniel Cole. Everyone used to call him 'Nat' for short. Later, some folks added 'King' to his name. Do you know who he was?"

Again, James shook his head.

"That's okay. You just ask your momma. I'll bet she'll know. And then ask your daddy about the Harlem Globetrotters. Four of them boys that started that team, well, I taught them all in history class."

"The Harlem who?"

"Your daddy will know who I'm talking about. And speaking of firsts, tell your folks I also taught the first African-American to attend our nation's military academy—West Point." As they sat, Manny went on for several more minutes, telling James about other important black folks, some famous, some forgotten, that came from the Bronzeville neighborhood where they both now lived. "You see, James. I've known lots of black folks who'd been first at things and I wish your daddy could have been one of them, too."

"Well, my daddy's first in my book." James bent over and picked up a few loose stones scattered at his feet. He began tossing them one-by-one into the blue water below.

"Hey, James. Hyde Park Foods is going to be looking for a delivery boy once school's out. You think you might like a job like that?"

James continued tossing the stones. "Maybe." He took a moment before he went on. "Would I get paid?"

"Of course you would! You'd get paid for every delivery you make and if you're real good you might even make some tips. Why don't you talk to your parents about it and then let me know. I'm sure I'll see you in the park here again."

"You got that right. Got to do my travlin' every day, fo' sure." The boy tossed the last of the pebbles in his hand down into the lake.

Manny stood up. "I'd really like to talk more but I need to skedaddle now. Got to get to work." Manny held out his hand. "Nice to see you again, Mister James Overstreet."

They shook hands again and smiled.

"And, James. Thank you for your advice about that gang yesterday. But don't worry about me. Okay, son?"

Manny popped up his kickstand and effortlessly hopped on his shiny bicycle with its spotless, over-sized, white-walled tires. The wheels' polished spokes shimmered as they trapped the glow of sun's morning reflection off the glimmering lake behind them. As Manny turned and headed off south down the bike path, James watched him until he no longer could see him or the red Huffy.

Later that day as he sat at his family's kitchen table after dinner, James told his mother and father all about the conversation he had with his new friend who rode the shiny red Huffy bicycle.

"And this Mister Fleischman says there's a job for me this summer deliverin' groceries and stuff to the rich folks in Hyde Park. He said I can make a lot of money, Momma." He turned to his father. "Really, Daddy. He's a pretty cool ol' man. Knows a whole lot about baseball. And, he says he knows a lot of famous black people, too."

"Is that right?" his father said. James could only see the top of his daddy's head as his father continued to read his newspaper. "Jus' what kinda famous black people does he know?"

"He told me about the first doctor in the world to operate on a man's heart while he was still alive," James sputtered. "He was a black man, Daddy, and lived right here in Bronzeville, right near our house, a long time ago. Mister Fleischman says that very same doctor became the first black man in the country to start a hospital just so he could teach black folks how to become doctors and nurses."

"He said that, huh?" his father said, still not coming out from behind the paper.

James spoke nonstop, pausing only so he could catch his breath. "Daddy, did you know that during the Civil War there used to be a prisoner of war camp right here near our house. Right on the corner of our street?"

"You don't say." His father remained behind the newspaper.

"Yes, sir. There really was. And another thing Mister Fleischman told me was that he taught some famous black basketball players who go around the world to play hoops and stuff. He called them the Globetrappers or something."

His father dropped his newspaper to the table. "The Globetrotters? The Harlem Globetrotters?"

"That's it, Daddy. The Harlem Globetrotters. He said he taught some of them boys who started that team way back when."

His daddy cocked his head. "Well, I'll be."

"Says he even taught a black man named Nat, who's a king—a king of coal or somethin'."

"You mean Nat King Cole?" His mother hadn't participated in the conversation but gulped her first words as she wiped her hands on her apron, moving from the kitchen sink to the table.

"That's it. That's his name, Momma—Nat King Cole. Mister Fleischman said he grew up not far from here. Do you know him, Momma?"

"Oh my, he's one of my favorite singers." His mother's voice quavered. "I didn't know he was from 'round here." She stood over them at the edge of the table and turned her head to her husband. "Did you know that Earl Overstreet?"

"Can't say's I did," Earl replied, raising his newspaper and lowering his head back behind it.

"What did you say this old man did for a living, son?" his mother asked.

"He was a teacher, Momma. At DuSable High School. I'm thinkin' maybe I wanna' go to DuSable when I graduate Jackie Robinson. Can I take that job at Hyde Park Foods? Can I? Please?"

"Well, don't see why not. Not too soon for you to get a job and start setting aside a little savings for college," his father said. "Every little bit helps."

"I'm goin' there Monday then, after school, after I go travlin' to the park, of course."

James rose from the table and ran toward his bedroom just off the kitchen. Three steps into his run he skidded to an abrupt stop and turned back to the kitchen.

"Oh Daddy, can I be excused from the table?"

Earl Overstreet hadn't many rules in his house except that when done with their family meal he required all of his children to ask permission to be excused from the dinner table. That was his daddy's rule, and his daddy's daddy before that.

"Yes, you're excused, son," he replied, his back to the boy who had stood in the hallway off the kitchen, waiting for his father's reply.

"Oh, and thank you for supper, Momma. Sure was good."

James dashed off into his room, exhilarated by his parents' permission to pursue Manny Fleischman's job offer. As was his habit when excited about a new adventure, he began to turn the globe on the desk. Spinning it round and round, he thought of all the places he'd like to see when he grew up. In class that week, Miss Burns had lectured about the Seven Natural Wonders of the World and James remembered how she said the Grand Canyon was the only natural wonder in the United States. He ran a finger along the globe's outer edge and then stopped it on the United States, right on top of Arizona.

Remembering his daydream during her lecture, but also thinking about being the first black person in whatever he ended up doing to do something special, he said aloud, "I want to be the first black person to discover something new about the Grand Canyon. Someday, I'm going to go to Arizona!"

CHAPTER 8

Two months into his summer vacation, James had nearly completed his eighth week working as a delivery boy for Hyde Park Foods. He worked every day of the week, except Tuesday and Sunday, arriving at the grocery store by ten in the morning and working until all the deliveries went out for the day.

One of the first things James had noticed after only a week on the job was that Manny Fleischman had his share of run-ins with kids shoplifting. Manny wasn't afraid to chase anyone if he caught them using a five-finger discount. He seemed to be constantly on the watch for the actions of "bad apples," as he called them, all while he bagged groceries at the small, neighborhood establishment.

Two days ago, on Saturday—the store's busiest day—James had overheard Walter Sibley, the produce man, lecture him. "Manny ol' boy, no use chasin' dem typ'a kids. If ya' catch 'em probably won't do dem no good. Probably got no daddy at home to whoop dere behinds anyhow."

"I'll get them next time. Kids have got to learn there's no future in that sort of behavior," Manny told Walter, huffing as he walked through the produce section after another futile pursuit.

"Some kids jus' don' know right from wrong, Manny," the old black man with the deep Southern accent said as he placed more tomatoes into a produce bin.

"I would have never retired from teaching if it wasn't for those kind of kids."

"You retired 'cause you was just too damn old!" the raspy-voiced old Southerner cackled. "In Kentucky, white folks put a horse out to pasture when he can't run the race no more. Das what they did to you, all right. Put you out to pasture. Jus' thank God they didn't shoot you."

"I'm not out to pasture, Walter. Not me. Got a lot of years left in these old bones, my friend."

Walter struggled to lift a case of bananas from a wooden pallet in the aisle. "Well, the good Lord dun give you a strong body. Not like ol' Walter here. This roomatiz I got just 'bout killin' me today."

As James remembered the conversation of the two old men, a group of four boys entered the store through the front door. A tall, muscular fifteen-year-old James knew from his Bronzeville neighborhood led the gang. The leader's street name was "Ice Pick" although most just knew him as "Pick." Always carrying a very thin, six-inch switchblade knife tucked in the front of his pants, James had often heard the story of how Pick had gotten the nickname because once, during a gang fight, he had stuck his knife in another kid so many times it looked as if he were chopping a block of ice. Everyone James knew feared Pick and his gang.

James wasn't sure if Manny saw them come in since he was chattering away with Walter once again back in the produce section on the opposite side of the store. James watched from a distance as the young thugs went down the candy and snacks aisle. James followed behind them, staying out of sight. The gang grabbed chewing gum from the shelves, along with bags of chips and pretzels, stuffing them in their pockets and under their shirts.

At the end of the aisle, Pick stopped by the meat cooler. He grabbed a steak and tucked it inside his pants. Then he turned suddenly and his eyes met James's. James froze as Pick's cold glare gripped the delivery boy in fear. James thought of running, but his feet didn't seem to want to respond, like the way he felt during a bad dream when you wanted to run but your legs just didn't move. Not sure what to do, he turned to leave the aisle.

Manny Fleischman stood behind him, startling him. "What is it, son? You feel okay?"

Stuttering, James answered. "Yup . . . I'm o . . . kay."

"Well, you sure don't look too good. Maybe it's something you ate. You want—"

Manny stopped midsentence and looked past James's shoulder. James turned to see what Manny saw. One of the boys who had come in with Pick, wearing a patch over his eye, grabbed a steak, stuffed it in his pants, and began to walk away. James turned back to see what Manny's reaction would be. The old man's brow furrowed then he sprang past James, running down the aisle, shouting at the one-eyed boy. "Hey, put that back!"

As James stood there, Pick appeared at the opposite end of the aisle. He raised his right index finger and pressed it to his lips. Then he took that same finger, placed it under his left ear, and dragged it left-to-right along his throat, never taking his gaze off James, standing motionless.

Pick's clear threat sent a shuddering wave of fear through James as the gangbanger ran out of the store.

THE NEXT MORNING
10:00 A.M.

"I'm going to go out now, Momma," James shouted as he left their basement-level apartment.

"If you go travlin', you be careful. Watch out for them older boys in the park. You hear?"

His mother's caution warning made him remember Pick's threatening gesture from yesterday. There wasn't a day James went to the park or work that he didn't look over his shoulder. That was the normal way of life in his neighborhood. Today would be different, though, he told himself. *You see Pick, you run.*

James's methodical travlin' routine consisted of the same exact steps every trip. He left through the only entrance to their home: a heavy, wooden door equipped with three locks. The window on the top one-third of the door was laced with a protective layer of twisted, wrought iron metal. This doorway led to an enclosed area under the building's back porch. Once there he'd grab his Ted Williams, which he meticulously secured each night by locking it with padlock and chain to the six inch by six inch wooden beams that supported the porch. Depending upon the day's weather or upon the whim of his mood, he took his bike and rode to Burnham; or, he left it, and went by foot. Today, he decided to walk.

When James went travlin' during the summer, he frequently stopped and knocked on the door of his best friend, Clayton Thomas. Clayton lived just a block from Robinson Academy on the first floor of the fourteen-story Olander projects, a Chicago Housing Authority high-rise engulfing an entire block. Clayton hadn't been answering James's knocks at his apartment door for nearly three days. James always presumed Clayton to be there because he knew Clayton's momma, to protect him from gangs, usually only allowed her son out of their apartment for school. Now that they were on summer break, it meant Clayton should be home.

Getting no answer at Clayton's house once again, James decided to go alone to the lakefront. His route took him north from Clayton's apartment through an alley where he headed east until the passageway dead-ended at the Illinois Central railroad tracks. There, he followed a narrow footpath along the west bank of the tracks, heading south until he reached the long, pedestrian overpass that extended over Lake Shore Drive at 43rd Street. At that point a very short distance separated him from the lakefront.

James jogged across the hundred foot or so steel and concrete aerial expanse, then down the sturdy metal steps on the other side of the footbridge and into the park. He had his baseball bat with him today, the one given to him by his hero, former White Sox star Dick Allen. As a second job, James's father, Earl, worked as a part-time clubhouse security man for Chicago's South Side major league baseball team. He had promised his youngest boy that if he finished the seventh grade with no C's on his report card, he would take him to meet the team's famous slugger. When he did, Allen surprised him with the enormous memento.

As soon as James entered the park, he saw Pick and his gang running toward him. *Run now. Run as fast as you can.* But it was too late to flee. The gang was at his feet as soon as he put his first foot on the ground, coming off the steps. James stopped dead in his tracks.

"Little nigger, gimme some money for comin' in my park," Pick demanded.

"Ain't got no money," stammered James.

"You're nothin' but a little nigger squealer. Aren't you?" Pick accused James as he poked him in the chest with a bony index finger. "You snitched on us to that nosy old man you work with at that store. Didn't you?"

James didn't speak, knowing Pick wouldn't believe anything he had to say.

"So you ain't got no money. Maybe I'll just take that bat of yours then."

James had carried the Dick Allen Louisville slugger with him hoping he'd see his friend Clayton in the park and that, if he did, they might be able to hit fly balls to each other there. Clayton had the glove and ball, James the bat.

Pick snatched the bat from him and tossed it to an even taller boy. "Hang on to my new bat for me, Tyrone."

"That's my Dick Allen Louisville," James pleaded.

"Dat thang too big for your little Pygmy black ass anyhow," Tyrone laughed, hopping into an impromptu batting stance and swinging away a few times.

Pick shoved James to the ground. As he laid there, a member of Pick's gang, the one with the patch over his eye, came over and kicked James in his ribs, and said, "We're gonna throw your sorry little nigger ass in the fuckin' lake."

Before he could get up off the ground, another member of Pick's notorious crew grabbed one of the park's wire mesh trashcans. With one swift motion, he turned it upside-down, emptying its contents over the fallen James.

"That's it, Bobby D!" Pick shouted. "Perfect!"

"Now we got your little black ass!" Bobby D yelled to James through the can's metal screen. "That'll teach you to squeal on us."

Caught like a caged animal in the steel container, James could not stand since the basket only stood about four feet high. He crouched like a catcher behind home plate, fingers laced through the basket's mesh. Discarded trash lay strewn over and around him. The boys outside circled the can and ridiculed their terrified captive. James tried to push the basket off of him, almost succeeding, but another boy jumped on the top of the basket.

"That's it, Jumbo. Hold him down tight. Don't let that little nigger squealer get out," Pick cried.

Wham!

Tyrone smashed the side of basket with a powerful swing of James's bat, just missing his fingers.

Tyrone passed the bat to the boy with the patch.

Wham!

James pulled his hands from the desperate grip he held on the basket and placed them over his ears to protect them from the piercing sound the bat made as it smashed against the surrounding metal. His captors laughed and hollered as James cringed inside his steel-walled jail.

"Lemme have a whack at it, Pokie!" Pick shouted, pulling the bat from the one-eyed boy.

WHAM!

The crushing sound sent tears flowing from James's eyes. He contorted into a fetal position and whimpered as the boys passed the bat to each other, taking turns pummeling the basket with James underneath. Then they started spitting on him through the wire mesh, landing globs of slimy mucus on his head and back. He cried for them to stop but with each plea, they laughed louder, whooping and hollering, continuing their relentless barrage.

"I got something you'll really like!" Pick said. With those words, he backed his ass to the wire and farted as close as he could toward James's face. The other boys squealed with laughter at their leader's crude action. Another pushed his own ass against the wire. Then they all took turns, passing gas into James's face as he cried louder and louder for them to stop.

"I'm gonna piss on him!" Bobby D shouted as he began to unzip his jeans.

James looked up and begged them to stop. When he did, he noticed Clayton Thomas, standing about ten feet behind the others. Shocked to see his best friend, James's heart leapt with hope of rescue.

"Clayton!" James shouted. "Clayton! Get me outta here. Make 'em stop."

But his friend did not reply. "Can't he hear me?" James wondered aloud as Pick's gang continued to taunt him.

Pick knelt down next to the basket and pushed his face inches from the wire mesh. "Clayton no help to you any more, Pygmy. He's a Ranger now!"

James didn't believe Pick's words. *Clayton would never join Pick's gang. Never.* Yet James watched in disbelief as Clayton made no effort to help him or attempt to stop the gangbangers from continuing to beat on the basket with the bat.

"Leave him alone! Leave him alone!" a voice called out.

Peeking between his fingers as his hands covered his face, James's heart leapt when he recognized Manny Fleischman's red Huffy bicycle racing toward the group.

"I'm calling the police! Leave him alone I say!" Manny yelled.

Startled, the gang looked up at the old man, who flailed away with a small brown club in his hand raised high above his head, riding swiftly toward them. The man's wild and reckless approach caused them to scatter in every direction, like startled rabbits. Manny stopped and jumped off his bike as it crashed to the ground. The old man ran to the upside down basket and began to lift it.

Still terrified that Pick and his boys might still be out there, James closed his eyes and wrapped his arms around his head. "No! Stop! No more. Please stop!"

"James. It's me. It's Manny, son." Manny picked up the basket and tossed it aside, kneeling next to the frightened boy. "It's okay. It's all right now. They're gone. They ran away."

James pulled his head up slowly, afraid to look. Manny stretched out one arm and James fell against the old man's chest. Shivering, he clung to Manny, wiping his tears on the old man's jumpsuit sleeve.

"Those are the same boys who came into the store yesterday, aren't they?"

James didn't answer.

"Now I wish I had caught them." He pulled a crisp handkerchief from his pocket and handed it to James. "I'm calling the police."

James tugged at Manny's sleeve. "No! Please don't, Mister Fleischman. *Please don't.* It'll be worse if you do." He stood up and brushed himself off, straightening his disheveled clothes. "I'm okay. Honest." He handed Manny's kerchief back to him.

"But, James, we can't let this happen—"

"Mister Fleischman. *Please.* You can't tell anyone what happened. *Please!*" James held back the tears, refusing to cry anymore. "All that matters right now is that they're gone."

But James wasn't telling Manny the truth. What really mattered most to James was figuring out why his best friend, Clayton Thomas, didn't help him. *Was it true what Pick said? Was Clayton now running with Pick's gang, the Oakwood Rangers?*

"Thank you for saving me."

The old man placed a firm hand on James's shoulder. "That's all right, James. I know you'd do the same for me."

CHAPTER 9

ONE WEEK LATER

At precisely 9:45 a.m., regimented by a finely tuned Swiss watch given to him as a memento for his retirement almost a dozen years before, Manny Fleischman started out on his daily bicycle ride. From his apartment on Martin Luther King Drive, he headed east toward the 31st Street entrance of Chicago's Burnham Park about four blocks away. Once there, Fleischman wheeled his Huffy down the park's almost half-century-old asphalt paths that paralleled the Lake Michigan shoreline.

Dressed in his blue jumpsuit and a post-World War I-era baseball cap, Fleischman's one-hundred-and-forty pound, eighty-five-year-old, still-toned body reflected a long-lived, healthy lifestyle. Undaunted by the lakefront's stifling midsummer air, he rode south with one purpose. His mind drifted as he passed the location where he had rescued James from the attack last week. The attack traumatized the boy so much that it was several days before he had begun speaking again at work.

"What's wit James?" Walter had asked Manny the day after the attack. "He ain't actin' hisself."

Manny had shrugged off the produce clerk's questions, pretending he didn't know what James's problem might be, though he knew James was still suffering from the pain and embarrassment of the vicious attack. By the third day after the incident, Manny had decided that getting James to talk about what happened was better than keeping it inside, festering in the boy's mind.

"James," Manny called to the boy as he walked back into the store after delivering some groceries to a customer, "you want to go on break with me?"

James shrugged and then nodded. The two headed into the small employee canteen behind the store's deli.

"Would you like an orange pop?" Manny asked James. "I happen to have an extra one."

James nodded again, still not speaking.

Manny passed the lukewarm can to him, then sat down and began eating an apple with some peanut butter. He held out the apple to James. "Would you like some?"

James shook his head as he sat down across the table.

"James, it wasn't your fault what happened in the park. You know that, don't you?"

He didn't answer.

"Those boys are going to end up in some pretty serious trouble someday. They're going to hurt someone real bad and then they'll get their just punishment. Cream like you, James, good boys, well, they float to the top. Crap like them sinks. You remember that." Manny paused a moment, taking a swig of his drink. "I know you saw those boys stealing from the store last week. And I know you were afraid to turn them in. I understand. But you'll come to see someday that it's always better to tell the truth than to live a lie. I know this, son, because one time, long, long ago, I was in the very same situation, a very serious situation. I knew something wrong was going to happen and it did happen, and I didn't say a word to anyone. I never spoke about it. And, you know what, I've regretted that decision every day of my life for the last fifty some years."

James looked as though he didn't comprehend what Manny was trying to tell him. So the old man went on to share with him the secret he had held for over fifty years, never having told it to anyone, not even his wife or daughter. When he was done, James stared at him, still looking bewildered. Manny wondered if he had gotten through to the boy, hoping that by clearing his conscience after five decades of silence he had made an impression on his young mind. Then James finally spoke.

"My best friend Clayton, he was there when Pick and those other boys jumped me. He's in their gang now." He paused a beat. "Mister Fleischman, I talked to Clayton. He told me them boys are plannin' on getting' you back for helping me."

As Manny rode his bike to work through Burnham Park, he ran over and over in his mind that conversation with James a few days ago in the store canteen. Manny had chosen not to focus on James's warning but rather on helping the boy deal with not only the pain and humiliation of the beating, but having his best friend desert him when he needed him most.

Then suddenly, out of nowhere, two boys jumped in front of Manny's bicycle, surprising him, grabbing his handlebars and abruptly stopping his progress. At the same time, leaping at him from behind, two more boys pounced upon him and took hold of the rear of his cherry red Huffy. One of these four boys wore a patch over his eye; Manny recognized him as the kid who stole the package of meat from the store. Then, a very tall, gangly boy leapt out from behind a row of bushes. He held an enormous baseball bat perched on his scrawny shoulder. A last boy then sauntered out from behind the bushes. Tall, too, but not as tall as the first, this boy's pronounced swagger sent a clear signal to Manny he was the ragtag bunch's leader.

This has got to be them—Pick and his Oakwood Rangers! While the four surrounded him, the giant pair approached the surprised prey, the boys' backs to the glaring sun. Manny remained cautiously still, all six boys eerily silent.

"So, you must be Pick," Manny said to the tall boy without the bat. "I was wondering when I'd get the chance to meet you in person."

"The one and only," replied Pick.

Without warning, Pick threw a punch at the old man, but Manny, still strong for his age, stopped the boy's scrawny hand midstrike. He held it and then twisted Pick's fist, tossing him back like a rag doll. The other gang members roared with laughter.

Glaring at his mates, Pick snatched the baseball bat from his taller sidekick's shoulder. He turned the piece of wood in his hands, standing sideways, cockily emulating the motions of a big league ballplayer. Without the briefest hesitation between respective movements, he swung at the old man. Manny raised his arm to block the blow, but the brute force shattered his forearm. The impetus of Pick's vicious blast threw Manny from the Huffy, screaming in pain.

Mind spinning from the pain of the bat's crushing blow and the adrenaline now pumping through his body, Manny experienced the next moments as if in a dream. One boy grabbed the sparkling red prize and attempted to jump on it as two of the other boys fought the first for rights to it. The fourth boy ran off, terror on his face. Pick and his sidekick laughed as they watched the three remaining Oakwood Rangers foot soldiers battle for possession of the bicycle booty.

Manny lay prone, face turned sideways, moaning, unable to move. Pick taunted the old man as he stepped closer, balancing the bat on his bony shoulder. He shouted down at Manny. "You shoulda kept your white-haired Jew ass out of my park!"

Then, like Lazarus rising from the dead, Manny seized Pick's leg with his good arm, clenching his attacker with a grip just above the ankle. Startled, Pick struggled to free himself from the old man's strong hold. The gang's leader panicked. The boy with the patch over his eye rode Manny's Huffy in rings around the fracas, closing in around the pair of combatants. Another boy sat on the handlebars while the third stood on the axle of the rear tire. They whooped and hollered, taunting their leader as they watched his futile effort to break free from Manny's grasp.

"That fool's got your silly ass, man!" cried one boy.

Another shouted, "Stomp his head, man! Stomp him!"

"That fuckin' ol' man whoopin' your ass, Pick!" yelled the boy with the patch.

Unable to pull himself away from Manny's vice-like clamp, Pick spun, pivoting, as he supported himself with the bat. But he still could not break loose. Scowling, he raised the bat over his head and swung it downward full force, striking the old man square on the back of his head.

The Huffy's driver slammed on the bike's brakes, tumbling the other two boys from the bike. Dumbstruck, the trio stared as Pick began a vicious thirty-second pounding of the prone Manny. Then, as abruptly as he began, Pick, blood splatters covering his entire body, halted his bat barrage and stared down at his victim. Dazed, his eyes were as glassy and dark as the shimmering, sapphire lake behind him.

The old man, lying in a pool of his own sticky, gray-colored brain matter, managed to somehow open his eyes. He struggled to focus his vision through blood, though it skewed his sight. He reached a limp arm out, pointing. Pick, watching his victim's every move, looked in the direction of Manny's outstretched limb. The leader's eyes widened. He pointed with the Louisville toward a park bench off the path about fifty yards away. The gang turned their eyes to where Pick raised the bloodstained weapon.

"Hey, do you see who I see?" shouted the boy with the patch. "That's our little nigger squealer! Let's go get him!"

"No," Pick snarled, freezing the group. "We'll deal with his sorry ass later. Right now, everyone book it. Then meet at ten back in the bone yard tonight."

Following their still-crazed leader's directions, the members of the gang dashed north while blood from Manny Fleischman's wound continued to flow, oozing into the crevices of the park's black asphalt path. Then Pick raised the bat, turned his head toward the park bench where the boy crouched, and slammed the bat down on the head of his prone victim one more time.

CHAPTER 10

10:34 A.M.

Earl Overstreet sat at his kitchen table in the family's basement apartment on Ellis Avenue as he did every morning, reading the newspaper. In a couple of hours, he'd be leaving for his afternoon shift as a security guard at Goldblatt's Department Store. His wife, Eva, busied herself collecting the family's dirty laundry, preparing for her weekly trip down to the turn-of-the-century building's dingy cellar. When their son James came running through the apartment's back door, the boy's feet barely hit the floor. He ran nonstop through the family's stark kitchen and straight into his room.

"James Overstreet! Don't you be runnin' through this here house with your shoes on!"

James never looked back to reply to his mother's demand. As the door to his room slammed shut behind him, she looked up from her laundry basket and turned to Earl.

"Earl, I told that boy a thousand times to take those shoes of his off before he comes runnin' through my house. Maybe you can get through to him 'cause I sure don't seem to be able to lately. He's been actin' awfully strange this past week. Go see what's wrong with that son of yours."

Earl had already thrown his paper down as soon as his son streaked by him. He went to the door of the boy's room. His wife had been correct in her observation. James hadn't seemed his usual talkative self, keeping himself locked up in his room for nearly a week, only coming out to eat or go to work.

"James, boy. Get out here," Earl said through the door. "What the heck is going on with you, son?"

No sound came from behind the closed door. Earl inched a little closer and spoke through the thick, wooden door. "James?"

Again, no response.

"Boy, your daddy's asking you to come out here before I come in there." Earl waited. "Son? Do you hear me?"

No sound.

"James!"

His father turned the old brass handle slowly, opening the squeaking door. He peeked in through the small crack he created, large enough for Earl to see his son's tear-filled eyes.

"What is it, boy? What's goin' on? You in some kinda trouble?"

As James stood there, hanging his head, shaking it back and forth, Earl gently pushed the door open wider. Whimpering, the boy said, "They killed the ol' Jew-man, Daddy. They *killed* him."

Eva's clothes basket thumped to the kitchen floor. She rushed over to the doorway. "*Who* killed *what?*" she asked, pushing her husband aside.

"The ol' Jew-man, Momma. The man I work with in the grocery store. Mister Fleischman. They killed him. They took his bike and then they beat him with a bat."

"Oh my Lord," Eva gasped, pulling James close to her in a protective embrace. "Not Mister Fleischman!" she wailed.

James struggled to nod, his head buried in his mother's chest.

"Dear God," Earl murmured. "Who did this?"

"Ice Pick and his gang—the Oakwood Rangers. They took his Huffy bike in the park, right where he always rides, and then they beat him. They said they was gonna beat him and they did," James said, looking up, sounding as if he was about to cry.

"Whatchew mean 'they said they's gonna beat him'?" Earl asked, raising his eyebrows toward the top of a furrowed brow.

"Earl? Please?" she said, clutching James even closer. "Ease up on the child."

"All right. Okay. Everybody just calm down. Now, come over here with me, boy, and explain to me what happened," said his father as he returned to the kitchen table, sitting back down.

Still under the protection of his mother's shielding clench, James followed her as she sat across the table from her husband. James's sisters and brothers had gathered in the kitchen now, too. Everyone remained silent as James described what he had just seen: how the gang had stopped Manny Fleischman, taken the man's bike, and then how Pick had beaten the old man repeatedly with a baseball bat while the other boys in the gang stood by and watched. When he finished with his tale of what had happened, no one said a word.

Earl broke the eerie silence. "Did you help the man, boy? Did you call an ambulance?"

For the first time since he started telling the sordid tale, James began to weep openly. "I ran, Daddy."

"Ran? That man's your friend. You work with him."

"All I could think of was gettin' out of there as fast as I could," James said through his tears.

"That means that poor man's still lyin' out there. Probably bleeding to death!" Eva declared, squeezing James.

James's two sisters started to cry. One brother groaned.

"Well, then, we gotta tell the police, boy. That's all there's to it," Earl said.

"Over my dead body!" Eva shouted, standing up. She grabbed James and pulled him away from the table.

"Whachew talkin' about, Eva? This boy's been a witness to a crime, possibly a murder."

Eva stood firm. "He ain't tellin' no police. He ain't tellin' no one. Those boys'll kill him if he does."

"Did those boys see you, son?" Earl asked him.

James answered with a short nod.

"Oh my Lord," Eva whispered.

"If that's the case then he has to go to the police 'cause they might kill 'im even if he don't," Earl added. "Those boys know he saw them. He ain't got no other choice."

"But Momma's right, Daddy," James's other brother said. "If James flips those boys, they'll be after him for sure."

"There's no place he'll be safe," the other brother said. "I know those boys, Daddy. They's badass dudes."

"Now you watch your language. You hear, boy?" Earl stood up from the table and looked at all of them. "I can't believe what I'm hearing from my own family. What about Mister Fleischman? What about his family? If James don't go to the law then he's no better than those boys who beat that poor old man. James gotta tell the police. They'll help him. Protect him."

"Don't try to sell me on the police helpin' or protectin' black folks, Earl Overstreet," Eva persisted. "Just like they helped my poor brother down in Little Rock, I suppose? They ended up killin' my baby brother. That's what the police did. Killed him."

The argument continued for several more minutes as to whether James should go to the police station or not. After much discussion, Earl made a final statement. "Let's just all calm down now. I'll find out exactly what's happened to Mister Fleischman and then I'll make a decision for this family of mine."

There were two local hospitals in Bronzeville and Earl had hoped by calling them he'd be able to find out if Manny Fleischman had received help and been taken to one of their emergency rooms. First, he called Michael Reese Hospital, but the staff refused to provide him with any information over the phone. Undaunted, he dialed Bronzeville's other local hospital.

"Mercy Hospital."

"Yes, ma'am, my name is Earl Overstreet. I live over on Thirty-ninth and Ellis. I'm tryin' to find out if an old man was brought in to your emergency room today?"

"Hold, please. I'll connect."

"ER nurse's station. Nurse Piper."

"Yes, Miss Piper. Could you tell me, ma'am, if an old man was brought in there recently to your emergency room—an old man who might have had his head badly beaten?"

"May I ask whom I'm speaking with, sir? Are you family?"

"No, ma'am, I'm not, but my boy knows him, works with him."

"I'm sorry, sir. But I can't release any information like that over the phone. Confidentiality and all."

"Please, miss. We gotta know. My boy—I think my boy seen this man get attacked."

"Then let me get your name and number and I'll have the police call you, sir."

"Police? So, he is there?"

"I'm sorry, sir. I really can't say. Please give me your contact information and I'll have someone call you."

Earl dropped the receiver from his ear and placed the handset back in the phone's cradle. Avoiding the family's puzzled looks, he mumbled, "I gotta go to work now 'cause I'm gonna be late." He turned to his wife, still seated at the table, holding James to her side. "We're gonna have to wait until I can find out exactly what happened." He tapped his index finger several times hard on the kitchen table and continued. "James, stay right inside this house until I come home, you hear? Matter of fact, I don't want anyone leaving the house till I come home from work. Ya'll understand? That's—"

Earl's words were interrupted by the telephone's ring. He picked up the phone.

"Hello? Oh, hi Clayton. Yes. Hold on. I'll get him." Earl turned to his son, covering the receiver with the palm of his hand. "James. It's Clayton. Don't stay on the phone too long, okay, and don't say a word to him about what you saw today!"

James nodded as he got up from the table and took the receiver from his father's hand. He then grabbed the phone from the small table it sat on in the hallway and pulled it inside his room, closing the door behind him.

The next morning, James awoke very early after a night of restless sleep interrupted by nightmares of Manny Fleischman's beating in the park the day before. When he walked into the kitchen, his momma stood at the stove. James took his seat while she continued stirring a boiling pot. She didn't speak nor turn to greet him with a "good morning" as she always did. It was as if she knew, he thought, what he was about to tell her. James watched her robotic-like moves as she pulled the pot from the burner and very deliberately dished out hot cereal into a bowl. When done, she grabbed the heaping bowl and placed it in front of him.

Gazing at the steaming porridge, James felt his heart quicken in his chest. It took him a minute to find his voice. "Momma," he muttered, "I've decided I'm going to go tell the police what I saw."

CHAPTER 11

Being a cop on the South Side of Chicago in the early seventies was a job for the very brave—or the very foolhardy. The 21st District, known to its officers as simply "The Prairie," was one particular police precinct on the city's South Side considered an especially forbidding war zone. Predominantly black, this section of the city a few miles south of Chicago's famous Loop included some of the city's poorest housing and was home to some of the most incorrigible citizens of the Windy City.

The Prairie possessed one of the more irregular police district boundaries: 61st Street on its southern end, 14th Street on its north, and Lake Michigan on its east. On its west side, The Prairie jutted as far as the Penn Central and the Chicago, Rock Island & Pacific railroad tracks, then narrowed down to Cottage Grove Avenue as it moved south. Quite large, The Prairie held numerous neighborhoods with such names as Bronzeville, Douglas, Oakland, and Hyde Park. Also within it borders: the iconic Burnham Park.

Edward Hanley, a detective in Area 1's Aggravated Assault Unit, arrived to work at his usual time. He occupied one of the desks on the second floor at the 51st Street and Wentworth Avenue detective division headquarters. His desk was in a massive room containing many desks, all facing back-to-back in several adjoining rows. Area 1 encompassed five police districts, including the 21st.

He strode immediately to the pot of coffee sitting on a beat up, wooden cupboard, a relic left over from the 1920s. Disheveled, sporting uncombed hair with an unknotted necktie over an open-collared, badly wrinkled dress shirt, he grabbed his Chicago White Sox coffee mug and poured a cup. His partner, Detective Timothy

Boscorelli, seated at his desk a few feet away, was already on his second cup of joe.

The duo, known to all their coworkers as "Stick" and "Timbo," called Area 1 their home away from home. Both had graduated on the same day, almost a decade earlier, from "dick school," the name cops affectionately called the police department's detective academy. As well, both were born and raised on Chicago's far South Side. Stick's Irish Catholic family had served the Chicago Blue for four generations. Timbo's Italian-American father had been the first Boscorelli on the force. Over the past eight years, Stick and Timbo had become two of Chicago's toughest and most streetwise cops—and best friends.

Timbo always had a smart remark first thing in the morning for his bleary-eyed partner. When he wanted to get a rise out of Stick, Timbo would call into question his athletic partner's baseball skills. As Area 1's softball team captain, the lanky Irishman loved to play the game, always leading his team in hitting—hence his well-deserved nickname.

"Too much coffee makes your bat speed slower, Stick."

"Fuck you, Timbo," Stick replied, not even looking up from his java pour.

"No, honest, Stick. I just read in the most recent AMA journal that coffee drinkers have a reflex response time three-times slower than non-coffee drinkers."

"Double fuck you, Timbo, because first of all, what the hell are you doin' reading a fuckin' AMA journal? And second, why ya always messin' with me when you know I worked security last night at Comiskey? Was it a full moon last night? There were some seriously crazy guys out there. Me and O'Hara musta thrown out at least twenty idiots."

Overtime pay for homicide dicks didn't exist, so most guys ran up huge amounts of comp time they had to use or lose. Most worked second jobs, like security at local sports venues. These side jobs not only helped make ends meet but for many carried a stronger incentive: moonlighting gave a guy an excuse from staying home with the wife. Cop marriages, especially in Homicide, had a high rate of failure. Stick's, thankfully, wasn't one of them—yet. Timbo's, on the other hand, was definitely on the rocks.

Stick took a sip of his coffee then stopped. "Did you make this shit? Almost ten years we've been together. When the fuck you gonna learn how to make a decent goddamn pot of coffee?"

"Don't look at me. I didn't make it. That rookie, Vallis, did," Timbo replied, picking up the morning paper. "So if you gotta complaint, go see him. Anyway, don't try and change the subject. Whadja expect over there at Comiskey last night anyhow? A convent full of nuns? All you Sox fans are crazy assholes."

"Just because all you homos root for those pansy-ass Cubs in that pansy-ass Wrigley Field—"

"All right you two. Knock it off. Don't you guys ever get tired of that Sox-Cubs bullshit?" The interruption came from Area 1 Homicide/Sex Division Lieutenant Jim LaFrance. "Listen up. I got a kid out here in the hallway says he saw that old guy get whacked with the bat yesterday in Burnham Park over in The Prairie. Report is the old man's still in a coma. He's at Mercy. Since you two seem to have nothing better to do than to argue about fucking baseball, take this one."

"C'mon, Jim. I'm juggling six cases right now. My wife and kids haven't seen me for more than eight hours straight in three weeks," Stick pleaded.

"And I got a foot-high stack of case reports on my desk," Timbo added.

"Sorry. Got nobody else. Bufano's on sick leave and Tumpich has been put on temporary assignment with the mayor's office. That leaves you two jokers," LaFrance rebuffed their pleas. "Anyway, you guys know you're my A team, so get at this one while it's still fresh. Victim's family's already posted a reward. Stick, you're the lead on this."

Without any hesitation, or another word or a gesture of any kind, Stick took his notepad from his desk and tucked it under his arm. He then refilled his White Sox coffee mug and headed for the double doors that led out into the hallway. His husky partner followed right behind him.

Timbo punched his buddy in the back between his shoulders. "Fix your collar and tie for crissake."

Stick ran an open palm through his hair and clumsily pulled up on his tie.

"How does your wife let you out like that in the morning?" Timbo added. "Doesn't she dress you like the rest of the kids?"

Once they arrived in the corridor, Stick observed a black boy about eleven or twelve, he guessed, dressed in a neat pair of navy slacks and a crisp-pressed, powder blue dress shirt, complete with a clip-on navy blue tie. His feet were encompassed in a pair of shiny black shoes. Had it not been for a tattered, sweat-stained baseball cap on his small head, standing out like a sore thumb, the boy looked like he could have just come from, or was just going to church. A well-dressed man and woman, also black, flanked the boy on each side. All three sat like park statues, motionless, on the long, wooden bench right outside the busy investigators' office as uniformed police officers marched several handcuffed individuals back and forth in front of them.

With coffee cup in hand, Stick approached them and asked, "Are you the boy who saw the attack yesterday in Burnham Park?"

"Yes, he is," replied the black man, standing as he addressed the cops, his fedora in hand. "I'm Earl Overstreet. This is my wife, Eva. My son, James here, says, well, he—"

"Mister Overstreet, is it? Why don't we just let the boy speak for himself? Okay?" Timbo interrupted.

"Of course. Excuse me," replied Earl, lowering his head. "I understand. Of course."

Stick looked directly at the boy. "James is it?"

James nodded.

"Well, James. Why don't we just step in here and you can tell us in your own words what you saw? Okay?" Gesturing with his coffee mug, Stick motioned toward a door to the left of where the family sat.

James didn't respond to the tall cop's request but rather looked up at his father, still standing and clutching his hat in his hand. His father nodded his approval.

"We're going in there with him," Eva Overstreet stated, as she sat on the bench, an arm clutched tightly around her son.

"Of course. No problem," replied Timbo. "Are you his mother?"

Patting moist eyes with a white, lace hanky, Eva nodded and stood up with the boy. While they conversed, several more police officers hustled prisoners, both male and female, through the cramped corridor.

"This way," Stick said, directing them through the commotion into the room. "It's more private in here."

The Witness Interrogation Room, a rectangular room more wide than deep, had one six-foot blond wooden table in the middle. The backside of the table had a chair tucked under it while the front side held two. A row of identical chairs lined the back wall. Waist high, bar-covered windows bookended that same, dirty-white wall. Bolted shut, the windows looked as if they had not been open since Prohibition, making the dingy room seem more depressing than it already was.

Chicago lay gripped in a longer than usual July heat wave, coupled with oppressive humidity. The air in the room was stale and thick. A large industrial-type fan stood in the corner, noisily dominating the dank space as it whirred away, oscillating on its aluminum stand. Fluorescent lights hung from the ceiling, buzzing, making the shabby green painted walls appear even drabber.

A screech echoed in the room as Stick pulled out a chair, scraping it against the worn linoleum floor. He motioned for James to sit down.

"We wanted to come in as early as possible, Investigator, but—"

Timbo interrupted the family patriarch in a superior tone, "Actually, we're detectives, Mister Overstreet. The title investigator—"

It was an honest oversight for the man to call them investigators, which they were, but a sore point with many cops like Timbo in the Aggravated Assault Unit. Memos went out recently by police brass proposing to change these cops' official titles to "investigators" since some other major cities were adopting this term, too.

Stick knew Timbo thought the idea was horseshit, hence his

terse retort to the father. In order to keep things on track, he interrupted. "Why don't we let James start telling us what he saw now? Okay?" Stick smiled at everyone in the group, including Timbo. "Please. Everyone have a seat."

Timbo effortlessly lifted two chairs from the back wall and set one on each side of the boy for his parents. The cops then took seats opposite the three of them and they all sat down.

Stick started the questioning, flipping open his notepad. "Now, James. Where would you like to begin? What happened? What did you see?"

Stick Hanley and Timbo Boscorelli had interviewed eyewitnesses to felonies hundreds of times before in their short but illustrious careers. Their first order of duty: make the witness feel as comfortable and calm as possible, yet at the same time look and listen for signs of truth or falseness in the story told. Good cops searched for inconsistencies.

"Can I get you a cup of water, James?" Stick asked, grabbing his own coffee mug and taking a sip.

James shook his head.

"Maybe a bottle of orange Fanta? I even have some Green River," Stick offered, knowing his own kids loved those drinks. "I got some right in the fridge across the hall."

James said, "No."

Timbo butted in. "Okay then. Well, let's get on with this. So, what happened yesterday in the park? Just what did you see, kid?" After making a few scribbles, Timbo turned his eyes up to look right at James, then flipped to a clean page in his notepad.

James watched him, and following a long pause, he swallowed once, took a deep breath, and spoke in a meek voice. "I was travlin'—" He stopped, cleared his throat and said, louder this time, "I was travlin' to the lake, like I do every day, 'cept when I stopped by my best friend Clayton's, like I usually do, there was no answer."

Timbo jotted as James spoke. "Yeah. Go on," Timbo said, not looking up from his pad.

"So, like I said, I went alone, like I been doin' a lot lately. And I was walkin' this time 'cause I wasn't ridin' my Ted Williams—"

"That's his bicycle we got him for his birthday last year," Earl interjected.

The investigators nodded their heads in unison. Stick took simultaneous notes, too, which, along with Timbo's notes, he'd later combine to become part of the official General Progress Report, or GPR, which every lead investigator was required to keep on a case. As he listened to the boy's story, Stick continuously moved his eyes up and down between his notebook page and across all three of their faces. Timbo did the same but kept his eyes especially glued on James.

"Yeah, my bike," James continued. "I left it at home and walked to Burnham Park. When I walk I always go across LSD, over the footbridge at Forty-Third Street, ya see, 'cause I can get down to the lake faster that way."

"When you say, LSD, you mean Lake Shore Drive, James? Is that correct?" Stick asked.

"Yes, sir. Lake Shore Drive. I was headed to the playground there, at Forty-Fourth Street. When I got to the top of the footbridge, I saw them messin' with the old man. They had his bike—his red Huffy."

"Who is 'they'?" Timbo asked.

Lifting up his head, James went on. "Ice Pick and his gang. They had the old Jew-man and his bike and they started messin' with him. Next thing I see is Pick—that's what everyone calls him for short—he has a bat and takes a whack at him while the old man is still on the bike. I knew the old man was in trouble then." James turned and looked right at his mother. "It all happened so fast, Momma."

Eva, whimpering now, wiped her eyes.

"Take your time, James. Just go slow and tell us exactly what you saw," Stick said. "Did you know the man they stopped?"

"Yeah. The old Jew-man. Mister Fleischman. Everybody in the park knows him. The old man sticks his arm up to block the bat. He must have known Pick was going to hit him 'cause he timed it so sweet. But Pick hit him so hard—"

James paused again.

"—he hit him so hard that the old man fell from the bike

screaming. Then he just laid there. The other guys, they hop on that bike and start to ride it around the old guy, whoopin' and hollerin', while he's just lying there, on the ground, not movin'. He looked dead."

"What happened then, James?" Timbo asked.

"Well then . . . then next thing I see is that Mister Fleischman's not really dead. I mean, I guess he musta' been playin' possum. Because he grabs Pick's ankle and won't let go. I mean, he's holding him real tight. I was happy to see he wasn't dead and all, but I could see Pick spinning, trying to get away from him, and he can't. He can't break away 'cause Mister Fleischman is holdin' him so tight and this time he won't—"

Eva grabbed her son. "Please don't make him talk about this—please!"

"Eva. James wanted to do this. Remember?" The husband's reply was a clear indication to Stick that Eva and Earl were not in agreement on being there this morning.

"James, are you sure you don't want a glass of water?" Stick asked.

The boy shook his head back and forth and looked at his mother, "It's okay, Momma." He turned back to the two detectives. "That's when Pick really hit him. He just raised that big bat over his head and came down on the old man like . . . like he was crazy or something. He hit him again—and again."

"What were the other boys doing?" Timbo asked, jotting notes as he spoke.

"They just stopped what they was doing and watched Pick beat him." James stared, looking between the two cops. "I never seen nobody get beat like that before."

"What happened next, James?" Stick interjected, knowing that the next bits of information would be crucial to finding the killers.

"While all this was goin' on, they didn't see me but I had come down off the overpass and hid behind a park bench right on the path that goes by the playground. The old man was just lyin' there, all bloody an' everything, but then he sticks his arm toward me and I'm pretty sure he sees me behind the bench. They looked like they were both starin' right at me just before Pick hit him for the last time."

James stopped his story and became silent for a moment. He swallowed hard.

"How far away were you then?" Stick asked him.

"Less than a half block away. I can show you."

"That's not necessary. We can do that later," Timbo jumped in.

Timbo's dismissive tone surprised his partner. Stick looked at him then turned back to his notepad and jotted with his pen. Stick picked up the next question. "And then what? What happened next, James?"

"That's when I think they saw me. I think they know I saw what they did but I'm not sure."

"So what did you do?" Timbo asked.

"I didn't move—didn't budge. I waited to see if they'd come after me."

"What did they do next?" Stick asked.

"They started to run toward the Oakwood Boulevard overpass. I watched them until I couldn't see them no more. Then I got outta there as fast as I could. I came right home, same way I got there," James replied.

"You mean you didn't help the man they attacked? Go over to him to see if he was dead or alive?" Timbo's voice rose with each question.

James shook his head.

"He was frantic when he came home. He just kept saying, 'They gonna kill me, Momma. They gonna kill me.'" Eva cried harder, her voice rising louder, "You gotta protect my child!"

Earl got up and went over to his wife, embracing her and kissing the top of her head.

"Nobody's gonna hurt your child, folks. That's why we're here, to take animals like these off the street and put them away for good," Timbo instructed them matter-of-factly.

"Could you identify all of these boys if you saw them again, James?" Stick asked.

James nodded that he could. "I know five of them for sure, but the other one I didn't see real good 'cause he ran away when the whole thing started."

"Is that so?" Timbo said, writing in his book.

"Would you folks please stay here? We'll be right back," Stick said, pushing his chair back from the table and standing up. Timbo did the same. The detectives left the room and stood outside in the hallway. Stick looked at Timbo as his Italian partner placed his pen inside his coat pocket.

"So, whadya' think, *coomba*? This eyewitness should make it easy for us to solve this old guy's mugging. If this kid can positively ID the attackers, we got ourselves a dunker. We could use one right now. We need some clearances and I need to get home to Katie."

"Yep." Timbo answered without looking up, flipping through his notes. "That is—" He stopped before finishing his sentence.

Stick knew his partner was holding back and prompted him for a reply. "That is what?"

"That is, if you can believe this little nigger."

"C'mon, Timbo. I heard the tone of your voice in there. He's a goddam kid for crissake. Why don't you fucking believe him?"

Timbo looked up from his notepad and looked his partner in the eye. "It's all too rehearsed. He's too cool. He made it sound too easy to tell us. And you heard what LaFrance said. There's a reward out for the fuckers who did this. A nigger'll turn in their fuckin' grandmother if they think there's something in it for 'em. This little shithead's folks probably set him up to do this. They probably have the fuckin' money spent already."

"Christ, Timbo. You are one sorry son of a bitch. Why the hell would this kid turn in somebody's who's not guilty? He ain't gonna get no fuckin' reward if we don't find somebody guilty."

"Well, that may be. But, shit, don't tell me you've turned into some kinda goddam nigger lover all of a sudden."

"Fuck you. You know that has nothin' to do with it. If this little kid saw that old man get whacked in Burnham yesterday then we gotta treat him as our goddamn eyewitness. Period." Stick punched his own notepad with the tip of his pen to emphasize his point.

"All right, all right. Don't get so defensive. I'm on your side for crissake. What the hell's eating you anyway? Katie cut you off again? Let's just find out if the victim can talk yet—if he's come out of his coma. Why don't you go to Mercy and see what you can find out and I'll stay here with the kid and the parents."

Stick knew that Timbo knew him better than anyone. Only his long-time partner was aware of the fact that Stick and his wife, Katie, were having serious problems, something he'd kept hidden for months from the other Homicide dicks. Stick loved his big, fat Italian partner, but he also knew Timothy Boscorelli was one of the most prejudiced sons of bitches on the Chicago police force. He raised an eyebrow to Timbo's comment, knowing better than to leave his partner alone with the Overstreet family.

"Don't worry," Timbo said, "I won't fuck with your little spook. Like I said, why don't you go over to Mercy and check on the old man's condition."

He looked right at his partner and said, "No, LaFrance made me the lead on this case. You contact Mercy. I'll stay here with the eyewitness. But first, I need to take a leak and piss out this shit you claim is coffee."

Timbo watched Stick walk down the hallway and turn into the men's room then went back to his desk in the detective's office. The big cop plopped himself down in his swivel chair, picked up the phone, and dialed Mercy Hospital. He identified himself and inquired about the Burnham Park beating victim. The hospital operator connected him to a nurse's station.

"Four west ICU, Mulcahey," the voice on the other end of the line crackled through Timbo's receiver.

"Hey, Fran. It's Timbo."

"Hey, Timbo. How's it hangin', big guy?"

"Just the way you like it, darlin'."

"So, you calling to pick me up when my shift's done? How is it you can tell when I'm so hot for that Italian sausage of yours?"

"Not now, babe. Later. Okay? This is police business. I'm calling about the guy brought in there yesterday. The old man that got mugged in Burnham. Fleischman's the last name. I understand he's up in your ICU. When do you think we'll be able to talk to him?"

"Oh, jeez, Timbo. I'm sorry. Didn't you guys get a call? He died about forty-five minutes ago."

There was silence on the other end of the phone.

"Timbo, honey? You okay?"

He slammed down the phone. "Fuckin' niggers."

CHAPTER 12

"James, boy, what did you mean yesterday when you said, 'They said they was gonna get him'?" Earl asked his son as they sat, waiting in the muggy interview room for Detectives Hanley and Boscorelli to return.

James didn't answer.

"Earl, I think this was a bad idea to bring the boy down here," Eva whispered as she clutched her son toward her.

"The boy had to tell the police what he saw, Eva."

"Momma, it's the right thing to do."

"I'm just worried those boys will come after you and hurt you. Are you sure you know who they are?" she said.

"I know them, Momma. I *know* them."

Knocking at the door before he reentered the room, Stick returned alone to resume the questioning. He sat back down at the table.

"Folks, I'm going to need James to stay and look at a few pictures with me."

"Sure, Detective," Earl replied. "Whatever you need."

"Wait a minute," Eva said. "I don't want my boy left alone in no lily-white police station. Too many things can happen down here. Too many racist cops be turnin' their heads the other way on him. Like that fat partner of yours."

"Please don't talk like that," Earl said to his wife. "This ain't Little Rock. It's Chicago. Our home."

"So was Arkansas. Those police down there killed my brother, sure as I'm sitting here today. Police said he 'resisted arrest' but I know better. That's our child now you're leavin' here, Earl. Our own flesh and blood."

"Eva. Please." Earl turned to Stick. "I apologize for my wife's remarks, Detective." But Earl knew his wife's remarks were probably not far from the truth. The atmosphere around Chicago police stations toward blacks, be they criminal or witness or even fellow cop, was certainly biased. Even though Earl didn't hear them, Timbo's remarks out in the hall to his partner a few minutes earlier proved that point. Earl tried to imagine what Eva might be feeling; he tried to put himself in her position of a mother, leaving her young son in a strange and intolerant environment.

"No need to apologize. Let me assure you both that I will personally take care of your son all the time he's here," Stick said. "I'll treat him like he's one of my own. He'll be safe with me."

Earl and Eva looked at each other and then at their son. James shrugged and nodded, indicating he'd be okay. Eva looked at Stick Hanley and, after a moment, nodded her approval.

"How long you gonna have my child down here?" she asked.

"You better give us an hour or so, ma'am. I have a lot of pictures for him to look at and then I'll need to get his account on paper and into my GPR."

Eva reached across the table, laid her hand on Stick's forearm, and gave it a tight squeeze. "Okay. But Detective Hanley, the next time I see my child he better look exactly the way he does right now. You understand me?"

Timbo sat at his desk talking on the phone. "So time of death was seven a.m. then, huh? Okay, Fran. Thanks. Hey, I'm sorry I hung up on you earlier. Can I make it up to you? How about that Italian sausage you wanted for dinner?" Sensing someone was walking up behind him, he lowered his voice, "Yeah, maybe Friday night, we'll see." He hung up the phone and wrote a note on a small piece of paper. He glanced up as Stick and the boy witness walked up to his desk, handing the scribbled note to his partner.

"Sit here," Stick said to James, pointing to the chair behind his own desk, facing Timbo's. He read the note, looked over at Timbo, and shook his head. Stick walked up behind his partner, bent over, and whispered, "Don't tell the kid."

Timbo looked up and whispered back, "It's murder now, so you better be sure about this little shithead's story."

As the two spoke in muffled voices, James twirled in circles in Stick's swivel chair. Timbo watched the boy spin for a few moments, looking at James and his tattered cap revolve around. The burly cop motioned his big head upward and said, "So, you're a White Sox fan?"

James kept spinning.

"Don't like the Cubbies, huh?" Timbo prodded him. "They're the better team, ya know."

James didn't answer but after a few more spins finally replied, "Well, I don't know about that. The Cubs finished sixth in the NL East last year with a sixty-six and ninety-six record. The Sox finished fourth in their division and played five hundred ball."

"Yeah, but we had some bad luck. Lots of injuries."

Still going round and round, James replied to Timbo's excuse. "I don't think injuries was the problem, sir. More like pitching. The Sox had two twenty-game winners. Wilbur Wood and Jim Kaat. Your best pitcher, Bill Bonham, lost twenty-two."

"Whadya got here, Stick, a ringer?" Timbo asked, a tinge of anger in his voice.

James stopped his spinning but didn't let up with his statistical onslaught. He looked right at the big detective.

"And, the Sox beat the Cubs last year in just about every major category—hitting, pitching, and in every fielding position." The boy emphasized each statistic by counting them off on his fingers. "So, I'm not really sure what you mean when you say that the Cubs are the better team."

"Ouch, Timbo! Looks like we're gonna have to take you to the Cook County Hospital burn ward 'cause James here just lit you up, my man." The lanky cop high-fived James as they both grinned wide smiles. "Looks like we got another knowledgeable baseball fan here. And, guess what? No surprise—he's a White Sox fan."

Timbo dismissed them both by swinging his chair around, away from them.

Still grinning ear-to-ear, Stick went on. "C'mon, James, my man. Let me get you outta here. Nothin' worse than having to look at a pissed-off Cubs fan. Anyhow, I need you to take a look at some photos to see if you recognize any of the boys you saw in the park yesterday."

"Don't need no photos, sir. I know all of them. See 'em every day on the street."

Stick looked right at the boy as he still sat in the lead detective's chair. "You do? Do you know their real names, too?"

"No, sir. Just their street names. It was Ice Pick and his gang, like I told you in that room with my momma and daddy," James said. "Aren't you gonna arrest them?"

"Sure, James. If you say you saw them do it, then we can arrest them as soon as I know their names. But first I'll need to know if you're positive who they are and, more importantly, if you're willing to tell this someday in front of a judge in court."

"Yes, sir. I seen them do it. I know it was Pick and four of his Oakwood Rangers."

Stick paged through his notes. "Didn't you say there were six of them all together?"

James paused for a moment, looked down, and replied, "Uh, I don't know that last boy, sir. The one that ran off."

"Do you think if you saw his picture, though, you could identify him?"

Head still down, James paused again before answering Stick. He shrugged his shoulders.

"Well, that's okay," Stick said, looking down at him. "Once we get the others, they usually flip on their friends. Let's get you over to Youth Division to see if they know these boys you're talking about. Okay?" He looked over to Timbo, who still had his back turned to them. "Hey, Timbo, call up to Juvie, wouldja? Ask them if they have anything on this kid Ice Pick and the Oakwood Rangers. If they do, have 'em start putting together a photo array. Tell them I have a witness I'm bringing up to look at it. See if your

Cubs buddy, Cyclops Murphy, is there. If he's not on another one of his six coffee breaks, put him to work on it."

Timbo's face still burned red under his tight-collared shirt. He wanted to tell Stick and his little nigger Sox fan witness to go fuck themselves, but bit his tongue as Stick led the boy out of the office.

When Stick and James reached the elevator at the end of the hallway, Stick pressed the white plastic UP button on the wall. He looked down at James, smiled, and tugged the brim of the boy's White Sox cap past his eyes. James tilted his head up and nudged the brim back in place. He smiled back, looking up at the tall cop. As they waited for the building's vintage contraption to make its way down to the second floor, Stick leaned against the hallway wall and spoke to him. "So, you're obviously a very big Sox fan."

"Yeah. My daddy works part-time for them in the home team locker room."

"Is that right? You know, I thought he looked kinda' familiar. I work there, too, ya know."

"You do?"

"Sure do. I work crowd security for night games to make a little extra money for me and my family."

"You got kids?" James asked.

"Four." He held up his hand and counted them off on his fingers. "Kaitlin, Karen, Kevin, and Brian. Brian's about your age. What are you? Eleven? Twelve?"

"Gonna be thirteen, August first."

Stick paused a moment in thought, then asked, "August first, huh? Nineteen sixty-two then. Right?"

"Yes, sir."

"Bill Monbouquette, Boston Red Sox, no hit us that day," Stick said. Most Sox fans liked to forget the bad memories, especially something as significant as a no-hitter against them. He sounded proud of the recollection. "I was at that game."

"Really? You was?" James said, his voice echoing in the hallway.

"Yep. I was there. It was my first summer after high school," Stick reminisced. "Bunch of the guys from my neighborhood,

Avalon Park, went to that game. Big Monboo really shut us down that day. Next summer, I was off to Vietnam with the Marines."

"My daddy was a minor league ballplayer with the Red Sox. He played with Monbouquette in 1958," James said. "The Red Sox said daddy was gonna be the first black ballplayer for them to get to the big leagues. He busted up his knee, though. The year after he got released the Red Sox brought up Pumpsie Green to the big leagues. They was the last major league team to have a black player. Shoulda' been my daddy."

Impressed with the boy's knowledge of baseball and the story about his father, Stick took a liking to the boy. As he watched him, he noticed James begin to fidget. The boy started cracking his knuckles as he looked up and down the hallway. Then James blurted in a high-pitched voice.

"It was my bat that Pick used to beat that old man with."

Stick jerked himself up erect from the wall, turning his eyes right on James. "What did you say?"

"My Dick Allen Louisville. That was my bat Pick used when he attacked the old Jew man," James rattled. "Mister Allen gave it to me last summer when my daddy took me to meet him in the club-house for my report card."

"Hold on, James. Slow down a minute. You're telling me that Dick Allen's bat was used by this Pick kid to kill Mister Fleischman?"

James's eyes widened. "So, he dead?"

Stick crouched down, bringing himself to the boy's level. He laid his hand on James's shoulder. As he looked at him, eye-to-eye, Stick replayed Eva Overstreet's clear threat in his mind. At the same time he also thought about his partner Timbo's doubt and not wanting to trust the Overstreets. He harbored no animosity toward the mother and, at least as a fellow parent, understood her concern. As for his partner, he knew his bigotry clouded his vision, but, in the end, he also knew Timbo would back his decisions 110 percent.

Even with all those thoughts spinning through his mind, another more pressing question took precedence: was James sure he understood all the implications of what it meant to be an eyewitness to a murder and the future he was about to face?

"Yes. He died a short time ago from the hemorrhaging in his brain. It's murder now, so you need to be absolutely sure about what you saw and what you're telling me here."

"I know what I saw, sir, and Pick and his gang jumped the old Jew-man and beat him with my Dick Allen bat. I know it for sure."

CHAPTER 13

The elevator came to a bumping halt when it reached the sixth floor. The physical jolt seemed small in comparison to the emotional blow Stick felt from James's shocking revelation in the hallway four floors below. The doors creaked open and the two stepped off.

"Juvie" was the nickname given by the Homicide dicks to the Youth Division at Area 1. The busiest juvenile department in the City of Chicago, it handled thousands of cases every year. Its staff of Youth Division cops knew just about every bad kid by first name in the neighborhoods within The Prairie. If they didn't know the guys James saw, no one did.

They would also know whether any of the kids who attacked Fleischman had a YD Record, meaning they had a prior arrest as juveniles, requiring a photo to be taken of them at the time of their arrest. If the kids James saw attack Fleischman were actively involved in local gangs then the guys in Gang Crimes South, part of the CPD's Gang Crimes and Investigation Division could help, too. And, if that was the case, then Stick could take James to their office, also located in the Area 1 headquarters building, to look at more photos.

Stick led the boy to the opposite end of the fluorescent-lit corridor where the bold stenciled words, **YOUTH DIVISION**, highlighted the frosted glass of a large double door. Stick pulled one of the doors open for James to enter, the boy's tattered White Sox cap still perched on his head. The tall cop motioned with a quick nod for James to go in and the boy entered the room, gliding under the detective's long arm. He pointed him to a desk and pulled out its metal chair for him. As he did this, a muscular man about six-foot tall, wearing a gun strapped to his shoulder, approached them.

"Hey, Hanley. Is this the little bro' your fat partner just called about who said he saw that old man get whacked over in Burnham yesterday?" asked the cop, working his nicotine-stained teeth with a toothpick.

The two men did not shake hands.

"This is James Overstreet, Youth Officer Murphy," Stick said, his tone pointed. Still struggling to understand all the possible implications of James's bat statement divulged just before their elevator ride, Stick didn't have the fortitude at the moment to deal with Murphy's sarcastic lip. "He witnessed the attack of our victim, Mister Fleischman, yesterday. Homicide needs you to help him ID some of the kids he says he saw commit the crime."

"No, problemo, Stickaroo. You got Mike Murphy on the case now. Best cop on the South Side, maybe even the City of Chicago."

Murphy turned to James. "C'mon over here, little bro, and we'll look at photos of some of our wonderful city's most likely to commit a crime."

"His name is James, Officer Murphy. And mine is *Detective* Hanley," Stick replied, looking directly at Murphy and staring at his close-set eyes separated by a huge nose—hence his office nickname, "Cyclops."

"Sorry, *Detective* Hanley. Little testy, aren't we, Stickaroo?"

The two cops had always played a tense game of placating each other but underlying this ostensible accord brewed a seething, mutual animosity. Over the years, there had been no love lost between the two men. Each man possessed a temper with a very short fuse and had a history of behaving unpredictably in each other's presence.

Murphy went on. "Oh, that's right. Tough loss last night. Your sad White Sox just can't seem to put it all together this year, huh? No more Dick Allen to save your sorry asses."

Stick ground his teeth, holding back, wanting to punch Murphy in his smug face, right in his third eye. Even though he was fighting unrelenting fatigue from working nonstop Area 1 homicides along with his part-time security job, Stick still noticed James's head drop when Murphy mentioned Dick Allen's name. From now on the All-Star baseball player's name would be forever associated in James's mind with the beating of Manny Fleischman.

Ignoring Murphy's snide remark, Stick said, "Let's just help James, okay, Murph, so I can get him home to his parents."

"Roger dodger, Stick ol' boy."

Murphy turned to James. "Okay, James, let's see if we can help you positively ID who you say whacked that old guy." Then he prodded the boy. "Hey, I see by your sad-looking Sox cap, you're pullin' for the bad guys. What year is that cap from? Seventy-three?"

"Actually, it's a nineteen seventy-four Sox cap," James replied. "Ron Santo finished his career wearing a cap just like this one. But I'm sure you already knew that, Mister Murphy, sir."

Stick held back his laughter, not sure how Murphy would respond to James's dig. He knew nothing could be more brutal for a Cubs fan than when reminded of the fact that their former team captain—"Mister Santo" as aficionados of Chicago's North Side team reverently referred to him—finished his baseball career in a White Sox uniform. Most Cubs fans couldn't even bear to think about this fact let alone talk about it.

"That's *Detective* Murphy," he snapped, glaring at the boy.

"Uh, your official title, according to CPD General Orders, is youth officer, not detective," Stick smirked.

The Youth Division dick turned away and reached for a piece of paper with six pictures clipped onto it. He placed it down in front of James.

"Here's a quick photo array I put together on the name Timbo gave me when he called up here earlier."

James studied each snapshot. "This is him. This one right here." He pointed to one of the pictures.

Murphy went to his desk and leafed through a pile of manila folders, stopped, and picked one out. He brought it back, opened the file, and laid out a larger picture of the boy James picked out. "Well, Stickaroo. The bro your boy James here pointed to goes by the street name of Ice Pick. Pick for short. Real name's Monroe Clarke." Murphy jabbed at the photo then read from inside Clarke's manila folder. "Couple of collars for assault, one for possession, two breaking-and-entering, one arson. Seems he really likes trespassing at Oak Woods Cemetery." Murphy leaned over to Hanley and chortled, "I thought spooks didn't like spooks."

Stick glared at Murphy. He hoped James hadn't heard the youth officer's derogatory remark.

"Boy's sharp, though. He's had a rock-solid alibi on every single collar," Murphy continued. "Mays and LeDonne over in Gang Crimes South have been watching him real close recently. They haven't been able to put him away on anything yet. If this is your bat boy then his luck may have changed with your boy James's ID here."

"Knock off the boy stuff, okay, Murph."

Murphy shook his head and continued reading from the papers in Clarke's folder. "He's got an older cousin, Julius Clarke. Runs the P-Stones out of the Olander Projects. He's one bad dude that Julius. Looks like little cuz might be following in the family tradition."

"Maybe Julius was the sixth kid you saw?" Stick asked James.

"No, sir. It wasn't Julius," James replied. "He don't run with those boys."

"Your boy's right there, Stickaroo. According to Gang Crimes, Julius runs with the older P-Stone Rangers. He's too big-time for these little shithead Oakwood Rangers. They're just punks who report to the Nation," Murphy added.

The P-Stone Rangers, originally formed as the Blackstone Rangers, had united scores of Chicago street gangs in organized violence, later renaming themselves the Black P-Stone Nation. Their members wreaked havoc everywhere in Chicago, and Gang Crimes believed they controlled many smaller, subset gangs, like the Oakwood contingent. According to Murphy's statement, the attack of Manny Fleischman seemed to prove that theory.

"Let's see if James can ID the other four boys then," Stick said.

Stick led James to a table with dozens of three-inch binders

lined up between two large bookends. Each binder was sorted
with a gang affiliation and the respective precinct within Area 1.
Murphy pulled one out labeled RANGERS—DISTRICT 21, opened it,
and pushed it in front of the young witness. The binder, stuffed
with plastic sheets of mug shots exhibiting juveniles with YD numbers in The Prairie, overflowed. As James leafed through the
pages, Murphy also pulled out some Polaroids from a separate
folder on the table.

"These are some recent snapshots we have of aspiring up-and-
comers we think are ready to make the leap into more heinous
crimes on the *sous-side* of Chicago, James ol' boy."

Stick once again let Murphy's last comment slide then watched
as Murphy laid out the Polaroid snapshots, one by one. As Stick
looked on, James slowly scanned each photo placed in front of
him.

"If you see this sixth kid you didn't recognize from the gang,
too, you'll let me know right, James?" Stick reminded his eyewitness.

James didn't speak but nodded his answer without looking up
from the Polaroids. Eventually he picked out the four other boys
who had attacked Fleischman, pointing at them with a short nod
and quick finger tap on the photo as he recognized each of them.
Murphy set the photos aside as he did. When finished, James still
hadn't identified the sixth boy.

"You're sure you don't see this sixth kid in any of these pictures?" Stick asked him again.

James shook his head no again. "Maybe he ain't got no police
record or nothin'. Huh?"

Stick wondered if the boy's question sounded more hopeful
than curious.

Murphy jumped in, "Your boy could be right there, Stickaroo.
First offenders usually get community adjusted, sent home to their
parents with a warning to not let us see their sorry little asses again.
We give these losers two chances at community adjustment. If they
screw up after that, then it's strike three and we arrest them. That's
when we give 'em their very own YD number and they get to have

their pretty little pictures taken. Maybe this sixth kid just hasn't posed for us yet."

Murphy went over to a desk and leafed through a handful of manila folders. As he found the Youth Division reports for each of the additional four boys James had IDed, Murphy read aloud from each of their rap sheets.

"Looks like all four have been involved in mostly small stuff. A little schoolyard and street corner extortion, a few collars for B and E on vacant buildings." Murphy stopped and pointed at two pictures on the table. "These two here are Bertrand Rhodes and Bobby DeSadier. Their street names are 'Jumbo' and 'Bobby D.'" He opened another folder. "And this one's name is Tyrone Witherspoon. They call him 'Stretch.' Seems he's a shadow of your batboy, Pick. Same exact collars, same time, and same outcome. Nothing stuck."

He paused on the next folder, reading it silently first to himself, and then continued aloud, shaking his head, right before he threw a large photo on the table of a boy with a patch over one eye. He tapped on it hard.

"'Course, every cop in Area 1 Youth Division and Gang Crimes South knows this little prick. His name's Porter Turner. He a real beaut, too. Street name's 'Pokie.' Wanna know how he got that cute little nickname? A classmate accidentally hit him in the eye once at school, so he returned the favor by poking the other kid's eye out with a ballpoint pen during recess. He was eight years old. Mean little bastard. Other kid didn't press charges. What a surprise."

"I think we got enough here for probable cause so I'll put out a stop order on these kids," Stick said as he scribbled in his notebook. Turning to James, Stick asked, "If we brought all five of these boys in for a lineup, do you think you could positively ID all of them?"

James nodded yes. "Can I go home now?"

"Sure, son," Stick replied, motioning him toward the door. "See ya later, Murph. Oh, and by the way, I'll make sure I tell Timbo you said to say hello to my *fat* partner."

As Stick and James approached the doors leading back to the hallway, Stick bent down and whispered into the boy's ear. Hand on the doorknob, they both then shouted in unison, "Go, Sox!"

When they returned back down to the detective's office, Timbo had the phone to his ear.

"Yes, sir. Right away, sir." He hung up as Stick and James walked up behind him.

"Edward Seamus," Timbo said in a lilting voice. A routine they played throughout their partnership, each called the other by their full baptismal names when something surprising, or official, or both, had developed in one of their cases.

Playing along, as always, Stick answered, "Yes, Timothy Joseph."

"Lieutenant LaFrance wants us to find these perps pronto and he wants a murder-one collar. City Hall's all over this one. Seems like this Fleischman guy was kinda famous."

"Whadya mean, 'kinda famous'?"

"Well, Stick. You better sit down 'cause you're just not gonna believe this."

Stick gave his partner an impatient look. He had no time for Timbo's little guessing games. "What, Timbo? Spit it out."

"Okay. Okay. You remember the Black Sox, don't you? Of course you do. Well, it seems that Manny Fleischman was the last surviving member of that team. So, I mean, he's kinda famous, in a sad sorta way, that is, considering it was the only time a World Series was ever thrown—ever, ever, that is."

As Stick stood with his mouth agape, his face turned ashen, not able to reply to his partner's news. What concerned the lead detective more, though, was what effect this news would have upon his eyewitness. He looked over at James who stared at him, eyes widened.

Timbo went on. "Seems the media got wind of this little known fact—a sports reporter from WGN radio just broke it—and now City Hall has it. So downtown is all over LaFrance's ass." Timbo motioned with his head toward their superior's corner office. "That was him on the blower. Looks like we got ourselves a heater here, pardner. They want these little bastards found and locked-up *yesterday*."

Stunned, Stick shook his head. He'd been a cop a long time and the remarkable unfolding of new developments in the attack of Manny Fleischman made his head spin, wondering what surprising discovery might come next in this murder investigation. He turned to the boy. "Let's go, James. Maybe it's a good idea to take you home now."

CHAPTER 14

When Stick Hanley drove up to the Overstreet apartment at 3938 South Ellis, James politely asked, "Wouldja like to come inside my house?"

"Some other time, James. I have a lot to do right now. We really need to find these kids—and fast."

"Okay. Yeah. I guess you're right." After a pause, James spoke again. "Detective Hanley, I didn't know baseball had an all-black team. Is that why people like Detective Boscorelli didn't like them?"

Hanley, staring off in thought, paused a moment until he caught the significance of the boy's innocent question.

"No, no, James. That's not what they mean by Black Sox. Actually, the Black Sox were a bunch of white guys long ago who really screwed things up—pretty bad as a matter of fact."

"What'd they do, kill somebody?"

"They may as well have." Stick paused, considering the irony in the boy's question. "No . . . no . . . but in a way, it was actually worse than that. They cheated. Then, they lied about it. And then, even worse yet, they tried to cover it up. They did something no baseball team ever did before or since."

"Did they go to jail?"

"No. No one went to jail. But they received a punishment much worse than jail. They got banned from baseball for life."

"Sounds pretty bad, but how can that be worse than killin' someone?" James asked.

"Well, in a way, James, they did kill something." Stick stared out the large windshield of his four-door Chevrolet Impala sedan.

"It just wasn't a person. They killed a spirit." He turned his head and looked at James. "It's a long story, son, and hard to explain. Maybe you'd better have your dad tell you that one."

"I think I know what you're talkin' about," James said. "I kinda feel the same way about me and Mister Fleischman. I mean that spirit thing you're talking about."

"How well did you know Mister Fleischman, son?"

"I used to see him and talk to him in the park every day. Then he got me a job at the place he worked at in Hyde Park, deliverin' groceries for the rich folks there. He was very good to me. He didn't treat me different like most white folks do. He taught me about the good things black people do, what some famous ones have done, things people don't know about or maybe even forgot about. He also told me he was a baseball player. A long time ago. That he played with a guy whose nickname was Shoeless Joe. He told me he was on a White Sox team with him."

Stick focused now on yet another new fact: his eyewitness intimately knew the victim before the attack. And James's last statement seemed to confirm this guy Fleischman was actually on the same team as the eight men thrown out of baseball for life from the 1919 White Sox—the infamous Black Sox. *What the hell is this kid gonna tell me next?*

"Maybe then tomorrow you can come by my house. My brother, William, wants to be a policeman, just like you."

"Sure, kid. Okay, tomorrow for sure." Stick knew the likeliness of this happening was slim. But it seemed easier to lie to the boy right now than to tell him the truth. More likely the scenario: Stick would only be back to visit James should he or his family decide they didn't want to cooperate with the investigation after having another night to sleep on the prospect of what lay ahead of them by testifying against a local gang. It was most probable Stick wouldn't be back in his own bed, for that matter, for at least the next twenty-four hours, possibly even longer. Heater cases had a tendency to keep investigators chained to their jobs until someone got arrested. Stick wouldn't be sleeping anywhere comfortable, he guessed, for at least the next few nights.

James exited the tan-colored unmarked police car, slammed

the vehicle's big door shut, and ran off down the gangway toward the brownstone's rear entrance. Stick waited until James took the sharp turn at the end of the brick three flat's narrow passage. He sat there for a moment, making sure nothing happened to this brave boy, the only eyewitness to the murder of the last surviving member of the 1919 Black Sox team.

He wondered if he should station a blue-and-white at the curb of the Overstreet home. Neither James, nor his parents, had mentioned threats of any kind being made against them, but once the gang found out an eyewitness had come forward—and that was only a matter of time—then the boy and his family's safety would be in jeopardy. Stick thought of moving the family to a safe haven, as a precautionary measure, but nothing warranted that step right at the moment. And anyway, with James's positive ID of the five youths, he and Timbo would have these little pricks locked up and off the streets pronto, making his concerns all for naught.

Mayor Daley's office would bring a lot of heat on the police department now to find these killers. Homicide investigators didn't like to handle these high-profile cases. It distracted them from the job at hand. And with a twelve-year-old witness, Stick's job would be even tougher.

What a fuckin' mess. I hate goddamn heater cases. They'll never let us sleep on this one. And what if Timbo was right and the Overstreets are in it for the reward money?

He questioned himself as to why he let that last thought of his partner's cloud his thinking. Yet, Stick couldn't help but wonder what would make a boy James's age act in such a courageous manner. *Should I really trust James and his family?* A kid like James always did what their parents said. It didn't help that Stick could still hear the anger in Eva Overstreet's voice, regarding anyone in her family wanting anything to do with helping the police. She had left a clear impression on Stick with her little, threatening squeeze of his forearm, reminding him to keep her son safe—or else.

Suddenly, the words of his own dad, Tom Hanley, preaching to his kids at the dinner table, popped into his mind. *"You can't trust a damn nigger if there's somethin' in it for them."* He hated when his cop father had spoken that way, teaching his son not to trust blacks, especially when one turned against another. Stick couldn't help but feel this kid looked and sounded different from the biased stereotype of blacks his father had instilled in him. His gut told him James spoke the truth. And one sure thing he did learn from his father was that a good cop followed his gut.

But what made James come forward?

Stick continued to ponder this thought as he sat in his Impala cop car at the curb outside the Overstreet apartment. Stick couldn't deny he liked the boy. And, it didn't hurt that James was obviously a die-hard White Sox fan—a huge mark in his favor. *But didn't my dad use to say most blacks liked the Sox anyway?*

Yet, putting all these thoughts and conjectures aside, Stick couldn't overlook the fact that getting eyewitnesses to come forward for any type of crime in Bronzeville, let alone a murder, defied explanation. In The Prairie, nearly 100 percent of all crime involved black gangs. Swift and merciless retribution awaited those who decided that their civic duty served a higher purpose than protecting their own skin—even if it was black.

Stick also knew, 100 percent, that James Overstreet's life would never be the same. From this point forward, the boy would live every day, probably for the rest of his life, looking over his shoulder. Whether these perpetrators would be found guilty—*I have an eyewitness, so why wouldn't they?*—or not guilty, James's future in his neighborhood would be uncertain. So, too, would be that of his entire family. Chicago Homicide Investigator Edward Seamus "Stick" Hanley fully understood this and hoped that James fully understood it, too, even if he was only twelve, and whether he was black or not.

CHAPTER 15

The Chicago Police Department dispatcher had released a city-wide bulletin about an hour before Stick Hanley returned back to Area 1 Headquarters at 51st and Wentworth. The boys James identified were well known by most of the Youth Division cops as well as to the guys in Gangs Crimes South, but not to the dicks in Homicide. Since this was a murder investigation now, Fleischman's name got added to the board on the wall of the Homicide/Sex/Aggravated Assault Unit's office, listing the open and cleared homicide cases in Area 1.

The clearance rate of murders in Area 1 was the second lowest in the city. The brutal summer of 1975 had all of the area's homicide dicks working ungodly hours on all types of violent crimes but predominantly murders. Most murders involved one black gang member killing another. The workload was overwhelming.

Last year's city record of nearly a thousand homicides hit the communal psyche of Chicago's inhabitants hard and by the end of this year, even though declining, the Chicago Police Department had projected there would still be more than eight hundred homicides. Relentless pressure from City Hall had been put on Police Superintendent James M. Rochford to lower this grim statistic. Ward aldermen clamored that murder within their respective borders had become all too commonplace and, hence, unacceptable to the proud city's image.

The Prairie, the most expansive district in Area 1, had one of Chicago's highest crime rates since many of the city's toughest black street gangs called it their home. Identified by Chicago PD as a "maximum patrol area," it required three times as many patrol cars as compared to any other section in the City of Chicago. On most Saturday nights, emergency rooms at the two hospitals in the district—Mercy and Michael Reese—teemed with victims of beatings, rapes, and gang-related shootings. To the Area 1 Homicide cops working The Prairie, it was considered nothing less than a jungle.

Stick knew the first forty-eight hours after a murder were the most critical in solving the crime, so he promptly delegated investigative tasks. Other departments in Area 1, as well as the district beat cops, would serve an assisting role to him and Timbo. He would need all the help he could muster in quickly rounding up the kids James identified. Now a little over thirty-one hours old, in all likelihood they'd be in hiding with help from elder P. Black-Stone Nation gang members.

On top of that, Stick had on his hands a heater, and "Downtown" wanted someone—*anyone*—apprehended immediately. He and his partner, Timbo, would work nonstop until they caught and arrested the vicious murderers.

"Our parks must be safe for da children and for all da people," Mayor Richard J. Daley proclaimed in his terse Chicago-ese on the local TV news the day after Manny Fleischman had died. "We will not stand for dis type of ting in our parks or in our streets or in our neighborhoods where old people—all da people of Chicaga—are not safe to move about dis byoodeeful city of ours."

The faithful who voted for Richard J. Daley the last six elections referred to their mayor as "King Daley." Such was the place of honor he had achieved, running the city with big shoulders. This was *his* city. Under his reign for nearly the past quarter century, Chicago had existed as its unofficial motto implied, "The City That Works." Within the Daley regime, that's all that mattered. "Hizzoner," another one of the pretentious nicknames given to him by his undying constituents, would not tolerate murder in his Chicago parks. The Fleischman slaying had occurred less than three months after his record sixth inaugural address, one that focused on promising a crime-free Chicago. Yet the fact of the matter remained: Daley's city was not safe.

There was another untold story, though, roiling in Chicago's political underbelly; a way of life unspoken about but all too real. In Chicago, where whites still outnumbered blacks, the unwritten law stated blacks killing whites would not be tolerated.

The mayor himself took a special interest in the Fleischman murder since he, too, like the slain former ballplayer and retired public school teacher, lived on Chicago's South Side. The Mayor's home was just a few short miles due west of the violent crime scene. The murder of an elderly white man by black street thugs so close to his own family's home in the safe and tidy neighborhood called Bridgeport did not go unnoticed by Hizzoner.

The political fire flared even higher with the revelation the murder victim was the last surviving member of the infamous Chicago Black Sox. City officials knew this murder could make national headlines, or at the very least, be a byline on sports pages throughout the country. This scarlet-lettered team, and the ill-chosen actions of eight of its star players, had forever left a blemish on the City of Chicago, upon its baseball sports scene, and, for that matter, upon America's pastime.

And now, the last survivor of the ball club, a heretofore unknown and obscure player by the name of Manny Fleischman, who played a mere four games during the 1919 season, had been murdered in one of Mayor Richard J. Daley's "byoodeeful" parks near his own backyard.

The *Chicago Tribune*, Stick thought, would have a front-page spread about his case in tomorrow's paper. No doubt they'd reprint headlines from the 1920 trial of the eight ball players covered that year by the same illustrious newspaper. "Fucking Cubs fans will have a field day with this," he swore to himself.

Stick had sent Timbo to Mercy Hospital to speak with the staff there and to meet with the victim's family. After dropping off James, he radioed his partner to tell him first the news about the bat and then to tell him about learning of the eyewitness's and the victim's close friendship. Not only had James known the victim, Stick told a stunned Timbo, but the boy worked with Fleischman at Hyde Park Foods.

How did we miss that?

Good cops looked at every angle during a murder investigation, trying to make the connection between victim, killer, and witness. Stick realized he hadn't been doing as thorough a job as he should investigating a crime of this magnitude. *Maybe it's because I'm so fucking tired from working nonstop the last three months.* Too, his initial interview with James had been shortened after his difference of opinion with his partner on the motive behind the Overstreets coming forward. Stick didn't like the fact he needed to question his own work and the weak job he was doing on the case so far, yet he didn't want any more surprises either. *I wonder if there are any more connections between everyone involved here?*

With plenty of summer daylight still left, he headed to the crime scene to meet rookie Patrolman Sal Abbatti. According to what Stick had read after Lieutenant LaFrance had handed him "the runner"—the name given in the Homicide unit for the paperwork file of a murder case—Abbatti had been the first officer on the scene. He also read that CCR, the Central Communications Room, had taken the inbound call on the city's recently deployed 9-1-1 system.

Abbatti's patrol area, Beat 2122, covered the section of The Prairie where the crime had been committed. According to the Youth Division reports, it also happened to be within the beat where four of the alleged perps lived—the Olander Housing Projects at 41st and Lake Park Avenue.

"A jogger said he found the victim's body near the bike path," the first-year cop told Stick as they walked together along the park's asphalt path toward the scene of the crime.

"What time was that?" Stick asked.

"The call came into CCR at ten twelve a.m. They dispatched Chicago Fire and those guys arrived here on the scene at ten twenty-two." The patrolman pointed to a nearby telephone booth along Lake Shore Drive not far from where Fleischman's body lay lifeless when Abbatti had arrived. "The caller dialed the new nine-one-one number from that pay phone."

"Where's this jogger now and what's his name?"

"Don't know. But CCR said the voice sounded like a very young male, presumably black. The caller didn't give a name. Said he was out running, saw a man lying on the ground, called it in, and then hung up the phone."

"So much for Good Samaritans."

"I was on patrol near Thirty-fifth and Lake Shore Drive when the call came in from dispatch. I was here within three minutes of the jogger's call. I saw Fleischman, went to him, checked his pulse. It was faint. He was alive but unconscious. His head was covered in blood. I was certain it was no accident by the extent of the damage. He had to have been beaten. From what his skull looked like, it was probably some type of blunt instrument. I radioed a supervisor and cordoned off the area."

Stick nodded as Abbatti relayed his details. The rookie had done everything by the book, and from what Stick saw, the scene hadn't been compromised.

"I made a sketch," Abbatti said, handing over his notepad to the detective.

Surprised at the rookie's thoroughness, Stick smiled as he looked at the patrolman's drawing. Abbatti had indicated the location of the body in relationship to some stationary objects nearby in the park—a light pole to the south and west of the body, the phone booth due south, two park benches due east, and a playground with a basketball court to the east and north of where the victim lay.

Just like they taught us in dick school.

"Hang on to that in case I need it," Stick said, handing the rookie's notepad back to him. "Did you show this yesterday to Detectives Dimmick and Sternberg?"

"Nope. But from what I hear, those two couldn't find sand if they were in the desert."

Stick wasn't surprised at Abbatti's comments about the two detectives who had first arrived on the scene after being notified by 21st District dispatch that a suspected attack had taken place in the park. The two veterans hadn't cleared a case in over six months, and Stick was certain that's why LaFrance had handed the case to him and Timbo. Near 90 percent, Stick and Timbo's clearance rate was the highest in Area 1.

Stick then looked in his notepad and read from the notes he had taken during the interview with James earlier that day. The detective walked the area, noting some of the key points James had mentioned, like the footbridge he had crossed to enter the park at 43rd Street, and the park bench he had hidden behind. Stick's gut told him something didn't add up.

"Is this where you found the body?" Stick asked Abbatti, pointing to a bloody spot on the asphalt.

"Yep. Right there," Abbatti said, pointing to the same spot as he walked over to where Stick stood. "The vic's body was laying here with his head facing southwest, toward Lake Shore Drive." Abbatti oriented his own frame to show the direction. "His clothes were blood soaked as was the asphalt bike path beneath him."

Stick shook his head. Something wasn't right with the description of how far James was from the scene after he came down from the overpass. The park bench he said he had hid behind was no more than fifty feet from where Abbatti found Fleischman's body. James had clearly said in his interview he was about a half block away. "That's more like fifty *yards*," he mumbled.

"Excuse me?" Abbatti said. "Did you say something, Detective?"

"You're sure this is where you found the body?"

"As sure as I'm standing here," Abbatti replied.

Maybe the boy just made a mistake, Stick thought. *He was probably scared shitless. He* must *have meant feet. But if he was fifty feet away, he would have gotten so close he would have certainly put himself in harm's way. Something's just not adding up.*

Stick stared north, looking down the bike path toward the Chicago skyline, five miles away. The sight was nearly identical to any one of a number of picture postcard versions a tourist could pick up as a wonderful memory of their trip to the magnificent city along the lake. With Lake Shore Drive winding gracefully along the western edge of Burnham Park, landmark Chicago skyscrapers in the distance, and a grassy shoreline, hugging the azure lake, it was a view like none other in the world.

A car and pedestrian overpass four blocks north at 39th Street, followed by a twin structure four more blocks north at 35th Street, gave ample access to park enthusiasts. The 43rd Street footbridge, the bottom of which Stick and Abbatti stood at now, gave additional egress to the lakeshore park.

"The boy said the gang ran north over the next overpass from where they attacked Fleischman. He must have meant this one," Stick said to Abbatti, pointing to the 43rd Street footbridge.

Abbatti read more notes from his pad to Stick, telling him that there were no signs of a struggle in the immediate area. He saw no ripped turf in the grass on either side of the path, nor had he observed discarded material of any kind, although he did notice something on the victim's jogging suit, which consisted of a blue pair of pants and blue windbreaker.

"His wallet and money were still on him, but he had grass stains all over his shirt and pants," Abbatti said. "Do you think it's possible they dragged him?"

He scratched his head after Abbatti's last remark, then replied, "Let me do the detective work, okay, Rook." Looking full circle at the crime scene, Stick went on. "Wallet and money still on him, huh? So they killed a helpless old man for a fucking bicycle."

Flipping his notepad closed, Abbatti gave a terse reply, "Looks that way, Detective."

Paramedics on the scene, emergency room nurses and doctors who had treated Fleischman—as well as the intensive care staff who spent only a brief time with him once he had arrived up on the Fourth Floor West ICU—detailed for Homicide Detective Timothy Boscorelli the severity of the victim's beating. Not easily shaken, Timbo nonetheless winced as Four West head nurse Francine Mulcahey described the trauma Fleischman had suffered and the victim's condition when he was admitted. She and her staff had provided what little treatment they could for him as they tried to comfort his devastated family.

"You're gonna catch these little nigger pricks, aren't you Timbo?"

"We'll catch 'em, Fran," he replied, as he placed one of his fat, thick hands on her shoulder, sincere in his intent.

She inched closer to him. "That was fun the last time we were together. When we gonna do it again?"

"Not now, Fran. I'm on duty and all I want to do right now is catch these little niggers."

Timbo had seen many beating victims in his years in Homicide, but after seeing Fleischman's smashed skull later in the hospital's morgue, coupled with his hangover from drinking too many beers at Fox's Pub after last night's softball game, he got sick to his stomach. Anger swept through his convulsing body as he hurled a bacon and egg breakfast into a nearby slop sink. After regaining his composure, he left the morgue and got in his unmarked Impala, driving to the nearby Hyde Park home of Fleischman's family members to interview them.

Bobbi Fenton, Fleischman's daughter, answered Timbo's knock at the door of her three-story brownstone. After he identified himself, she invited him into the living room. Timbo offered his condolences to the trembling middle-aged woman. She then proceeded to tell him how she and her husband had kept vigil outside Mercy Hospital's emergency room and later by her father's bedside after hospital personnel had transferred him to the Four West Intensive Care Unit.

X-rays taken immediately upon the victim's arrival at the hospital showed severe swelling in his cerebral cortex, making his condition critical, Fenton told Timbo. Emergency room doctors attending the octogenarian had decided surgery was out of the question until the swelling in his brain subsided. Unfortunately, the intense beating her father had suffered proved insurmountable, even though the tough old man had clung to life for nearly a day. He had died, she said, without recovering consciousness early the next morning.

"My father didn't have an evil bone in his body. You know that, don't you, Detective?" said Fenton, as Boscorelli squeezed himself into one of the room's overstuffed chairs. "He wouldn't have hurt a fly. He was a calm and peaceful man. He had relatives who died in the Holocaust, yet still he held no animosity in his heart for those who killed his own family."

Timbo, still pale from his viewing of her father's crushed head, nodded. Fenton spoke softly to him as they sat in the expansive parlor that faced Cornell Avenue, three blocks from the University of Chicago, where she and her husband, Lars, both taught.

"He loved to ride his bike in the park," Fenton went on. "He often rode fifteen, twenty miles a day and never had a problem. But I worried about him all the time. I told him, 'Papa, be careful where you ride. Please be careful.' He paid me no mind. He would always say to me, 'Who would want to hurt a little old man on his bike?' He was right, you know. Why would anyone want to hurt him, Detective Boscorelli? What did he ever do to them?"

Timbo waited for Fleischman's red-haired daughter's sobbing to subside before he continued his questioning, notebook in hand and ballpoint pen to paper. "Can you tell us any more details about your father than we already know? We want to know if he had a particular route or a special routine you're aware of? And if so, was it the same every day?"

"He only worked the midday shift, from ten thirty in the morning until two thirty in the afternoon," she replied.

"A creature of habit is what you'd call him, Detective," Lars interrupted, handing Timbo a cup of coffee he had carried in from the nearby kitchen. "My father-in-law was a creature of habit. He always left his Prairie Shores apartment precisely at nine forty-five every morning—never later, never earlier."

"Did you find his cap?" Bobbi Fenton asked. "He always wore that silly gray cap." She shook her head, a small smile appearing as she spoke.

"No, ma'am, we haven't found it yet. But we will. I know this may sound odd, ma'am, but did your father ever have any problems with anyone? Any incidences or run-ins with anyone at work?"

She nodded and began to cry again. "He told me about some boys at the park—those black boys who had put James in that garbage can." Timbo raised his brow and immediately jotted a note. Lars moved closer to her and hugged her as she sobbed. She wiped her eyes and softened her next words to the detective.

"He did love that boy, James, though," Fenton added. "My father talked about him all the time. Papa had been depressed for so many years, especially after Mama died. That boy gave him new life." She wiped the tears away from her eyes again, this time with a hanky Lars handed her.

Timbo shook his head, holding his anger back, wishing he wasn't causing this anguish for the survivors by interviewing the victim's family but rather out catching the killers.

"I can't imagine what James will do," she added, "how he'll react when he finds out his friend, Manny Fleischman, was murdered in the park they both loved so much."

Timbo realized, as he listened to her words, that she didn't know James had allegedly witnessed the murder of her father. Not sure whether he should release this information to her at this time, he chose at the moment to keep that bit of news to himself.

"Who will tell him, Detective Boscorelli?"

Not exactly sure what to say next, he gave her a puzzled look.

"Papa said the boy called him 'the old Jew-man.' Who's going to tell James Overstreet that his friend, Manny Fleischman, the old Jew-man, is dead?"

At that point it was clear to Timbo that it would be best if he did tell her. "Mrs. Fenton, James was in the park when your father was attacked. He saw the whole thing. He's our eyewitness."

CHAPTER 16

Based on an eyewitness who had positively identified five of the six alleged attackers of Manny Fleischman and with the assurance of his witness's willingness to participate in a lineup and testify in court, Stick Hanley phoned Felony Review at the Cook County State's Attorney's Office. He told them he had probable cause to request a warrant for the arrest of Monroe "Ice Pick" Clarke and his gang.

On-call for the Felony Review Office that night was second-year Assistant State's Attorney Norbert Dushane. Since Dushane had only been an ASA for two years and never been involved in a heater case, he immediately called his supervisor, Assistant State's Attorney Ronald Spencer. Heater cases had a tendency to become unwieldy beasts from the moment they happened. Every agency's respective protocol called for every *t* crossed and every *i* dotted when handling one of these hot potatoes.

An hour later, Dushane and Spencer went before Cook County Night Court Judge William F. Peters, requesting warrants for the arrest of the five boys James had IDed via the photo array produced by Youth Division Officer Michael T. Murphy. Based upon the police work performed so far, the nature of the crime, and the positive identification of an eyewitness, Peters granted the warrants.

Stick pulled his Chevy Impala alongside Patrolman Sal Abbatti's blue-and-white squad car, already parked at the curb next to the alley behind the Chicago Housing Authority's Olander Projects. The cars faced opposite directions, driver's door next to driver's door. Stick rolled his window down; Abbatti cranked his down, too.

"I just pulled up to the curb a few minutes ago. I patrolled the whole area for about an hour. Doesn't seem to be much goin' on around here," Abbatti informed Stick. "Just waiting for your orders."

"Okay," said Stick. He felt good hearing Abbatti's assessment but knew trouble could erupt any second at the Olander. Local authorities knew the CHA's fourteen-story, red brick building was home to some of The Prairie's most notorious street gang members. He and Timbo alone had investigated five shootings at this hot spot last month alone, three of them ending in deaths. Stick wondered where his partner was with the Tactical Team backup he'd requested. Last he spoke to Timbo, they were on their way. He wanted this arrest to go down fast and smooth, and sitting at the curb too long was never a good thing.

"Let's sit tight and wait a few minutes. We've still got a little bit of daylight left." Stick lit a smoke. "Do these little shitheads all live on the same floor?"

"Youth Officer Murphy radioed me and said Clarke and Witherspoon are on twelve, DeSadier and Rhodes on eight," Abbatti said. "I've already notified the CHA police like you told me and got them on our radio frequency. Two of their officers should be inside, waiting for us."

"Okay. But just double-check to make sure they'll be in there. Those guys have a tendency to get lost when we're busting their bros. When you do, remind them we'll lead once inside." Stick inhaled on his cig then blew the smoke out the side of his mouth. "And Abbatti. Take it real easy. You stay close to me."

The rookie smiled. "Roger that. Are we waiting for your partner?"

"Yeah, he's rollin' in with the tac guys. I also got a couple of Gang Crimes guys rolling in here, too. They told me dinnertime would be the best time to grab these burrheads. My gang guys told me one thing these gangbangers are definitely afraid of is missing their auntie's dinner—"

A call on Stick's car radio interrupted their conversation.

"This is twenty-one-sixty. Over."

The Tactical Team's call numbers cracked the silence of Stick's car radio. He picked up his handheld mic and replied.

"Twenty-one-sixty," Stick paused a beat, his brow furrowing, then spoke, asking their location. "Ahh, roger, this is fifty-one-fourteen. What's your twenty? Over."

"Forty-third and Cottage. Twenty-one-sixty ETA . . . three minutes. Over."

"Roger that. Fifty-one-fourteen. Out."

Stick slammed the radio handset back to his dash, flicking his cigarette to the pavement through the open window, and exited his vehicle. *He's got that other hot-headed dago with him!*

"You okay, detective?" Abbatti asked as Stick got out of his squad car. "Something wrong?"

"Yeah, there's something wrong," Stick snapped while he twisted the discarded butt into the pavement under his black oxford. "If I can teach you one thing, Rook, about being a good cop, it's make sure you are where you're supposed to be when you're expected to be there."

Stick grabbed his .38 service revolver from his shoulder holster, checked the load, and slid it back into its harness. Then Stick bent over and checked the .38 snub-nose in his ankle holster.

Minutes later, a second Impala pulled up right behind Abbatti's squad. Timbo exited the vehicle along with four other plainclothes cops from the Tactical Team. Stick noticed that Timbo looked different, his skin a chalky white, his eyes bloodshot.

"You okay?" Stick queried.

"Fine," he grumbled. "Why?"

"Don't look so good. That's why."

"Just want to get these fuckers off the street. That's all. You gotta problem with that?"

Stick knew what Timbo's terse reply meant: *Stay outta my way if I want to rough these little niggers up a bit.* Stick let his partner's comment slide, choosing not to embarrass him by calling him to task in front of the now-assembled team. "Just follow my lead. I want this one to go down sweet and easy. Let's make it a clean collar. No rough stuff here with these kids." Stick looked directly at his partner. "Agreed?"

Stick was unyielding when it came to cops under his command breaking the CPD's official rules of engagement. In particular, he worried about some hard-ass cop deciding to act out their own version of a *Baretta* episode, or worse yet, a scene from *Starsky and Hutch*. This was *his* investigation, *his* collar. Once LaFrance had handed it to him, he controlled every aspect of the case. His orders were absolute and final.

As Stick's seven-man team formed a semicircle in front of him, he lectured them. "I don't want any loose cannons here. No fuck-ups. Got that?"

He looked at each again, scanning for any hint of dissension among this contingent of highly skilled cops. As he did, another unmarked Impala screeched to the curb. Youth Division Officer Michael Murphy, accompanied by another cop, jumped out, each slamming their car doors behind them.

"Let's get this show on the road," yelled Murphy to the startled group.

"This isn't a fuckin' show, Cyclops." The team snickered at Stick's dig. "And who the fuck asked you to be here anyway?" Stick shouted back at him, looking over the approaching pair's shoulders, watching their backs as Murphy and his partner walked toward the group.

The first thing seasoned cops taught green cops was to never look a fellow cop in the eye while working on the street, especially when outside one of the CHA's gang hot spots. Out here, cops always needed to stay alert, eyes trained on their surroundings, and most importantly, watching their partner's back. Murphy was making eye contact with Stick as he strutted toward him and had broken a basic street rule. Cyclops had crossed the line—an unforgiving mistake in a homicide cop's world. Once Stick realized Murphy wasn't covering his back, Stick took a challenging step closer to the him.

"You and your mealymouthed, pussy sidekick Accardo here—" Stick said, staring eye-to-eye with his nemesis while at the same time pointing at Murphy's closed-lipped partner, "get your Juvie asses back in that car. This is a Homicide matter. Go look for a fuckin' truancy case or whatever it is you do. I don't have time for this shit. I gotta job to get done here and you two are in my way."

Stick did an about-face and headed toward the Olander's main entrance. He snapped his head for Timbo, Abbatti, and the four soft clothes from the Tac Team to follow. Murphy and Accardo stayed behind, standing at the curb, watching Stick and his men head off on their mission. Striding away, Stick heard Murphy mutter to Accardo, "Fuck that motherfucker. I'll deal with that skinny piece of shit later."

Stick moved his men in double-time, knowing that as soon as the project's suspicious residents spotted unmarked Impalas alongside Abbatti's blue-and-white police cruiser, a bust must be going down in their building. Before he got too close to the red brick structure, Stick scanned the nearly two-hundred-foot-high CHA behemoth for open windows as his men followed behind him in single file. It wasn't unheard of for suspects to jump from windows—from any level—once they knew cops were entering their building to make an arrest.

On one of Stick's first busts in the projects, a nineteen-year-old murder suspect jumped from a seventh-story window to avoid arrest. The perp landed on his head, hitting a large Dumpster. The kid splattered so hard when he hit the steel container that one of the cops in the arrest team jokingly suggested that they just throw what was left of the teenager's body in the Dumpster since there was so little left of him intact.

Stick stopped and turned to his men. "McGovern, you go around back. Watch the upper floor windows from there," he directed one of the Tac Team officers, his hand stabbing with thumb squeezed tight against four, closed fingers in military fashion. "All of you. Keep your eyes up, too!" he barked.

Stick knew The Prairie claimed the most number of cops killed in the line of duty, a discomforting distinction. Besides gunfire, when police appeared at a housing project, they commonly encountered projectiles like rocks, bottles, or anything else tenants had on hand thrown down on them as they stood below ready to make their entrance.

"Look out!" Timbo yelled, pushing Patrolman Abbatti to the ground and covering him with his massive frame. As he did, a cement block crashed within inches of the two of them.

Timbo jumped up, pulling Abbatti up with him, grabbing him

under his arm. The entire team dashed to the building's entrance. When they got there, Stick held his hand up for the team to halt.

"You okay, Rook?" Stick asked Abbatti.

"Thanks to this guy I am," he replied, nodding at Timbo.

Stick thanked his partner with a quick smile, knowing Timbo running on two cylinders was better than most cops running on eight. Seconds mattered now so Stick entered the front lobby alone. He had learned early on that the ground floor lobby of a "shit hole," the term cops from The Prairie gave the projects, is where most ambushes took place. As lead, it was his job to go in first. He reconnoitered the interior, scanning the lobby for any signs of a surprise attack. The first thing Stick noticed: the two CHA cops who were to meet them inside the lobby were not at their post.

"Shit. Those chicken-shit cocksuckers," he muttered to himself, sweat dripping now from his brow. His heart racing, he had guessed right. The CHA cops were nowhere in sight.

Stick scampered back to the entrance and waved for Abbatti to join him. "Abbatti, radio those CHA cocksuckers again and find out where the fuck those dogs are."

"Roger that," the patrolman replied.

Stick then motioned to Timbo and the three remaining guys from the Tac Team to enter the lobby. As they passed him at the doorway, he patted each on the shoulder and whispered, "Keep close to the wall. Stay alert."

The three Tac guys slowly entered, scoping out the entire ground floor. Each had their six-shot .38 Colt Specials drawn. Timbo trailed them in.

"That's a lotta firepower," Stick told his partner as Timbo paused before following the last Tac guy into the lobby. Timbo was carrying his .457 Colt Python for the bust and had the monstrous gun drawn, pointing it ahead of him into the lobby.

"Yeah, and it's got a magnum load in it, too. You gotta problem with that?"

Stick didn't answer his partner. He knew Timbo was aware of the first unwritten rule of engagement on an arrest in the projects: *Ask no questions, I'll tell no lies.*

"Thanks for saving my ass back there," Stick said to him, nodding to the spot where the brick would have almost certainly killed the rookie cop, Abbatti.

"Your ass?" Timbo smiled his frown. "Anyway, whadjoo expect? He's a *paisano*. We look out for each other."

Stick grinned and shook his head as he followed the other cops who had already entered the lobby. "Well, try to keep that fat dago ass of yours from getting shot at, wouldja?"

Stick watched as Timbo and the other cops methodically checked the elevators and the doors to the stairways on either end of the ground floor as he remained by the entrance with Abbatti. With perfect timing, two more cops rolled up to the scene. When Stick saw them at the curb, he waved them to come forward and join the team.

As the two new cops reached the building, Timbo's team had finished clearing the lobby. Stick called the team back together. "You guys. This is Johnny LeDonne and Barry Mays from Gang Crimes. They know this place like the inside of their church."

"If that's true, then you guys are fucked," Mays replied.

The group laughed and grunted their hellos to each other, nodding with quick upward jerks of their heads, all the while keeping a close eye around them.

"Okay. Let's get this done." Stick flicked another cigarette away and barked out his orders, emphasizing each directive with the use of a pointed hand gesture. "Timbo, Rossi, you two dagos take the back stairway and head up to twelve. Kircmarich and Popovak. You two follow them but wait on eight. Abbatti. You stay right next to me. Johnny. Barry. You're with me and the rookie."

Stick was keeping a close eye on all of his team, but particularly now on Abbatti. He didn't want any more close calls for the virgin cop making his first collar under Stick's charge. He looked at the guys from Gang Crimes and pointed to the steps in front of him.

"Follow me and Abbatti up this stairway and then head to twelve."

"Why don't we just use the elevator?" Abbatti asked.

"No, kid. Never use the fuckin' elevator in a shit hole,"

LeDonne cautioned him. "They'll jam it on you when you're inside and then you're really fucked."

"Fuckin' 'ey," echoed Mays.

"That's why I got you two here, so that kinda shit don't happen," Stick said. He appreciated the two veteran Gang Crime dicks, teaching Abbatti the ropes, especially about busts in the projects. It also helped break the tension. White Chicago cops never felt comfortable in the projects. Never. "Abbatti? Have those CHA guys answered you yet?"

The rookie shook his head.

"Fuck it then. We move up without 'em. Let's roll."

The arrest teams took off simultaneously up their respective stairwells. Stick guessed it would take his team four minutes to reach the eighth floor. Once there, LeDonne and Mays would continue past them up to twelve. The seconds seemed like minutes now. Chicago PD cops never knew which CHA cops were on their side or just shills for the gangs. Their absence in the lobby, as well as the brick thrown from above, burned a message in Stick's gut that the guys they had come to arrest were well aware Chicago's finest were there and coming after them in force.

Timbo's four-man team had reached the eighth floor vestibule. Per Stick's orders, Timbo and Rossi continued up to twelve while the other two Tac guys stayed at eight. The two veteran Italian cops clambered up the next four stories on the clammy concrete steps strewn with garbage and reeking of urine and feces.

"Look at all this shit," Rossi hissed. "Fuckin' *titzoon* animals."

"These *mullanjohns* give me any problem, I'm smokin' their little nigger asses," Timbo scowled, looking right at his unholstered Colt Python.

"Ditto that, *coomba*," said Rossi.

Back in the other stairwell, Stick paused when his team got to eight. "All teams—once you get to your floor, stay on the landing until I give the order to move in." Stick's clear instructions from the tiny speaker on each cop's Motorola hand radios echoed in the empty stairwells.

"I hope those two dagos don't run into Pick's cousin Julius up there," Mays said to Stick as he and LeDonne paused before continuing up to twelve. "If they do, this won't go down pretty."

"That's one bad motherfucker," LeDonne added. "One-bad-mother-fucker."

"Timbo's got his orders. He'll do it by the book," Stick answered them, although he knew his and Rossi's quick tempers often short-circuited when confronting anyone with black skin.

"When we get the order to go, *coomba*, you take Witherspoon in twelve-thirteen, I'll take that little cocksucker Pick in twelve-eighteen," Timbo told his arrest partner, Rossi. Both huffing, they rested on the landing of the twelfth floor.

Rossi nodded in agreement, catching his own breath. "Just say the word, *paisano*. They don't listen, they're *morte*."

"Hey. What's that?" Timbo whispered, laying his ear against the closed, steel door to the apartment hallway.

After waiting a few more minutes, Stick gave his next command into his Motorola. "Okay. Everyone in place? Kircmarich and Popovak?"

"Kircmarich, roger"

"Popovak, roger."

"LeDonne? Mays?"

"LeDonne, roger."

"Mays, roger."

"Timbo? Rossi?"

Silence.

"Timbo? Rossi?" Stick repeated. Only static came out of his and Abbatti's radio speakers.

"Detective Boscorelli! Officer Rossi! Come in!"

Still, no answer.

"Fuck! All units! Move in now! Move in! Move in!"

CHAPTER 17

The four suspects were apprehended without incident—for the most part. They were loaded into a paddy wagon, taken to Area 1 for interrogation, and prepared for an eventual lineup. As this was taking place, Stick and his arresting team stood in the street outside the Olander Projects, hearing the story once again from Timbo and Rossi as to why they didn't answer Stick's frantic radio calls.

"Stick, baby, you had to be there. It was too fuckin' funny," Timbo said.

"Yeah. Timbo hears this huge commotion right outside our door as we stood in the stairway, waiting for your 'go,'" Rossi chimed in. "We weren't sure what the fuck was going on out there in the hallway but we heard these *titzoons* screeching like fuckin' baboons in the fuckin' zoo.

"So, we figures the little bros are making a break for it down the elevator, knowing we're comin' and all—see? Now we know the fuckin' CHA dogs aren't down in the lobby doin' their cop thing, so me and Timbo we figures we gotta' stop these little *mullanjohns* right now before they get away."

Rossi rambled on with the story, laughing in between his stilted breaths.

"So, I says, 'Timbo, let's roll right now' and we bust into the hallway. That's when we see those two tall cocksuckers, Clarke and Witherspoon, with their foot-long black fuckin' dicks, pissin' down the elevator shaft."

Rossi stopped talking for a moment, losing his breath because he was laughing so hard, the other cops in the arrest team guffawing in anticipation of hearing the story's punch line for the third time since the arrest.

"And I says, 'Stop! Police!' Pointing my piece right at 'em with Timbo running beside me pointing his Python, ready to pop the first little soul brother that says, 'Boo!' "

Timbo roared with laughter as his dago buddy cop continued with his tale.

" 'Stop! Put your hands up and move away from the elevator doors,' I says again and they both put their hands up, but their big black dicks are still squirtin' away, pissing down the elevator shaft. Then, one of 'em asks, 'Can I put my Johnson back home, Officer?' and that's when Timbo here loses it and starts fuckin' laughin' so fuckin' hard I think he's gonna start pissin' his pants!

"So I says, 'No! Move away from the elevator and put your fuckin' hands against the wall, raised over your fuckin' heads,' and they both do as I say. So, then, while I'm keeping one fuckin' eye on them, I walk over to the elevator and look down the shaft."

Rossi can't continue because he's laughing so hard. That's when Timbo interrupts and continues with the story, laughing only a little less but able to finish.

"Right. And Rossi walks up to the elevator shaft and sees fuckin' Murphy and Accardo stuck in the elevator six floors down. Someone below musta jammed them on their way up and then opened the trap door above them. Before they could get out they were both drenched in nigger piss!"

The whole team laughed uproariously, unable to control themselves. McGovern, the Tac guy chain-smoker who had covered the back of the building, laughed so hard he coughed up gobs of phlegm. Mays from Gang Crimes held a handkerchief to his eyes, wiping away tears from his uncontrolled laughing spasm. The others shook their heads, trying in vain to recover from their own laughing jags.

"So, whadya think?" Stick asked the group, recovering from his own laughter. "I say, next week those two should get promoted to fuckin' Youth Division Commanders. Don't you?"

"Fuck you, Hanley!"

Stick turned around. There stood Murphy and his partner, Accardo.

"Fuck me?" Stick said. "I'd say you're the one who got fucked, Murphy, and it couldn't happen to a nicer guy. I told you two to keep your silly Juvie asses out of big man's work, but you just couldn't listen. Couldja?"

Murphy lunged at Stick, but before he could reach him, Timbo grabbed him in a bear hug.

"I think you've already lost one battle today, Murph. Let's not make it two. Heh?" Timbo said.

"Get your fat fuckin' hands off of me you fat fuck. Let me at that skinny little motherfucker!" Murphy shouted. "Let me at him! Let me at him!"

CHAPTER 18

Pokie Turner, the fifth boy James Overstreet had earlier IDed, remained on the loose and his whereabouts were unknown. The police surmised he had left town with his family as officers went to his apartment on South Drexel Avenue and discovered no one at the boy's home. A Gang Crimes Tac Team, search warrant in hand, had broken down the door and entered the squalid, four-room flat, finding half-emptied drawers with clothes and other articles strewn about, presumably in an unplanned, hasty exit.

The others were brought to Area 1 Aggravated Asssault Headquarters in a 21st District paddy wagon. Upon their arrival, detectives placed the arrested youths into separate interrogation rooms. On heater cases, the whole Homicide unit dropped what they were doing and offered help. Stick asked fellow Detectives Bill Rhino, a twenty-two-year veteran, and Joey Manfish, a fifteen-year vet, to each separately question Bertrand Rhodes and Bobby DeSadier.

"Let me take the Clarke kid, Stick," Timbo said, leaving Stick to question Tyrone Witherspoon.

Uncharacteristically, Assistant State's Attorney Norbert Dushane joined Timbo in Pick's interview, which started by reading the alleged bat-wielder his rights again, as was done at the scene of his arrest. Pick snapped gum and looked up at the ceiling as Dushane recited Miranda.

When the ASA finished, Timbo began his questioning. "So, knowing these rights that have just been read to you by Mister Dushane here," Timbo nodded at Dushane and then looked back at the boy, "Monroe Clarke, do you want to talk to us about your whereabouts on Tuesday, July 29 at approximately ten in the morning?"

"They call me Pick. And yeah. I ain't afraid to talk to ya'll. I was in Burnham, protectin' my turf, that's where."

"Okay, Pick. And just what turf is that?" Timbo asked.

"*My* turf, fool. Can't you hear or sumpin'?"

"I know you don't want to be here, son, and that this must be hard for you. I understand. Honest. I do. But if you talk to me that way, I really can't help you. And I want to help. Really. So talking to me that way isn't really in your best interest."

"Whachew gonna do, big man? Beat me? My daddy used to beat me until he learned his lesson." Pick leaned back on the two rear legs of his chair. "Maybe I should git me a lawyer or sumpin'? Yeah, that's it. I need one of doze dee-fense lawyers—"

"Of course you can talk to a lawyer," Dushane interrupted. "Do you want a lawyer or would you rather make a statement to us?"

"I don't need no fuckin' lawyer to talk to you two fools. Whachew wanna know?"

"So you *do* want to talk to us then?" Timbo asked.

"You must have shit in yo' ears, fool. Diddenchew hear me?"

"Yes. I heard you." Timbo paused, jotted a note on his pad, and then continued. "Okay then. Good. Let's talk. So exactly where were you this past Tuesday at around ten a.m. when you said you were in Burnham Park?"

"Like I already told you, watching my turf, man, on the bike paths wif my boys—like we do every day. Nobody comes through our turf without us knowin' about it. You dig, fat man?"

"Did you see this man there, Pick?"

Dushane slid a picture of Manny Fleischman across the table in front of him. The photograph showed the old man sitting on his red Huffy bicycle. It had been taken on the dead man's last birthday, a little less than three months earlier. Fleischman, coincidentally, wore the same clothes in the picture he had on the day of the attack.

"Yeah, I know that dude. Dat's the ol' Jew works up at Hyde Park Foods," Pick said.

"Did you see him this past Tuesday morning?" Timbo asked.

"Maybe I did. Maybe I didn't. Who wants to know?"

"Did you or didn't you see him, Pick?" Timbo asked again.

"Yeah, I seen that ol' fuckin' Jew. Motha's always riding that fancy, cherry red Huffy o' his up and down my turf. We warned the mo' fo' to stop ridin' his silly white-haired ass up 'n' down Ranger turf."

"You *warned* him?" Timbo repeated, making a note in his book. "Are you saying that you threatened this man?"

"Wassa matter whichew, man? You better have yo' fuckin' hearin' checked by some mother fuckin' poe-leese ear-checkin' fuckin' doctor, man, 'cause you can't even fuckin' hear me." Pick jerked forward, bringing the chair to the floor with a thump. "Maybe you got too much fuckin' fat between yo' fat ass fuckin' ears?"

Dushane raised his eyebrows with Pick's last rant. He looked over as Timbo cracked a smile. The youngster possessed a large set of brass balls, particularly since Timbo outweighed the boy by at least a hundred and fifty pounds. His Italian temper began to run short. Had the assistant state's attorney not been present, Timbo would have long ago pummeled the boy for his belligerence, smacking him around the room a few times. Every officer in Homicide might have done the same, or at the very least would have seriously considered it.

"That's some big talk for such a little man like you, Pick," Timbo said, getting up and circling behind the boy. "Maybe you'd like a piece of me, too, just like you got a piece of that old man, huh?"

Pick didn't reply but rolled his eyes upward, staring again at the ceiling while the detective stopped and stood in back of him.

Timbo felt the boy's indifference. He bent over him and whispered, "'Course, I'll bet that old man woulda whooped your black bony ass had you two been alone, huh?" Timbo snickered and continued his hushed tone. "Yeah. Whooped by an eighty-five-year-old man on a bicycle. I woulda paid to see that."

"Fuck you!" Pick shouted, trying to get up from his chair, but Timbo put his big paw of a hand on Pick's right shoulder, holding him down in his seat. The youth fought to get at the big cop, grunting as he tried to push himself away from the table. The chair's legs screeched on the damp cement floor but stopped when Timbo laid both hands on Pick's shoulders.

Pick became rigid. Timbo reached over him and picked up one of Pick's hands in his own. It was as small as a child's in the cop's mitt-sized hand. "Who could you possibly beat up with these puny little fists of yours?" Timbo asked him.

"Whatchew talkin' about, man?"

"What you gonna do, Pick? You got no friends here. No bat."

The boy tried to pull his hand away from the detective. Timbo leaned in ever so close. He whispered again, prodding the youth as he held him down with only one hand now. "You know what I'm talkin' about, my little bro. You beat that old man with a baseball bat. A Dick Allen Louisville slugger to be precise. We found it in your apartment with bloodstains all over it."

Pick shook his head back and forth repeatedly.

"You're just like every other stupid killer I've known—you kept the evidence. Our lab is running tests on it right now to see if it matches the blood of that—what did you call him—oh, yeah, 'that ol' fuckin' Jew' you beat to death Tuesday morning on your *turf*. I mean you must know about all that because it is *your* turf. Right, Pick?"

Pick didn't reply but kept shaking his head. Timbo wondered if the talkative youngster had lost his bluster.

"Do you wanna make a statement, son?" Dushane asked.

Pick kept mum. The investigator released the boy and came back around the table, sitting next to Dushane.

"Mr. Dushane. Would you leave me alone for a few minutes with Mr. Clarke here?"

The boy squirmed in his seat as Dushane stood up and left the room. Timbo knew from his many interrogation experiences punks like Pick wanted to brag about what they had done. This kid was like all the rest, he thought, and would soon lose his composure, and, along with it, his ability to keep his mouth shut.

Timbo knew that the next person to talk would be the one to break first—and it wouldn't be him. He would sit there, perfectly still, all day and night if he had to. He raised his gaze to the ceiling and crossed his arms.

Patience, Timothy Joseph. Patience.

Timbo could hear his partner's words repeating in his head. Stick Hanley had much more patience than he did when it came to not speaking in these situations, in *all* situations, and biting his tongue. A good homicide cop could wait a very long time for his perp to speak first; Stick could wait an eternity. "That's something they don't teach you in dick school," Stick had always told Timbo. This *something* was waiting for the perp to cave in. Timbo had struggled with this all the years he had been a detective. But now he held fast and continued to stare at the ceiling, occasionally glancing at his watch.

After an hour, the boy snapped. He jumped up out of his chair, knocking it hard against the wall behind him. Dushane ran back into the room in time to see Pick, standing now, thump his chest, alternating blows against it with each of his diminutive fists.

"I *warned* that ol' Jew. I told him, 'Stop usin' *my* park without *my* permission, ol' man,' but the *motherfucker* never listened. Just kept ridin' that sweet cherry red Huffy up 'n' down my turf. We had to do sumpin'. We has to show everyone this is Rangers turf. Oakwood Rangers turf. Ain' nobody crossin' that turf wiffout our permission—*nobody*."

"So you took his bike and beat him? Is that what you're saying, Pick?" Dushane asked as the boy stood behind the table.

"Yeah, I whacked the motha' fucker. Whacked him good. He ain't never comin' through my turf again—ever." Then he stood in silence, fists still clenched. Timbo could feel the attacker's hatred as it filled his deep brown eyes.

With that statement, Dushane got up and walked out of the room, leaving Timbo alone again with the boy.

Outside the room, standing behind a two-way mirror where they had been during the entire Monroe Clarke questioning, watching and listening: Headquarters Commander Gerald Lyons and Cook County Lead Assistant State's Attorney Ron Spencer. Typically, an audience with these two in attendance wouldn't have occurred during an interview such as this, but this heater case had brought the brass out of the woodwork.

"Let's get this in writing from him and have him sign it," Spencer said to his underling, Dushane, as he exited the interrogation room.

"Shouldn't we get a court reporter over here for this one?" ASA Dushane asked the lead state's attorney.

"No time for that. State's Attorney Carey's gonna want to get this news to Mayor Daley's office before the press finds out that we have a confession. Just have Detective Boscorelli write it all down and get the kid to sign it. Do the same with the others, too, since they'll start singing when they know their leader caved in."

Shrugging, Dushane replied to his boss Spencer, saying, "Okay. Whatever you say."

"What about the Turner kid? Any word on his whereabouts?" Spencer asked, turning to Commander Lyons.

"Yeah. I just got word from Jim LaFrance they found him. He was holed up over on Berkeley Avenue in his aunt's flophouse."

"And what about this phantom sixth kid?" Spencer asked. "Any word on who he is yet?"

"Nothin' yet."

"Okay. Let's get that Overstreet kid in here right away to ID these punks in a lineup. I'll also need him to ID that bat, too. And get Detective Hanley to get his witness's statement on paper as to what he saw and have him sign it, too," Spencer added.

"We probably have time to get a court reporter for that one, don't we?" Dushane again asked his superior.

"Yeah, yeah. Roust somebody up and give 'em a little overtime."

"You got it," said Dushane.

"Oh, and Gerry," Spencer said, turning his attention back to Commander Lyons. "Good work roundin' up these little pricks so fast. Downtown's gonna like that. But keep a lid on this for a little while, would ya, until we get our all our ducks in a row back in the County Attorney's Office. Okay?"

As Spencer finished his words, Stick walked up to the group outside the interrogation room.

"Timbo get a statement from the Pick kid yet?" he asked.

"Yeah," said Spencer. "He sang to your partner and my man Dushane here just a few minutes ago." Spencer, inhaling on a cigarette, nodded toward his assistant.

"Did he ask for a lawyer?" Stick asked.

"Nope," Spencer said. "The little smart-ass said he didn't need one."

"What about his family? Or someone from Youth Division? Were they called over yet?"

"Got no time for that," Spencer puffed his answer to Stick around the cigarette in his mouth. "Media's all over this and so is downtown. We gotta move fast."

"Juveniles are supposed to have a parent with them when questioned or at the very least a Youth Division officer," Stick said, eyeing Dushane with raised eyebrows.

"We got our perps, Hanley. This is an open-and-shut case. You just make sure that little nigger eyewitness of yours shows up for the lineup. My office'll do the rest." Spencer doused his smoke in a nearby ashtray, and walked away.

CHAPTER 19

ABOUT A MONTH LATER

Later in the morning of July 31st, the day after police arrested the suspects, during a lineup James had easily identified the five boys who attacked Manny Fleischman. With his father at his side, the boy had positively IDed all five of the alleged offenders in custody. Besides the witness and his father, also at the lineup: Assistant State's Attorneys Ron Spencer and Norb Dushane, Commander Gerald Lyons, Detectives Stick Hanley and Timothy Boscorelli, and the court-appointed public defender for the accused, attorney Mare-Beth Siegel.

Siegel, a prim, thirty-something, prematurely gray-haired graduate of UC–Berkeley School of Law, had only been a Cook County Public Defender for six months when Juvenile Court Judge Cecil B. Parsons appointed her to the case file. She had been a Public D.A. for a total of five years, first serving in Marin County, California. The *Chicago Tribune* had quoted her at the time of her appointment as saying that what propelled her to take the job in Chicago was, "An opportunity to work in the largest and most active judicial system in the nation." The case would be the most highly publicized she would ever defend in her position at the CCPD office.

Her next order of duty, after the lineup had taken place, had been to appear at her clients' detention hearing the next morning, regardless of the fact that it was only one day after she received the case file. At the hearing, Judge Parsons had denied Siegel's petition to remand the children to the custody of their parents, and incarcerated the five alleged offenders in the Audy Home, the juvenile detention center at 1100 South Hamilton Avenue.

But Siegal won a major battle a week later against her opponent, Assistant State's Attorney Ron Spencer. Her victory came in the 702 hearing, the proceeding where the court determines whether or not juvenile offenders should remain in the jurisdiction of the Juvenile Court for trial versus the State's desire to have them tried as adults.

Also during that same week, Monroe "Pick" Clarke's aunt had called the police and alleged that her nephew's civil rights had been violated when he was taken from her apartment, in her words, "For no reason other than he was black and the man that been killed was white." Aunt Della Clarke didn't trust the court's appointment of Siegel, a white woman, and called the local office of Operation PUSH, the Reverend Jesse Jackson's neighborhood watchdog group. Shortly after she had contacted them, the Chicago headquarters of Jackson's Operation PUSH—People United to Serve Humanity—released a statement that read, in part:

> Proper legal counsel for the five innocent, African-American boys unlawfully incarcerated by the Chicago Police Department will be provided at no cost to these young men and their upstanding and law-abiding families at the expense of Operation PUSH and its founder, the Reverend Jesse L. Jackson. PUSH cannot sit idly by and watch the destruction of innocent young lives along with the abominable perpetuation of black genocide imposed by the Daley administration and illegally executed by our city's Aryan-like police department in collusion with State's Attorney Bernard Carey's equally biased county attorney's office.

As a result of this news release, Quinella Poindexter, a prominent Chicago defense attorney, had come forward from her private practice, offering PUSH pro bono legal support from her

LaSalle Street firm for "The Fleischman Five," as the *Chicago Sun-Times* had labeled the alleged attackers of Manny Fleischman.

When the Cook County State's Attorney's Office had failed in its attempt earlier in the 702 hearing to try the boys as adults, the State's Attorney's Office had immediately petitioned Judge Parson's court to try each individually for Fleischman's murder. However, when the petition had come up for review another week later, Poindexter had argued and won in her preliminary hearing that the defendants should stand trial as one. A week later, she had dealt the prosecution another blow in winning the court's rejection of the State's 702 appeal to try the juveniles as adults.

Once Poindexter had won these critical battles for the defense, she returned the defense of the five boys back over to Public Defender Siegel, having convinced Pick's Aunt Della and the other boys' relatives that this was in their best interest. Siegel's "whiteness," as Poindexter had called it, would be, in her words, "Beneficial to convincing the court that this is not a case about black versus white but a clear case of misidentification and misinformation on the part of the Chicago police, the Cook County State's Attorney's Office, and by their only eyewitness."

Preferring to take her chances with the long-time Juvenile Court Judge Parsons, whom she knew to be a fair and honest member of the bench, Poindexter, and later Siegel, chose to downplay the racial sensitivity of the crime.

Newspapers stories, however, had continued to dwell on the race issue, since the eyewitness was black, too. To Poindexter's knowledge, Parson's, also black, was beyond reproach—she had been quoted in the *Chicago Tribune* as having called him "an uncompromising stickler for upholding the letter of the law" and she believed in his ability to find truth and justice, a rare commodity in Cook County's legal system. She knew him to be one of the fairest and most honest judges serving on the bench and she knew that Parsons's judicial modus operandi would not allow his courtroom to be influenced by the cultural issues muddling this case.

The prosecution presented its opening arguments in the Fleischman murder trial on September 1, 1975, less than two months after Manny's interment in a family plot in Oak Woods Cemetery. Cook County Assistant State's Attorney Ron Spencer presented the prosecution's opening arguments. The bench trial began in front of a courtroom filled with family representatives of both the defendants and the victim at 1100 South Hamilton Avenue in the Juvenile Court Building of Cook County. But Spencer didn't get to deliver his opening until presiding Judge Parsons had given these instructions to attorneys on both sides of the aisle as an overflowing gallery looked on:

"Understanding the publicity that has already surrounded this trial and due to the notoriety of the victim, I am going to take great strides in precluding this court from turning into a media circus. As my first order of duty, I'm declaring a gag order on all court participants in these proceedings, prohibiting any direct or indirect interaction with the news media."

When the attendees loudly scowled their displeasure, the veteran judge gaveled the courtroom back to order. "I'll have the bailiffs remove anyone in my courtroom participating in another outburst such as that. Do not test my patience!"

Parsons understood the gravity of maintaining secret the juvenile eyewitness's identity and his family's safety throughout the trial. But keeping this information undisclosed had somehow been compromised when a portion of the porch at the rear of the Overstreet's basement flat had been set on fire by a Molotov cocktail just days after a *Chicago Daily News* headline announced: BRONZE-VILLE BOY WHO WITNESSED BLACK SOX MURDER COMES FORWARD.

A few days later, Earl Overstreet had found a dead cat, sliced and mutilated, lying outside the door to their basement flat. Cook County Sheriff's Deputies were baffled at how this second threat could have taken place since they had stood guard 24/7 outside the family's apartment after the firebombing incident. But it was clear they were woefully unprepared to deal with the unique challenges brought forth by gang retribution in the 'hood. When yet another threat was phoned in to the *Chicago Tribune*, deputies decided to roust the family in the middle of the night and move them to a suburban safe house. Although safer, the family found themselves residing in a run-down apartment complex thirty miles from their neighborhood and home where they had lived for the past sixteen years.

As a result, James was not able to continue his last year at the Jackie Robinson Language Academy. His dream of attending DuSable High School, where his deceased friend Manny Fleischman had taught for so many years, would also vanish.

As well, Earl Overstreet was forced to give up his part-time job at Comiskey Park for the remainder of the season. That was because he spent most of his time at the State's Attorney's Office, driving his son back and forth, and helping him prep for the trial.

Once the actual trial started, the county provided transportation for the family as they made the daily commute from the distant suburban location to court. Deputies picked them up at eight in the morning in order to make sure they arrived in plenty of time before Judge Parsons gaveled the court to order promptly at ten a.m. each day for the next thirteen weeks.

As things would turn out, the number thirteen would be an unlucky number indeed for the Overstreet family.

CHAPTER 20

THIRTEEN WEEKS LATER

Promptly after Judge Parsons announced the "Not Guilty" verdict, acquitting Pick and four other defendants of the murder of Manny Fleischman, the Cook County Juvenile Courtroom erupted. Looking over the aisle at the defendants and their families as they celebrated their victory, James Overstreet couldn't help but feel utter disbelief. More so, though, he felt betrayed by the law and order system. James wasn't sure why these killers were set free—a "loophole" is what he would later hear it be called by the main prosecuting lawyer, Ron Spencer.

How could these guys get away with murder? he asked himself, knowing they were guilty. He had seen them commit the crime himself. The other lawyers on the prosecution's team, as well as the cops, had all told James and his family the case was "a dunker." James had seen the gang stop Fleischman in broad daylight, the lawyers had reminded the family, and observed the crime firsthand a very short distance from the attack. The prosecutors had the bat with traces, albeit minute, of Fleischman's blood type on it when police found it in Pick's possession less than forty-eight hours after the crime had been committed. And, James had positively IDed the weapon as his own Dick Allen bat, the bat Pick had taken from him a week before the Fleischman attack.

James also didn't understand why the confessions of all the boys had been thrown out of court and made inadmissible. All he remembered was how angry his father had become when Assistant State's Attorney Dushane, who was in the room when Pick was in-

terrogated and had personally heard his confession, called Earl
Overstreet several weeks before the trial started and told him that
the killer's statement would not be admissible in court. Pick's defense attorney had successfully argued in pretrial hearings,
Dushane said, that the confessions be declared inadmissible since
an attorney, nor parent or guardian, nor anyone from the Chicago
Police Department's Youth Division—which was required by law if
the previous two parties were not available—had not been present when he and Detective Boscorelli had questioned Pick.

"Not admissible? *Not admissible?*" Earl had shouted, banging
the phone's handset down on the receiver after speaking to the
assistant state's attorney. He circled the living room where his family sat watching TV.

"What's not admissible?" Eva asked him. "Who was that, Earl?"

"Dushane. He called about that gangbanger Pick's confession.
Judge Parsons threw it out. Ruled it was '*illegally obtained.*' Says that
killer's '*rights were violated.*' Legal mumbo jumbo. That's all it is!"

"How could they let this happen?" Eva asked, the news bringing a crackling sound to her voice. "My boy, Earl. They gotta protect my baby!"

James had remembered his daddy—a big and proud man, not
afraid of anything or anyone—shaking his head as he lowered it to
his chest, muttering to himself as he walked out of their basement
apartment, slamming the heavy wooden door behind him so hard
that it shattered its glass.

"Yes!" the acquitted Pick shouted and pumped his fist into the air.
Tyrone Witherspoon, Pokie Turner, Bertrand Jones, and Bobby De-
Sadier all jumped up, too. Once again free, they shouted and
hugged each other, as did those from their families, who had taken
seats in the gallery directly behind them throughout the entire trial.

"Rangers rule! Rangers rule! Rangers rule!" supporters shouted.

On the opposite side of the aisle the silent James sat between
his mother and father. Eva had cried out when the judge read
aloud his decision to the packed courtroom, joined by her husband, Earl. James turned and stared into the jubilant crowd across
the aisle. His eye caught sight of Julius Clark, Pick's older cousin.

As their gazes locked on each other, Julius drew a finger under his throat in a slitting motion. James wasn't sure if anyone had seen the threatening gesture. Then Cook County Sheriff's Deputies grabbed him and whisked him out through the front door of the courtroom.

"This is an outrage!" cried Bobbi Fenton, Manny's daughter, right before her husband, Lars, caught her as she collapsed in his arms. The rest of Fleischman's family sat stunned. Newspaper reporters dashed from the room, no doubt in an effort to reach the nearest pay phone, hoping there still might be time to meet the deadline for the late evening editions of their respective papers. Electronic news media people, too, began to set up lights in the hallway to capture footage for their evening broadcasts. During the commotion, deputies hustled the remainder of the Overstreet family out of the courtroom and toward a doorway to a small room across the hall.

"What will happen to James?" a reporter shouted as the underguard family pushed their way through the crowd of reporters and spectators who had jammed the hallway.

"Where are you taking them?" shouted another, jabbing a microphone out in front of Earl.

"No comment, no comment," fired back Assistant State's Attorney Ron Spencer, leading the entourage.

"Out of the way folks. Out of the way," one of the deputies said, shoving aside reporters so he could open the door to the room.

Once they were all inside, Spencer stood in front of them, straightened his red silk tie, and addressed the family. "Folks, I'm terribly sorry about this but I don't have time to discuss what went wrong. The most important thing right now is to get James to safety. I don't think it's a good idea for anyone to go back to either apartment tonight. We're going to get a van and have it waiting for you in the lower-level garage."

"You're sorry? That's all you have to say is 'you're sorry?'" Eva yelled. She then turned to her husband with venomous eyes. "It's your fault, Earl. It's your entire fault. I told you James should keep his mouth shut. Police never been good to any kin of mine," she shouted. "Now what? We can't even go back to our home. Now what, Earl?"

James watched his daddy pace back and forth on the room's terrazzo floor, his heels clicking a tedious tap. Spencer's emotionless words had quickly vanished against the room's bare plaster walls, still echoing from Eva's tirade.

The attorney had blown the case. James knew it. Moreover, he knew his parents knew it.

The only option left for Earl was to get his family to safety. He realized, though, that Spencer still controlled the destiny of the Overstreets, leaving the once proud and doting father feeling emasculated.

As Spencer dragged on his filter-tipped cigarette, beads of sweat formed on his upper lip. He turned and moved toward one of the sheriff's deputies, standing a few feet behind him. The man, Chester Borwinski, had been the Overstreets's main bodyguard during the trial. It looked to Earl, as he paced on the other side of the room, that Borwinski wanted to be as far away as possible from the losing attorney. As Spencer came up to Borwinski, he leaned in close toward him and spoke through his exhale of smoke. Earl overheard Spencer tell Borwinski, "I think it would be best if we moved them right away. I'll go call my office to get the paperwork going. Like I said, I don't even want them going back to their apartment for their stuff."

In a still small voice barely above a whisper, James's eight year-old sister asked, "Daddy, when can we go back to our home?"

After the girl's faint plea to her father, Spencer dipped out of the room, leaving Borwinski alone with the family.

Borwinski took a deep swallow and then spoke. "Okay, folks, just sit tight now. Mister Spencer will be back in a moment. Can I get anyone a glass of water?"

Over the thirteen weeks of the trial, Earl felt the sheriff's deputy had become more caretaker than protector of the patriarch's family. Borwinski had become very close to the Overstreets inasmuch as one could during the omnipresent tension of a murder trial. Earl had watched many times throughout the last few weeks of the trial how his youngest daughter had often played a game with the deputy, tugging on his nose.

"Missus O, ma'am. How 'bout you? Can I have one of my men bring you a cool drink? Would you like that?"

Eva looked up and shook her head, barely mouthing the words, "No, thank you."

"Okay. Well then bathroom's back there on your left. Like I said, State's Attorney Spencer'll be right back. He had to make a call. Long trial for all of us, I know. Just ain't right what happened in there. Just ain't right."

Earl appreciated the deputy's heartfelt expression. Yet, his stilted words were not quite adequate for the job. Earl knew the deputy had spent extra time, much of it on his own, to get to know each one of them as he and his men shuffled them back and forth, morning and night, from their apartment. He had watched Borwinski pay close personal attention to the individual needs of his family and knew the old-timer's heart ached for all of them, particularly for James.

"Just sit tight now. I'll be right outside the door here with the other deputies. You're safe in here now. Okay?"

Borwinski left the room, closing the door behind him. Outside in the hallway, his two deputies had taken their places, rigid armed sentinels, guarding the room's only entrance. He spoke to them. "It's a cryin' shame what's happened to these folks. State's attorney really screwed the pooch on this one. I seen a lotta things in my forty years but this one tops them all. The system's broke when it lets killers get away scot-free and the eyewitness gets the shaft. Just ain't right." Borwinski shook his head and rubbed his chin, then placed both hands on his hips. "I'll radio the office to bring up an unmarked van and we'll take 'em all outta here as soon as Spencer gives us the order of where to move them. I want you to take them down through the basement," he instructed his men.

Spencer, cigarette dangling from his lips, returned from his phone call and met Borwinski and his men in the hallway. "Okay, here's the plan. You're gonna drive them to O'Hare. I'll meet you guys out there at the airport and take over from there. I've got a Chicago blue-and-white en route to escort your van."

"Just ain't right what's happening to these folks, Ron," Borwinski told him.

"Just do your job, Borwinski, and I'll do mine. Okay?"

"Well, maybe if you *did* your job, these folks wouldn't be in any danger and those gangbangers would be behind bars right now."

"I did my job. The police didn't do theirs so there's not much I could have done. I can only try the case with the evidence presented and the CPD screwed up this one royal."

"You're blaming the cops? You're supposed to be a team. You think someone in your office would have listened better to the boy's story, taken him back to the scene of the crime—"

"Don't you think I feel terrible we lost this case? That an innocent man died and now an even more innocent boy's life will never be the same? I don't have time to spar with you, Deputy. Just have the van ready and get these folks down the back stairway. And keep 'em away from those fucking reporters out front."

Spencer reentered the cramped, stale-aired room. Earl paced the floor in front of his family with his arms folded tight across his chest, shaking his head left and right. Tears streamed down Eva's face. James sat next to her, as he did throughout the entire trial, but now slumped in his chair. Earl watched his family's wounded faces stare at the attorney as he closed the door behind him.

"How you gonna protect my boy now?" Earl demanded. "Where will my family be safe? Where are we gonna live?"

"That's complicated," Spencer replied.

"Complicated? What the hell do you mean, 'complicated'?" Earl demanded. "I tell you what's complicated. Explaining how my fist ended up in your face."

"Are you threatening me, Mister Overstreet?" Spencer asked, picking up his briefcase and holding it in front of him as if to shield himself from Earl's imminent attack.

"Where are you takin' my family?" Earl demanded.

"Arizona. We have a very safe place we can relocate you and—"

"Arizona?" Earl eyes popped. "What in the name of the sweet lord Jesus you talkin' 'bout?"

Without answering, Spencer turned and rushed out of the room. In the hallway, Borwinski shouted into his handheld radio for deputies to bring a van to the front of the courthouse where he would meet them. Hearing this, the reporters left the hallway, following him as they pushed to be the first to meet the vehicle at the curb. Borwinski's decoy statement did its trick. With the hallway cleared of reporters, Borwinski's other two deputies opened the door to the room holding the Overstreets and escorted them out to a back staircase that led down to the building's basement garage.

When they reached their destination, the transportation had already arrived, sitting with its motor idling . Earl opened the passenger-side door and sat up front next to the driver while the deputies crowded the rest of the family into the back.

The Overstreet family leader looked straight ahead, any sign of emotion now missing from his face. No one would have questioned him, though, if he had said he felt as if he and his family were like lambs being led to slaughter. The van's driver was a young black man, looking to Earl to be in his early twenties. He wore dark, aviator-like sunglasses, which Earl thought strange inside the poorly lit underground garage. Borwinski startled Earl from his thoughts when he tapped on the passenger-door's window, motioning for the father to roll it down.

"We don't have much time before those reporters find out you're down here. I just want to say good luck, Earl."

Swallowing hard, Earl nodded and blinked his eyes in a silent "thank you" to the dedicated deputy.

Borwinski nodded back, then slapped the windshield, signaling the driver to go. The young driver put the van in gear and the beige Ford Econoline headed up an exit ramp to the street. Once out of the garage, the van merged into Chicago's late afternoon rush hour. Earl noticed in his large, side view mirror that a Chicago Police car had pulled behind them as soon as they entered into traffic.

Earl reflected upon Spencer's instructions to Borwinski's men that they were not to take the family back to either apartment. *They can't be taking us to Arizona right away. Could they? And why Arizona?* Earl asked himself. *Was this Spencer's idea? Did anybody care what his family thought about this choice? Did anybody care what happened to them and where they were going? Did Deputy Borwinski? Judge Parsons? How about the family of Manny Fleischman? Did any of them care what was now going to happen to the family of Earl Overstreet?*

Earl kept asking himself what went wrong, still not wanting to admit that he should have listened to his wife. James had seen the murder with his own eyes and did what he should have: he came forward. Yet, at the conclusion of the bench trial, Judge Parsons said that he "deeply regretted" his decision and that he "had no other choice" but to find Pick and his gang not guilty of the murder of Manny Fleischman.

What does it take to find justice in this world? How could the guilty be set free and the righteous made to suffer?

Within minutes, the driver entered the John Fitzgerald Kennedy Expressway and headed out of the city toward O'Hare. The vehicle's stop-and-go motion bounced the van's cramped occupants to and fro as the driver alternated between tapping his brake and applying the gas. Eva clung to James in the backseat, sobbing loudly. Her children remained silent as their mother's sorrowful wails dominated the space.

James bobbed with the jerking motion of the vehicle, his mind working on comprehending the outcome of the trial. *What is going to happen to us now?* Like his daddy, he didn't have any answers. He really didn't know what emotion to feel the most. Anger? Confusion? Fear? He felt all three, each wrenching his gut. If he had listened to his momma, he wouldn't have caused all this trouble for his family. Because of him, no Overstreet could ever be safe in Bronzeville again.

It was because of him now, too, they would all have to move to Arizona. He recalled how he had dreamed of travlin' to Arizona someday, dreamed of it since Miss Burns told the class all about the Grand Canyon and the "Copper State," as she called it. But he had never imagined going there like this, against his will, trapped like a prisoner. *If anyone should be a prisoner now,* he thought, *it should be every guilty but free member of the Oakwood Rangers.*

According to the globe in his bedroom and the map Miss Burns had pulled down in front of his classroom's blackboard, Arizona sat between California and New Mexico. He could hear his teacher's voice describing it as a mostly hot and dry place—a desert. An "arid" state is what she had called it. Now he silently asked himself, "How could he live in a place with no water?"

What about Burnham Park and the lakefront? He imagined the cobalt water crashing against the limestone rocks and outrunning the waves as he did so many times. Closing his eyes, he imagined the glorious smell of the freshwater lake and the fragrance of Burnham Park's newly mowed grass, wafting through the humid, summer air. He imagined the sound of his Ted Williams bicycle whirring away along the park's asphalt paths, the feeling of its tires gripping the smooth, black pavement.

Then he recalled the thudding sound his Louisville Slugger bat had made while Pick ferociously pummeled Manny Fleischman's skull as his friend laid helpless on the ground. James snapped his eyes open as the shuddering memory ran the length of his body. The pain was deeper than anything he could ever imagine.

As he gazed outward, he saw his own reflection in the tinted windows of the van. At that moment, what became most clear to him was the memory of Manny Fleischman's desperate look the day their eyes last connected. It had been nearly four months since that dreadful day, the moment he lost the friendship of the old Jew-man forever. Manny had become like a second father to him. He admired and respected the retired teacher, even loved him, he thought. Not having him in his life anymore was, by far, James's deepest loss of all.

"Fuckin' rush hour," Chicago Police officer Henry Gaston mumbled as he tried to maneuver his squad car closer to the Sheriff's Department Econoline van. "How do people drive in this shit everyday?"

Traffic was heavy on the outbound John F. Kennedy Express-way. It was after five and the late afternoon mass exodus of work-ers from the city to the suburbs was in full swing. The Chicago Police cruiser, shadowing the van, stayed as close as it could, but ag-gressive drivers furiously tightened even the smallest gap between the busy roadway's crawling vehicles.

As the van approached Hubbard's Cave, a quarter-mile long tun-nel the JFK burrows through just north of the Loop, the accompa-nying blue-and-white fell several car lengths behind. Gaston's partner, Lou Darcy, perused the sports page of the *Chicago Sun Times*, head buried in the paper as he sat in the passenger seat. Even the darkness cast upon the car's interior from being inside the ex-pressway's man-made cave didn't deter him from his reading.

"You think the Bears are gonna win Sunday?" Darcy asked his partner.

"Quit readin' the goddam paper wouldja, Lou, and keep your eyes on that fucking van."

"That fuckin' van ain't goin' nowhere fast, Henry. Where the hell is he gonna go in this mess?"

"God, I hate tailing these stupid Cook County assholes," Gas-ton complained. "Why the fuck did he take the goddam Kennedy? Procedure is to use the side streets till we get outta the Loop. Now we're both stuck in this shit." Gaston slammed his fist against the steering wheel. "And what's he doing in that right-hand lane? What the fuck kinda moron is this guy driven that van?"

CRACK. CRACK. The distinct sound of two gunshots echoed against the tunnel's walls.

"Fuck! Fuck! Someone just shot at the van!" Gaston roared as he heard the two quick pops. He saw gun flashes come from the passenger's-side back window of a silver Buick Electra 225 that had pulled beside the driver's side of the van. Glass from the Econo-line's driver's-side rear windows shattered, and shiny shards flew onto the pavement.

Darcy dropped his paper and grabbed the car's two-way radio.

"Dispatch. This is twelve-zero-two. We've got shots fired in Hub-bard's Cave—shots fired—I repeat—shots fired! Over!"

Gaston flipped on the squad's blue Mars lights. He then toggled another dash switch, making his siren blare. Police dispatch did not respond to his partner's frantic radio call.

"We never get a signal when we need it in this fuckin' tunnel!" Darcy yelled. He jumped from the crawling car as Gaston attempted to maneuver his police cruiser closer to the van.

As his partner ran toward the van, Gaston grabbed the radio. "This is squad twelve-zero-two. Shots fired—repeat—shots fired. Over!"

Still no response from main police dispatch at the Central Communications Room.

"This is car twelve-zero-two—come in dispatch—twelve-zero-two—shots fired in Hubbard's Cave—*come in dispatch!*"

The Cook County Sheriff's van transporting the Overstreets had come to a halt. The cars ahead of it continued moving, seemingly unaware of what had transpired. The roadway was now empty in front of the stopped van. Drivers in cars behind and to the side of the van came to a complete stop, seeing the police car's flashing blue lights and hearing the siren's familiar whooping sound bounce off the tunnel's white, ceramic-tiled walls.

The deuce-and-a-quarter from which Gaston saw the shots fired had swung around the front of the van and made an abrupt, angled stop. Not able to move his car any closer, he threw the car into park, grabbed his scattergun from the dash, and jumped from his vehicle, running after his partner. As he did, the back door of the Electra flipped open. The van's driver got out and jumped into the sedan's backseat. Once inside, the four-door deuce-and-a-quarter screeched away, exiting at the Ohio Street ramp just ahead.

Weapons drawn, Gaston and Darcy finally reached the van, scrambling to the passenger side first. The windows had been shattered on that side, too, as the bullets went straight through the vehicle, missing, Gaston prayed, their intended targets inside.

Earl jumped out of the van just as the two Chicago cops arrived alongside the shot-up vehicle. "Where the hell were you guys?" he screamed. "They tried to kill my son! Where the hell *were* you?"

CHAPTER 21

A freshly carved-out community in the Arizona desert about thirty miles northeast of Phoenix, the town of Fountain Hills was still in a somewhat secluded part of Maricopa County. Developed as a haven for snowbirds in the late 1960s and early 1970s, Fountain Hills bordered both the Fort McDowell and Salt River-Pima Indian Reservations. On its other sides, the town bumped up against the outreaches of the ever-growing city of Scottsdale.

If the intent was to become or remain anonymous, then this town fit the bill as the perfect place. Fountain Hills was a place where a person could live and never have to talk to anyone; it was a place where someone could stay distant from his neighbors, and nobody would ever ask why. Holding true to its reputation, when the Overstreets arrived there the night of the last day of the Fleischman murder trial, the town's less than two thousand residents—still virtually 100 percent white—didn't pay much attention to the black family's appearance.

The first few weeks after they arrived, James read a notice delivered to their mailbox, warning residents to be on the lookout for a black bear that had roamed down from the high country in search of food. The bear's unwelcome visit brought out the news media as well as excited neighbors into the town's oft-deserted streets. The surprising result: for the very first time folks met each other, some after spending years of living together as strangers on the same block of homes.

At night, wild javalina roamed the town's mostly unpaved streets. Once, his mother found a diamondback rattler huddled inside the front screen door to their house. The family was warned by another flyer that those with swimming pools should be on the lookout for bobcats intruding their secluded, brick-walled yards in search of scarce water from their sparkling pools. Left outside unattended, pet cats or small dogs became easy prey for not only the bobcats but for foraging coyotes and hungry owls.

James remembered how his teacher, Miss Burns, had described Arizona as being a place that was "sparsely populated" and filled with all types of cactus. He also remembered how his best friend, Clayton, then asked Miss Burns if parsley was the only vegetable that grew there besides the thorny plants, and how the class laughed after Miss Burns explained the definition of sparsely versus parsley.

On that day back in May, some seven months ago now, she had gone on to tell them during their geography period that the 1970 U.S. Census had counted only 900,000 people residing in Arizona and that the vast majority lived in Maricopa County, home to the state's capital, Phoenix. Comparatively, she explained, the county they lived in—Cook County, Illinois—boasted a population of over five million. She wrote the large number with all the zeros side by side on the blackboard, and James daydreamed about what it would be like to live somewhere so uncrowded, so distant from your neighbor. It all seemed so unreal to him as Miss Burns described to her class that day long ago all about "our nation's forty-eighth state."

James discovered soon enough that his new home state of Arizona was a place where new people moved into everyday from somewhere else, many folks choosing to go there to begin their lives over again and "get a fresh start" as he would hear them later describe their motives. New neighbors didn't turn the heads of native "Zoners"—the name used for those born in the arid state.

In school, James met kids from families who had migrated for reasons that were innocent enough, such as to get away from harsh Midwest or Northeast winters. He also met kids from California, their parents moving the family because of the Golden State's outrageous cost of living. He met others whose families simply came to Arizona on a lark, adventure drawing them to one of the country's last uncluttered regions.

James would find out much later in his life that Arizona had long been a favorite place for the feds and other law enforcement agencies to send people into witness protection. The U.S. Marshal's Office monitored all of the country's witness protection programs, and the Cook County Witness Protection Program, or CCWPP, was no different. With the guidance from this government agency, Assistant Cook County State's Attorney Ron Spencer had picked the town of Fountain Hills, Arizona, for the new home of the Earl Overstreet family. The Overstreets, of course, had no choice in the matter.

The CCWPP arranged for Earl Overstreet to fill the newly created position of meter reader for the growing town's water department. Eva stayed home with the children as she did back in Chicago, and volunteered at the Four Peaks Middle School two days a week. As for James, it was difficult for him to make friends at school because he was anxious about getting too close to anyone, always fearful of being discovered. Perhaps contributing more to this hardship of fitting in was that James and his siblings had the distinction of being the only blacks in the town's entire school system. This uniqueness, though, would ultimately help them become friends with white kids, since many hadn't laid eyes on a black person before the Oversteets's arrival and their curiosity propelled them to reach out to the new black kids.

The Overstreets, each given a new first and family name, were instructed by the CCWPP to tell everyone they hailed from Gary, Indiana, a city in the northwestern part of the Hoosier State known for its one-time prolific steel-making industry. The premise given to them by CCWPP: they were starting a new life after their father had been laid off from Gary's U.S. Steel plant.

James despised his new name but he had no choice but to accept it. Their names had been changed without any of their input, and so, like many other things he disliked about his new life in Arizona, James accepted his, burying his feelings along with sad memories of his loss of his former home. He had to survive, he told himself, so one day he could be free and find justice for the murder of his friend. But surviving in Arizona as a black person would not be an easy task.

One thing that would help him, though, was the common bond provided by the nation's pastime, baseball. At the time when the Overstreets arrived in Arizona, the state had no professional baseball team but did host some teams for their spring training seasons. As a result, the kids he met in school who liked baseball— and that was most children—still followed the team from their original hometown.

"My favorite team is the Chicago White Sox," James told class-mates. Then, he'd deluge them with a litany of player stats from Pale Hose teams from the mid-sixties up to the present day. James knew his baseball. He'd come to find out that most kids were Yan-kees or Dodgers fans since so many of the early settlers of Fountain Hills had come from either New York or southern California.

"We gave you Tommy John for Dick Allen," James told the Dodgers fans. He smirked over that trade, which, at least in the beginning, turned out to be a huge success for Chicago's South Side ball club and a mistake for the National League team from the City of Angels.

But talking about his team wasn't the same as seeing them in person. He missed sitting in the old, green, wooden grandstands at Comiskey Park and wondered if he would ever be able to watch his beloved White Sox again. From this standpoint, the witness re-location move crushed him more than any other, but not as much as his inability to do his travlin' any longer in Burnham Park along the shores of Lake Michigan.

"Fountain Hills has a lake you can go to, James," his mother told him many times during those early days after their arrival. He sensed his mother had hoped visiting this land-locked, recycled wastewater lake could appease him in some way. The thirty-acre body of water, which spewed a geyser every fifteen minutes from a man-made fountain in its center—hence giving the town and the lake its moniker—was to Lake Michigan what a grain of sand was in a child's play box.

James never responded to his mother's urgings. Although he

secretly traveled to the quaint lake many times, he considered it a puddle of piss. James knew he couldn't stay long in a place like Fountain Hills. He dreamed of leaving from the moment he arrived. Maybe the people at the CCWPP thought their make-believe person with a name he despised would live happily ever after in this godforsaken Arizona town with its pathetic lake made out of recycled urine. But James Overstreet never would.

CHAPTER 22

Those first years of living in Arizona led James down a path of secluded isolation and despairing loneliness. As a result, he withdrew deeper and deeper inside himself. James knew he was different from any of his classmates. Not only was he in witness protection, making his true identity lost, but he was black.

Maricopa County had a black population of less than 50,000—barely 3 percent of the country's population—James discovered doing research for a school report he titled, "Black Folks in the Valley of the Sun." He had done the paper as a freshman at Chaparral High School in 1977. His research also told him that by contrast Chicago alone was 20 percent black at that same time, equating to almost 1.5 million blacks in the greater Chicago-land area. No wonder James felt like a fish out of water in Arizona.

Nor was it any better for the rest of his family. The Overstreet parents had started fighting back in Chicago well before they left their apartment on Ellis Avenue for the suburban safe house. By the time they had settled in their austere home on Caldera Drive in Fountain Hills, Earl and Eva fought nearly every day. The arguments had first become violent when the prosecution team from the Cook County State's Attorney's Office started to lose the murder case against Pick and his gang.

"Stupid goddamn lawyers," James had heard his father shout one day from behind a closed bedroom door where he and Eva had gone to take a phone call from ASA Ron Spencer. This particular fight ensued after the defense had blasted lead Homicide Investigator Edward Hanley's testimony earlier that day in court, concerning his interpretation and description of the escape route of the alleged offenders. The defense lawyer had pointed out how Hanley's testimony clearly contradicted the version of the prosecution's own eyewitness—their son, James.

"You've hung my son out there like a fool," Earl had protested to Spencer on the phone after the day's court proceedings. "You might as well have given those gang bangers the goddamn rope to lynch him."

Eva then expressed her displeasure to Spencer on the phone that the Chicago police had blown the case by never taking James to the scene of the crime and by the police assuming their boy must have been mistaken about the path the killers took after the attack on Fleischman.

"How could you be so goddamn stupid?" she screamed, her voice coming through the bedroom door.

James was more shocked, though, at the intensity of the couple's ensuing arguments and distressed at the constant tension between his parents. During the whole ordeal, James watched his doting mother change into a bitter, uncaring woman. Just as often, he had asked himself the very same questions that she had asked about Chicago PD's handling of the investigation. James knew Burnham Park better than the police did, she kept saying. He knew every bike path, every park bench, every water fountain, and every entrance to the park between 31st and 55th Streets.

How could they have screwed this up? he too had wondered.

From that point forward, the trial, the marriage, and the Overstreet family deteriorated. Once the judge said "not guilty on all counts," James knew, even at his young age, that something was terribly wrong with the judicial system—a system that could let murderers like Pick and his gang go free. The way he saw it: the gang's lawyers were smarter than his lawyers.

He had told the truth. He had volunteered to come forward. He had done the very two things his father had always preached to him he must do in life: tell the truth and never be afraid.

He had testified against one of the most feared gangs in his neighborhood. Now there would be no way he would ever be safe again in Bronzeville nor in any of the surrounding neighborhoods the gangs controlled. If there was one thing that was certain, it was the gang's determination to extract retribution for those who turned against them. And, it didn't matter how long it took. Popping James Overstreet, or anyone in his family—already attempted that day in Hubbard's Cave during their van ride to O'Hare Airport—would be not a matter of if, but when.

As he struggled to adjust to life in Arizona, James gravitated toward his favorite sport—baseball. He played on his Little League team in Fountain Hills and then later played ball for the Chaparral High baseball team—the Firebirds. After high school graduation, James chose to attend Arizona State University and commuted there for his four undergrad years. James's higher education was on the government's dime since one of the promises made to Earl and Eva after the family was placed into witness protection had been that their children could attend the university in Tempe, Arizona, free of charge, for both undergraduate and graduate degrees.

James would one day try to walk onto the ASU Sun Devils baseball squad but wouldn't make the team. He dearly loved the game his father and Manny Fleischman had taught him so much about that he stayed on as an equipment manager. The job enabled him to be around a wide range of different people, something the witness protection folks had always discouraged. They constantly warned his family not to join social groups, since membership would risk exposure. For years, James and his family maintained the lowest of profiles, greatly exaggerating their isolation.

To insure the family's compliance, witness protection authorities had always kept a distant but close eye on them and would visit them at irregular intervals. An unassuming, four-door sedan would pull up in front of their house on Caldera Drive and a lone man would get out. He would stride up the family's walk and ring their doorbell. The man made himself especially conspicuous when he visited, dressing in dark, long-sleeved clothing even on 110 degree days. Sometimes he'd come on a school holiday, James recalled, like Lincoln's Birthday or Memorial Day, because the children always seemed to be home when the frequent, unannounced visits occurred.

"Ma'am," the gentleman would begin, tipping his hat when Eva opened the door. "How are you and your fine family doing today?"

She would answer "Doin' okay" or "All right" or some other emotionless, terse answer, standing in the doorway, one hand resting on her hip, the other propped up against the doorjamb like a nightclub bouncer.

"Well, you just call our twenty-four-hour emergency number if you need anything. Okay, ma'am?"

He'd always make sure to hand her his card. She'd oblige him by taking it and he'd tip his hat once more. Then he'd be on his way, as quickly as he'd appeared, not to be seen until the next surprise visit.

"Momma, what's this one say?" James would ask.

"Here, look for yourself," she would answer, passing it to him and walking away, waving her arm in the air. "Put it with the others when you're done with it."

This visitor's card had read:

SCOTT SANDSTORM
Adobe Air Conditioning
Serving the Valley of the Sun for Over Three Years
24-Hour Emergency Number
602-555-9999

As directed by his mother, James would then stick the card to the left of the door, against the jamb. There it joined about a dozen other similar cards, most fading from the length of time they'd been stuck there without ever being pulled out again. All were on white, heavy cardstock imprinted with slightly raised letters in thick, black ink. Each, though, had a different company name, such as "Valley Sun Screens" or "Desert Landscaping" or "Agave Pool Cleaning" or some other similar-sounding, innocuous Arizona-like business name. Yet, every card had Scott Sandstorm's name and the same identical phone number on it.

"Why do they always use a different company but the same guy's name and phone number?" James wondered his thought aloud so his momma could hear him.

"Damned if I know," she'd answer, shaking her head. Then she'd always end by saying, "Stupid is as stupid does."

Why do we have to stay in witness protection? Why would anyone still want to come after my family or me? James would ask himself. *Who in the hell was going to travel from Chicago to Arizona even if Pick and his gang knew where I was? And who could ever find us in this godforsaken place?*

Another sad memory James had was when the entire family went to see a school play in which James's little sister had a part. Eva had insisted that the family sit in the empty first row in the auditorium. But Earl argued with her, telling her they'd be "too exposed" in front of such a large crowd.

"Who in the hell is going to recognize us, Earl? Do you see any other black folks from Chicago other than our family here?" Eva waved her arm around the room, bringing attention to herself and her family as she raised her voice to her husband.

James watched as his parents argued over where they should sit before he blurted out, "Why don't we all just sit in the middle like everyone else?"

The boy's simple yet poignant request quickly put a halt to his parent's embarrassing actions in front of his classmates, and the family quietly took the center seats.

As the years went on, these constant eruptions diminished into complete silence between his parents. James knew everyone in his family hated the situation they had been thrust into as a result of his coming forward as a witness to Manny Fleischman's murder. He could feel and sympathize with their pain even though the final result of their feelings of anger, loneliness, separation, and desperation would be to shun their brother.

ELEVEN YEARS LATER: AUGUST 13, 1986

Through the ensuing years, James's own rage grew, not knowing whom to hate. But he had buried the pain and the anger in a very deep place within his heart.

Graduating with honors from Arizona State University with a Bachelor of Science degree in Sociology, he applied to the university's fledgling law school. If he could become a lawyer, he thought, then maybe he could prevent what happened to him from ever again happening to anybody. James knew he wanted to be a lawyer from the day Cook County Juvenile Court Judge Cecil B. Parsons found Monroe "Pick" Clarke and his four fellow gang-bangers not guilty of the murder of Manny Fleischman. He hated what had occurred to him and his family, forcing them to leave their home in Chicago for their own protection. He hated the fact that his parents had continuously fought about his fateful decision to go to the police station and tell Detectives Hanley and Boscorelli about the tragic event he witnessed in Burnham Park.

By the time James started his second year at ASU School of Law in the late summer of 1986, he was one of less than a literal hand-ful of blacks enrolled in the young school. Being black, he was ad-mitted under a cloud of assumption and innuendo by fellow students as well as by some faculty and staff. The doubters believed he received some type of special treatment for admittance, per-haps benefiting from an assumed lowering of the qualifications due to the government mandate for equal opportunity.

To answer the critics and skeptics, James plunged into his stud-ies with an unrelenting tenacity. Even before law school, he placed at the top in every class. But it was during his pursuit of his Juris Doctor where he'd excel. In moot court—where skills in oral ad-vocacy and brief writing are first honed—his efforts were unri-valed. Unflinchingly, he dealt a deft blow to every opponent in his opening remarks, setting a tone from which they never recovered. The preparation of his legal briefs and his organizational skills proved flawless. His unending research for the mock cases turned over every possible stone. He always looked for historical prece-dents in his student cases, looking to the past to see who had sim-ilar cases to his. He relied upon precedent and studied what approach was taken there and, most importantly, whether it failed or succeeded.

Especially adroit at thinking on his feet, James became a su-perb listener. Candid about his ignorance of things he didn't know or understand, he welcomed questions from fellow students. To the chagrin of his opponents, though, he many times used this ignorance to his advantage by transitioning answers to his questions into brilliant insights or questions of his own, weaving them seamlessly into his own oral argument.

However, more than anything, his persuasive style revealed a deep sense of conviction to his case and to his client—a confidence and a fervor opponents found impossible to overcome. His eye contact with the bench, along with his posture and gestures, mesmerized all who watched him. His precise vocabulary and punctuation, both written and oral, left most opponents and all who observed him in action with the feeling that he had been Harvard trained rather than ASU schooled. This perception would follow him throughout his career. Learning the law consumed the former James Overstreet, but what ultimately drove him to greatness would be his unending desire to find justice for his client.

If he did have a flaw, it may have been his arrogance, which could consume him as he arduously pursued his case. He was prone to summarily dismiss those who weren't on his intellectual level by jumping into black, Chicago street slang to make his point—usually under his breath or out of earshot of opposing counsel and the bench. In one particularly exciting collegiate moot court competition, his assignment was to argue the merits of overriding the protection of double jeopardy. As preparation, James buried himself in pages upon pages of court cases where the double jeopardy provision took effect, looking for a way to legally challenge and overturn one of the most basic tenets of the judicial system founded in the Bill of Rights.

His passion to win, even in a no-win situation such as double jeopardy, brought admiration not only from his law professors but from fellow students. In the mock case, James truly believed he had found a loophole, but when the judge questioned the validity of his argument based upon Fifth Amendment protection, eventually ruling against him, James openly scoffed at the moot court judge's decision. Fortunately for the young law student, his guttural, street-like utterances occurred out of earshot of the professor presiding over that day's moot court proceedings. The bench never heard James mutter under his breath, "You're a silly-assed mother-fuckin' fool."

PART THREE

PIECING IT TOGETHER

CHAPTER 23

FRIDAY, NOVEMBER 11, 2005

Sitting at his desk a few hours later back in his downtown Phoenix office, Stan Kobe tried to comprehend how he felt after seeing Turner and DeSadier earlier that morning at the Maricopa County Fourth Avenue Jail. As his mind raced, the phone rang. The quick double ring indicated it was an interoffice call. The caller ID display on his telephone read: THOMAS, A.

Shit. He's probably heard what I did.

Stan picked up the phone and answered, "Stan Kobe."

"Hey, Stan. Got a minute? I need to discuss something with you."

"Sure. Be right there."

As Stan hung up, he pulled on each his fingers, cracking the knuckles. They popped loudly as he jerked every joint. A nervous habit he had since childhood, he remembered how his mother hated when he did it, moving methodically from index finger down to pinky. The panicky tick helped distract him from his current worry as to why the big boss wanted to see him. Andrew Thomas, head Maricopa County attorney, only called staff to his office for bad news. Since there were 126 capital cases on the docket, he easily could have been calling Stan to talk about any one of those. But as Stan took the one-minute walk down to Thomas's office, his instinct told him the head honcho wanted to talk about the two Chicago gang members being held in their custody at the Fourth Avenue Jail.

"Come in. Come in," Thomas mouthed to him as he cupped

the mouthpiece to the phone he held up to his ear. Thomas motioned with a couple quick tilts of his head for Stan to enter and at the same time pointed to one of the two chairs in front of his desk.

"Okay, Governor. Yes. No problem. I understand," Thomas said as he spoke into the phone. "Yes. I understand it's a matter of homeland security, too. Yes. We'll make sure it happens. Certainly. Thank you."

Thomas hung up. Sitting now, Stan looked him in the eye from across the desk and nervously waited for Thomas to speak.

"I guess you gathered that was the queen bee," Thomas said. Stan nodded.

"I don't like to get calls from her. You know that, right?"

Stan repeated his nod. He knew Thomas and Arizona Governor Janet Napolitano, political adversaries, rarely spoke.

"She was calling about those two guys arrested on the Gila Reservation we're holding over at the 4th Avenue Jail. She wants me to charge them immediately and send them to trial before Illinois moves extradition papers to get them back."

"We'll have to wait on that, boss. They've been picked up already. The Gila Rez police has 'em."

Thomas rubbed his chin a few times before leaning forward in his leather chair. He looked Stan in the eye. "Why does Gila have them? Who authorized moving them there?"

"I did. The tribal police called me and wanted them back, especially since they were caught on the reservation." Stan hoped his weak excuse would deter further questioning.

"Really?" Thomas paused before continuing. "Tom Terry tells me he got a call from Detective Hanley down in Chandler. Hanley told him these guys spooked you over at the jail. Is that true?"

Stan couldn't believe Brian had called and reported this to Terry, the charging attorney in the Maricopa County Attorney's Office. Beyond the fact that he went over Stan's head, he felt blindsided by his best friend's betrayal, wondering why he would do such a thing.

"Hanley's a cop, not a prosecutor. You want him to try your case?" Stan snapped. He realized this was probably not the best choice of words when speaking with the chief county attorney, but it was too late to reel them back in. If the next words out of Thomas's mouth were, "You're fired!" Stan wouldn't have been surprised.

"For the moment, I'll ignore your last remark, Stan. In the meantime, the governor is about to announce a new statewide effort to prevent the smuggling of various types of contraband back and forth across the border. She especially wants us to go after the heavily organized groups conspiring to do this. What the governor asked me—no—what the governor *told* me during that phone call just now is that she wants this office to prosecute these two guys, and she wants our best, you, handling it."

Stan nodded without speaking. Feeling trapped, he moved to get up, but Thomas stopped him with his next words.

"Wait. I'm not done yet. As for your little outburst a moment ago, I'm willing to overlook it because you're my number one guy in this office. I'm not sure what this argument is all about between you and Detective Hanley, but this effort is something none of us can afford to screw up." He tapped his index finger hard on top of his desk. "I need you to make an example of these two, so get them back over to 4th Avenue and initiate them. Pronto."

Stan pushed his chair away from the front of Thomas's desk. He nodded to him and walked out of the room before he allowed Thomas to see any glimpse of the anger brewing inside him.

Still fuming over Brian's phone call to Tom Terry, Stan immediately left his downtown Phoenix office building and drove out to the Gila River Indian Reservation ten miles south. With pressure thrust upon him directly by the governor of Arizona via the county attorney, he was out of options. When he arrived at the jail, he asked Police Chief Jimmy Nejo if he could speak to the prisoners. Stan and Jimmy knew each other well and had become close friends since their days together as undergrads at ASU.

"Thanks for picking these two up for me so quickly, Jimmy."

"Hey, you sent up a smoke signal, I came a runnin'," Jimmy paused. "Hanley's not with you?"

Prosecutors always sent cops or had cops along with them to interrogate prisoners. Stan ignored his question.

"You gonna talk to them without their counselor here?" Jimmy asked his friend.

Stan still didn't answer.

"I ain't supposed to let you do that, you know. Could mean a lot of trouble for both of us."

Knowing he had to give his old friend some kind of explanation, he finally answered him. "I know, Jimmy. I don't want to get you in any deeper than you already are. All I can tell you is it's a matter of life and death."

The Indian stared at him but gave no verbal response, yet his eyes told Stan he'd do whatever his friend asked. Inseparable during their days at ASU, the two shared a common bond as outcasts in a white man's world.

"Have they requested to make any calls yet?" Stan asked.

"Been askin' since they got here, 'specially the guy with the patch over his eye. He keeps saying he gets one phone call. Told him, no problem. He's welcome to use the phone, but the phone don't work."

Jimmy's wink brought a smile to Stan's tense face.

"I'll have two of my boy's bring 'em into the old interrogation room, the one we're not supposed to use anymore," Jimmy said, pointing down the hallway. "It's the very last door on the right."

Stan raised an eyebrow, not wanting to get anyone else involved in his potentially criminal action.

"Don't worry. They're my nephews," Jimmy assured him. "As far as anybody around here's concerned, you was never here."

"Thanks, pardner. I owe you."

CHAPTER 24

Brian had fumed over Stan's odd behavior at the 4th Avenue Jail. Why had his friend been so reluctant to bring charges against those two Chicago criminals, Pokie Turner and Bobby DeSadier? Brian was even more disturbed by the conversation he had with Stan and his insistence on the pair's extradition back to Chicago.

His anger with Stan and his stance prompted him to do something he'd never before had to consider during the scores of cases he'd worked on over the years with his best friend—go over his head and call the Maricopa County Attorney's Office. Brian didn't take lightly his decision to share their private conversation with Tom Terry, Stan's immediate boss and the charging attorney for the county. He knew when Stan found out his buddy would likely pop his cork, but Brian felt compelled to challenge his best friend's actions.

When he finished his phone conversation with Terry, Brian had turned his attention back to the two rap sheets, looking at them in more detail. Stan had left the manila folders he had on the two men before he stormed out of the observation room. As Brian leafed through their rap sheets now, each fifteen pages thick, it was obvious that Turner and DeSadier were no small-time hoods. Both had spent significant time in prison and had perpetrated just about every major crime: arson, armed robbery, aggravated assault, resisting arrest, drug possession, and grand theft. All the felons lacked on their sheets were murder charges.

Something else stood out: Turner's last known address in Chicago was on South Langley Avenue, DeSadier's on South Rhodes.

I know where that is. That's the Twenty-First Precinct. Dad worked that district!

He popped open his cell phone, speed-dialed his office, and asked his assistant to get him the name of the district commander for the Twenty-First Precinct. He then went over and stared at the two incarcerated men through the small glass window. He wondered what secrets they held in their corrupted minds and why they were in Arizona now, bringing their criminal actions into the Copper State.

His cop's gut told him his best friend, Stan, knew these men. Somehow, their paths must have crossed in the past. But how that happened was anyone's guess. He knew his buddy, though; he knew him better than anyone did. And Brian's gut also told him Stan was lying.

"*When you lie to a friend,*" Brian's dad once told him, "*you're lying to yourself.*" That saying never meant much to Brian before this day, not quite fully understanding the depth of his father's wisdom. If Stan Kobe was lying to Brian, then he was lying to himself, and Brian had decided to find out why.

When Brian arrived back at his Chandler office, his assistant had left him a note with the name and phone number he'd requested. He looked at the name on the Post-it and raised his eyebrows. Grabbing his cell phone, he made the call right away.

"Twenty-first."

"This is Detective Brian Hanley, Chandler, Arizona, Homicide Division. Can I speak to Commander Abbatti, please?"

"Hold on. I'll transfer."

"Prairie District. Commander Abbatti."

"Hello, Sal. It's Brian Hanley."

"Wow! Brian Hanley. How the hell are you, kid? How's Arizona treating you? Hot out there?"

"Yeah, it's hot. But it's a dry heat."

"Yeah, dry heat. Right. That's like being a little pregnant, son."

Brian heard Sal laugh, then abruptly stop. "Hey, Brian. Sorry to hear about your old man. Salt of the earth. A cop's cop. You know what I mean?"

"He always said the same about you. Said his dago friend would make commander someday. Looks like it happened."

"Well, they couldn't fire me, so they just kept promoting me," Sal laughed aloud again. "What can I do ya kid? I'm sure this is no social call."

"Can't fool a good cop I guess. Yeah, you're right. It's police business. I need you to fill me in, if you can. What do you know about a couple of hoods named Turner and DeSadier?"

There was silence on the other end of the line. Brian thought that maybe his cell had dropped the call. "Hello? Sal? You there? Sal?"

"Yeah, yeah. I'm here, kid. Sorry." Stammering, Abbatti continued. "What did you say those two names were again?"

"One's street name is Pokie Turner. The other is Bobby De-Sadier."

"Where on God's green earth did you come across those two?"

"So you know them?"

"Oh, yeah. I know them. What's up?"

"We arrested them out here on one of our Indian reservations. They were planning to purchase and move a big shipment of Mexican meth, probably up to your neck of the woods."

"I'm not surprised. They're three-time losers. Lotta bad history around these parts with those jokers."

Brian heard the tone of Sal's voice change. He had known Sal since way back, when Abbatti was a beat cop. Homicide dicks like his dad became close to the beat cops—the good ones that is—relying upon them to gather critical information at crime scenes since they were the first on the scene. Not like other guys who came to work and hoped nothing came their way, Abbatti relished assisting the detectives. Looking back now, Brian knew that, besides his father, Sal Abbatti had influenced him the most in becoming a cop.

"Whadya mean 'bad history'?"

"That's goin' way back, kid, maybe thirty years."

"Hey, Sal. It's me. Stick Hanley's kid. What aren't you tellin' me?"

"Aw, it's dead and gone now, Brian. No sense bringing up the past."

"Hey, I wouldn't be calling unless I needed your help. I think my best friend is somehow connected with these guys."

"Then all I can say is—stay away from your best friend."

Brian didn't like the answer. He prodded for more. "Give it to me straight, Sal."

After another longer than normal pause, the commander continued. "Back in the seventies, I remember your old man bringing you around on Saturdays. You were just a little shit. Always asking questions. I knew you'd make a good cop someday, just like your old man.

"Anyway, the Twenty-First was a cesspool back then. Your dad and his partner, Timbo Boscorelli, collared those two you're holding now on a murder over in Burnham Park. A big heater. Even the mayor got involved. But their case was thrown out. Turner and DeSadier got away—scot-free."

"I don't remember Dad talking to me about that one. He told me about every murder case he ever worked on. That is, at least I thought he did. I'm sure I would have remembered it. What happened? What were the particulars?"

"This old man got whacked riding his bicycle on the way to work. Good news, we had an eyewitness. A little kid, 'bout same age you were then, maybe a little older. Sharp kid. Bad news, we didn't get the facts straight between the kid, the detectives, and the Cook County Attorney's Office. The killers walked and our witness had to be put into a witness protection program."

Brian didn't immediately respond to Sal Abbatti's particulars about the case. Rather, the wheels turned in his head in an attempt to grasp the significance of all these details and how they might possibly relate to the men in a holding tank at 4th Avenue Jail, his best friend Stan's aversion to charging them, and that same friend's eagerness to send them back to Chicago.

After a few moments of silence, Brian said, "I need the files on that case. I'd like to take a look at them while I still have these two hombres in custody here in Arizona."

"I'm not even sure where those records would be, kid. Remember, that's in the days before computers."

Brian recognized Sal's hesitancy to help. If what he said went down the way the new commander said it did, Brian was sure there would be lots of people who wanted to forget this crime ever happened, let alone stir up the feelings again of those still alive who had worked on the case. Even though homicide cops have thick skins and short memories for the cases they never cleared, like his dad did, there were some cases that stayed with them a very long time.

"Do the best you can, wouldja?" Brian asked.

"Okay, kid. I still owe your old man for watching my back all those years. Maybe the files are in our basement archives. Gimme a little time on this, okay?"

"Sure, Sal, whatever you need. Hey, what about the trial records? Got any contacts over at Cook County courts?"

"Can't help you there. All five of the perps were tried as juveniles. Their records are sealed shut, kid."

"Did you say five? So these two weren't the only ones in on this?"

"Oh, no. There were five of them and, if I remember correctly, a sixth who was never IDed. It was a whole gang who jumped him. P. Stones. Those evil bastards never did anything alone. Always made sure the numbers were in their favor. Took a lot of real brave little nigger pricks to kill an eighty-five-year-old man."

"Eighty-five? The person these black kids killed was eighty-five years old?" Brian paused a moment. His fascination with the case rose with each new detail. "Do you remember his name?"

"Oh, sure, kid. Nobody around here will ever forget him. The guy actually played for the nineteen-nineteen Black Sox. His name was Manny Fleischman."

CHAPTER 25

After his phone call with Sal Abbatti from Chicago, Brian's mind spun trying to put together the pieces of the fascinating yet troubling puzzle laid before him. His best friend, Stan Kobe, who had fearlessly and successfully prosecuted some of the most heinous criminals in Arizona, had suddenly become squeamish about throwing the book at two losers from Chicago held in custody in the Maricopa County Jail. In past situations, Stan would have looked for the tiniest loophole to keep scum like this behind bars for as long as he could. Now, uncharacteristically, he wanted nothing to do with them, maintaining they should be sent back to Illinois.

Still not sure why Stan supported extraditing Turner and De-Sadier when he could initiate charges and try them here, he did know that if Maricopa County decided not to bring forth charges, then the state would be required to implement extradition very soon and send the two felons back to Chicago.

Brian dialed another number. When that call ended, he placed another.

"History Department. Professor Kobe."

"Maxine. I'm glad I caught you."

"Hey, Brian sweetie. How are you? What's up?"

Not in any mood for small talk, Brian hurriedly replied. "Can we meet? How's your afternoon look?"

"I'm in class till two. What's up? You forget Claire's birthday again? If you want to know what to buy her to get out of the doghouse, I can tell you right now over the phone."

"No, no. It's not that. This is serious, Max. I need to see you right away. It's about Stan."

Her voice rose. "Stan?"

"Don't worry. He's fine. It's just important that I speak to you as soon as you got a few minutes. Alone. Okay?"

"Okay. Sure. I go over to the Rec Center for my karate workout after my last class today. Why don't we meet over there about two thirty?"

"Great. See you then."

Brian hung up, not giving her a chance to ask more questions or even to say goodbye. He didn't have time to waste. If the two thugs being held at the 4th Avenue Jail lawyered-up soon—and there was no doubt they would after Brian noticed their connections in Chicago on their rap sheets—they'd surely be out of lockup very soon. On top of that, if Stan's charging unit under Tom Terry's direction didn't bring charges against the two men, then he'd have no way of keeping them behind bars since, by law, they'd have to be extradited within seventy-two hours.

He picked up his desk phone and made still another call.

"Federal Defender's Office, Dianna Cherry. May I help you?"

"Dianna. It's Brian Hanley. Hey, I need a favor."

Over the next hour, the fax machine in Brian's office whirred, spitting out sheet after sheet of information on the murder case of one Emanuel "Manny" Fleischman. Sal Abbatti sent over everything he had regarding the involvement of Turner and DeSadier as it pertained to the thirty-year-old murder. Brian figured Sal's conscience must have gotten the best of him since the documents Abbatti had thought would be hard to find had started to appear soon after their phone call ended. Abbatti's mysterious change of heart did puzzle Brian, though, as he began reading the faint pages as fast as they spewed from the fax.

The initial pages were copies of the original reports filed by the first officer on the scene, Patrolman Sal Abbatti. *He had to be a rookie in seventy-five. No wonder he remembers this case. That's also probably why he wants to keep it in the past.* As he read further, Brian learned about the arrest of the five boys after the eyewitness, a twelve-year-old boy by the name of James Overstreet, had picked each from photo arrays shown to him in the Youth Division offices at Chicago's Area 1 Headquarters. According to the reports, the collars on the five perps seemed clean. Detective Edward Hanley—*Dad busted these guys!*—had read them their Miranda rights when arrested at The Olander Housing Projects.

Each alleged offender had been brought into Area 1 and interviewed individually. Because it was a heater case, a Cook County Assistant State's Attorney had also been involved in the interrogation. Most glaring to Brian as he read on was that counsel did not represent the alleged offenders during their interviews.

They were juveniles. Why weren't their parents there when they were questioned?

Brian read where each boy had confessed to being at the scene of the crime. During the interviews, they had individually told police interrogators the boy wielding the bat was a kid by the name of Monroe Clarke, known by his street name as "Ice Pick," or more commonly "Pick," the alleged leader of their gang.

It says here in the interrogation notes that Pick had asked for an attorney. I wonder why they didn't give him one?

As he read on Brian thought it noteworthy that the eyewitness Overstreet had mentioned seeing six attackers, but when questioned, each of the five arrested had stuck by his story that they were the only ones who had participated in the crime. Brian didn't give much weight to this tidbit because he knew as a seasoned homicide investigator an eyewitness can be notorious for getting things wrong.

As Brian continued to read the details of the case, it became clear to him that the detectives made major mistakes when they gathered evidence at the scene. He found errors, too, in the interviewing of the witness and the interpretation of subsequent facts necessary to initiate charges against the alleged offenders in order to bring them to trial.

I don't see here where anyone ever took the Overstreet kid back to the scene of the crime. Could Dad have possibly overlooked this? Why wouldn't he have confirmed before the trial what James actually saw and where he saw it?

Brian paused in his reading. Head spinning, his mind drifted back to the day he had decided to become a police officer those many years ago, making him the fifth generation of Hanleys in law enforcement. At the time, Edward Hanley took his son under his wing and had taught him all he knew about being a good cop. The father shared his experiences about working in Area 1, in particular about the notorious Prairie District, the Twenty-First on Chicago's near South Side, and his war stories as a homicide investigator there in one of the city's most dangerous neighborhoods.

Brian still remembered his dad's long-time partner, Timothy "Timbo" Boscorelli, so it came as no surprise how often his name appeared in the old police reports he had just read. His dad and Timbo had been inseparable during most of their careers, especially during their early days together, both on and off the job. But in later years, particularly after Brian's dad's forced retirement due to his health and the Hanley family's move to Arizona, the two had stopped communicating with one another. The connection had broken completely when Timbo, who left the Chicago PD back in the late eighties, ended up in private security, protecting high-profile Chicago politicians.

It dawned on Brian that his Saturday trips with his dad to the police station abruptly stopped. As a boy, he hadn't understood why. Thinking back now and doing the math, Brian deciphered it had been right around the time of the Manny Fleischman case. Almost nine then, he figured his dad was just too busy to bring him down to the office anymore. Like most boys his age, Brian had started to play Little League baseball, so his weekends left him little free time what with games and practice.

At this very moment, he struggled to understand why his dad had never told him about this particular case, but it was becoming clearer to him as he read on that he might have just found out why. First, though, he needed to follow a hunch he had about a particular item displayed prominently on the wall of his deceased father's baseball memorabilia collection.

Brian's phone rang, interrupting his thoughts.

"I've got Pat Bobko from the U.S. Marshal's Office on hold," his secretary announced. "Says he's returning your call."

"Put him through."

"Hey, Pat. Brian Hanley. I'm fine. How are you? Great. Got a minute? I need to pick your brain about something."

Brian pulled up to a handicap parking spot right next to the ASU Rec Center exactly as his car's digital clock displayed 2:15. He placed a placard reading CHANDLER POLICE DEPT on the dash of his unmarked car, allowing him to park wherever he wanted, one of the perks of being in law enforcement. Five minutes after his arrival, he watched as Maxine Kobe strolled up to the building, making her way toward the main entrance. Workout bag slung over her shoulder, her tall, curvaceous physique and dark olive complexion exuded the epitome of good health.

Brian always loved to watch how his best friend's wife carried herself as she walked. He admired how she held her head high—confident, strong, self-assured. Maxine, he knew, not only loved her career but her freedom, too. He knew that she and Stan had a solid marriage, one based upon trust and openness. If what he planned to tell her proved right, then that trust and openness would surely be tested, and tested very strongly.

"Max!" he shouted, jumping from his unmarked car, startling her from behind as she strode by.

"Brian. Don't do that. I almost karate kicked you right in the family jewels. Don't you know you shouldn't do stuff like that to a girl walking alone on campus?"

"I'm sorry. You're right. Just anxious to see you."

She paused a beat before she said, "What's going on?"

Brian discerned a furrow in her brow. Not knowing how to begin, he looked down at the ground and bit his lip.

"Sweetie, you're starting to creep me out. If you're about to tell me you want to leave Claire—"

He held up his hand in a halting gesture, feeling his face turning red. "No, no. It's nothing like that. I just want to ask you a few questions." He moved his hand around to her back and gently urged her toward his car. "Here. Please. Take a seat in my car."

Brian hadn't meant to frighten Maxine, but the crevices deepening in her brow indicated he had, so he blurted out what he came here to tell her. "Look. I'm concerned about Stan. Have you detected anything different about him lately? Any odd behavior?"

Maxine pulled her gym bag off her shoulder and set it on the hood of his car. "You've noticed it, too?" Her response seemed to be one of relief, but then her expression went from bewilderment to concern as he spoke.

"So you think he's acting funny, too. I knew it. He just doesn't seem like the friend I know. I mean, it all started with that baseball bat of my dad's he—"

"Not that goddamn bat again," she jumped in. "First, he tells me that night it wasn't about that stupid bat and that it was about a case you two were working on—which I knew was a lie. Then, the next morning he admits it *was* about the bat but won't tell me exactly what it's all about. We had a huge fight. I told him that if he couldn't be honest with me, then I was going to leave him."

"You said that?" Brian asked, shocked at the revelation of a chink in the armor of what he had always thought to be a strong marriage.

"Yes, I said that, thinking that my husband would never allow that to happen. That he'd snap out of whatever was bugging him and just tell me what was going on."

"And what'd he say?"

"You wanna know what he said? He said, 'If you gotta go, I'm not stopping you.' Can you believe my Stan said that to me?"

"No fuckin' way!" Then quickly he added, "Oooh. Sorry for my French."

"Fuck your French. That son of a bitch really said that to me."

Brian took a deep breath before going on. He knew that what he was about to say could further shatter this woman's faith in the man she loved. He laid a hand on her shoulder.

"I'm a cop, Max." He paused a full beat. "And cops are trained to be suspicious. Right?"

She nodded her head. He could see by the look on her face she wasn't quite sure what he was about to say next.

"The reason I wanted to see you is because I'm here to tell you that I don't think Stan's the guy he says he is."

He awaited her reaction, but none came. *Does she suspect the same thing, too?*

Unsure of what to do or what approach to take next, he took another deep breath. Brian took his other hand and put it on top of her other shoulder, bracing her, and staring into her emerald-colored eyes.

"Max. I also wanted to tell you—" He paused until she focused on his eyes.

"What?" she asked.

"I've found Barbara Reyes."

CHAPTER 26

Maxine jumped away from Brian with a jolt. She shook her head, narrowed her eyes, and her face contorted.

"What do you mean, you've *found* her? And just where *is* she?"

Maxine's mind spun with this latest news, though she wasn't sure whether maybe she should first be asking Brian about the other bombshell he had just dropped, the one regarding her husband, questioning her perception of the man she loved.

"Just what I said. I found her," he replied. "She's living in a small city in Idaho. College town again. I'm sure she's okay."

She rattled questions at him nonstop, feeling the rush of an adrenaline surge pump through her body. "Where in Idaho? Did you get her address? Her phone? How did you find her?"

"Whoa, slow down, slow down. Look, Max. I really can't say any more. I shouldn't have even told you what I just did. But you're a great friend, and I thought it might ease your mind to know."

She struggled to deal with the surprise of Brian's news. "Brian, what's going on? First you tell me you don't think my husband, the father of my children, is who he really is, and now you tell me you found Barbara Reyes but can't tell me the details. What is all this? What's all this got to do with my Stan?"

"Please, Max. Let's take this conversation into the car. I'll tell you all I can in there. Honest."

She had no reason to doubt Brian's concern for her and for Stan. And hearing that he found Barbara Reyes did bring her some comfort. Brian had already opened the front passenger door to his vehicle and waited for her to get in. As she did, she settled in the seat and watched him walk around the front of the car, then get behind the wheel. The car's police radio squawked with chatter. He turned it down to a barely audible level.

"Sorry," he said as he shrugged his shoulders. "I'm still on duty."

As she looked at him, he paused a moment and then locked onto her eyes.

"I'm gonna cut right to the chase. Recently, I've been part of a multiagency task force working on stopping the smuggling of illegal crap across the Mexican border. I've been working real close with some federal agencies as part of this project, especially with some folks from the U.S. Marshal's Office. They're the people in charge of all our country's various witness protection programs. I made some connections high up in their chain of command. That's how I was able to find out about Barbara."

Maxine listened to him intently. "Is she okay?"

"She's fine. I really can't tell you much, though. But the bottom line is, Barbara's in a federal witness protection program—"

"So Stan *was* right," she interrupted. "He told me that's what he thought but he wouldn't talk about it."

"Well, it's not that he wouldn't talk about it. He—we—didn't know for sure. I just found out for certain myself during a phone call earlier today."

"Why? I mean, what did she—?"

"She didn't do anything, Max, if that's what you were going to ask. But, for your own safety, I can't give you any specifics. As a matter of fact, I really don't know all the details myself. All I know is that Barbara once lived in New York and worked at a big accounting firm. She discovered some improprieties with her firm's accounting practices and blew the whistle. There was a trial and her client was found guilty on all counts.

"Unfortunately for her, the company she worked for was laundering money for some very bad people. The hammer then fell on those people, they were arrested and convicted, and now their "family," shall we say, blames it all on her for coming forward. Those people are out for revenge, and after she was threatened, the feds decided to put her into the protection program."

Maxine reeled with the news, pressing her palms against the

sides of her face. "Oh my God. What about her child? And her husband? Are they in danger, too? Can anyone really protect them?"

"That's why they were relocated so quickly. Her identity was compromised and the feds moved her and her family for their own safety. I'm sorry to say, but that's sometimes the down side of being a good guy," Brian said. "Sometimes you end up with the shittier life. I don't know if people ever have a normal life again or will ever be safe when they go into that program."

Brian shook his head, then stared out through the windshield of his unmarked police cruiser. Maxine dropped her hands to her lap. Her heart felt for Barbara and her family. It didn't seem fair that her life had become forever changed because Barbara did the right thing. She paused and took a slow, deep breath before she spoke.

"So, what's all this got to do with my Stan?"

Waiting patiently for Brian to respond, Maxine believed she would learn more from him by what he didn't say next than by the actual words he would speak. As a teacher of college students the past eighteen years, she had become an expert on body language. She looked at him closely for any telltale signals from his limbs, face, or torso, revealing if he was or was not about to utter the truth.

"Yesterday, I met Stan down at the 4th Avenue County Jail. We're holding two known Chicago gang members there. We have them on tape conspiring to transport illegals, drugs, guns, and cash back and forth between Mexico, move it all though Phoenix, then on to Chicago. When Stan saw these guys for the first time, he acted like he'd seen a ghost. Max, he could barely look at these two guys."

She listened intently. As he told his story, he never lost eye contact with her. As he sat sideways, facing her, he held the steering wheel with his left hand while his right hand laid on the back of the front seat just above her left shoulder. She sensed from his composure that what he was telling her was the truth to the best of his knowledge.

"I also found out the County Attorney's Office is being encouraged by the governor's office to bring local charges against these guys while the feds are working out a parallel investigation on their end. The feds even told us they wouldn't stand in our way, letting the state prosecute this to look good on Arizona's war against border crime. Yet, we need to move now on charging them before they get extradited back to Chicago or, worse yet, get sprung by a high-priced defense attorney from Chicago. And Stan? What does your husband want? Well, your hubby wants them gone. Now. Out of his hair. Vamoose!"

Brian pulled his left arm from the wheel and waved his hand as if shooing away a pesky fly. "He wants them out of town as quickly as possible. You should have seen him. Maricopa County's most ruthless prosecutor? Huh! Not yesterday. I swear he shit his pants when he saw those two in lockup."

Confused by his description of Stan's actions, she propped herself up in the seat. "That's not like him. My Stan would never do that. He'd never allow these two to go free. Never."

"You're exactly right. So, maybe, just maybe then, he's not your Stan. As a matter of fact, I don't really believe he is who he says he is. I'm beginning to wonder if he's really the man we think we all know."

Not waiting for her reply to his accusation, Brian pushed a button under the dash near the driver's door, opening the car's trunk. He hopped out and went behind the car. Dumfounded, Maxine turned to watch him through the back window. All she could see was the rear trunk lid propped open. She felt the car move to and fro as he dug around in the trunk for a few seconds. Then he slammed the lid and came back around the side of the car. He carried an object in his hand. Her heart pounded as he got back behind the wheel, finally seeing what he held in his hand.

"What's that?" Maxine asked as she inched ever so slightly away from him and the huge object, back toward the passenger door. "Why do you have that baseball bat?"

"Well, this isn't just any baseball bat. I think what I have in my hands is a thirty-year-old murder weapon that may hold a clue to all this."

"Murder weapon? A clue to all *what*?" she asked, her right hand now reaching for her own door handle.

If she had been confused and troubled by everything he had told her to this point, now she felt even more perplexed. The gigantic piece of turned lumber almost spanned the width of the car's interior. A black tar-like substance covered its worn handle from near the bottom to the lower mid-point of the barrel.

"Wait," she said. "I've seen that bat before."

"That's right. You have. This is the bat Stan saw in my dad's trophy room at Kaitlin's party last Saturday. Remember?" He pointed it toward her. "Recognize it?"

She flinched slightly but then nodded. Brian went on.

"I may have had a few too many beers that day, but when Stan saw this bat and freaked out, I knew something had to be up. And then, when he spazzed on us and took all of you out of there so quickly, well, that really made me wonder."

"I don't understand. What is this all about?"

"Here. I'll show you. Look, Max. Look closely at the tip of the barrel."

He took the bat and carefully raised it closer to her so she could see the fat end of the bat. There, carved into the ash hardwood were two, faint letters.

"Is this what you want me to see?" she asked. "These initials?"

"Yes. I think they're initials, too. Exactly. What do you see?"

She squinted and grabbed the barrel of the bat, bringing it closer to her. "Well, it looks like a J and an O. Yes. It looks like the initials J.O."

"That's right. J.O. You see it then, too."

"All right, Brian. I give up. Who's J.O.?"

CHAPTER 27

Stan Kobe watched Jimmy Nejo's two Native American jail guards escort Pokie Turner and Bobby DeSadier into an old interrogation room no longer used at the Indian jail. The two were bound with hand irons chain-linked to foot shackles. The bigger guard, built like a fullback with tattoos covering his arms and neck, pulled DeSadier by the arm and moved him to the table.

DeSadier resisted. "Git your motherfuckin' hands off me, Injun!"

The three-hundred-pound, six-foot-plus jail guard didn't respond, but merely continued shoving DeSadier toward the table, holding him at bay with a saguaro cactus rib nightstick. The second guard, at least six inches shorter than his partner and easily more than one hundred pounds lighter, had the much more subdued, one-eyed Turner in a similar hold. He escorted him, holding his nightstick at his side, to a seat next to DeSadier.

After the guards shackled their ankles to the floor and their wrists to the top of an old wooden table, Stan entered the room with trepidation in his heart. He didn't want to show his deep-seated fear of the two men in irons but, nonetheless, cracked a knuckle. He had never been in this interrogation room before and now he knew why. It looked antiquated, like a relic dating from before the turn of the century, a remnant of bygone days. The newer interrogation rooms at the Gila jail didn't allow shackling of prisoners to the floor.

Stan dragged a creaky, wooden chair over from the sidewall and sat opposite the two prisoners across the four-foot-wide sturdy, mesquite wood table. The first guard finished double-checking to make sure the prisoners' chains were firmly secured. Stan acknowledged the guards with a thankful nod as they walked out of the room, locking the door behind them with a throw of a deadbolt.

Stan put his finger between his collar and his neck, stretching it a bit before he spoke.

"Mister Turner. Mister DeSadier. My name is Stanford Kobe. I'm a prosecutor with the Maricopa County Attorney's Office. I'd like to ask you both a few questions."

Turner hung his head, staring at the tabletop, not looking at Stan. DeSadier, however, looked straight at him.

"Hey, blood, you say my last name perfectly: dee—sah—dee—ay," DeSadier said. "That's very cool. You impress me." The prisoner pulled on his chains while he spoke. "A French brother with the same name discovered Chi-town, ya know. I think I'm related to him. Yeah. That's right, I'm goddamn Chicago royalty is what I am. So? Where's my fuckin' chambermaid?"

DeSadier laughed aloud at his own remark. Turner still remained silent, unmoving.

"For your information, Mister DeSadier, his name was DuSable, and I don't think you're related to him. And I don't think you're royalty, either. As a matter of fact, I'd say your more like *merde*."

Knowing DeSadier had no idea what the word meant, Stan waited a moment before he went on. "That's French for shit."

DeSadier jumped up from his chair and lunged at the prosecutor, but the tight chains yanked him back like an angry dog on a short leash. The guards rushed in and grabbed him, forcing him back into his seat.

"Hey, can't you see us black brothers don't want your red Injun asses in here?" DeSadier cackled, angrily thrusting his shoulders away from the big guard's grip. "Can't you see we's havin' ourselves a revival meeting?"

Although he attempted to look unshaken by DeSadier's chain-thwarted leap, Stan had unknowingly pushed himself back several feet from the table. He straightened his suit, pulled his shirt cuffs down, and regained his composure.

After he rechecked their chains, the smaller guard glanced at the prisoners and nodded to his partner. Then both left the room, closing the door behind them again.

"You have a right to an attorney. Do you know that?" Stan continued, adjusting his tie and pulling his chair back up to his side of the table.

Neither responded, both staring away in silence.

"Okay. If that's the way you want to play it. We can make this easy or we can make this hard. Which do you prefer?" Stan knew his question was rhetorical. He hoped these two weren't smart enough to realize he was biding his time. If he didn't charge them soon, a federal defender might spring them, or at the very least their own lawyers would begin to look for them in an attempt to get them back to Illinois.

Once again, no answer from either. Stan decided to plod on.

"Right now, you're both looking at several counts of conspiracy in the commission of proposed felonies, breaking both federal and state statutes. If you're found guilty, you're looking at spending a lot of time in prison. Do you both understand that?"

Turner slowly lifted up his head. His unpatched eye gazed into Stan's. Stan could feel the hatred and contempt in the man, honed from spending more than twenty years of his life behind bars. Still, Turner didn't speak.

"We've done time before, we'll do it again. Even if it's in an Injun jail," DeSadier said, spitting on the floor.

"I don't think you should be so cavalier about this, Mister De-Sadier."

Once more, Stan could see the puzzled look on the boastful man's face.

"Cavalier. That's a French word again, Mister DeSadier. But I'm sure you knew that."

"Yeah, I knows that. Just because you're some Uncle Tom don't mean you're smarter than me, nigger."

"I assure you, Mister DeSadier. I'm no Uncle Tom. And I ain't your nigger. I'm an officer of the court now. You may have gotten away with murder in your past, but this time I promise I will see you two go down. Straight down to hell."

Stan had put his career on the line. Even a first-year law stu-

dent would understand the legal ramifications of the line this prosecutor had crossed by visiting the two men without their counsel
present. And his clear threat was not only immediate grounds for
disbarment but also risked the suppression of any statements the
incarcerated men might make in future charges leveled against
them.

Turner still hadn't spoken, but with Stan's last threat he began
a more intense scrutiny of the attorney, sitting four feet away.
Turner's gaze made Stan feel uneasy. Sensing Turner's one eye
scan him from mid-torso to the top of his balding head, to distract
himself Stan looked down and rifled through a manila folder.

"I see, Mister DeSadier, you're on parole—"

"How long you think you gonna play this game, *Mister Prosecutor?*" Turner interrupted.

Stan looked up at him, but didn't respond to his question.

"You think you're so smart? Think you know a lot about me
and my fool here?" Turner said, twisting his head toward DeSadier.

"Who you callin' a fool, fool?" DeSadier snapped. "Don't be
dissin' me in front of this Tom!"

"Don't you see what the man's doin'? Don't you see the game
he playin'? Don't you know who this man is?"

"Watchew talkin' about, Poke?"

"Yes, Mister Turner. Why don't you inform us both just what it
is you're getting at?" Stan said.

"I never forget a face, Tom. Work twice as hard at it, seein' as
I got me only one eye," Turner replied, running his tongue across
his puffy lips. Each time his lips parted, a gold front tooth glis-
tened.

Stan rested his arms on the table and folded his hands together. As Turner stared at him, Stan didn't realize he had started
pulling on each his fingers, cracking all of his knuckles.

"This where you been all this time? Out here in the sunshine?
Playin' golf, I'll bet. You a big golfer now, Tom? Think you're Tiger
Woods?"

"What the fuck you talkin' about, Poke?" asked DeSadier.

"Take a good look at Tom, here, Bobby D. Take a real good
look at him."

DeSadier looked at Stan as the attorney propped his elbows on the table and clasped his hands together, then pointed across at Stan with cuffed wrists. "All's I see is an Uncle Tom workin' on keepin' two brothers in a fuckin' Injun jail is all I see," DeSadier said.

"That's why you's a fool, Bobby D. Hadn't been for you screwin' up, we'd be back in Chi-town right now, sniffin' taint, and poppin' cherry till dawn."

"What the fuck you talkin' 'bout?"

"Take a look at this man, fool. Look deep into his eyes, Bobby D. You know who this is? This is the little mo' fo' from Thirty-Ninth Street. He's alive and well and a big time lawyer in Arizona."

"No mothafuckin' way!"

"Ain't that right, Mister Prosecutor? Ain't you our little squealer?" Turner asked.

Stan didn't reply, not biting on Turner's lure.

"You got to be kiddin' me. James motherfuckin' Overstreet? It's really *you*?" DeSadier shook his head as Stan looked straight at him. "Wait till we tell Pick you's still alive and where you been hidin' all this time."

"Shut the fuck up, fool!" Turner shouted.

"No, please, gentlemen, please. Keep talking. It's fascinating what one can learn from such educated men as the two of you." Stan's sarcasm went over their heads.

"I tole Pick the day after he whacked that old Jew I shoulda' done a little Fred Astaire on your face and beat your little nigger ass, but he said you'd never go to the poe-leese," Turner said. "Said you'd know better than that. That fool Pick's a fool, too."

"Well, it's just too bad Pick will never find out. Will he now?" Stan said. Grabbing his papers, he turned an about-face and stepped the four paces to the door, knocking for the guards to release him from the room. As he waited, he could feel the shackled men's burning stares at his back.

When the guards opened the door, Stan moved aside as they entered the room.

"I want a fuckin' lawyer!" Turner shouted. "Gimme my phone call!"

CHAPTER 28

By the time Stan reached his vehicle, perspiration had soaked through his starched white shirt and onto the lining of his gray, three-piece suit. He paused for a moment before he got into his Acura, placed his palms on the car's sunbaked black roof, and took a deep breath. He didn't know how long he could keep Turner and DeSadier in Police Chief Jimmy Nejo's jail. But that was precisely why Stan had arranged for his longtime Indian pal to pick these two up and transport them to his reservation's lockup. Stan knew that because the reservation is a sovereign nation, the tribal police could do anything they wanted. Questions would be asked, but answers weren't guaranteed when something took place on the rez.

Before he left the Gila Reservation Police Station, he had asked his longtime friend, Jimmy, to keep the two out of sight. "Keep them isolated for their own protection," was they way Stan had phrased it.

"Veteran's Day tomorrow, ya know. I'm takin' a long weekend. Gotta march in the parade and all. So, I'm shuttin' off my phone. Nobody'll be able to get a hold of me," Jimmy told him. "You're right, too, this place can get a little rough, 'specially for tough guys like these two from Chicago. Salt River and Fort McDowell Rez jails are full, so I might have to send 'em up to the Yavapai Rez Jail, to keep 'em safe and all for you, ya know."

Stan smiled at Jimmy's clear understanding of the situation.

Jimmy grinned back at him, then continued with a shrug. "Plus, that Yavapai jail's so far out on the rez their phones rarely work up there."

Stan got into his car and drove off the Gila Reservation, but his mind wouldn't stop dwelling on his confrontation with Turner and DeSadier. Meeting them face-to-face for the first time in over thirty years brought back a rush of painful and unbearable emotions. He felt confused, wondering how he would explain his unethical—if not outright unlawful—interaction with them, especially to Andrew Thomas. He'd been way out-of-bounds, talking alone to Turner and DeSadier without counsel at their side. Disbarment for such an action was probably the minimal consequence; a significant fine and even jail time were distinct possibilities if he ended up with a contempt ruling.

At this point, Stan didn't care.

As he felt the sweat ooze from his pores, he realized he felt the same way he always did when he woke up from a recurring nightmare he had in childhood. The dream had always been the same:

James stood on one perfectly round, brilliant white flat rock along the edge of Lake Michigan. Ahead of him lay about thirteen more identical rocks out in the water. On the last sat his seventh-grade teacher, Miss Burns. But the stone she sat on would magically turn into a green lily pad. With legs hunched behind her, she looked like a frog, darting her tongue out, trying to catch flies.

"No, Miss Burns! You're not really a frog. I just think you look like one with your hair pulled back and your big, brown eyes that open so wide when you talk."

He'd shout these words to her, but she'd never reply, his small voice absorbed by the waves crashing up against the shore.

I've got to tell her she's not a frog!

At that very moment each time in the dream, he would mysteriously be transported into the audience of "The Grand Prize Game" on the popular *Bozo's Circus* show. It was his favorite television program and he and Clayton would watch it every day at noon when they went home for lunch from school.

"One boy! One girl!" Ringmaster Uncle Ned would bellow, holding up a single finger on each hand to the TV and studio audience who anxiously waited for the "magic arrows" as Ned called them, to land on one of them. That was how you were picked to play Bozo's Grand Prize Game.

Randomly generated arrows would repetitively flash on-and-off across the TV screen while the camera scanned the studio audience. Only those viewing at home could see the white, magic arrows. But, when they stopped flashing, Ringmaster Ned somehow knew whom the magic arrows landed upon. He was a grown-up after all, so that made perfect sense to James, he would think.

Then, to the boy's amazement, the magic arrows landed on him.

Uncle Ned would cry, "The magic arrows have landed on a boy! Come on down!"

In the dream, James would come down from the studio audience and stand next to Uncle Ned.

"What's your name, young fella?" Ned would call out.

"Ja . . . Ja . . . Ja . . ." James had never stuttered before in his life but suddenly he couldn't speak his name.

"What was that, pardner?" Ringmaster Ned would prompt him again, microphone gripped firmly in his fat, adult hand, sticking it right below James's mumbling mouth.

"Ja . . . Ja . . . Ja . . . no . . . no . . . it's . . ."

"I'm sure you're nervous. Don't worry, son. Let's go over to the Bozo Drum and see who you're playing for at home today!" Ned would bellow.

The star of the show, Bozo the Clown, would then enter from behind a curtain, pushing in a huge wire basket on wheels as he strode before the cameras. The drum overflowed with postcards sent in by boys and girls from all over the country.

"Spin the Bozo Drum real good!" Ned would scream, as the clown turned a big handle, whirling the metal basket round and round. As Bozo cranked and cranked the Bozo Drum, James would watch it spin and spin and spin and morph into a Chicago Park District garbage can, just like the wire basket the Oakwood Rangers had trapped him in that day in the park. Bozo would stop turning the Bozo Drum when the basket metamorphosis was complete. Garbage spilled from inside, mixed in with all of the postcards.

"Reach in there and pull out a card, Ja!" Bozo would scream his first words. "We need a boy's name!"

Hesitant to get too close to the basket, James would stretch his arm only far enough to get his hand just inside, turning his head away and closing his eyes. His hand pushed through the garbage until he was able to feel for a postcard and grab it from the trash. He quickly pulled it out and handed it to Uncle Ned, while the make-believe ringmaster deftly grabbed his reading glasses from his front vest pocket.

"Why, this is a blank card! Try again, Ja!" Ned would yell.

Resisting, James would do it again until he found another card, but this one would be blank, too.

"Tee-hee! Let's try that again, Ja!" the red-haired Bozo would scream.

Rummaging through the garbage, James would pull another card, and another, and another. But all the cards would be blank.

"Well I'llllllllll be!" cried Bozo. "Nobody in this world has got a name! I'll fix that!" At this point in the recurring dream Bozo would always pull a huge baseball bat out from under his floppy clown suit and start banging it on the wire basket, saying, "The next card you pick out better have a kid's name on it, Ja, or I'm going to make you pay! Tee-hee-tee-hee-hee—"

At that very moment each time he had the dream, James would wake up, his pajamas drenched with sweat.

CHAPTER 29

As Stan drove back to his office on Interstate 10, his cell phone rang. Startled, he snapped back to reality, out of the semidaze of his haunting childhood nightmare. The cell continued ringing. He looked at the caller ID: his home phone number.

I've got to get my shit together.

Regaining his composure, he answered. "Hey, hon."

"Hi, babe. Whatcha doin'?"

"Nothin'. Just workin'."

"Are you real busy?"

"I'm always busy, Max, but what do you need?"

"Would you come home right now?"

"Now? You want me to come home now?" he asked, eyebrows rising. "Sure. What's up? Did I forget we're supposed to go somewhere tonight?"

His wife's voice cracked through the phone's tiny receiver. "No, I just want you home, that's all."

Only three thirty in the afternoon, Maxine's request puzzled him. Why did she want him back home so early in the day, since he normally didn't arrive home until well after six? Had this been ten years earlier, he would have thought his sexy wife was calling him home for a quick roll in the hay. But since the birth of the twins, their nooners had become few and far between, actually nonexistent, he thought, trying to recollect the last time they had an impromptu roll in the hay like that.

"Okay," he said, glancing at his watch while trying to hold his cell in the crook of his neck. "It'll take me about an hour. Maybe more. I'm pretty busy."

"An hour? Why can't you come home right away? Where are you?"

"I'm down at Gila River Jail."

"What are you doing down there?"

"I told you, I'm working. What do you think I'm doing? Look. I'll explain later, Max. See you in a bit. Love you. Bye."

As he drove toward home, his heart pumped out of control over what he had just done down at the Gila Jail. Although Stan knew no Arizona statute could overcome releasing suspected felons from an Indian reservation without the cooperation of the Indian police, it would only be matter of time before a sharp federal defense attorney or their own defense lawyer would get Turner and DeSadier out of Jimmy's lockup. More pressing on his mind, though, was finding an explanation for the question Andrew Thomas was sure to ask when Chief Nejo told the County Attorney's Office that they weren't ready yet to return these guys back into the county sheriff's custody.

And on top of all this, Maxine wants me home? Now? For what?

Worse yet, though, for Stan was the bigger worry of the possibility that the publicly elected Thomas would get another call from the Arizona governor's office, asking for an update on the county's arraignment of these two border smugglers. If Stan didn't come up with a solution, and a quick one, then he knew a phone call would take place between Andy Thomas and the president of the Gila River Indian Reservation. At all costs, Stan wanted to avoid that from happening. He would have to stall Thomas for as long as he could. Meanwhile, Jimmy Nejo would play a human shell game with the two gang members from Chicago.

Stan sped past traffic, heading north now on Phoenix's Loop 101 toward his Scottsdale home. He worried what he would tell Maxine if she asked him to talk about the current case he was working on, as she normally did. He knew she would find a way to get to this subject especially since she now knew about his unusual visit down to the Gila Reservation Jail.

Why did I mention that to her? I should have lied.

He asked himself if he could keep the news from her about

these two thugs, his intimate knowledge of their past criminal life back in Chicago, and what they really meant to him. More importantly, he worried how he would keep his family safe when these two murderers got word back to Monroe "Pick" Clarke in Chicago that they found the kid who squealed on them over thirty years earlier.

As he neared his exit, Stan felt the world closing in around him, squeezing him hard. He found it difficult to breathe. News would be out soon, too, he worried, from the Maricopa County Attorney's Office, reporting the arrest of two more border smugglers and with it the release of their names. When Thomas took center stage at his news conferences, he always made sure to have Stan Kobe next to him at the podium, signaling to the media that "Arizona's Most Ruthless Prosecutor" was on the case.

Stan knew he had to delay that press conference, as well as any word about it in the *Arizona Republic* as long as he possibly could, since the case no doubt would make headlines not only in his hometown of Phoenix, but in Chicago newspapers, too.

When Stan arrived at the corner of his block, he could see Maxine standing on the large, flagstone patio that bordered the circular driveway in front of their home. As he pulled his car up next to hers, she waved at him.

"Hi, honey," she said as he got out of the car.

"Hi, baby." He pecked her on the cheek. "Been a long time since you called me home in the middle of the afternoon," he said as he pulled away, winking at her.

"I swear, the older you get, the hornier you get."

As they entered the front door of their home, he closed the door behind them. As soon as he got in the foyer, he came to an abrupt halt.

"Hey, Stan."

"Brian! What are you doin' here?" Surprised to see his buddy standing there, Stan turned to Maxine. "Max?"

She looked back at her husband, but didn't answer.

He questioned her again, "What's goin' on?"

"Brian and I wanted to talk to you. Together."

"Is that right?" He paused a second, then turned away from her and looked Brian straight in the eye. Seeing him standing in the foyer of his home had rekindled his anger about the call Brian had made earlier in the day to Tom Terry. "'Bout what?"

"About this," she said, stepping in between them. Maxine reached behind the chair in the foyer and pulled out the Louisville Slugger. She held it up in front of her husband's face.

Stan stared at the bat, unable to take his eyes off it. After a prolonged pause, he shook his head and looked at her. "You wanted to talk to me about his dad's bat? That's why you called me home? I said I was sorry to him about that comment I made." Stan snuck a quick look at Brian but then turned his attention back to his wife. "I *told* you I was sorry. What is this really all about?" He furrowed his perspiring brow and pointed at the Louisville. "Please don't tell me *this* is what you called me home for?"

"You know what it's about, Stan," Brian replied. "Or should I call you James?"

Stan looked at him, bewildered, and then turned back to his wife, shrugging. "Do you know what he's talking about? 'Cause I don't."

"You don't?" Brian asked. "Well then, why don't we try a different subject? Let's talk about Manny Fleischman."

"What about Mister Fleischman?" Stan replied.

"Tell us how you know him?"

"You know how I know him. I knew him when I was a kid. I worked in the same grocery store with him." He shook his head. "But I've told you all that already."

"What grocery store would that be?" Brian continued.

"Hey, what is this?" Stan brushed past the both of them and walked into the kitchen. "What's going on? What's this all about?" he asked over his shoulder.

"Answer him, honey," Maxine said, following him. "Just tell us the truth."

"This is ridiculous!" Stan shouted. He shrugged off his suit coat and tossed it on the back of one of the kitchen table chairs. When he turned around, Maxine and Brian were right behind him.

"You can't sweep this under the carpet, Stan," she challenged.

Stan knew, had they been alone, a full-blown argument would have followed since that was how he always chose to deal with her badgering. It was either a fight or give answers to her prodding questions.

"Just answer Brian. What grocery store did you work at with Mister Fleischman?"

"Hyde Park Foods," he scoffed, turning his back on both of them again.

"Hyde Park?" Brian said. "Why, that's in Chicago, if I'm not mistaken. I thought you told me you were from Gary, Indiana."

Stan paused a beat and then walked toward the kitchen sink, not looking at them as he did. "I *am* from Gary . . . that is . . . we lived in Chicago, too . . . I mean . . . "

Maxine eased to Stan's side as he stared out the window above the kitchen sink and laid her hand on his shoulder. "Stanford. I love you. *We* love you. Brian and I want to help. But we can't help you if you don't tell us the truth. We want the truth."

Stan felt trapped. He turned and walked to the table, pulled-out a chair, sat on it, and started to crack his knuckles.

"I'm your wife. I deserve the truth."

"You don't understand," he mumbled. "You just don't know who you're dealing with. No one can know."

"Know what, pardner?" Brian asked.

"Know about me. Who I am. I can't tell you." Stan looked up to meet his friend's stern glare. "I can't."

"We already know, James," Brian said.

"There you go with that *James* thing again."

"Stan, I've told Max everything. We've sent the twins to California in an unmarked car. They'll be safe there with Maxine's mother."

Stan bolted up from the chair. "You did what? What do you mean? Why did you—? You had no right—I need them near me. I can't protect them if—"

Stan rubbed his temples with his trembling hands. His wife came up behind him and put a hand on his shoulder, urging him back into the chair. He obliged her. Then she stroked the top of his slightly balding head.

"It's all right, honey. It's okay. Brian and I are here for you."

He raised his head and looked back at her with dark eyes.

"You just don't know. No one can or will *ever* know."

CHAPTER 30

The kitchen at the Kobe house would have been completely silent if not for the ticking of a clock on the wall. Sweating more profusely now, Stan stared blankly across the room's big, round table. He pulled a handkerchief from his back pocket and wiped his brow.

Brian stood where he'd been since he first entered the kitchen. He had the Louisville in his grip now, tapping the bat in the palm of his hand. Maxine sat down at the table next to her husband. No one spoke. She reached for Stan and embraced him.

Her hug gave him needed comfort, much the same way his momma had done those many nights he'd awake, sometimes screaming, from his provocative, recurring nightmare. As a child, he'd describe the details of his dream to his momma and she would console him, lulling him back to sleep with her tender words. He had buried the raw feelings the dream unflinchingly reproduced and pushed them into a deep part of his soul, wanting to forget all of his pain, anger, and frustration and, most of all, grief.

"There's no way I could ever explain to you," Stan said, breaking the silence, "or to make you understand." He took a deep breath and looked at his wife. The safety of his children and Maxine's love—and trust—had become, besides his job, the only thing that mattered to him in his life. Somehow, Stan Kobe had overcome all the challenges, creating a life where he could make his own decisions; far different from the life James Overstreet had as a child, hiding under the wary shield of witness protection. Stan Kobe had risen to a position of prominence and become a top prosecutor, a man feared by every felon and defense lawyer who faced him. Stanford James Kobe was a survivor and he did not want the refuge, the haven, he struggled to achieve in Arizona to come crumbling down in front of him. Not now. Not after all he had done. Not after overcoming the identity he had lost.

Stan felt trapped—the same way he felt the day he rode in the back of the tan, Ford Econoline van when an imposter Cook County Sheriff's Deputy drove him and his family away after the not guilty verdict in the murder trial of Manny Fleischman. He recalled the way his mother had cried as she held him close to her chest, protecting her "sweet baby boy," the way she had always referred to him. He didn't know then what she must have known in her heart as she wailed inconsolably in the back of the van: that the family's life would never be the same again; would never be a life where they could make choices freely and without fear.

He knew that feeling now, though. He felt the same gnawing her gut must have felt; the pain she had held within her from the day the family arrived in Arizona, only to leave her the day she died in a nursing home from—as he always believed—a broken heart. His brothers and sisters must have felt the same way, too, since they had all long before stopped talking to the brother who went to the police and ruined their lives. No longer in touch, Stan didn't even know where they lived. Nor did he know the whereabouts of his father, a man who had walked out on his family not long after being set up in Fountain Hills with their new identity.

As his mind returned to the challenge that faced him this late afternoon inside the kitchen of his north Scottsdale home, Maxine and Brian offered him little choice but to answer these accusations. The tables turned on him now, Stan felt like he was the criminal under interrogation. Yet, still, he fought. He would do the thing he knew best. Lie. He took another deep breath and said, "I have no idea what you two are talking about." Then he snapped his head around and looked squarely at Brian. "And it pisses me off you getting my wife all worried here. You have no right to butt your nose into our personal business. Why did you do this?"

Brian didn't respond. Stan knew Brian's experience as a cop

exposed him daily to criminals who tirelessly denied accusations made against them in their desperate attempt to avoid facing the truth. Many denied it even more fiercely when the evidence was clearly stacked against them.

"I did it to help you, Stan, that's why. I'm your friend. But maybe you've forgotten that."

"A friend wouldn't call another friend's boss. Go behind his back. You had no right to call my office and speak with Tom Terry."

"Didn't I?" Brian barked back at him. "I'm an officer of the law. There's no way those two guys over at 4th Avenue Jail should be extradited back to Illinois like you want to do. You know that. You're wrong and I had to put a stop to it. I didn't risk my life, wearing a wire, to capture those two pieces of shit, just to have you run and turn tail."

Stan leapt at Brian, tackling him around the waist and wrestling him to the ground. The jolt dislodged the bat from Brian's grip and the ash wood clattered as it hit the room's Saltillo tile floor.

"Stop it, you two! Stop!" Maxine screamed, pouncing upon them both, attempting to pull them apart. "Stan! Stop! Please! Stop it!"

She pounded on his back, but the men continued to wrestle until Maxine shouted, "I'm calling the police!" She got up and rushed across the room, picking up the phone on the wall.

Stan immediately jerked himself away from Brian and stood up. "No, Max. Don't do that. That's a *very* bad idea."

"I mean it, Stanford. Stop this fighting or I'm dialing." She hovered her index finger over the keypad.

"Please, Max. Don't." Stan held his hands up in the air as if under arrest. "I'll stop. Honest."

Brian pulled himself up off the floor and stood silently, looking as if he were waiting for Stan to say something to him. When Stan didn't speak, Brian broke the tension. "I'm sorry, Stan. I was only trying to help, trying to do what was right."

Stan dropped his head, eyes going down to the silent, discarded bat. "Hang up the phone, Max. I won't cause any more trouble. Promise."

Maxine hung up the receiver and pulled a chair out from the kitchen table. "Sit down, honey. Please. Just sit down and cool off."

Stan went to the table. Brian picked up a chair Stan had pushed to the floor and sat down next to him.

Avoiding their gazes, Stan asked sullenly, "How'd you two figure it out?"

"It was Brian. He did it. He dug until he found the answer."

Stan looked up and inched a smile at the meticulous cop.

"Even though I was three sheets to the wind that day at my house, your reaction when you saw that bat just wasn't like you," Brian said. "And then when you lost it at the 4th Avenue Jail seeing Turner and DeSadier, well, those two led me to my dad's old precinct. The Chicago PD sent me everything they still had on the Fleischman case."

"Stan, I'm so sorry what happened," Maxine said. He felt the tight clench of her hand around his as she pulled a chair out and sat down on the other side of him. "I can't even imagine what it must have been like. You were just a little boy. I mean, all of them getting away with murder. And then what happened to you and your family. It's just awful."

Her arms pulled him closer. His heart melted as he thought of his own mother the day she hugged him in the back of the van, protecting him from the bullets and the shattering glass all around them, smothering him in her embrace. He had never wanted his wife to mother him, but couldn't deny that Maxine's love and comfort right now made him want to crawl inside her, to retreat into the protection of her maternal womb.

"It was terrible," Stan sighed, hanging his head, choking back tears. "But not nearly as bad as having to keep the secret from you. I've mistreated you because of my fears all these years, not knowing how to or what to share with you. Wanting to tell you but also wanting to protect you from all the pain—from all my pain."

"It's okay, honey," she whispered into his ear, cradling him.

The warmth of her breath against his skin eased him. "Now that it's finally out in the open, I feel like a huge weight has been lifted from my chest." Stan cried openly. Thirty years of living another person's life had taken its toll on him, making him regret so many of his actions and behaviors, especially with his wife, children, and friends. He was filled with mixed emotions. Sad for all the things he had done but joyful that it was finally out in the open, able to be talked about freely, and with no fear.

He had lost so much. His psyche had been damaged so badly. He had never fully mourned everything he had lost in the blink of an eye the day Monroe Clarke took Manny Fleischman's life. Now, he had to work on repairing the damage he had done to his relationship with his wife and best friend.

"How did you piece it all together?" he asked them, looking up, tears rolling down his cheeks.

"All I had to go on was what my contact at Chicago PD told me and the newspaper clippings," Brian said. "What I can't figure out is exactly what went wrong at the trial?"

Stan pulled away from Maxine and got up so he could pace the floor and think. "I came forward. Told the police what I saw. I met with the state's attorney. I told every one of them I had witnessed Manny Fleischman's attack, but they really didn't listen to me. I was just a little black kid. Just some little nigger. 'What the fuck does this shithead know?' That's what they thought."

Stan increased the speed of his pacing, his voice growing louder. "They didn't listen to me when I told them Pick and his gang ran toward the Oakwood Boulevard overpass at Thirty-Ninth Street. They just figured I must have had it wrong, 'cause Mister Fleischman's body was found next to the Forty-Third Street footbridge.

"Our side made the wrong assumptions. They didn't even walk the crime scene with me before the trial. It wasn't until we were three days into testimony that our team realized they misinterpreted my version of what really went down versus the version they presented in court. The gang's defense lawyer tore us a new ass. It wasn't until I entered law school that I fully understood all the holes in the prosecution of our case."

"That's unbelievable," Brian said. "I also read they didn't provide counsel to this Pick kid when he asked for a lawyer. What could they have been thinking?"

Stan stopped and looked straight at Brian. "I guess that's a question only your father can answer."

Brian's eyes widened. "How long have you known I was Stick Hanley's kid?"

"I've known since the day we executed Tisdale down in Florence, back in 1992, when we first worked together," Stan said. "When you mentioned your dad had been a detective, a lightbulb went on in my head. I had my office run your background. When they came back with the results, I couldn't believe you were who you were. What were the chances of that happening, I asked myself, a million to one? Who would have believed I'd end up working with the kid of the cop who ran the Fleischman investigation?" Stan paused. He walked over and stood in front of Brian, placing his hand on the cop's shoulder. "And then become his best friend."

Brian smiled back at his buddy.

"Your dad was a good cop, Brian, and he was good to me. There were so many times I wanted to tell you." Stan paused once more, recalling the times the two had worked together side by side, catching and prosecuting bad guys and sending them to jail, then having a beer together in celebration. "You know, you not only look at lot like your dad but you act a lot like him. He protected me and watched out for my family, too. "

Brian shot up from the table. "Oh my God!" he cried. "It all makes sense now."

"What?" Maxine asked.

"Dad moved us out here so he could be by you!" Brian said as he pointed at Stan.

Stan stared at Brian, his mouth agape.

"It's gotta be why we moved to Arizona. We all thought it was because of his health and that he wanted to retire in the sun, get away from the Chicago winters. But it was because he was watching you, Stan! He was still protecting James Overstreet, the kid he let down. His eyewitness who got screwed!"

"You really think your dad moved you and your family out here to be by me?"

"It makes perfect sense. It has to. Dad was married to his job. And after we moved out here, our family could never figure out why he'd always take us to watch kids play baseball all the way out in Fountain Hills. Then years later, he took us to watch the base-ball team at Chaparral High School. Come to think of it, you're the only black kid I remember seeing on those teams now."

Stan stared blankly at Brian then replied, "So someone was watching over me all those years. I really wasn't alone, was I?"

Stan flashbacked to all the years he felt alone in Arizona, aban-doned, discarded, just like the pieces of trash strewn all over him the day Pick and his gang turned the wastebasket on top of him in Burnham Park.

He sat back at the table, thinking of the effort Stick Hanley made to keep on eye out on his witness, to "cover each other's back," as he had often told the boy. Overwhelmed with the emo-tion of knowing someone cared for him that much, he dropped his head in his hands and sobbed.

CHAPTER 31

Stan cried for a few minutes before choking back his tears. Head in his hands, he remained seated at the kitchen table. After he had come forward as a witness to Manny Fleischman's attack, Stick Hanley often told James they were "partners in this now" and partners always had to watch out for each other—watch each other's backs wherever they were, wherever they went. What Brian conjectured made sense. That's the kind of cop his father, Stick Hanley, had been.

He could only imagine now what Brian must feel, knowing that his dad uprooted his entire family to make good on his promise to James to always protect him. Was he angry with his father? Or was he proud? Maybe he was a little of both. Nonetheless, Stan was thankful whatever the reason. Thankful to have Stick Hanley's kid today as his best friend.

Stan thought back to the first day after Manny Fleischman's murder and recalled more details for Maxine and Brian. "Your dad knew, Brian, that I was his only hope for a conviction. But there was a lot of pressure on these cops to find the killers fast."

Brian shook his head. "That's just not like dad," he said. "He went by the book. He woulda offered those kids counsel. I know it."

Maxine dabbed her eyes with a napkin she pulled from the holder on the table. "You saw the crime with your own eyes. You IDed them all. And Brian told me the cops found the bat used to kill Fleischman in that Pick kid's apartment. What could have gone wrong?"

"DNA gathering wasn't around then," Stan shrugged, getting

up from the table. "Not only that, but they never took me to the crime scene before the trial to corroborate my story. I guess they heard what they wanted to hear." He nodded toward Brian. "And, it didn't help that his dad's partner, Timbo Boscorelli, was a racist fat prick son of a bitch. He didn't trust blacks. Not even me, his star witness."

Stan paced back and forth in the huge kitchen. "I don't think he ever really believed anything I said." Stan shook his head, staring off into the distance. He then recounted to Brian and Maxine how he had inadvertently overheard the hurtful words Boscorelli had spoken the day Stan came forward to the police. How the two detectives had left him and his parents in the witness interview room. He was thirsty and decided to slip out of the room to get a drink of water from a fountain in the hallway. When he pulled open the door, he heard the two cops discussing his description of what he had witnessed the day before and heard Boscorelli's cruel words, accusing him of making up the story so his family might cash in on the reward money.

"Your dad defended me and my family against Boscorelli's accusations. And your dad was right. We didn't even know Fleischman's daughter had offered any reward money," Stan told Brian and Maxine. "But the truth didn't matter to his partner, I guess. I'll never forget how painful it was when I heard Boscorelli's hateful words. He was supposed to be on my side!"

Stan walked to the cabinet above the kitchen sink and grabbed a bottle of Jack Daniel's he only opened for a celebratory toast at Thanksgiving and Christmas. He filled a glass nearly to the top and took a hefty swig. The sour mash liquid burned his throat, bringing a grimace to his solemn face. Glass in hand, he looked at the startled faces of his wife and friend. He wondered if what he was saying was making any sense to them. All he knew right now by seeing their stunned and painful reactions was that it was time to let them know everything, to spill his guts like Brian and he had coerced so many of the perps they had arrested and prosecuted to do. He began pacing the room again.

"Mister Fleischman saved me from that gang a few days before they jumped him. The Oakwood Rangers had me caged inside a trash basket and were pounding on it with my Dick Allen bat." Stan pointed to the bat Brian once again held in his hands.

"Pick took my bat away from me right before Bobby DeSadier put me inside the basket. Then Pick, Tyrone Witherspoon, and Pokie Turner all took turns, smashing the side of the basket with the bat. I really thought they were going to kill me. I can still hear the crack of the wood on the wire cage, over and over." Stan clenched his fist and squeezed his eyes shut. "I begged them to stop. That's when Manny Fleischman showed up and scared them off."

He blinked his eyes a few times and stared out the large kitchen window, then took another gulp of booze before placing his glass down on the kitchen counter.

"Pick and his gang were going to teach Mr. Fleischman a lesson for that—for saving me." Stan tapped his finger on the rim of the glass. "They planned his murder."

"What do you mean planned the murder?" Brian asked.

"It's the one thing—"

Stan didn't finish his thought, but instead drained the remainder of his Jack with one big swallow. He reached for the bottle and poured himself another four fingers of the Kentucky bourbon. He was thankful for the liquor's numbing effect on the pain he felt from his escalating release of emotions.

"What are you talking about, Stan?" Maxine asked as she got up from the table and walked toward him. His back to her, she pulled him by the shoulder, spinning him around. "Stan?" she asked him again.

Their moist eyes looked square into each other's. Knowing that not answering her now would hurt her even more, he blurted out, "Mister Fleischman had told me how he had regretted not coming forward his whole life. How important it was to tell the truth when you know it."

Stan saw the puzzled look not only on her face but also on Brian's as he glanced over at his buddy.

"You see, a few days after the gang had jumped me, Mister Fleischman was trying to console me, trying to convince me to go to the police. I still refused, thinking it was better to keep it secret for fear of more retribution from Pick and the Oakwood Rangers. Mister Fleischman explained to me how it would be the wrong decision to remain quiet. It was right then he told me he knew the fix was on for the nineteen-nineteen World Series.

"What?" Brian cried. "Did you just say what I think you said?"

"I know. It's unbelievable, isn't it? Here was a man who was a bench warmer on a Chicago White Sox team with guys so good he knew he'd never get a chance to play. He tells me he overheard his teammates Chick Gandil and Eddie Cicotte plan the championship fix and, if the fix were on, Cicotte, the pitcher for the series opener, would hit the first Cincinnati batter he faced. When Cicotte hit him, Manny never said a word to anyone—not to any of his teammates, not to his manager, Kid Gleason, not even to the team owner, Charlie Comiskey. He told me that in those days, you kept your mouth shut unless someone spoke to you first."

"He actually *confessed* all this to you?" Brian asked.

Stan nodded, staring into his fresh glass of Jack.

"He explained to me how important it was to live your life with no regrets. To tell the truth in everything, no matter what you thought the consequences might be. He hadn't, and it had haunted him his entire life. He was more ashamed of what he *didn't* do than of what a few of his teammates *did* do. He kept that secret with him, buried forever, eating away at him like a cancer. That's why he never talked to anyone about being on the Black Sox. *Ever.* He was glad he was forgotten."

The kitchen fell silent. The three of them stood there like statues in a park, motionless, until Brian broke the pall.

"But what's that got to do with you and those five boys?"

"Everything. It's got everything to do with what I'm talking about. You see, there weren't five boys in on Fleischman's attack. There were six there," Stan said as he sat down at the kitchen table once more, hanging his head, clutching his drink in both hands.

"That's right. I recall that detail in the reports Sal Abbatti sent over to me," Brian said. "He said you had seen a sixth boy when they first interviewed you but that you weren't able to recognize him. I never read where you ever positively IDed a sixth attacker, though."

"Yeah. That's right. I never did." Stan took a deep swig of whiskey, then looked right at Brian. "But I could have."

"What?" Brian gulped.

"Stanford. You could have identified one of Fleischman's attackers but you didn't?" Maxine exclaimed. "I don't believe you. That's not true. That's just not like you." She took a breath, then sighed, "But then I really don't know you. Do I?"

Pained by her comment, Stan continued on nonetheless. "But it *is* true, Max. And I've lived with that secret and the guilt from keeping it my whole life. Manny Fleischman's voice has haunted me ever since. There isn't a day that goes by I don't replay his words over and over in my head."

"Stan, do you know what you're saying?" Brian said. "You're admitting that you withheld evidence in a lethal felony investigation."

"Don't you think I know that?" he snapped back, jumping up from the table, the liquor taking its full effect upon him now. "Why do you think I've dedicated my life to upholding the law, doing everything in my power to send guilty people to jail, even to their deaths?" He took a swig from his glass and lowered his head again.

"Honey. It's okay," Maxine jumped in. "That was a long time ago. You were just a boy. You did a very brave thing coming forward and identifying the kids who attacked and killed your friend." She stood up next to him and pulled one of his hands away from the glass, holding his open palm tight. "It's okay. It's okay."

"She's right. There's nothing that can be done now," Brian said. "Anyway, if that sixth kid was smart—which I doubt very much he was—maybe he turned his life around, knowing how lucky he was you didn't ID him."

Stan shook his head, then threw it back, gulping the remainder of the booze. Wiping his mouth with the back of his hand, he stared into the bottom of the empty glass.

"What?" she asked her husband. "What is it?"

"That sixth kid was my best friend. That's why I didn't squeal on him," Stan answered with a blank stare. At this point, he had drunk more bourbon than he ever had in his entire life.

Looking over at them, Stan saw Maxine and Brian look at each other, neither saying a word. Even though his head spun, he saw the unmistakable look in both their eyes, knowing they were wondering what he might say next, afraid that more secrets would come spewing forth.

Stan sat back down and stared into the bottom of the empty glass while he rolled it in his hands on the table. "And you're right, Brian. He was smart all right," Stan said, nodding. "And, I guess you can say he did turn his life around." He paused and looked back up at them. "Does the name U.S. Senator Clayton R. Thomas ring a bell?"

CHAPTER 32

The kitchen at the Scottsdale home of the Kobe's had become one big confessional for Stan Kobe, as his wife and his best friend listened to him recount his childhood tale, unraveling all the details he had kept secret for the last thirty years.

"Are you shittin' me?" Brian blurted.

"I wish I were," slurred Stan.

"*The* Clayton R. Thomas?"

"Yes, *the* Clayton Thomas. The one and only. The guy that's supposed to be the first black to get a real shot at running for president of the United States."

"Clayton Thomas was at Mister Fleischman's murder?" Maxine asked. "Is that what you're saying?"

"Yes, that's what I'm saying," he shouted, the whiskey coursing through his body, causing him to speak louder than he intended. He tipped the glass for another gulp, forgetting he'd already downed the last drop.

"I think you've had enough," she said, pulling the glass away from him.

He grabbed futilely for the glass, but the alcohol made his reflexes slow.

"Stan?"

Stan didn't look up nor respond to Brian's voice.

"Stan, buddy. Tell us what happened. What else do you know you're not telling us?"

"I need another drink." He garbled his request.

"No. No more," Maxine said. "Talk to us. Finish telling us."

Stan attempted to sit up straight. He massaged his head back and forth with both hands, then stopped and began cracking his knuckles. Not only had his last lingering swig burned his throat but it had also inflamed his memories. He jumped up from the table and began pacing again. The whiskey's power released his repressed memories so fast that his words raced to keep up with the flashbacks.

"Clayton was my best friend. We used to go to Burnham Park every day when we were kids, walk up and down the shoreline, race the waves along the rocks." He stopped and aimlessly fingered the table's placemats. "But all of a sudden, Clayton stops going to the park with me. I thought it was because his daddy used to whoop him. Wouldn't let him come out to play. His old man drank an awful lot. My momma said Mister Clayton was just on hard times. Hard on his family was what he was, beating his wife and kids at the drop of a hat."

Stan stopped momentarily. The booze made his mind swirl. He tilted his head down toward the floor. Then he looked back up again. Slurring a bit more, he continued.

"Then one day, Clayton shows up, see, at the park with Pick. Seems overnight he and Pick is best friends. I know this can't be true. No way. Clayton ain't no gangbanger."

Stan turned away from the table. Eyes feeling dry and blood-shot, he leaned back against the sink, staring back past the two of them, hugging himself with arms crossed protectively in front of his chest.

"My friend broke my heart. He joined the gang, and I didn't know why. But then it all made sense."

Maxine handed her husband a bottle of water she had taken out of the fridge. Stan took the cold plastic container from her but didn't drink.

"I didn't find out why he joined until Clayton called me that same day they attacked Fleischman. It was him who had run off before Pick started beating the old man. He told me he didn't care if Pick came after him, but he wasn't going to be part of no murder. That's why I never IDed him. 'Cause he didn't do nothin'!"

"You know he was a material witness to a felony," Brian said.

"I do now," Stan said. "But I didn't know all the legal implications then. All I knew was my best friend didn't take any whacks at that old man. He didn't stay there like Bobby D, Pokie, and the others, and pull Mister Fleischman's bike out from under him. He didn't taunt him and watch Pick beat him to death with that bat, my bat, and not try to stop Pick."

Stan picked up the bat Brian had laid on the kitchen table. After more than thirty years without seeing it, he had held it in his hands two times in the past week. He ran the palm of one hand softly along the barrel as the other hand clutched its thin handle. After all these years, some pine tar remained, clinging to the middle of the bat, permanently staining the patina of the ash wood. As Stan held the bat, he thought of Manny Fleischman the first day he met him in Burnham Park and how the old man took swings with his own make-believe bat. He wished at that moment he could be back in the park again, watching the old Jew-man, listening to Manny tell his story about Ted Williams— *The Splendid Splinter— You see, ol' Teddy, well, he had one of the finest swings in the game—Great hands with the splinter. The wood. The* bat.*"*

Stan looked over at Brian. "Your dad must have kept this after the trial. The prosecution presented it as evidence. Called it 'Exhibit A.' When I took the witness stand, the Cook County State's Attorney asked me if it was mine. I positively IDed it. Said, 'Yes, that's my Dick Allen Louisville. Mister Allen gave it to me last year. My initials are on the tip of the barrel.'

"On the stand, Pick admitted he stole the bat from me a week before the crime. But we didn't have any DNA back then so they couldn't positively tie in the bat as the murder weapon even though they found traces of Fleischman's blood type on it. The cops were certain Pick must have washed it clean with bleach when he got back to his apartment. But unfortunately, Manny's blood type was the same as mine. So the defense raised reasonable doubt that the blood on the bat could have been my own."

"But you said earlier 'they planned it.' What did you mean by that?" Maxine asked.

"Just what I'm saying," Stan replied, setting the bat down, and finally taking a sip of his water. "Clayton told me everything when he called my house. It was the last time we had spoken to each other. The first time was the day after the gang had put me in that wastebasket. I told him I was angry with him for running with the gang, for not helping me the day I got jumped.

"He told me he had no choice. That Pick had threatened to kill him if he didn't join his gang. He cried and begged me to forgive him, telling me he'd make it all up to me someday.

"I didn't know what to tell him. What to say to him. He was sobbing like a baby. He was so scared of Pick. I assured him we were still friends. That nothing could change that and not to worry. I said we could think of something together or maybe I could go to my daddy and ask him what to do.

"Clayton begged me not to do that. He said that Pick and his older cousin, Julius, were too dangerous to turn against. The second time we spoke he said he had just left a meeting of the gang at a local cemetery. That's where they had planned the attack on Manny. Clayton said Pick was going to teach the old man a lesson for butting in when they trapped me in the wastebasket. Pick and Julius made everyone swear secrecy to not let the police or anyone ever know who was in on the plan. They reinforced upon all of them how Rangers don't turn on each other, and to keep their mouths shut. If they didn't, they'd never be safe in the neighborhood again.

"The last time we spoke he had called me from a pay phone right after the attack on Mister Fleischman. He told me Pick caught up with him and knew I saw them attack Mister Fleischman in the park, but Pick didn't think I'd go to the police."

Stan paused a full beat.

"What?" Maxine asked.

Stan shook his head. "Pick and Julius also said they'd kill me if I ratted them out again. And they told Clayton they'd make him do it as part of his final initiation into the gang."

"That's a conspiracy," Brian said. "You know that, right?"

"I do now that I'm a lawyer. But what good does that do me now? Had I known that thirty years ago, well, maybe it could have been different."

"But you knew—everything," Maxine muttered.

The Jack Daniel's had taken its full effect as Stan struggled to maintain his composure, but he could still feel the disappointment in his wife's voice. He set his water bottle down on the table and rubbed his eyes with the palms of his hands.

"That's why I decided to come forward the next day—because I did know everything. Mr. Fleischman's story about how he held his secret about the Black Sox kept repeating over and over in my mind that night when I tried to go to bed. I had to go tell the police what I saw, I had to."

"Why didn't Clayton come forward, too?" Maxine asked.

"How could he, Max? He was in the gang. They would have killed him for sure. He had no one to protect him. Why do you think Clayton would have been safe?"

"Because the police could have protected him," she replied.

"Police? Shit! What are you talking about? The police were almost one hundred percent white back then. To them, we were all just niggers—*motherfuckin' niggers*. Don't tell me you two don't know all about that. Look what happened to me!"

Stan turned away and walked over to the kitchen sink. As he peered down at his reflection in the stainless steel basin, he barely recognized himself. He looked and felt like a man about to fall apart. He had never spoken like this before. Never to Brian and especially not to his wife. But for the last thirty plus years, he felt as if he were the lone black man in a white man's world, always conforming, never expressing his feelings about how he was treated, or how he felt about the biases toward him in Arizona.

Not speaking for almost a minute, an uneasy silence befell the room. Then he turned and spoke again, looking at them both.

"I'm sorry about what I just said. You know I don't really think you two—"

"I used to believe that, Stan, but now I'm not so sure," Brian interrupted.

Maxine stared at her husband. He knew he had hurt her deeply and her next words proved it.

"You think that's how I think, too, Stan? Do you really know how or what I think about you. Or how I *feel* about you? Do you really care? Do you think I've been insulated from all the stares and all the innuendos? Do you think it's been easy for me to be married to a black man? And what about the stigma on our children?"

The liquor's power made Stan suddenly unresponsive, although there was no mistaking the anger and hurt in his wife's voice. Staring at Maxine, he blinked his eyes, trying to focus.

Then Brian broke the tense silence that had once again set upon the room. "We need to figure out what to do next. We need a plan."

CHAPTER 33

Over the next several hours, fortified with many cups of strong coffee, Stan, Maxine, and Brian sat together at the kitchen table as Stan told them more of his memories of the murder trial, its painful outcome, and the surprising and swift relocation of the Overstreet family to Arizona. He recounted the dreadful story of the bungled police investigation and interrogations, and the prosecution's assumptions and miscommunications, coupled with scores of occurrences of the mishandling of evidence and the improper execution of the rights of the juveniles in their custody. Those mistakes would eventually culminate in the handing down of a not guilty verdict for the five defendants accused of murdering Manny Fleischman.

But, the most intriguing part of the story came with the bombshell revelation that the Oakwood Rangers had not only conspired to kill Fleischman and cover up their crime and those that participated in it, but to kill anyone who squealed to the police.

"Where did you say they went those nights to plan your attack and Fleischman's murder?" Brian asked.

"To a cemetery. I think it was called Old Woods or something like that," Stan replied. "Clayton told me the P. Stones used the place for gang initiations at the base of some monument."

Maxine jumped up from the table, startling both of them. "Wait." She held up the palm of her hand. "Don't say another word until I'm back." She then ran into her home office just off the kitchen. She came back a few minutes later with an unbound manuscript in her hands. She dropped the stack of paper on the kitchen table and leafed through its pages. "What did you say the name of that cemetery was again?"

"Old Woods? No. Oak Woods. That's it. I'm sure that's the name," Stan said. "Clayton told me they used to meet near a huge statue with cannons around it. I'd never been there, but Pick's gang used the cemetery for their night meetings, knowing they'd be safe there."

Maxine abruptly stopped flipping through the loose pages, scrolling down with her index finger to the bottom of the page. "Here it is. Oak Woods Cemetery. Chicago, Illinois. I knew that name rang a bell." She read from the page as her voice escalated with excitement: 'Site of the largest Confederate mass burial grounds outside the South. Dedicated by President Grover Cleveland, Memorial Day, 1895.' I thought this place sounded familiar. Barbara Reyes discovered it doing the research for me on Chicago's Camp Douglas for my latest book on Civil War prisons of the North."

"Chicago had a prisoner of war camp during the Civil War?" asked Brian. "I never knew that."

"Oh, yes. One of the most notorious," she replied. "During the course of the war, it may have held up to twenty-six thousand prisoners. Nearly six thousand rebels died there. Douglas's dead were all eventually interred at Oak Woods."

"I remember that now. Mister Fleischman told me about that camp," Stan said. "He said the apartment where our family lived at Thirty-Ninth and Ellis actually bordered part of the prison grounds. Stretched all the way to the lakefront."

"Where Fleischman was killed?" Brian asked.

"No. Not exactly. He was jumped south of there. At Forty-Third Street."

"It's too bad they didn't kill him on federal land," Brian added. "Then maybe we'd still have a case against those two we're holding now."

"Why? What are you saying?" Stan asked.

"Well, I'm studying federal conspiracy cases right now in my evening law school classes," Brian said. "Our teacher, Professor

Stengel, discussed a rare federal case the other night about ongoing conspiracies and the statute of limitations. In this particular case he used as an example in class, the court ruled that there's no statute of limitations limit on an ongoing conspiracy to cover up a crime committed on federal land."

Stan rubbed his chin. "Really?"

"Yeah. But, we're out of luck here since the conspiracy wasn't committed on federal land," Brian added. "According to what you said Clayton told you, the gang planned everything at the cemetery. Probably privately owned or owned by the city, I'm guessing."

"It's private. But if my memory serves me correctly that's what's so unique about Oak Woods," Maxine jumped in, spilling some coffee as she poured herself more. "As a matter of fact, we spoke to the management office of the cemetery a few months back. Barbara called them when she found their website after doing a Google search. I remember talking with her specifically about this burial site within their grounds and that is was managed by the federal government."

"You're sure of that?" Stan blurted.

"Yes. I'm sure the federal government is still involved somehow, but I don't remember the details off the top of my head. It's too late to call Chicago now, but I'm certain that Barbara added the complete notes in the file she created on the site about what she found out from her conversation with the cemetery manager. All the details from what she discovered should be in it."

Brian gestured for her to refill his empty cup. "Do you still have the file?"

"I don't know. I mean, I should. Barbara was meticulous. She kept all our research in password-protected files. But since she disappeared, I haven't had time to check where she left off with everything."

"Do you know where she might have kept the file and what she named it?" Brian asked.

"More importantly," Stan interjected, "what the password is?"

"She would have only kept it in one master folder, and I assign the passwords since everything is on a shared external hard drive in my ASU office."

"Take that coffee to go, babe," said Stan, bolting up from his chair. He felt like a new man, revitalized after unloading thirty years of shame and guilt, but more so from the legal implications now churning in his mind. "Let's go find that file and get the details of exactly what Barbara found out." He turned to Brian. "Pardner, why don't you get ahold of that professor of yours and pick his brain on this a bit more, make sure we're on solid legal ground to possibly charge Pick and his crew on a federal conspiracy charge."

When they arrived on campus, Maxine and Stan headed directly to the Social Sciences Building, a brown brick edifice that housed Maxine's office in the History Department.

Standing at the elevator, she asked, "How's your head?"

"Spinning."

"Mine too." They simultaneously grabbed for each other's hand and held tight.

She pressed the up button and the lift's doors opened, creaking all the way. As the elevator rose, the hum of its wire-rope cables, pulling the massive machine skyward, was the only sound she could hear besides that of her own pumping heart.

"I had Jimmy Nejo's guys pick up Turner and DeSadier at the 4th Avenue Jail and take them to his lockup on the Gila Indian Reservation," Stan blurted, breaking the silence of their ascent.

Not believing what she just heard, Maxine looked at him. Confused, she didn't speak.

"That's why I was down there. I went to see those two. To talk to them."

"You did what?"

"I had to see them face-to-face, make sure it was really them."

"You're not supposed to speak to defendants without their attorney present are you, Stan?" She already knew the answer to her rhetorical question. Being the wife of a prosecutor, she understood the law better than some of her husband's coworkers. She also was well aware that he and his Indian pal, Jimmy, were close friends and had helped each other before when in a jam. Jimmy would do whatever he could to help the "Lízhíní Lawyer," Stan's Navajo nickname used by all his Native Americans friends.

"Nope. You're absolutely right. I'm not. But I don't give a damn." He pulled his hand from hers and waved it in the air. "As far as I'm concerned, they can rot in Jimmy's jail forever."

"You've got your friend Jimmy involved in this now. Does he know why he's sticking his neck out for you?"

Stan shook his head. "All he knows is that I needed help."

"So, what do you two plan to do with these guys? You both know this is illegal. Once their lawyer finds out, he'll make a motion to release them, won't he?"

"Their lawyers will have to find them first. Anyway, don't worry about Jimmy. He's a big boy. And besides, tribal police can do what they want, you know."

"Well, what about your office? What happens when the County Attorney's Office finds out what you two have pulled off?"

"If and when the County Attorney's Office does find out, pulling them from the reservation will take a call to the president of the Gila Rez. And that just happens to be Jimmy's cousin. Anyway, first they'll have to find these two pieces of shit. Who knows, maybe these scumbags will just disappear? Stranger things have happened in Indian jails. Who would miss—"

As the doors opened, the elevator's bell interrupted Stan's words at the same time Maxine did. Barely able to get the words out, she choked back her shock in his revelation as they stood in the elevator.

"Stan? What's gotten in to you? Even though I'd like to see these guys fall off the face of the earth, too, you can't take the law into your own hands. If you do, then you're no better than them."

"No better than them? What the hell you talking about? These guys got away with murder. I saw them attack Mister Fleischman with my own eyes. They laughed as Pick pummeled him senseless and then got away with it. And because they were juveniles, their records were sealed shut forever, as if it never happened."

Maxine glared at the back of her husband's head as he walked off the elevator and into the hallway. But he wasn't finished with his tirade.

"You call that justice?" he shouted to her over his shoulder.

"I call it revenge," she yelled back, stomping behind him. She caught up and tugged on his arm hard, spinning him around. "I didn't fall in love with a man who has revenge in his heart. Justice is one thing, Stan. An eye for an eye is another."

Stan jerked away from her grasp. Without answering, he continued walking down the dimly lit corridor and stood at the door to her office. He waited for her to open it, hands tucked deep into the pockets of his pants.

She brushed him aside, unlocked the door, and entered her office. She flipped on the light switch, crossed the room, and booted up the computer on her former assistant's desk. Stan came up and stood beside her, not speaking.

"I think you owe Brian an apology," she said, breaking their brief silence as she clicked through a list of Word files now displayed on the monitor. "He's been worried sick about you. You just don't know how hard he's worked to find all this out about you."

Stan still didn't speak.

"And don't you think he feels bad, too, maybe even a little guilty, about what his dad and his partner and the Cook County Attorney's Office did to you and your family?" Stan didn't answer as she continued her search for the files. "I think this is it. Yes. Here it is."

"Here's what?"

"The goddamn information we came to get, that's what," she snapped.

"All right. Easy. I'll apologize again to Brian if that's what you want."

She bolted up and looked him square in the eye. "Apologize to Brian? You think that's all I want? How about apologizing to me? Your wife. How could you keep this from me all these years? I thought you loved me. How could you have never told me about all of this, not shared it with me? How could you possibly accuse me of not feeling the prejudices against you? Worse yet, you actually think I feel the same way others do. The way they feel down deep about blacks, don't you?"

"Max. Please. C'mon."

"C'mon, what, goddammit? I've been married to a man for almost twenty years who's been in the goddamn witness protection program and I didn't even know it." She deepened her look. "And then, what you said earlier, to me and Brian. Do you know how that makes me feel? How deeply you hurt me?"

He didn't answer, making her angrier.

Her eyes widened. "And what about the twins? Did you ever consider their lives? Their safety? Their future? You should have told me this the first time we met—"

"The first time we met? Right. C'mon. Would you have continued to date me if I had told you? Would you have even given me a second chance?"

"I loved you the first time I saw you, Stan. Or is it James? See what I mean? I don't know who you are anymore. I—"

She stopped abruptly and turned away, but he pulled her to him.

"Maxine. I'm still just *me.*"

She struggled out of his grasp, brushed the tears from her eyes, sat back down, and went back to the screen.

"What are we looking for again?" he asked.

She hated when he could so easily change the subject like that. But she knew retrieving the information they had come here to get was more important than trying to correct his behavior. More than frustrated, she decided to just answer his question.

"We're looking for the specific details Barbara recorded when she spoke to the folks at Oak Woods Cemetery." She struggled to focus on the monitor's display as she wiped tears from her eyes with the back of her hand. "Here. This is what we're looking for. I thought so."

She read from Barbara Reyes's notes in the Word document:

> The cannon, shot, and shell ornamenting this government lot in which both Union and Confederate soldiers are buried were purchased by the War Department under authority of an Act of Congress in 1893. Two acres of government-owned property

have been set aside and are maintained to this day by Oak Woods Cemetery personnel, holding the monument and graves of those that died at Camp Douglas.

Stan stared at her, his mouth agape. "Do you know what this means?" he blurted. "This means they committed their conspiracy on federal property. If Brian's professor is right, then we might have found a loophole to retry these guys and finally send them all to jail."

"But how are you going to prove this?" she asked. "The only one who can corroborate your story is one of the five killers or Clayton Thomas himself."

"I know. So I've got to find some way to make those two we're holding come forward and tell me the whole story."

"How can you do that now since you've already spoken to them without their lawyer being present? They'll throw the case out faster than—"

"Yes, I know. I know." Stan said, grumbling his reply, knowing Maxine's understanding of the law was second only to her knowledge of the Civil War. "The only one who can help me now then is Clayton."

"Clayton? And how do you propose to do that? He's on track to be the first black candidate for President of the United States. Why would he jeopardize that?"

"Because he owes me, that's why. Because he said he'd make it up to me some day. It looks like I'm going to have to pay a visit to my old best friend and call in my mark."

CHAPTER 34

Before Brian left the Kobe's home last Friday, he had called his
law school teacher, Professor Stengel, and set up an appointment
to meet him the following Tuesday at the professor's office in the
Ross-Blakely Law Library on ASU's Tempe campus. He had briefly
explained to Stengel what he was looking for, prepping him for
the meeting.

When Brian arrived at the professor's office, Stengel welcomed
him from behind a meticulously clean desk.

"Hi, Brian. I'm glad you're on time. Nothing worse than
people who aren't punctual, you know. I'll need to keep this brief.
I've got a class in forty-five minutes across campus."

"Of course, Professor. I really do appreciate your time on this,"
Brian said as he sat down across from him.

"So, how can I help?"

"Well, sir, I'm working with the Maricopa County Attorney's
Office. It's somewhat involved, but I will keep my inquiry as brief
as possible. I'd like your opinion on something."

The detective retold Stengel the story of James Overstreet wit-
nessing of the murder of Manny Fleischman over thirty years ago
in Chicago's Burnham Park. He detailed the Chicago Police Department's impetuous pursuit of the alleged juvenile offenders,
the authorities' subsequent hasty arrests and interrogations, and
their misinterpretation of the escape route of the attackers. He
also described the prosecution's key oversight in not taking the
eyewitness back to the scene of the crime prior to the trial to corroborate his story.

"Well, I must say, Brian, the case does sound intriguing. And the police didn't provide the alleged offenders counsel, you say? Even when they requested representation?"

"That's right, sir. The judge in the case had no choice but to throw out their confessions."

"I can understand why the confessions would've been thrown out, but Miranda didn't exclude the bat."

"The bat was introduced and the eyewitness IDed it as the weapon. But the prosecution was never able to prove it was used as the murder weapon," Brian explained. "The theory is that the primary suspect must have cleaned the bat of any residual blood traces. They were never able to positively type it against the victim and, unfortunately, the bat's owner had the same blood type."

"That's right. You said this happened in nineteen seventy-five. Pre-DNA days," Stengel observed, nodding. "So, if I might ask, what's your involvement in this case, Brian?"

"I'm not really at liberty to say at this point. Let's just say I have an interest in seeing this brought to justice."

"Well that's all fine and good but I don't need to remind you, Brian, that double jeopardy applies here, do I?" Stengel proceeded to count off his other legal concerns on his fingers. "Not to mention statute of limitation issues, the fact that they were juveniles, and the fact that juvenile records are sealed."

"No, no. Of course not. We're not looking at retrying them for the murder. But we think we can overcome the statute of limitations issue."

"How?" Stengel asked.

"We might be able to show we have grounds to file a federal conspiracy charge against them." Brian inched forward in his seat toward him. "You remember that case you talked about in class a couple of weeks ago, United States versus Masters?"

"Yes, I remember."

"Well, I've read and reread the court's decision. It held that a conspiracy can include an agreement to conceal the conspirators' conduct and such concealment can continue the conspiracy for statute of limitations purposes."

"Yes. That's correct. But how do you propose to introduce that in court?" his professor asked.

"We believe we can show that the gang had intended from the beginning to prevent discovery of a planned crime and had conspired to commit murder, and that this concealment was part of the original conspiracy."

"But as that case stated," Stengel added, "you'll need to show that their actions weren't the result of a spontaneous reaction to their fear of arrest and prosecution. In U.S. v Masters, the court stated that a distinction must be made by the prosecution to infer the existence of a conspiracy and must show that the perpetrators took care to cover up their crime in order to escape detection and punishment. Can you prove none of these conditions existed?"

"We believe we can."

"And that's just the first hurdle," Stengel went on. "Then, if I remember correctly, you would have to show that an original agreement was made among them to continue to act in concert in order to cover up, for their own protection, traces of the crime after its commission took place."

"Yes, I know," Brian said, his voice trailing off, sensing the immensity of the burden of proof.

"And, besides," Stengel added, "according to what you've already told me, the murder wasn't committed on federal property."

"Yes, but the conspiracy was," Brian said. "The gang planned the murder on a piece of federally owned property inside Oak Woods Cemetery in Chicago. There's a Confederate burial mound there that the U.S. government acquired in eighteen ninety-five and still owns to this day."

"Well, that's remarkable luck, but do you have proof of this conspiracy because coincidences don't win trials," Stengel chided. "Do you have any witnesses to this alleged conspiracy or participants who are willing to come forward?"

"We've got two of the actual participants locked up on unrelated charges here in Maricopa County. But I don't think they'll volunteer to roll over on this. They're both three-time losers."

"Maybe they'll sing a different song when they realize the penalty if they're found guilty," Stengel said.

"I don't understand. Why?"

"Because the conspiracy to cover up a murder may hold the same sentence for the crime itself," Stengel said.

"Really?" Brian struggled to keep up with notes he had been taking since they started their conversation, but after Stengel's surprising remark he made sure to double underline his last statement, annotating CHECK FURTHER in his notebook's margin. When he was done writing, he asked, "So, if they're found guilty, then it's the death penalty for them?"

"Not so fast. I didn't say that. You said this act was allegedly committed in nineteen seventy-five. There was a moratorium on federal executions back then. Your case is unprecedented if they're found guilty. If we use today's law, they'd get the death penalty. If we revert to the time of the commission of the crime, then they'd get life."

"Either way, it's win-win," Brian said, sounding somewhat relieved.

"Don't get your hopes up, Brian. You've got a lot to prove. And U.S. v Masters is the only case of its kind that has tried this legal theory. That's not much of a precedent. It's too bad you don't have someone who'll come forward voluntarily," the judge added, looking at his watch.

"That's what we're working on right now. We know the whereabouts of a witness to the original conspirators," Brian replied.

"I'd say that's very fortuitous for your side," said Stengel, "but what makes you think he'll cooperate and come forward without a federal subpoena?"

Brian had no reply, not knowing what strategy Stan planned in leveraging Senator Clayton R. Thomas to come forward.

"We haven't quite figured that out yet, sir."

"Well, I suggest that if and when you do convince him to come forward, based upon the history of this gang and their current criminal involvement, you might want to offer him witness protection as an enticement."

Brian chuckled, shaking his head as he wrote in big-blocked, capital letters in his notebook: OFFER SENATOR WITNESS PROTECTION?!?!

"What's so funny?" his professor asked.

"Irony, Professor Stengel. The unbelievable irony, that's all."

PART FOUR

SWEET HOME CHICAGO

CHAPTER 35

From his vantage point in the window seat of Southwest Flight 543 to Chicago, Stan Kobe was provided a view he had never heretofore experienced. A few thousand feet below him Lake Michigan stretched out as far as the eye could see. It lay like a blue velvet carpet tousled gently by a northwesterly wind, its prevailing direction at this time of year. He calculated that it had been thirty years, two months, and twenty-nine days since he had laid eyes on the inland body of water. Her embracing blueness reached far off onto the horizon, mimicking, albeit weakly, the zero edge swimming pool in his north Scottsdale backyard. Needless to say, this magnificent body of freshwater held far more than the twelve thousand gallons or so of his man-made play pool back in Arizona. And it held many more memories, too.

As a boy, he had only been able to see the lake from the shore, imagining what must exist at her outer edge, unfathomable to grasp at such an immeasurable distance. As he gazed through the airplane's cold Plexiglas window he reminisced, remembering how his seventh-grade teacher, Miss Burns, had explained to her class that Lake Michigan was a prehistoric remnant of the retreat of glacial ice. A body of water probably more than fourteen thousand years old.

"That's almost as old as my great-granny," Clayton Thomas had wisecracked to James Overstreet, making him laugh that day after school when James walked with his best friend in Burnham Park so many years ago.

James Overstreet was someone Stanford Kobe barely remembered now, the boy's identity lost. He and Clayton had stared at the old lady lake as they sat on the edge of the limestone steps that jutted out from the shoreline, tossing small stones into her indigo waters. The best friends shared a dream that day, promising each other, as naïve, innocent boys often do, that when they got older they'd sail across the lake to find out where it ended; to find out what adventures lay out there, waiting for them on the far side of Miss Burns's ancient, mysterious lake.

The Boeing 737 banked steeply to the left on its final approach to Midway Airport. Stan watched as the horizon dipped below his view, making the vast freshwater lake's edge vanish. He stretched from his seat as high as his seatbelt would allow him until the massive body of water disappeared from his view. Now only clouds rushed past the plane's windows.

Losing sight of the lake filled his mind with another vivid childhood memory. He recalled the day he had watched his mother walk out of sight when she dropped him off for his first day of kindergarten at Oakenwald Public School. He had stood inside the school and stared out through the building's steel-meshed glass doors for what had seemed like an eternity, watching her walk away. In his mind, he knew she was still out there, somewhere, yet the experience of losing sight of her made his heart skip a beat, not knowing and wondering, when—or if—she would return.

As the plane touched down, he had already internally rehearsed his speech with the current U.S. Senator from Illinois, Clayton R. Thomas, a hundred times. Stan had found out after making a call to the senator's Washington, D.C., office on Tuesday that the senator would be in his Chicago office this week in between a session of Congress. As a ranking Democrat on the Senate Judiciary Committee, Senator Thomas would be holding a town hall meeting in Chicago, dealing with the recent announcement by the Department of Homeland Security that the Windy City had become the #1 destination for illegal immigrants from Mexico.

Stan's office had contacted the senator's office and asked for an emergency meeting between a representative from the Maricopa County State's Attorney's Office and the senator prior to the public assembly. It was to discuss, as the formal e-mail read, "Chief

County Attorney Andrew Thomas's announcement to make every resource in his office immediately available to the senator's committee in order to stem the tide of illegal immigrants funneling through Arizona to Chicago." Stan just hoped he could pull the sham meeting off prior to his boss getting wind of his maneuvering, instructing his own secretary to set up an auto reply to any incoming e-mails while he was away.

Stepping out of the terminal to hail a cab, the late fall but still humid Chicago air engulfed him in a warm embrace. He was finally home. He stopped for a moment and closed his eyes, taking time to savor the fact that his dream had come true—he had returned to the place of his roots. As a youth, autumn in Chicago had been his favorite time of the year. Actually, James had loved all the seasons except the bitter Chicago winter, which prevented him from taking his daily treks to the lakefront. Standing on the curb, he held the emotion for a moment, heart open, wrapping his arms around the sensation. He was back in the city of his birth, back to the hometown he had been ripped from as a boy.

He told the cab driver his destination: "Forty-three hundred South King Drive."

"Bronzeville. Yah, sir. No problem."

Stan didn't recognize the cabbie's accent, not that he would. This was actually his first cab ride, never having need of the service while living in Phoenix his entire adolescent and adult life.

"Bronzeville," Stan repeated.

"Yah, sir. Bronzeville. Very nice. Good place now. Not so good many years ago. Now? Okay. No problem."

Stan recalled the lectures given to him by Manny Fleischman about the famous people who emanated from or were drawn to this formidable enclave of black entrepreneurship and leadership. People like turn-of-the-century feminist and civil rights activist Ida B. Wells and Daniel Hale Williams, the father of open-heart surgery. Or the founder of the Negro National Baseball League, Rube Foster, and world-renown poet, Gwendolyn Brooks. Once called America's "Black Metropolis," from the late 1800s until after World War II, the area had been home to many of the nation's most significant African-Americans.

His old Oakland neighborhood within the Bronzeville district, glutted with gang-infested Chicago Housing Authority high-rises when he lived there, had since come under the wrecking ball of urban renewal. The area had now become the "in" place for DINKs—double income, no kids—and yuppies—young upward professionals. Urban gentrification had taken over full force in this, at one time, most blighted of neighborhoods on Chicago's near South Side—helping it experience a renaissance driven by unprecedented new construction and building rehab and renovation.

Thirty minutes later, the cabbie pulled the car up to the curb of Stan's destination.

"Here yah go, sir. Forty-three hundred King Drive. You want me wait, sir?"

"Yes," Stan replied, grabbing his attaché case from beside him in the backseat. "Please do. And, would you do me another favor?" As he said this, Stan handed the driver a fifty for the twenty-five-dollar fare and along with it a small piece of paper.

"Ah, thank yah, sir! No problem! I wait, no problem, sir."

Stan stepped away from the yellow taxi and walked up to the storefront, its aluminum-and-glass door decaled with the official emblem of the United States Senate and the following:

CHICAGO OFFICE

U.S. SENATOR CLAYTON R. THOMAS

HOURS BY APPOINTMENT ONLY

Stan opened the door and walked in. A young, twenty-something black girl sat behind a desk with a nameplate that read: RECEPTION.

"May I help you?" she asked.

"Yes, Stanford Kobe, Maricopa County State's Attorney's Office. I have an appointment with Clayt . . . uh . . . Senator Thomas."

"Yes, Mr. Kobe. The senator's been expecting you. Won't you have a seat while I let him know you're here?" She gestured toward two brown leather chairs to his left. "Did you have a good flight in?"

"Yes, I did."

"Can I offer you coffee or a bottle of water?"

Stan shook his head and replied, "No, thank you." He took a seat in one of the chairs that flanked a circular teak table, displaying a variety of literature on top of the dark wood's oiled finish. All the pieces described in some manner the senator's efforts in the local community. He picked up one that had Clayton's picture on the cover. *I see he still has that scar over his right eye. I remember giving him that. Guess that thing never kept him from getting elected.*

"Senator Thomas," the receptionist said into the phone, "Mr. Kobe is here to see you. Yes, sir." She hung up and pointed to her left. "Right through there, Mr. Kobe, sir. End of the hall, last office on your right."

As Stan opened the door for the hallway to the senator's office, he wondered just what Clayton's reaction would be when he saw him. *Will he recognize me? Of course, don't be silly. But he hasn't seen me in over thirty years. Well, you recognized him, didn't you? Yeah, I did recognize him. Clayton hasn't changed a bit.*

A recurring thought popped into Stan's head. It was something that had occurred to him many times, especially after he became a high-profile prosecutor. His picture had been published dozens of times in the *Arizona Republic,* especially over the last ten years. And once or twice some legal articles he had been asked to write were published in a Washington, D.C., think tank publication. If he Googled himself, his picture was all over the Internet. *Why haven't I ever been recognized all these years I've been in witness protection?* He tapped the top of his balding head. *Have my looks changed that much?*

He stopped and turned back to the receptionist. "May I use your restroom to freshen up a bit first?"

"Of course," she said, motioning behind her desk. "Right over there."

Stan entered the restroom and locked the door behind him. He ran the water full force in the sink. As he did, he pulled out his cell phone and dialed his office back in Phoenix.

"Yvonne. Hi. It's Stan. Yeah. I had a good flight. Do me a favor, would you? Would you please get me a list of all the subcommittees

Senator Clayton R. Thomas from Illinois serves on for the Senate Judiciary Committee? Yes. That's right. Text it to my cell stat. Okay?"

Stan hung up, flushed the toilet, ran the water in the sink a few more seconds, and then exited the restroom. The receptionist smiled at him as he went back to the door that led to the hallway to Senator Thomas's office.

When he got there, Clayton's door was open. Stan peered in and saw the senator sitting in a leather swivel chair behind an impressive wooden desk. His back was to the door and he was speaking softly into the phone as he wrote some notes on a pad sitting on top of a smaller desk against the wall. A huge map of Africa covered two-thirds of the wall, which was filled with about a dozen colorful masks. Two large shields also adorned the wall and two long spears placed over each of the shields dominated the space. The African-motif items looked like authentic tribal artifacts. Stan walked in but wasn't sure if Clayton heard him come into the room.

He stood for a moment while Clayton continued to speak in whispered tones. Stan cleared his throat. The chair spun slowly around. Clayton smiled and waved for Stan to take a seat in one of the two chairs across from his desk. Stan obliged him. Clayton turned back and continued his conversation for a moment longer and then hung up the phone. He then turned back to Stan, stood up, and extended his hand across the huge desk.

"Mr. Kobe, is it? I'm Senator Thomas."

"Senator Thomas."

"Welcome to Chicago. First time here?"

Stan hesitated. "Yes. Very first."

"Well, well. You're in one of the finest cities in the world. None better. You can have New York. And L.A.—well, too many Hollywood types out there for me. Chicago's the heart and soul of this country. It's my home. And also, I might add, home of the new World Champion Chicago White Sox!" Clayton paused a minute to pick up a picture from his desk. It showed the senator shaking hands with a White Sox player. "You should recognize this player," he said as he pointed to the picture. "Paul Konerko. He's from your neck of the woods."

"Yes, Senator. He graduated from the same high school I did, Chaparral. Like to think the White Sox couldn't have done it without him." As Stan spoke, he couldn't help but feel cheated he wasn't able to be in his hometown when the White Sox won their first World Series in eighty-eight years. He and Mr. Fleischman had always dreamed of the Sox making it to the Series, promising each other that if it ever happened they'd go to Comiskey Park together to watch every game. Hearing Clayton boast now about the White Sox winning the most recent World Series surprised him. The more significant feeling Stan had was the pain from the memory of the loss of Mr. Fleischman, rather than savoring the glory from the momentous victory of their beloved team.

The senator's deep voice broke into Stan's past thoughts. "And how is my old friend Andy Thomas down there in the great city of Phoenix? He hasn't become a Democrat like me now, has he?"

"Oh no. No. I don't think so, sir. I think Governor Napolitano would have let you know that," Stan answered as they both chuckled.

"Well then. What is it? I understand you folks have taken some new initiatives down there to halt this rampant invasion of our country by these undesirables and their illegal drugs?"

"You're right, sir, we have done that. One way has been via a very hard-working multiagency task force we've had intercepting this criminal element as they move or plan to move various contraband back-and-forth across the border. We're talking guns, methamphetamines, cash, and, of course, human cargo."

Senator Thomas shook his head. "As a ranking member of the Senate Judiciary Committee, you know my commitment on stemming the tide of illegal activity across the border. My record speaks for itself." The senator got up from his desk, walked over to a side table, and grabbed some papers. As he did, he looked back at Stan. "Have we met before, Mr. Kobe? Possibly at a hearing on Capitol Hill? You look awfully familiar."

Feeling suddenly uncomfortable, Stan squirmed in his chair

and began cracking his knuckles. He didn't immediately reply to Clayton's question, although he was tempted to blurt out: *Don't you remember me? Don't you recognize me? Clayton—it's James!*

"No, I don't believe I've ever met you at any hearing, Senator. I'm certain I'd remember that."

"Well, you just have one of those faces. You know," Clayton replied, sitting back down at his desk. "So why are you here exactly?"

"As I mentioned, Senator, our task force has been working on intercepting this activity and recently picked up a couple of very unsavory characters. We're holding them in Arizona. They were caught conspiring to transport illegal goods back and forth across the Mexican border."

"Good job," Clayton said. He opened a humidor on his desk and turned it to Stan. "Cigar? They're Cuban."

"No thank you."

The senator took one for himself, he snipped the edge with a gold cigar clipper, then clamped the huge cigar between his teeth. He struck a match and pulled the cigar from his mouth. "You don't mind?"

Stan shook his head. The senator put the cigar back to his lips and lit it, puffing at it until it was fully ignited. Stan had never seen a cigar that long and that fat. The stogie reminded him of the photographs of Fidel Castro and his ever-present signature Cohiba cigar.

"Go on, go on. I'm always interested in hearing stories of the fine work of the patriotic men securing our borders," Clayton said, puffing away. "Men *and* women, that is," he chortled.

"Yes. Of course." Stan forced a smiled at the senator's obvious attempt to be politically correct. He went on. "Well, speaking of someone being from 'your neck of the woods,' these two losers, Senator, are from right up here. From your Oakland neighborhood. They have outstanding warrants out against them here by Chicago PD."

"Is that so? Have our local authorities started extradition proceedings for them to get them back from your state?"

"That's just it, Senator. If they do, we won't cooperate. We don't want to extradite them back here. Governor Napolitano and our county attorney want them charged and tried in Maricopa County first. They want to make an example of them. Show the nation how tough we are on border security and such. As a matter of fact, they want me to handle the case personally."

Stan paused and closely watched Clayton's body language. The senator rolled the immense cigar slowly in his mouth and squinted his eyes. Nearly twenty years of bargaining with defense lawyers told Stan that Clayton already knew all of this and that the two of them were now merely entwined in a game of cat and mouse. At that moment, a text message beeped on Stan's cell. He excused himself while he scanned the message, then he continued his conversation.

"I apologize. As I was saying, I'm holding them on an Indian reservation," Stan said. "Even their lawyer will have a tough time finding them."

Clayton stopped puffing and pulled the cigar from his lips, staring blankly at Stan. Based upon the text message he had just received on his cell phone, Stan wondered at that very moment if the senator already knew this information.

"Why, I believe that's illegal. Isn't it, Mr. Kobe? As a matter of fact, as a fellow lawyer, I'm certain it is."

Stan's cordial tone turned challenging. "Very illegal, sir. But we all do illegal things in our lives. Every one of us. I haven't met a person yet who hasn't done something that couldn't be considered illegal, sometime, somewhere on this great big earth of ours. Have you, Senator?"

"I'm not quite sure what you're referring to, Mr. Kobe."

"Well, I did a little research on you before I came in here today. I hadn't realized it until a few minutes ago before entering your office, but then it hit me like a brick in the head, or maybe I should say, like a bat in the head."

Senator Clayton took a deep puff and blew the smoke skyward. He tipped his head slightly downward and looked directly at Stan as the smoke slowly cleared.

"You're a member of a couple of Senate Judiciary subcommittees. One is Immigration, Refugees, and Border Security. The other is the Terrorism, Technology, and Homeland Security sub-committee. Isn't that correct, Senator?"

"That's right. That's common knowledge. What is your point, Mr. Kobe? I've got a town hall meeting later today I need to prepare for and I had hoped you were bringing me something meaty I could use there. Catching those two gang members is definitely something we should announce tonight."

"I never said they were gang members, Senator."

"Well, I just assumed—"

"We all make assumptions, Senator. Question is, what do we base those assumptions on, hearsay or inside knowledge?"

"You're trying my patience, Mr. Kobe. If this is some political maneuver by your Republican boss to gain headlines in my state—"

"That would be a wrong assumption, sir. As I assumed wrongly all these years that I was invisible, courtesy of the Witness Protection Program, a program I might add, under the jurisdiction of the U.S. Marshal's Service, which just so happens to fall under the Attorney General's Office."

"Spare me the civics lesson, Mr. Kobe. I've been in Washington over twenty years. I think I know the organizational flow chart of the United States Government!"

"Indeed you do," Stan shot back. "That text message I just received came from my secretary. You've also been a ranking member of the Senate Judiciary subcommittee on Crime and Drugs for the last twelve years, and chairman for the last six. That didn't register right away. That is until her message told me this subcommittee holds all the purse strings for the U.S. Marshal's Office, the folks who monitor the Witness Protection Program."

"And your point is?" the Senator asked.

"My point is, it's been you who's helped keep me alive all these years. Hasn't it, Clayton?"

CHAPTER 36

As Stan sat in the chair across from the senator's desk, he stared at Clayton, waiting for a reaction to his accusation. None came. The senior U.S. senator from Illinois merely continued to roll the cigar between his thick lips and waft billowy puffs of gray-white smoke into the room. The silence seemed deafening to Stan.

What if I'm wrong? Maybe the senator wasn't involved in protecting me all these years.

He began to crack his knuckles, nonstop, one after the other.

Clayton strode out from behind his desk and closed the door to his office. He walked over and stood behind Stan, no more than one foot behind him. Stan sat perfectly still, unable to see the senator behind his back. Clayton dropped his hand down hard on Stan's shoulder, clasping it in a strong grip. The prosecutor flinched.

"I never thought I'd ever see you again," said Clayton in a halting voice.

Stan jumped from his chair and faced his long ago friend eye to eye. Inches apart now, Stan noticed a faint hint of moisture, forming in the corners of Clayton's eyes. Stan embraced his friend, giving him a bear hug. Clayton returned the gesture, squeezing him hard.

"Whoa, big fella," Stan cried. "You don't know your own strength. Don't make me smack you upside your head again and give you another scar."

"Sorry, old friend," Clayton laughed. "I just—I—"

"I know what you're feeling. I feel the same way."

Clayton took a seat in the other chair next to Stan's. "Please,

James, sit down. I want to have a good, long talk with you now . . . now that you know."

"I never thought anyone would call me that again. *James*. It sounds so good. Sounds real good."

"You don't know how many times I wanted to contact you— you know, after I found out where you were," Clayton said.

"Why didn't you? I always wondered about you, too. And then, a number of years ago, right after I joined the Maricopa County State's Attorney's Office, I found out doing some pretrial research that you were the lawyer on a case that came up as a precedent. I couldn't believe it. Both of us had become lawyers. I followed your career from that day forward. And when you were elected to the House and then the Senate, well, no one was prouder."

" 'Ceptin' maybe my momma. She beamed when I graduated college and then law school. She always thought I'd end up like my brother. Dead with a bullet in the back of my head. Shot in one of the stairwells of the Olander Projects. After the Fleischman trial, she had enough with living in hell and sent me away, down south to her sister's in Springfield. She didn't want her family part of any more deaths, part of any more killings.

Clayton took a long pause and scanned his old friend from head to toe.

"But I don't understand something, James. Why now? After all these years? Why did you risk it all by showing up here at my office?"

"Fleischman," Stan answered.

"That was an unfortunate incident. It changed all our lives."

"Unfortunate incident? Is that what you just called it?" Stan stared at Clayton, waiting for him to finish pleasuring the cigar he rolled in his mouth, circling its wet end with his thick tongue, before he got an answer to his question.

"Don't tell me you haven't let go after all these years, James."

"Let go? Are you serious? They murdered him. They admitted it. And aren't you forgetting about my family and me being taken from our home? *Sent to fucking Arizona?* How do you let something like that 'go'?"

"James. We were just kids. Anyway, that was thirty years ago. It's the past. It's over. A long-gone memory. We've all moved on."

Stan furrowed his brow, attempting to comprehend Clayton's perception of these tragic events. He had truly become the quintessential politician, Stan thought, spinning, in his own mind at least it seemed to Stan, that the murder of Manny Fleischman was perceived by him as nothing but the unfortunate outcome of the senseless actions by some poor, misguided youths.

"How can you dismiss it like that? You seem to forget, Clayton, you were an accessory to a murder. I could have IDed you. But I didn't. You'd never be where you are—"

"James, James, James," Clayton interrupted, clenching the dwindling Cuban between his pearly white teeth. "I guess that heat must have shrunken your brain all those years out there in that relentless sun. How hot does it get again? Hundred 'n' twenty? Shiiiiit. How can a soul brother live in that kinda heat?"

Stan squirmed in his seat. "What's your point, Clayton?"

"My point is, old friend, those boys were found not guilty by an irreproachable judge in juvenile court. The case is closed. Their records are sealed. We've all moved on. Why, Monroe Clarke is an upstanding member of our fine community of Bronzeville now. He and Tyrone Witherspoon are on my payroll, running a youth program I sponsor at The Carondolet Center over on Thirty-Ninth Street. Those two are helping boys every day find the right path. Helping them get good jobs in our community.

"Matter of fact, even Bertrand Rhodes has turned a new leaf and is now the Third Ward alderman. Can you believe it? Now that's an accomplishment. Don't you agree? Did you ever imagine in your wildest dreams that these former bad boys would do good some day? Turn their lives around and make up for all the wrong they'd done? They're giving back to their neighborhood, not taking away any more."

Stan glared at Clayton as he extolled the virtues of the killer Pick and his henchmen's current exploits. His stomach turned, imagining the incorrigible gangsters in their new roles as stalwarts of the community.

A knock at the door interrupted them. "Yes. Come in," said the senator.

The door opened. The receptionist stood in the doorway.

"Yes, Janeequa. What is it?" the senator asked.

"Senator Thomas. I need you to come out to the lobby for a moment, sir."

"One minute, Janeequa. I'll be right there."

"Yes, Senator." She exited the room, but left the door ajar.

"I'll be right back, James. Make yourself comfortable. Help yourself to a Scotch with that water." The senator pointed to a fully stocked bar, then left the room.

When Senator Thomas got to the lobby, several of Chicago's finest stood in front of and around the reception desk.

"Senator," one of the police officers addressed him.

"Officer?" the senator leaned forward to get a closer look at the cop's name badge.

"Officer Leo Cronin, sir," the uniform replied, pulling his name badge toward the senator to make it easier for him to read. "We're looking for a Mister Kobe. The cabbie that dropped him off here earlier called our precinct commander."

"Is that so? What on earth for?" Senator Thomas replied.

"He said his fare, Mister Kobe, gave him instructions to call the number Mister Kobe had handed him on a piece of paper." Patrolman Cronin continued. "The phone number was to District Commander Abbatti's personal cell phone, sir. I was told by him that the driver sounded pretty anxious."

"Really?" the senator said, walking closer to Officer Cronin. "By the way, I went to law school with a Leo Cronin. Any relation, per chance?"

"My dad drove a garbage truck, sir."

"Admirable. Very admirable. Sanitation workers are the backbone of our city. Some of my most loyal constituents are—"

"Senator? Mister Kobe, sir?"

Unflustered by the cop's interruption, Clayton answered him. "Please tell your Commander Abbatti not to be concerned. Mister Kobe left for the airport a few minutes ago. Said he had a flight to catch. I had my personal driver take him. Get him there much faster." He winked at the cop. "He must have just forgotten to tell the cabbie."

Walking back down the hallway to his office, assured the police were satisfied, Clayton asked himself why James would have done such a thing. He couldn't believe his long lost friend gave the cabbie Prairie District Commander Sal Abbatti's personal cell phone and, evidently, with instructions to call Abbatti.

Why would he do that? What was that fool thinking? I've gotta find out what this man's agenda is.

Opening the door to his office, Clayton discovered James had disappeared.

"Where the hell did he go? What's with this guy?" He picked up his phone. "Janeequa, did you see Mister Kobe come through the lobby? Well, if you do, please ask him not to go anywhere and ask him to take a seat. Well, if he refuses, call me."

He hesitated for a moment and his pulse quickened as his thoughts welled in panic. He made another call.

"Yes. It's me. I need to see you right away. Thirty minutes. Yes. The usual place. Thank you."

CHAPTER 37

Clayton's revelation that several of the former Oakwood Rangers were now on the senator's payroll was beyond anything Stan ever expected to hear. It was incomprehensible, making it impossible for him to stay in Clayton's presence any longer. Not waiting for him to return to his office from the lobby, Stan exited out of the back of the building. He strode down the alley behind the senator's office building, constantly checking over his shoulder. After aborting the meeting with his old friend, Stan's mind went at a quicker pace than his feet as his brain worked to digest what he'd just been told.

How will I ever be able to convince him to turn against them now? Especially if I'm suggesting bringing conspiracy charges against guys he's still in cahoots with and weak conspiracy charges at that?

Before finally coming out of the alley and onto 43rd Street, dozens of thoughts ran through Stan's mind as he wondered what to do next. He needed time to regain his composure; time to be alone.

In one way, the corner of 43rd and King Drive looked and sounded much the way it did to him as a boy a little more than three decades earlier: heavily congested with traffic, thick air stinking of exhaust fumes, drivers impatiently blowing their car horns. One horn in particular repeated an incessant pattern. The blaring of the persistent driver's beeping tested Stan's frayed nerves. On edge, he looked to the street to see what could possibly be so urgent for someone to blow his or her car horn so unremittingly.

Thank God people don't honk their horns like that in Arizona.

"Sir. Sir. It's me!" the cabbie yelled from his car. "You okay? You need cab?"

Stan could barely hear the cabbie's shouts over the din of the street. He quick-stepped to the side of the car.

"Come, sir. Come. Get in." The cabbie hopped out of his car and opened the back door for Stan. "I take you wherever you need to go."

Stan climbed into the back of the cab not knowing what to do or where to go next. He nervously cracked his knuckles. His meeting with Clayton taught him a lot about what had transpired all this time with his best friend, who, according to national polls, had become the Democratic Party's front-running candidate for president of the United States.

Clayton Thomas's climb to the top was meteoric by any standard. It started by winning the Chicago alderman's race in his own 3rd Ward while still attending the local Kent Law School. His star then rose within City Hall when he staunchly backed Mayor Harold Washington during "Council Wars," the moniker given to the period by the news media for the first two years of the administration of the city's first black mayor. White and black aldermen unabashedly took racial sides as they faced-off in city council sessions after Washington won the mayoral election in 1983. Each faction desperately struggled for control of the City Council, their actions making national headlines. Presumably at stake: the future racial makeup of the City of Chicago.

"Burnham Park," Stan directed the cabbie. "Take me in through the Oakwood Boulevard entrance."

"Yes, sir. No problem, sir. I really happy to see you. I call number on paper you give me. I still wait, even when police come. When police come out, they tell me you leave with senator's chauffeur."

"The police said what?" Stan asked, talking through the small opening in the double-thick Plexiglas window that separated passenger from driver.

"Police tell me you leave in senator's car," he yelled back at Stan. "They say his driver take you to airport. Me confused. I tell them 'I no move from curb. No see senator's limo.'"

The cabbie drove east on 43rd Street to Vincennes Avenue then north on Vincennes to Oakwood Boulevard. Once there, he made a right turn, heading directly toward Burnham Park, now less than one-half mile away. As the car began its slight ascent approaching the Lake Shore Drive overpass, Stan unsuccessfully tried to roll down his back window. He knocked hard against the Plexiglas to get the cabbie's attention.

"Yes, sir?" the cabbie replied, throwing his words over his shoulder.

"Unlock the windows and roll them all down," Stan shouted. "Hurry. *Hurry.*"

"Yes, sir. No problem. Beautiful day. Yes, sir. Beautiful."

The obliging driver motored down the windows. Stan immediately leaned his head out and closed his eyes. He let the scented air wash over him—part air, part sky, part fish, part newly mowed grass.

It smells exactly the same. Exactly.

"Pull over here."

Stan stuck his hand through the Plexiglas opening and pointed to a small gravel area just past the park's main asphalt parking lot, immediately to the south of the entrance. The driver wheeled his yellow cab to the spot where Stan pointed.

"Wait here."

"No problem, sir. Meter not running for you. I got number. You not back in fifteen minutes—?"

"Give me thirty, my friend. Okay?"

Stan walked out onto the main bike path that dead-ended at the edge of the gravel. Heavy construction equipment surrounded by chain-link fences stood between him and the lakefront. Work crews moved large, smooth, white boulders along her shoreline, replacing the jagged rocks he once played on as a boy so many years before. Except for the current work, the area looked exactly the way he remembered it.

Stan continued south along the path for about a block before veering off and heading east over a large berm of grass, which separated bike path from lake. As he climbed to the top of the grassy knoll, Lake Michigan's expanse came into full view.

There you are. I missed you, ol' girl.

He had thought about this day from the moment Cook County deputies whisked him and his family out of Chicago into the suburban safe house prior to the trial of the murder of Manny Fleischman. Seeing and being at the lakeshore again had never left his mind. The thought became the only thing that gave him hope while he felt displaced and abandoned all those years in Arizona.

"Thank you, God," Stan whispered. He pulled his jacket close to protect him from the cool, brisk air coming in off the water.

"Figured I'd find you here."

Stan snapped an about face. Clayton stood behind him, alone, clutching a stub of a cigar between his fat fingers.

"What do *you* want?" Stan asked.

"So. What. No goodbye? Is that the way to treat someone you haven't seen in over thirty years?"

Stan didn't answer. He turned away, staring out over the open blueness, toward the vastness of the undulating water that extended as far as he could see. He turned away because he wanted to hide his displeasure, not only in Clayton finding him here and ruining his blissful moment, but to conceal his anger from hearing earlier that Pick and his gang were now employees of his long-ago friend.

"You might think you know all about me, but you don't," Clayton said. "You think you've got this all figured out. Don't you?"

Puzzled by Clayton's remarks, Stan still didn't answer him. He wondered what the senator meant, though, and why he came to the park to find him.

How did he know I'd be here?

"Maricopa County's most ruthless prosecutor. That's what they call you, right? You've never lost a case. Ever wonder if you judged a man guilty before you even tried him? Ever sent an innocent man to jail?"

Stan still didn't answer Clayton's questions nor turn around to look at him again, but the senator's words did intrigue him, wondering where his probing questions were leading.

"Remember this place? Remember how it used to look before they put all these silly fuckin' steps in here?" Clayton stepped down in front of Stan and swept his arm back and forth in front of them. Stan watched him, his eyes following Clayton's gesture. "There were hundreds of those big, beautiful jagged rocks all along here. I used to love to watch the waves crash against them. Go looking for frogs in the nooks and crannies with you. You showed me how to jump from rock to rock. It was you, James, who taught me how to balance myself and not be afraid of falling in the water."

Stan resisted but gave him a small nod of affirmation.

"Pick's still scared shitless of the water, ya' know. Still frightened of stepping out on those rocks." He paused a moment. "He hated that about you, James. Hated the fact that the water and the rocks didn't scare a little shit like you. Didn't scare you a bit."

So that was Pick who shouted—"Crazy nigger!"—*at me all those years ago!*

"I ran here when Pick started to beat him," Clayton said, pointing to an area on the current rock steps, which led to the water below them. "I sat right here and cried like a baby. I knew if Pick found me he wouldn't come out onto those rocks because they were so close to the water. I couldn't believe he actually did what he said he was going to do to that old man. I was so afraid of him." He paused and took a breath, shrugging his shoulders. "Still am."

Stan sat down on the rock step and stared out at the lake, listening intently to his boyhood friend's confession.

"I didn't tell you the whole truth when I called you on the phone the day they jumped Fleischman. I had told you the reason I had joined Pick's gang was because the Rangers had caught me alone in the park and threatened to kill me if I didn't join them right then. They said they'd also get my brother, Eldridge, too."

"And that wasn't true?"

"Not exactly," Clayton replied, turning his eyes to the ground. "What really happened was that I found out about a week or so before they jumped you in the park that Pick's older cousin, Julius, had killed my father."

"What?" Stan gulped.

Clayton looked right at Stan. "You heard me right. It's true that the gang did catch me alone in the park. I was waiting to meet up with you and play ball. But what happened was that Pick told me my brother, Eldridge, was the one who had come to him and asked him to do it, to kill our daddy, to put an end to the beatings our family was getting. He then told me Julius was the one who had shot my father and dumped his body in the lake. I didn't believe Pick. I didn't believe my brother could do such a thing.

"Pick didn't care what I believed. And he told me their deal with Eldridge was that if the gang killed our daddy, then he'd have to join the Rangers. He told me Eldridge agreed but never showed up at Pick's gang initiation. Pick told me to tell Eldridge if he wasn't at the cemetery that night then the Rangers couldn't be responsible for what happened to anyone in our family from that point forward, including my momma.

"Pick let me go but told me to take that message home to my family. I did and my momma locked us all up in our apartment. That's why we never answered the knocks at our door anymore. But after a while I knew we couldn't live like that. So I snuck out and went to Julius and Pick and told them I'd join the Oakwood Rangers if they'd leave my family alone. Julius and Pick agreed to my proposal and I joined them. That's why I couldn't help you when they trapped you in the basket. That's why we never traveled together out here any more."

Clayton pointed up and down the lakefront with a sweep of his hand, stumpy cigar still stuck between his fingers.

"But then after they killed Fleischman, I told Pick I wanted no part of his gang. I wanted no part of killing. Pick told me leaving the gang meant leaving this world. I was so scared. I didn't know what to do. I told my brother, Eldridge, everything. He told me not to worry, that he got me into this mess and he'd straighten it out, and that everything'd be all right. Later that same night, he went out to the store for momma. He never came home. The police found him the next morning, shot in the back of the head."

Stan's heart ached with sorrow, hearing his old friend's poignant tale, making it difficult for him to speak his next words. "Clayton . . . I . . . I don't know what to say. I'm so sorry."

"Sorry? My heart doesn't know the meaning of sorrow no more. Been closed shut too long. Too many years."

"Why didn't you tell someone the whole truth about what happened? About Pick admitting that his cousin, Julius, killed your father."

"Who could I tell?" Clayton replied. "Who'da listened? Who'da cared? Niggers in the projects was all we were. Who gave a rat's ass about us? Just niggers killin' niggers is all it was to white cops."

"You coulda told *me*."

Looking ashamed, Clayton paused and took a deep puff on the remainder of his stogie. "When you didn't ID me as being one of the boys in the attack that day, I didn't know what to do, what to think," Clayton said, lowering himself and sitting down beside Stan. "After the trial, I felt so bad that you got the raw end of the deal. I never forgave myself for not coming forward and helping you. Same way I felt the day they put you in that basket when I stood there, afraid, and did nothing to help you."

He took a last puff on his cigar and tossed it into the lake below. "I decided to come back to the neighborhood after all those years I spent away. I wanted to give something back, help the youth of my old community, help keep them out of gangs. I decided to run for city council from the Third Ward. What I didn't realize was that Pick was still around, still active, still doing his crime thing. He had become one of the top enforcers of the P. Stone Rangers. Ruthless is what everyone called him, and always one step ahead of the law.

"He got word I was back and paid me a visit. He threatened me, saying he would leak my involvement in the Fleischman thing. He said he'd ruin my career. Ruin everything I had worked so hard for. He'd stay quiet, though, he said, if I helped him while I was in office."

Clayton paused momentarily, stared out at the lake, and then continued. "I really didn't care about the job or my political future, but I had just gotten married. He told me if I didn't cooperate he'd kill my wife. I believed him. The gang killed my father and most likely my brother. Pick helped make the decision easier by welcoming me back to the 'hood with a beating given to me by his old sidekick, Tyrone. From that point forward, I did whatever he asked."

The senator hung his head. "There's an old saying and I know its meaning now. I sold my soul to the devil. And the devil's name is Pick Clarke. Lord help me."

"Clayton," Stan sighed, "I had no idea."

"No one did. When people asked me those first few days I was back what happened to me when they saw my punched-up face, I just kept my mouth shut and went about my business. But I've looked over my shoulder ever since. Pick keeps close tabs on me. Guess the saying's true, huh? Keep your friends close but your enemies closer?"

"I'll take that cigar now you offered me back in your office," Stan said. "Matter of fact, I think I need that Scotch too."

Clayton smiled and pulled back the lapel of his coat, grabbing a hand-rolled Cuban from the inside pocket of his tailored silk suit and handed it to his friend. Stan lit the cigar, its gray smoke dispersing in the gentle lake breeze. Lulling waves splashed against the limestone rocks about twenty feet below them. It was a perfect late fall day. As he puffed on his cigar, sitting there next to the lake, Stan felt a sense of calm flow through his body, even with Clayton's revelation that Pick had added blackmail and extortion to his long list of crimes.

Stan took a deep inhale of his stogie. After an equally long exhale, he said, "It's Turner and DeSadier I've got under arrest in Arizona."

Clayton turned to him, looking stunned. "Say what?"

"The two I told you about in your office that we nabbed on an Indian reservation. It's Pokie Turner and Bobby DeSadier I've got locked up. They were planning to smuggle guns into Mexico and methamphetamines and cash back out. A federal task force down there got tipped-off—" Stan stopped mid-sentence. He shook his head back and forth and continued. "—that's how it went down. It all makes sense now. That task force is funded by the Department of Homeland Security, isn't it?"

"What task force? Government's got a lot of those. Hundreds," Clayton replied, turning away, staring back out onto the water.

"You know perfectly well what task force. The Arizona Border Initiative Task Force. Those are the guys who nabbed Turner and DeSadier, who probably work for you too now, right? Along with

Witherspoon, Rhodes, and Pick, like you told me in your office. Do I have the picture about right?"

Clayton didn't respond.

"Was it you who tipped-off the task force? Leaked them information those guys would be down there to conduct their little transaction. Question now is, where's all the money they've been bringing back into the U.S. been going all this time? To Pick? Or to your presidential campaign's war chest?" Stan got up and stood directly in front of Clayton. He pointed his huge cigar in the senator's face. "It's time for you to level with me. Whose side are you on?"

"I don't really know any more," said Clayton. "I've been a politician so long, playing both sides of the fence. Ya know, I don't really know—" Clayton's voice trailed off.

Stan sat, his glare burning a hole to the side of the senator's head. Was this just another campaign speech? No politician today spoke more eloquently than his one-time boyhood friend, a candidate who cut equally across both racial and political lines. Senator Clayton R. Thomas stood a very credible chance of becoming the next president of the United States of America, leader of the entire free world. Right now, Stan felt like kicking his black ass across Lake Shore Drive, back to the projects where he came from.

"James, there is something I should tell you." The senator looked up at him, looking to Stan as if he were uncertain if he should continue.

"Well?" Stan prodded him.

"Pick knows I knew where they were hiding you all these years."

CHAPTER 38

Monroe "Pick" Clarke strode into The Negro League Café and took his regular seat on a stool at the end of a long, acrylic-coated bar. The Negro League Café had opened its doors for business a little more than fifteen months earlier. Local favorite son, U.S. Senator Clayton R. Thomas, who grew up a mile away, had participated in the ribbon-cutting ceremony that late July day in 2004— the 29th to be exact. A coincident fact not mentioned at the festivities was that twenty-nine years earlier, to the day, Manny Fleischman had been murdered only a half-mile east of the establishment's 43rd Street and Prairie Avenue address. Thomas had performed his dignitary's role at the café's opening far more honorably than his part as accomplice to murder in Burnham Park a lifetime earlier.

The 43rd street watering hole and eatery had become the regular meeting place for the 3rd Ward Democratic Committee. Members of the group included the ward's current alderman, Bertrand Rhodes, and the ward's precinct captain, Tyrone Witherspoon. These two typically sat in the café's lone corner booth under the "Wall of Fame," the title given to an almost thirty-foot-long mural of legendary Negro League baseball players. The painting had been commissioned by the café's owner and executed by a former, spray-painting-tagger-turned-hip-Bronzeville-artist-nouveau.

Pick's bar seat was directly in line with a portrait in the mural of the soulful stare of Ray Dandridge. The diminutive, bow-legged Dandridge, who spent most of his playing days in the Mexican

baseball leagues during the 1930s and 1940s, had become a favorite of his.

"Black folks got *respect* down south of the border. Yes, sir. No
Jim Crow down there to keep the black man down. No sir. Uh-uh."

Using phrases like this from his bar stool throne, Pick regu-
larly pontificated about black pride and expounded his knowledge
of the lives of the old Negro players. Those within earshot of his
preacher-like sermons who bellied up for a drink at the highly polished bar had a good chance of being recipient of his regular yet
uninvited soliloquies. And, if some unknowing patron possessed
the ignorance to be in his seat when Pick strutted in at his usual
time of two p.m. daily, then Pick would walk up to that person and
in his charming voice say, "Sir, that's the chair, *man*, for the chair-
man."

The politico, as it were, was referring to his unofficial title of
"Chairman, 3rd Ward Democratic Committee," of which he was a
member, ex-officio. Most whom he approached obliged him by
getting up, sensing as streetwise folks do that perhaps underneath
his seemingly innocent request lurked a devil who'd most likely
chuckle after slicing you with the switchblade he always carried
hidden in the front of his pants. Others, who didn't understand
the nuance of Pick's play on words, usually ended up being
asked—"told" the more appropriate word—by the bartender on
duty to take another seat at the bar.

When Senator Clayton Thomas entered the café, Clarke, Witherspoon, and Rhodes sat in the corner booth, coffee cups in hand.
It was exactly 3:00 p.m. Empty now, except for those three men,
the café would reopen for dinner in about two hours. Chatting in
confidential tones, Pick didn't look up when the senator entered.
As an ex-P. Stone and later El Rukn gang enforcer, he had the un-
canny ability to sense things 360 degrees around him, aware of
everything and everyone in his presence at all times.

Clayton walked through the dark customerless room, its window blinds drawn closed to block the mid-afternoon sun, passing
the diner's empty tables. He didn't speak until he reached the de
facto 3rd Ward booth.

"Good day, gentlemen."

"Afternoon, Senator," Alderman Rhodes said, standing and extending his hand.

"Alderman," Clayton replied, obliging him back by putting out his hand. He looked at Pick and Witherspoon.

"Senator." Witherspoon said, acknowledging the Washington politician, too, with a handshake though remaining seated.

Pick neither stood nor returned Clayton's salutation. "You wanted to see me?" Pick said without looking up.

"Yes. Seems we have a slight problem."

"Slight?" Pick replied, looking up at him. "That's an interesting choice of words. Are you using that word in the literal sense? For example, as in 'Oprah has a slight weight problem.' Or figuratively, as in 'Oprah has a slight problem. She just found out she's going to get audited.'?"

Rhodes and Witherspoon chuckled.

"I'm serious. It's about Arizona. I've been contacted," Clayton said. "He came by my office. 'Bout an hour ago. Said he needed my help—"

"And what, might I ask, did you say to him?" Pick retorted.

"I didn't say anything, just acted surprised. Ya know, seeing him after all these years."

"Let me get this straight," Pick said, leaning forward from his slouched position behind the table. "Our little nigger squealer shows up in your office, whom you haven't seen in over, let's see, thirty years? And, what? You two talk about the motherfuckin' weather?"

"What could I say? I told him I was surprised to see him—"

Pick slammed his cup of coffee down on the table. Clayton jumped back from the hot liquid that splashed in his direction.

"'Surprised to see him'? Did you actually say 'surprised'?" He pointed his coffee cup directly at the senator. "I told you I would keep him alive, didn't I? Aren't I a man of my word? An honest man? Hey. I'm an upstanding citizen of Chicago." He waved his cup at the others around the table. "Hell. I'm the goddamn *chairman* of this here organization."

Snickers rose from Rhodes and Witherspoon.

"So. Where is he now?" Pick asked, settling down and taking a sip from what remained of his double-shot almond latte.

"He's in Burnham. He went back there—you know—to where—"

Hearing this, Pick slammed his other hand on the table, rattling the salt-and-pepper shakers against the metal napkin holder.

"In the park? What the hell is he doing in the goddamn park?" Pick's eruption this time even made his two cohorts shrink back in their seats. "Did you let him know that if it wasn't for you, that if it wasn't for our deal—" His tone lowered to a whisper as he emphasized his next words to the senator. "—that he and that pretty honky bitch wife o' his and those two half-breed kids o' theirs would be dead by now?"

"What could I do?" Clayton replied. "The police came to my office looking for him."

"Poe-leese? What the goddamn hell the poe-leese doin' lookin' for him in your goddamn office for? What the fuck is goin' on here?"

Pick's boiling point drew closer.

"I don't know. But let me find out more. He trusts me. I told him to wait for me in the park. Told him I'd get back to him. But—"

"But, what?" Pick demanded.

"But, he knows."

"That's it. Fuck this shit!" Pick turned to Witherspoon. "We still got those two fools Turner and DeSadier down there, right?"

"Yeah. They should be back soon," Witherspoon replied.

"Soon my ass. They's probably smokin' and whorin' down there with all that Mexican pussy." Pick straightened himself up and sipped from his mug, nodding his head. "I'd be doin' the same thing myself. Damn straight. Black man's still treated like a king down there—*respected*." He jabbed his index finger on the table in front of him. "Maybe we need to have our boys Pokie and Bobby D pay a visit to that little mo' fo's house. Scare the shit outta that sweet little thang wife o' his. See if that'll get his sorry little squealer nigger ass outta' my park." Pick turned once more to his longtime sidekick. "Tyrone, get ahold of those two down in Arizona and tell them—"

"No. Don't do that!" Clayton jumped in.

Restraining himself, Pick asked, "What did you say?"

"What I meant to say is that I'd advise against that. This man's an officer of the law now. We can't be doin' any of that stuff. No way. No how."

Pick leaned over and grasped the senator's forearm. With a magician's deftness, the gangster pulled his switchblade from the front of his pants. A swift flick of his wrist revealed the knife's shiny, six-inch, stainless steel blade. He pushed the senator's hand down flat on the table and thrust the point of the stiletto between the man's spread fingers. The razor-sharp dagger stuck deep into the wood top, narrowly missing the web between the fingers of Clayton's hand. The senator froze.

"Don't you *ever* fuckin' tell me what I can or can't do! Ever! You understand?"

Clayton nodded, beads of perspiration forming on his upper lip.

"You do what I tell you to do. Just like it's always been." Pick's voice softened. "Okay?"

Clayton made another short quick nod. A bead of sweat dripped to the tabletop.

Pick pulled his blade out from the table where it had sunk in more than half an inch. He pointed the tip of the blade up in the air, right next to the temple of his own head, then went on. "You know. Better yet. Why don't I go to the park and meet with my old friend Mister James Overstreet myself?"

CHAPTER 39

Before the senator had departed, he suggested to Stan that he stay in the park for at least thirty minutes. Then, Stan should meet him at The Negro League Café, one block west of his office back on 43rd Street. While Stan sat there, waiting for the prescribed time to pass, his head swam with confusion. He stared out at the lake, thinking and wondering about Clayton's life under the control of Monroe "Pick" Clarke for the last three decades.

The deep blueness of the water had always had a calming effect on him as a boy, but today, the lake's mysterious powers didn't work as he tried to comprehend how Pick could've known about his whereabouts all these years and done nothing about it. Had he lived in fear all this time for nothing, he wondered?

Stan pulled out his cell phone. Brian Hanley should have arrived by now and the plan was for them to speak by phone within an hour of Brian's landing at Midway Airport. But Stan's cell phone wasn't able to pick up a signal down along the shoreline.

No signal down here on the rocks. I'll try again when I get back up the hill by the parking lot.

He picked himself up and double-timed it back to the parking lot where the taxi ran idling, sitar music blaring from within. The driver puffed lazily on an unfiltered cigarette.

"Twenty-ninth and Prairie!" Stan shouted through the cab's open front passenger window as he ran up to the car and jumped in the backseat. "Hurry, please!" Stan then flipped open his cell.

"Police station? Yes, sir! No problem, sir! I step on it—just like in movies!"

The cab driver threw the car in reverse and began to back out of the gravel lot. "Uh-oh, sir," the cabbie said. "Senator's limo coming behind me again. No look so good."

Hearing his words and seeing the shocked look on the cabbie's face, Stan turned to look out the vehicle's filmy back window. Clayton's limo had pulled up behind the cab and hemmed it in the small lot. In order to get out now, the cabbie would have to jump an eight-inch curb less than a foot from its own front wheels. Attempting such a maneuver would necessitate a now-impossible running start. Before Stan could make any suggestions to his driver, Tyrone Witherspoon stood outside the cab's rear door. He spoke through the open window.

"Going somewhere, James, my man?"

Stan didn't answer as Witherspoon opened the car's door.

"Someone back here wants to see you." He motioned his head back toward the limo behind them. "Why don't you come with me? Nice and easy. Okay, blood?"

Stan pushed the send key on his phone and slipped it in his pocket as he moved over to exit the taxi. But before he did, he glanced at the cab driver who Stan saw was watching his movements in the rearview mirror. Stan shot a wink at the cabbie. The driver caught his facial gesture and smiled back with a small nod.

"You packin'?" Tyrone asked him.

Stan shook his head.

"Good. Don' want no accidents out here in dis beautiful park of ours. We've worked real hard makin' this a family friendly place now, ya know." Witherspoon pointed to a tot lot about fifty feet from them filled with shiny new playground equipment. "Third Ward Democratic Club bought all these swings and bouncy horses. For all the poor children still livin' 'round here, ya know. Givin' back to the community is what they call it."

"That's very big of you. I'm sure there's a plaque dedicated to Manny Fleischman somewhere around here, too."

"Still the smart-ass little nigger? Still think you're better than any of us."

Stan didn't answer, but merely walked back toward the senator's black limousine, Witherspoon right behind him, one hand tucked inside his windbreaker jacket, the other holding a cigarette. The back door of the limo opened. Out stepped Pick.

"Well if it isn't James motherfuckin' Overstreet. How the hell are you, my man? Welcome home, blood!" Pick extended his hand for a soul shake. Stan stood motionless. "Well, now. Too big and important I see to shake a brother's hand. Is dat it?"

Stan didn't reply.

"So. What brings you back to the beautiful Windy City? Back to the old neighborhood here. Wanna see how us poor folk are doin'?"

Stan still remained silent.

"Whassa matter? Cat got your tongue? Or maybe you don't understand me or sumpin'? Huh? 'Dat it?"

"I understand you perfectly, Pick."

"Well, now. You *can* talk. And it don't sound like you talk none of that street nigger shit we talk here either. You got that educated sound. White bread is what real brothers like myself call it. Maybe you's an Oreo now. Huh? Is dat it?"

"Fuck you," Stan replied.

"Shiiiiiit. Listen to this mo' fo', Tyrone. Dat ain't no way for a big time, smart-ass, white bread, educated lawyer to be talkin'. Is it now?" Pick turned to Witherspoon, looking for a response.

Like a puppet on a string, he obliged his boss. "No, sir. Un-uh. Can't talk like that in no Arizona courtroom for sure."

"And I'll bet for damn sure you don't talk like that in front of that honky bitch wife of yours neither," Pick added. He pulled a pack of Kool cigarettes from inside his leather jacket and offered the pack to Stan.

"Those'll kill you," Stan said. "Of course, you've got nine lives, so I'm sure you don't worry about that."

"You got that right, Mister James Overstreet. Got me nine lives. Just like a cat. A real cool cat. Nothin' ain't goin' to keep ol' Monroe Clarke down. Always one step ahead of the man."

Pick stood there with the unlit cigarette dangling from his lips. He then lit it with Tyrone's smoke and took a deep drag on the filter-tipped Kool Light. He looked the epitome of a jive-talking, South Side Chicago, gangbanger, Stan thought.

"Well, I'm here to tell you, your streak of luck is about to come to an end," Stan said.

"Is that right? And how, might I ask, do you propose to bring about my demise?"

"Well, I think the phrase we use in my line of work is, 'That's for me to know and for you to find out.' "

Pick laughed, throwing his head back and looking up at the cloudless blue sky. "Shiiiit. Dat sounds more to me like schoolgirls talkin' on the playground, not big man stuff we's talkin' about here." He eyeballed Stan with a venomous look. "So, if you've come here to play some kind of game with me I'd think twice about it. See, you remember Pokie and Bobby? Don't you? 'Course you do. What am I thinkin'?" He inhaled again on the Kool and blew the smoke in Stan's face. "Well, dem two boys of mine is down Arizona way, doin' a little work for me and your ol' friend, Clayton. I asked Tyrone here to ring dose boys up and have 'em go pay a little house call on the pretty little honky bitch wife of yours."

Stan remained silent but began to crack his knuckles.

"Oh. Gonna' play brave now, thinkin' you won't let this news upset you. Very admirable. Very admirable." He nodded and shrugged his shoulders. " 'Ceptin', I got no control of Pokie when he gets mad. 'Specially all da way down there in, whadya you call it? Oh yeah—da valley of da sun. Dat's it. I like dat name." He dragged again on his Kool and spoke with the cigarette in his mouth. "Well, I mean to tell you dat man Pokie got no discipline. No self-control of his very bad temper. No, sir. It's a real shame. Real shame. Now, me? I got plenty o' control. Nothin' rattles my little world." Pick pulled the smoke from his lips and pointed the cigarette at Stan. "Not even James motherfuckin' Overstreet comin' back into it after thirty some years. The little cocksucker who went to the poe-leese and told them all about what he saw dat day in the park. Matter of fact, not too far from here, if I remember correctly." Pick pointed south down the path with his cigarette between his first two fingers. "Why don't we take a little walk down there to the—what'd our attorney, Miss Poindexter, call it again, Tyrone?"

"Scene of the unfortunate incident," Tyrone answered.

"Yeah. Dat's it! Scene of the unfortunate incident," mocked Pick. "Ya see, they can't call it 'scene of the crime' 'cause there was no crime. All the alleged suspects were found not guilty as charged. You remember that? 'Course you do. You see, James, sometimes things just aren't what they seem to be the first time you see them." They continued to walk on the asphalt path toward the spot of Manny Fleischman's three-decade-old attack. "You see, my man, what you thought you saw when you was just a small boy all dem years ago, may notta been at all what you thought it was. You dig? See, you thought you seen some young, angry, out-ta'control little nigger boys beatin' up an old white man, when what was really happenin' was dem proud black youths was just protectin' themselves."

Stan stopped and stared at him.

"What? You don't believe me? Well, it's true," Pick cried. "'Dat ol' Jew hated niggers like us. He really had it in for black boys, 'specially for yours truly here. Claimed I stole stuff when I worked at Hyde Park Foods as a delivery boy, just before they fired me and hired your smart little nigger ass. And here all I was tryin' to do was my part in helping out my auntie Della and cousin Julius. Two of my family who had to raise me when my daddy and momma were forced to abandon me in order to become secret agents for the government."

Tyrone snickered at Pick's sarcasm.

"You're nothing but a liar and a murderer, Pick," scoffed Stan.

"Whoa, James, my man. Watch what you're sayin'. I can sue you for dat. Libel is what they call it. Ain't dat right, Tyrone?"

"Judge Judy'd throw his ass in jail, for sure," Pick's sidekick retorted on cue from his leader.

"It's not libelous if it's true," Stan said. "And you gotta lotta fuckin' balls to stand here, look me in the eye, and tell me Mister Fleischman attacked you. What kinda silly ass fool you take me for, nigger?"

"Who you callin' a nigger?" Pick grabbed Stan by the lapels.

"I'll tell you what kinda' fool. You're the kinda fool dat thinks he can come back into my city—into *my* park—after all these years and raise up some ghost of an old Jew-man who got what he deserved. Dat's what kinda fool I think you are!" He spun Stan around and grabbed him by the arm, pushing him toward a spot he pointed to on the asphalt. "Look. Lookie here, you little cocksucker. Here's where I smashed that Jew motherfucker's head. Splattered his thick skull with your baseball bat." Pick threw his Kool to the ground near the spot to where he had pointed. He put his pointed-toed shoe over it and twisted his foot hard several times, snuffing out the cigarette. "I think they call that 'irony'—ain't dat right, Tyrone?"

"Oh, yeah. Irony. Dat's the word, my man," Tyrone repeated.

Stan stared down at the exact spot where Fleischman fell after Pick's first vicious blow with the bat. The location and the sight were indelibly etched in his mind. He watched now as Pick ground out his cigarette on the asphalt path. For the first time in years, the thought reentered his mind of how he much he wanted to kill Pick.

"Came in real handy dat bat o' yours. Never thought I'd be usin' it to protect myself when I took it from you. Often wondered where that Dick Allen Louisville ended up."

Stan turned to him. "Yeah? Well, I often wondered what happened to you, Pick. Wondered if somebody smoked your jive ass in the projects or took your pitiful mug to a cornfield somewhere out in Indiana and dumped you where nobody'd ever find you. I wished for that as a kid. Prayed you'd get the same thing you gave Manny Fleischman."

"But you forget, James, my man. I'm a cat. Got nine lives. Remember? Nine lives. And I still got plenty o' lives left, too. Nobody smokin' ol' Pick. Nobody. 'Specially no squealin' little sorry ass Arizona nigger lawyer like you."

Stan watched Pick turn toward the limo, which had crept slowly behind them along the park's wide path. Pick waved the driver to pull alongside the three of them as they stood there on the spot where the Fleischman attack had taken place so long ago. The driver rolled down his window.

"Tubbs, you remember James Overstreet, don't you?" Pick said. The driver nodded.

"Sure you do. That's right. And you remember Tubbs, don't you, James? The last time you saw my boy Tony Tubbs here was when my cousin, Julius, had him driving that van for the Cook County Sheriff's Office with you and your family in it. We missed our chance to kill you that day. This time we won't." Pick looked at Tyrone. "Why don't we take Mister Overstreet here for another little ride, 'ceptin' this time, let's do the job right."

HONK! HONK! HONK!

The three men, standing alongside the limo, turned when they heard a car's horn, blaring like that of a Coast Guard cutter on the nearby lake. A bright yellow car, its engine accelerating, sped toward them. The group stood frozen on the asphalt path like frightened deer in the headlights of the fast approaching cab. Less than ten feet from plowing into them, Pick and Witherspoon dove into a row of bushes along the path. Witherspoon covered Pick's body with his own as the cab came to a screeching halt.

"Get in! Get in!" the cabbie yelled through the open window of his cab.

Seeing a gun now clutched in Witherspoon's hand, pointing right at him from the bushes, Stan yanked the cab's door open and dove in, hitting the backseat hard with his face.

"Stay down, sir! I get you outta here! Just like in movies! No problem!" The driver throttled the yellow car's engine. "Oh, shit!" the cabbie yelled.

Stan heard the cab driver's yelp. In the next moment Stan felt someone jump on his back. Then everything went black.

CHAPTER 40

When Stan regained consciousness, he didn't know where he was. Stale cigarette smoke stung his nostrils, alternating with the pungent yet unmistakable reek of burned hashish. Dingy and dark, only a sliver of light coming from two small windows—blocked with what looked like large, cardboard boxes stacked floor-to-ceiling—which lit the room. His head throbbed like he'd been beaned by a major league fastball.

Where the hell am I?

Instinctively jerking his limbs, he couldn't move his arms, legs, or torso. He came to the quick realization he'd been hog-tied to a straight-back wooden chair. Squinting his eyes in the dim light, he recognized the figure across from him, tied-up in a chair as well.

"Hey. Hey." He called over to the lifeless figure.

The cabbie, dried blood smattered across his face, did not reply.

"What have they done to him? I'll kill Pick."

"James?" The voice sounded like it came from behind Stan. "James. It's me. Are you all right?" Stan didn't reply, though he recognized the voice. "I'm sorry I had to hit you so hard."

"That was you that clocked me?" Stan mumbled, cobwebs still clouding his head as he turned, trying to see behind him. "Just who the hell's side are you on anyway?"

"If I hadn't knocked you out and you had tried to get away, Pick and Witherspoon would have killed you both. I'm sure of it." Clayton Thomas walked in front of him into the faint light and pointed to a door about fifteen feet to Stan's left. He continued in his low voice, "Speak softly. They're all upstairs."

"What have they done to the cab driver?" Stan begged his whispered question.

Clayton stepped over to the slumping cabbie and pressed two fingers to his neck. "He's alive. Thank, God. Pick had some wild idea he was working undercover with you and had Witherspoon work him over pretty good."

"He was just trying to help me, for crissake."

"I'm sorry, James. Really. I am." He leaned over and began to untie Stan's hands. "But you've got to get out of here."

"Where are we anyway?" Stan looked up, reacting to the footsteps he heard on the wooden floor above his head.

"In the basement below The Negro League Café."

"What are they doing up there?"

"It's where they run their operation."

"What operation?" As Clayton loosened the ropes that bound Stan's feet, the prosecutor rubbed his wrists.

"Their smuggling operation in Arizona. They've been running guns into Mexico for a number of years now, trading them for pure meth from Sonora, along with smuggling in the human cargo they use to carry the stuff out of the country for them. That's why Turner and DeSadier were in Phoenix when you caught them. Those two have been coordinating all the trafficking down there. They're the guys who set up the deals, move the goods, and run the drop houses."

Stan struggled to comprehend Clayton's words, still coming out of his haze. "How did Pick and his gang get involved?"

"It all began when Pick went down to Nogales some time ago on one of his 'tequila and pussy runs' as he liked to call them. He discovered how eager the Sinaloan drug cartel was to get the heavy firepower they needed since Mexico's gun laws are so strict. Pick figured out he could swap guns for meth and make ten times the money he could get for selling the same hardware on the streets of Chicago. He makes hundreds of thousands of dollars on some transactions. I'm sure he's made millions." Clayton paused, shaking his head. "Not to mention flooding Chicago's neighborhoods with high-grade Mexican meth."

"Where is he getting all of these guns from?"

"That's a whole other story we don't have time for."

"He's got to be stopped." Stan tried to push up from the chair but halted. "Ooooh. What the hell did you hit me with? A park bench?" He gingerly rubbed the knot on the back of his head.

"That egg there is the least of your worries. When he finds out you got Pokie and Bobby locked up in Arizona, Pick'll kill you for sure."

"He'll never find out," Stan replied. "Unless you plan on telling him."

"Say what? Do you have any idea who you're dealing with? What's at stake here, especially for me?"

"Well, I'm not really sure who the bad guy is—you or Pick."

"You don't believe me, do you? *I'm* not the problem. Pick is. This man hasn't stopped killing for thirty-five years. And he'll continue to kill until—"

"Until, what?" Stan asked. The rumbling noise from an elevated train filled the dank room, its deafening drone exacerbating the pounding in his aching head.

"You've got to get out of here."

Stan didn't have the time nor the mental composure to figure out why Clayton evaded his question. He worried, though, about his bound friend across from him and nodded toward the cabbie. "What about the cabbie?"

"I'll make sure he gets out okay. You're the bigger worry for me right now."

Clayton flipped open his cell phone and punched in a number. Stan could hear a woman's voice answer through the tiny receiver.

"Janeequa," Clayton said. "Have Tubbs bring the limo over to the alley behind the café. Now!" He turned back to Stan. "As soon as my car gets here, I'm going to go upstairs and talk to them. Follow me. Right outside that door there will be a hallway. Take it down to the stairs at the end. They'll lead up to a door that exits to the alley. My driver will know where to take you."

"But Tony Tubbs is your driver!"

"Don't worry about Tubbs. He's on my side."

Stan shook his head in bewilderment, wincing as he looked right at Clayton. "I'm not afraid of Pick, you know. He doesn't scare me anymore."

"That may be, but you can't bring him down alone."

"I'm glad you brought that up." Like a good prosecuting attorney, Stan recognized that Clayton had opened a crack in the door. Now was as good a time as any for Stan to present his plan. That's why he'd come to Chicago, hoping to obtain Clayton's cooperation and help. Stan knew Clayton's answer to his idea would tell him once and for all whose side the politician was on. He inched closer to his oldest friend and put his hand on the senator's shoulder. "Clayton, you're right. I can't bring down Pick alone. At least not without your help. I have a plan to bring federal conspiracy charges against Pick and you're the only one who can testify against him. I need you."

"What are you saying? Conspiracy charges? Pick's distanced himself from every transaction south of the border. He's too smart."

"I'm not talking about what he's doing today. I'm talking about conspiracy charges pertaining to the murder of Manny Fleischman and the cover-up that followed."

"Are you crazy?" Clayton said, pushing Stan's hand away from his shoulder. "That was thirty years ago. Time's run out on those charges. Plus, they were found not guilty *and* they were juveniles. That hit on the head I gave you really did whack you silly, didn't it?"

"Just listen to me." Stan jabbed his index finger into Clayton's chest. "Remember how Fleischman saved me at the park that day when the gang corralled me in the basket, and how because of that Pick planned the attack on Fleischman?

"Yes. So?"

"That's a conspiracy to commit murder."

"But they've been tried for the murder. Double jeopardy protects them. And, besides, if I remember correctly, isn't there a statute of limitations on conspiracies?"

"Those points are true. You're right. But guess what? There's no statute of limitations if you conspire to commit or cover up a crime when that conspiracy takes place on federal property."

"Federal property?"

"Do you remember that you told me you were there at the cemetery when the gang planned the Fleischman ambush? And when they met again to cover up their crime? Well, Pick planned the attack and the subsequent concealments in Oak Woods Cemetery at the base of that Confederate burial mound there, right next to the monument."

"Correct. That's where the P. Stones held all their secret meetings. They made everyone go. Everyone who attended made a vow of silence about what went on there. That place still gives me the creeps every time I have to go there for a burial," Clayton said.

"Well that monument is on federal land." Stan placed his hands on the sides of Clayton's shoulder and shook him. "You know what this means? We've got him. We've finally got Pick!"

CHAPTER 41

As soon as the wheels of the plane hit the tarmac at Chicago's Midway Airport, Brian dialed Stan's cell number.

"He's not answering his cell phone, is he?" Maxine asked.

Stan's in trouble, Brian knew it. Concerned, but calm like a good cop, he nonetheless didn't want to frighten Maxine. "Don't worry. I'm sure he's fine. He said he'd call us by five local time, just as we planned." The plane had arrived thirty minutes late so Brian did wonder, though, why there was no indication on his phone of the voice mail notification he expected.

Two days earlier, Stan and Brian had put a hasty plan together of what they needed to accomplish once they arrived in Chicago, the place they hoped to find the firm evidence and the witness needed to bring a federal conspiracy charge against the original members of the Oakwood Rangers. Their plan had Stan leaving on an earlier flight and meeting alone with Senator Clayton R. Thomas, hoping to convince him to be that witness. After Brian tied up some legal loose ends in Arizona, Stan had suggested that he fly to Chicago on the next flight and meet him at the senator's office. From there, they had planned to visit Oak Woods Cemetery to confirm Barbara Reyes's discovery of the federal property within the cemetery's grounds before concluding their trip by meeting with Chicago Police Commander Sal Abbatti at 21st District headquarters.

Maxine's being in Chicago was never a part of the two men's plan.

Brian grabbed his and Maxine's carry-ons and headed for the terminal exit. He scanned up and down the taxi and shuttle bus lanes, looking for the driver scheduled to meet them. A conspicuous, gold Lincoln Town Car pulled up to the outer curb. "That's him, Max. There's our ride."

As Brian spoke those words, a tall, paunchy man emerged from the garish sedan. As he came around the front of his car, the guy shoved his meaty palm at Brian and pumped his hand up and down. "Brian Hanley. How the hell are you, kid?"

"Great, Mister Boscorelli. Just great."

"Hey! What's this 'Mister Boscorelli' stuff? I told you on the phone, you just call me Timbo," the ex-cop bellowed, his voice refusing to be drowned out by the surrounding street noise.

"Timbo, this is Maxine Kobe. She's the wife of my best friend back in Arizona."

"Pleased to meet you, Mrs. Kobe."

"Please. Call me Maxine."

"Okey-dokey. Maxine it is." Timbo tipped the red longshoreman's cap on his huge head. His massive frame was wrapped in a wrinkled, tan trench coat. "So, Sal Abbatti said you two needed a personal tour of the old stomping grounds. Whadya doin' kid, one of those genealogical things? Tracin' your roots are ya?"

"No, no, Timbo. Nothing like that. Maxine's husband, Stan, is in town for a meeting with Senator Thomas. We're here to meet Stan and then spend a coupla days in Chicago, seeing the sights."

"Great. Ya know, Maxine, this is the most beyoodeful city in the world. Ya know that, dontcha? Sears Tower. Michigan Avenue. The Magnificent Mile. The Art Institute. Burnham Park. Yep, beyoodeful. Like the song says, 'My kinda town.'" As they stood outside the car, Timbo kept talking, not coming up for a breath. He changed the subject. "I sure hope your husband's here to talk that nigger senator of ours outta runnin' for president, though. Last thing this country needs is a spook in the White House. Ya know, they didn't name it the White House for nothin'." The ex-cop laughed at his own joke.

Timbo grabbed their carry-ons and put them in the Lincoln's trunk. As Maxine got into the back of the vehicle on the passenger side of the car, Brian walked behind the car and grabbed Timbo by the sleeve as he placed the bags in the trunk.

"Timbo. Uh. Maxine's husband—my best friend, Stan—is black."

"Jeez, kid. That's too bad." Timbo shook his head, slamming the trunk closed and looking through the back window at his female passenger. He tried to lower his voice but his whisper was still a roar. "Why is it that these great looking white broads marry these colored guys. Never could figure that one out."

Brian narrowed his eyes and shot Timbo a disapproving look.

Timbo caught Brian's glare and replied, holding up three fingers scrunched together. "Okay, kid. Scout's honor. I won't say the N word no more."

Brian opened his door and slid in next to Maxine. "Just take us to Senator Thomas's office. Okay, Timbo?" He looked at Maxine and shrugged his shoulders at the ex-detective's insensitive comments.

"Don't worry," she whispered to him.

Brian smiled at her reply. Maxine Kobe's dedication to her husband was unshakeable, hence her insistence on coming to Chicago.

"I deserve to go to Chicago. After being married to you all this time and all you've put me through I think I'm as much a part of this as you are," she had insisted back in Arizona when the three of them hatched their plan and the ensuing trip. Brian watched as Stan stood his ground, forbidding his wife to go. It was the only time he had seen his friend lose his temper with her.

She had argued that, at the very least, she could be of value when they met with the Oak Woods Cemetery people, identifying the details of the monument, and verifying its location on federal land. Brian had agreed with Stan that Maxine should not go with them but knew Maxine would not be held back. Now that she knew all the details about Stan's past, she'd want to do everything in her power to help her husband right this wrong. A wrong that not only affected him but her and their children, too.

When Maxine had showed up at the airline gate with her ticket and overnight bag in hand, she confirmed Brian's suspicions and he knew nothing he could say would possibly convince her not to go.

"Senator Thomas's office is over on East Forty-Third Street. I'll have you there in a jiff." Timbo stuffed himself behind the steering wheel as he got in the car. "Cops know all the shortcuts. Me and your old man, God rest his soul, worked these streets for a long time, kiddo. Know 'em like the back of my hand." Timbo accelerated his Lincoln and merged into the heavy late afternoon airport traffic and headed toward the expressway.

"Is there anyone else who has offices in the senator's building?" Brian asked as he poked numbers into his cell phone then held it up to his ear.

"Nope. Just the senator. It's a tiny place. There's a small front lobby. I think it's his niece who's the receptionist."

"Entrances?" Brian asked, jotting some notes while checking his voice mail.

"Front and back. Jeez, kiddo, you sound like a cop ready to make a bust."

Brian didn't reply, putting his finger in his other ear. His eyes widened as he listened to the message.

Fifteen minutes later, Timbo exited the Dan Ryan Expressway at 43rd Street and turned east, heading toward the small, one-story brick building that housed Thomas's office at the corner of 43rd Street and Martin Luther King, Jr. Drive.

"Hey, if I ain't mistaken, that's Senator Clayton's limo right in front of us," Timbo called out to his two backseat passengers. "Matter of fact, I'm sure of it."

The limo, a few car lengths ahead of them, made a quick right turn on Prairie Avenue.

"Are you sure?" Off the phone now, Brian's voice turned urgent. "Is there anyone in it?"

"Can't tell with those smoked windows," Timbo replied.

"I think we should follow it," Brian suggested.

"Really?" Timbo replied. "Okay. Whatever you say, kiddo."

Timbo made his own sharp right-hand turn south down Prairie, driving several car lengths behind the stretch limo. He followed the black-windowed government-plated vehicle as it turned left on 44th Street, then left again when it reached the alley that paralleled the Chicago Transit Authority's commuter train tracks.

"Pull over here," Brian said to Timbo. "I wonder why he's going down the alley? Let's see where he stops."

They waited until they saw the limo come to a stop at the end of the alley. Then Brian asked Timbo to take the same route. Timbo drove down the narrow, gravel passageway lined with rusted-out garbage cans and strewn with litter. A train rumbled above them on tracks supported by ancient-looking steel girders, a trademark of the city's elevated commuter system. The chauffeur-driven sedan sat with its emergency flashers blinking. Timbo brought the gold Lincoln right up behind the idling limo and stopped.

"Senator's office is about a block east o' here. You want I should find out if the senator and the husband are in the car?" Timbo asked, turning back to his two passengers.

Brian and Maxine nodded in unison.

Timbo lumbered out of the car and waddled his huge frame up to the senator's limo. When he reached the driver's side of the black sedan, the window motored-down. Wearing aviator sunglasses that looked like two, shiny mirrors, the driver looked like he should be in the cockpit of an F-16.

"Yes?" the driver asked.

"Whatchew doin' parked back here, Tubbs?"

"Dunno. Just got the call to come over and wait out back. They don't tell me much. You know how that is."

Brian wondered what Timbo and the driver could be talking about. After listening to his voice mail, his cop's instinct grabbed his gut. He turned to Maxine and pressed a single index finger up to his lips for a moment, then opened the Lincoln's back door. "Let's get out of here," he whispered.

They slid out and crept away from the vehicle, sneaking into a yard two doors away. Once out of sight, Maxine tugged at Brian's shirt, stopping him.

"Where are we going?"

"To find Stan."

Rushing up the gangway between twin, three-story brownstone buildings whose fronts faced Prairie Avenue, they reached the city sidewalk that paralleled the street. Once there, they turned right and walked back north toward 43rd Street. When they reached the intersection, a metal sign on a steel pole hung from one of the corner buildings. It read: THE NEGRO LEAGUE CAFÉ.

"This is it," Brian said, turning toward Maxine.

"This is what?" she asked.

Brian paused for a moment, then chose his next words. "According to Sal Abbatti, this is where Senator Thomas is supposed to hold his town hall meeting later tonight."

Brian opened the front door and a small bell announced their entry. He scanned the room and at the same time reached for Maxine's hand. A few patrons seated throughout the joint looked up at them as they glided past several tables where people sat eating dinner. The couple grabbed two empty stools at the end of the café's lacquer-finished bar.

"Good evening," the bartender said, greeting them with a warm smile. "Welcome to The Negro League Café. Can I seat you folks at a table?"

"No, thanks," Brian said. "These two seats are fine right here."

Brian noticed the bartender's smile turn to a concerned look. "Well, okay then. So, what can I get you two?"

"Two coffees, please," Maxine replied.

"Two javas. Comin' right up. Would you like to see a menu? We serve the best soul food in Chicago."

"No thanks," Brian said.

Brian turned his head back toward the front door and scanned the room once again. As he did, he felt a tap on his shoulder and spun around on his stool. A tall, gangly, black man, dressed in a fine, brown leather jacket, stood next to him.

"That's the chair, *man*, for the chair*man*."

"I beg your pardon." Brian's reply was more a question than an apology.

"I said, That's the chair, *man*, for the chair*man*."

"Oh, I'm awfully sorry. Am I in your seat? I didn't realize—"

"Oh, it's no problem," the black man said. "You and your pretty friend here just go ahead and stay right there. I can sit with my friends at their table over there." He pointed to a booth in the corner where two men sat drinking coffee and smoking cigars. "So, what brings you to our wonderful café and our beautiful Bronzeville neighborhood?" the black man continued.

"I'm a big baseball fan," Brian said. "My lady and I are in town on business and I read about this café on the Internet, so I wanted to see it."

"Mixin' a little business with pleasure, huh? Nuttin' wrong with that, my man. What kind of business you in, might I ask?"

"Importing and exporting."

"Really. Isn't that a coincidence? I'm in that same business myself. Of course, you know what Oprah says, 'There's no such thing as coincidence.'" He chortled at his quip.

"Here you go. Two javas." Interrupting their conversation, the bartender set down two steaming cups of coffee on the bar. Then he slid over a bowl of sugar and a creamer for them.

"Rayford," the stranger said to the bartender, "I'll have my usual."

"One double-shot almond latte, coming right up."

"And put this nice couple's two coffees on my tab. You folks enjoy your coffee. And again, welcome to Bronzeville."

"Thank you, but you don't need to do that," said Brian.

"Oh. But I insist," said the man. "And we should talk more. 'Specially about baseball."

Brian watched the lanky fellow as he walked away toward the booth where his two friends sat, each staring over at Brian through puffs of creamy cigar smoke.

Once the black stranger was out of earshot, Maxine leaned over to Brian and murmured to him as she sipped on her coffee. "What was all that bull about importing and exporting?"

"Don't look now but I'm positive that's our man, Pick," Brian whispered back. "Sal Abbatti e-mailed me some recent jpegs of him."

"*That's* him?" Maxine said, looking tempted to turn around and eyeball him again. "But he's got such a sweet smile. Such a soft voice. He didn't look mean. Are you sure?"

"Looks can be deceiving, Max, especially with stone-cold killers—like Pick."

"Brian. I'm worried about Stan. My woman's intuition is off the meter."

"I'm sure he's fine." He patted her hand, trying to cover up his lie. "Wait here. I'll be right back." Brian caught the bartender's eye. "Men's room?"

Rayford pointed just beyond the bar. "Back through there, last door on your left."

Brian nodded. He turned to push away from the bar and off the stool, but Maxine tugged at his forearm, pulling him back. "Make it snappy. Okay?"

He squeezed her hand. "I'll be right back. Promise."

CHAPTER 42

Maxine prayed Brian wouldn't be long. *I hope he's working on some kind of plan.*

"Are you enjoying your *caffe* at the café?" asked the same black man who had approached her and Brian earlier.

Maxine turned and looked behind her. "Why, yes. Thank you for asking." She tried to hide how startled she felt by the man's unexpected reappearance.

"Mind if I—"

"No, of course not," she said, gesturing with a small nod for him to sit down.

He slid onto the stool next to her, placing his drink on the bar next to hers. "So you and your husband are big baseball fans, huh?"

"Yes . . . well . . . we are. But he's not my husband."

"Oh, I beg your pardon then. He introduced you as his 'lady' and ol' Monroe here just figured—"

"Monroe?"

"Monroe Clarke. At your service." He tapped a single index finger to his forehead, offering a quaint salute.

It is him! She took a sip from her coffee cup, trying to keep her hand from shaking.

"I'm a descendant of one of the slaves—I prefer to call them 'black explorers'—who traveled with Lewis and Clark. That's how I got my slave surname. I have an *e* in my Clarke, though. I always like to think that stands for 'eloquent.'" He produced a queer smile. "My daddy named me Monroe after James Monroe. Our fifth president. Eighteen seventeen to eighteen twenty-five. He's the fellow who really put together the Louisiana Purchase, ya know. Not that cracker slave owner Thomas Jefferson like all the history books say."

"So you're a history buff?" She hoped her voice hadn't quavered.

He grabbed his tall cup and took a slow sip of the steaming drink. "I'm a seeker of truth, ma'am. Monroe was the first president who believed slaves should be freed. But, most importantly, he believed they should be able to return to Africa, back to their rightful home."

As an undergrad history major, Maxine had thoroughly studied James Monroe and was well aware of his unpopular stance on the repatriation of slaves to Africa. She didn't take Clarke's bait, though, changing the subject.

"That's fascinating, Mr. Clarke. So you *are* a student of history then. Where did you receive your degree?"

He laughed, raising his eyebrows. " 'Receive my degree,' you ask? Well, I obtained my education right out there, ma'am." He pointed out the café's front windows. "I got my degree out in the streets. Got me a P-H-D. Only here on the South Side of Chicago that stands for Pushin' Hard Drugs. But that's all in my past. Now I study all types of history—American, African. I'm particularly interested in Civil War history, especially the period when my people achieved their emancipation from slavery."

Not sure what to make of this last statement, she smiled. "That's quite remarkable, Mr. Clarke."

"Please. Call me Monroe. I insist."

"Okay—Monroe."

"And what, may I ask, is your name?"

"Maxine. Maxine Kobe. My husband's is Stan Kobe. He's a county attorney in Arizona." She saw the look on his face change. Not quite sure what the look meant, nonetheless, it rattled her nerves. Her senses told her that she was sure this charming man knew the whereabouts of her husband whose phone call was now very conspicuously overdue. She decided to find out if her intuition was right. "Perhaps you remember him, though, as James Overstreet." Her protective instincts took hold of her. She paused for a moment before continuing. "If you've done anything to hurt my husband, Mister Clarke, I'll—"

The smile on his face transformed to a scowl. He leaned in toward her while at the same time putting a hand inside his leather jacket, reaching down toward his belt buckle. Then he whispered close to her ear. "You think you're playin' some kinda game here, bitch?"

His warm, almond-scented words washed over the side of her suddenly chilled face. He placed his other hand on one of her knees. His touch was ice cold, sending a shiver down her back. Repulsed, Maxine struggled to maintain her composure. Undaunted, though, she challenged him further, asking, "Where's my husband, Pick?"

He inched closer. As an involuntary defensive reaction, she shut her eyes, fearing his thin lips would at any moment press upon her now cold earlobe. As she imagined his next move she squirmed, but his small but strong hand, placed firmly above her knee, squeezed harder. She wondered if anyone in the café saw what he was doing, but she was too afraid to open her eyes to find out.

He whispered, "So you wanna see your squealer husband? Okay, just take it nice and easy and come with me and you won't get hurt."

He pulled his hand off her knee and jerked it under her elbow, urging her up from the stool. They walked together through the doorway to the back room, toward the restrooms where Brian had gone minutes before.

Please be coming out right now, Brian! Please!

Clarke walked behind Maxine, his hand grasping her under the bend of her arm, gripping her tightly. "Right through here. Nice 'n' easy now," he said softly. "Scream and you'll never see that nigger husband of yours again."

CHAPTER 43

"Who's there?"

Stan's voice cracked the silence of the basement room as the door opened to the dimly lit, clammy room. Seated back again in the wooden chair from which Clayton Thomas had freed him, Stan still felt groggy from the hit on the head. Still with him, Clayton crouched down behind him.

A male figure stood in the doorway, not answering. Bright daylight from the windows one floor above washed down the stairway, backlighting the form, putting the person's face in total shadow.

"Who is it?" Stan asked again, his voice rising.

The stark, human outline brandished a weapon, pointing it ahead of him as he walked into the room.

"What the—" Clayton said, standing up.

"Nobody moves and nobody gets hurt," the deep voice interrupted the senator.

"Brian!" Stan cried.

"You okay, pardner?" Brian asked, holstering his service revolver.

"Yes, I'm fine. But I don't know about him." Stan nodded over toward the lifeless man slumped in the chair across from him.

"Who's he?" Brian asked.

"He's my cab driver. He tried to save my life."

Brian looked at Clayton, standing behind Stan's chair. "Then I'm guessing you must be Senator Thomas."

"Yes I am. But who are you?"

"Just the best cop west of the Mississippi!" Stan stood up and bear hugged Brian.

"How'd you know I was here?" Stan asked, releasing his clutch on him.

"Clever of you to hit send on your cell phone. When it went to my voice mail I heard everything that happened to you in the park. It was still on when they made the plans to bring you over here in the Senator's limo. I know every bar in Chicago stores their liquor in the basement so I figured I'd check here for you first."

"Make that the best cop west and *east* of the Mississippi." Stan patted Brian on the shoulder.

Brian moved over to the unconscious cabbie and put two fingers to man's neck. "His pulse is weak, but he's alive. We need to get you both out of here right away."

"There's no way you'll get them out without my help," Clayton said. "I need to get back upstairs, before Pick and his men get suspicious. Once I'm up there, I'll distract them. Create a diversion. It should give the three of you time to get out. My limo should be here by now, waiting in the alley behind the café."

"It is. We saw it when we arrived—"

"Who's we?" Clayton asked.

Brian didn't answer. Stan looked at Brian, waiting for him to continue.

"Bri?"

Brian wouldn't look at him.

"No, Brian. You didn't? You didn't let Maxine—"

"Did you say Maxine?" Clayton interrupted. "His wife? She's here with you?"

Brian nodded.

"Brian, how could you? How could—?"

Brian interrupted him.

"She just showed up at the airport. She had a ticket. What could I do?"

Sounding panicked, Stan asked, "Where is she now?"

"She's sitting at the bar, waiting for me to come back from the john."

"You mean you left her alone up there with Pick and his men?" Stan cried.

"Oh, no," Clayton said, rushing past Stan toward the stairs.

"What?" Stan asked as the senator brushed by him.

"Pick *knows* her," he cried. "He knows what she looks like!"

Before Clayton could reach the bottom of the steps, a voice bellowed, bouncing off the stairway walls, echoing into the basement through the still open door. "That's right, Clayton. I do know what she looks like."

Pick flipped a light switch on the wall and entered the room. Walking behind him was Maxine, followed by Tyrone Witherspoon who held a Colt .45 against her head.

Brian slid his hand under his jacket, but Pick interrupted his movement. "I suggest you not reach for your weapon, Mr. Import-Export," Pick calmly told him, nodding back toward Tyrone and Maxine. "Lest you risk my friend here harmin' the bitch."

Brian froze.

"Thank you. Now, take your piece out, very carefully."

Stan stood motionless, knowing that the last thing any cop would do is willingly give up his service revolver. He wasn't sure what Brian would do, but Stan knew Brian was an expert marksman. He hoped if he fired his weapon, he'd blast Witherspoon right between the eyes, allowing him to lunge for Pick. As these thoughts whirred through his mind, Brian drew his firearm slowly out from the holster under his jacket and held it with two fingers, dangling the gun in the air.

"Brian! What are you doing? Shoot him! Shoot the son of a bitch!"

"That's a very bad idea, James," Pick advised. "Just do as I said and drop your weapon to the floor and kick it over here."

Brian did as told.

"Smart man," Pick said.

Stan looked at Brian, shaking his head with a disapproving face.

Pick nodded to Witherspoon who bent down and picked up Brian's gun, stuffing the cop's steel sidearm into the front of his pants. As he did, Pick grabbed Maxine and shoved her hard toward the rest of the group. She stumbled, falling into Stan's arms.

"Did he hurt you?" Stan brushed his wife's hair back, inspecting her face.

Maxine shook her head.

"Why would I want to hurt that pretty little honky wife of yours? 'Specially with an ass as fine as—"

Stan lunged toward Pick, but Brian intercepted him, throwing his arms around his buddy. Pick had already flicked his six-inch blade open. He pointed it now in Stan's direction.

"Let him go," Pick ordered. "Been waiting to Popeil this little motherfucker for thirty years. Slice and dice him 'til no one recognizes him."

"Let me go! Let me go! I want to kill him." Stan struggled with his friend, but Brian tightened his grip. "You didn't have the nerve to shoot him so let me *kill* him!"

"Not now," Brian said. He lowered his voice and whispered to Stan. *"Not now."*

"Your friend's smart, James. It's good to surround yourself with smart friends. Like me and ol' Clayton here." Pick walked around to the senator and wrapped his arm around Clayton's shoulder, pulling him close to him, still brandishing his knife. "Ain't that right, Senator?"

"Take your filthy hands off me," Clayton said, pushing away from him.

"Whoa, big fella. What's gotten into you? Did you spend too much time down here with your long-lost pal, James?" He turned and tapped the point of his sharp stiletto against Stan's shoulder. Then, turning back to the senator, Pick prodded him. "You're still my nigger, ain't you?"

Clayton didn't reply.

Pick looked at Witherspoon, who aimed his gun at the group. "I think our boy Clayton here might need a little attitude adjustment." He turned back to Clayton. "How 'bout it, Clayton? Been a long time since my boy Tyrone here gave you a good ass whoopin'."

"Go ahead, but I'm done doing your bidding, Pick."

"That's big talk from a man who's in no position to bargain," Pick told the senator. "You seem to forget our little arrangement, our little agreement. What if it ever got out to the press it's been you who's been helping me all this time run guns into Mexico.

Making sure all your committees in Washington are looking the wrong way. You seem to forget it's me who's holding all the cards."

"You can't hurt me anymore."

"Is that right? Well, it would sure be a shame, a *damn* shame, if that pretty little niece or that beautiful wife of yours ran into someone, late at night, with a blade just like this and had their pretty little faces all carved up." He dragged the blunt edge of his blade slowly across the senator's face. "Wouldn't it now?"

"I'm through with your threats. It's over. Your game is up. You're going down and I don't care if it means I go with you."

"So you're willing to throw it all away? For what? For this little squealer friend of yours?" Pick switched his knife closed and grabbed Clayton by his suit coat lapels, then pinched his thumb and index fingers together in front of Clayton's face. "We are *this* close, brother." Pick motioned with his head at Stan, still wrapped in Brian's clench. "This man can do us *no* harm."

"Yes he can! James is going to bring charges against you again for Fleischman's murder," Clayton blurted.

"He is, is he? For that old Jew we stomped thirty fuckin' years ago? Is that right?" Releasing Clayton from his grip, Pick turned to Stan and chuckled. "Did the heat get to you down there in Arizona or something? Just what did they teach you in that two-bit law school down there? Double jeopardy's in place here, my friend. And besides, we were all juveniles. All our records are sealed shut."

"Federal charges," Stan said back at him.

"Federal charges? Where in the hell did you come up with that one, Mr. Arizona Prosecutor?"

"That's right. Federal conspiracy charges," Stan said. "You planned Fleischman's murder and the cover-up at the base of the Confederate Monument in Oak Woods Cemetery."

"That memorial was and still is on federal land. President Cleveland dedicated it back in eighteen ninety-five. But I'm *sure* you knew that, being a student of history and all," Maxine scoffed at Pick.

"Don't smart mouth me, bitch, or I'll give you the slap you deserve."

Brian put a firm hand on Stan's shoulder as Clayton stepped in front of Stan. "All James needs is a cooperating witness and I'm his man."

"Is that right?" Pick said, glaring into the senator's face. "And what if this so-called cooperating witness just happens to have a very bad accident, maybe on one o' his last-minute junkets down to Cancun for some of that Mexican pussy he loves so much?"

"Your threats are useless. James's people have Turner and De-Sadier in custody in Arizona," Clayton said. "They've probably already flipped on you, just like they did when we were kids, after you killed Manny Fleischman. Those two losers are probably singing like birds down there right now." Clayton pointed in Pick's face. "It's over! You're through!"

"What's this jive-ass double-talkin' politician spewin' about?" Pick shouted as he whipped his head at Witherspoon. There was no misinterpreting the anger in Pick's voice as he heard Clayton's claim that Pokie Turner and Bobby DeSadier were in custody in Arizona. "Have we heard back from those two fools yet?"

Witherspoon shook his head.

Pick then turned back to Clayton. "If this turns out to be some trick, I'll make sure to kill the bitch first—that is—after I fuck that pretty little ass o' hers right in front of my boy James here." Pick turned back to Witherspoon and shouted an order. "Stay with them while I go upstairs and find out what all this bullshit is about with Pokie and Bobby."

Pick turned and walked up the stairwell. When he got to the top a man's voice stopped him in his tracks. "Where the fuck you goin', you skinny little prick?"

CHAPTER 44

As dusk waned, the black vehicle meandered through the quickly darkening streets of Chicago. Stan sat in the middle of the back-seat, flanked by Brian and Maxine, whose head rested on Stan's shoulder, eyes closed. Across from them sat Tyrone Witherspoon, holding his gun on the trio. The still-unconscious cab driver leaned against Senator Clayton Thomas, who sat on the seat next to Witherspoon in the rear of the stretch limo.

The long car slowed as the driver exited a side street and turned on to a narrow asphalt driveway. A pair of matching, twelve-foot-high brick pillars bordered the entrance, gargoyles perched on their respective tops. Six-foot-wide sides of opened, wrought iron gates were attached to each column. A brass sign on the front of each of the man-made sentinels guarding the entrance, displayed the words: OAK WOODS CEMETERY.

As the vehicle wheeled past the entrance and around the first curve, it proceeded on for a few more minutes, following the winding road before finally coming to a full stop.

"Where are we?" Maxine asked, picking up her head.

Witherspoon glared over at her when she spoke. "A place you'll feel real comfortable in real soon," he responded. "Now, don't no-body move or get any ideas." Getting out of the car, Witherspoon pointed his weapon back at Brian. " 'Specially you, pig." The thug slammed the door behind him, leaving the five of them alone in the back of the limo.

Headlights from a car behind switched off.

"There must be someone else with them," Stan said.

"Yeah, I noticed a pair of headlights following us, too, ever since we left the café," said Brian.

"Clayton, do you know why they've taken us here?" Stan asked. Clayton shook his head.

"What better place than this for getting rid of a few bodies?" Brian replied.

"Pick wouldn't kill us unless he created an alibi first." Stan said.

"I'm not sure he's thinking rationally any more," offered Clayton. "He'll do anything to protect the empire he's built and get me into the White House. Anything."

Stan squeezed his wife's hand. "Nothing's going to happen to us." Stan pulled his hand away from hers and began cracking his knuckles. "Nothing. I'll make sure of that."

"So what do you propose? A chat over a cup of coffee with these guys?" asked Brian. "I think we're a little bit past that stage."

"We wouldn't be in this mess right now if—"

"If what?"

"If you hadn't let Maxine come along!"

"Stan!" Maxine jumped in. "Brian couldn't stop me. Nothing would've stopped me from coming to Chicago to help you."

"He had his chance back in the basement. He could have shot Witherspoon," Stan charged, sounding frazzled.

"It wasn't the right opportunity. There was too much room for error. What if I missed?" Brian said.

"Well, I'm not going to just stand idly by. I'm going to do something."

"James, don't be a fool and try to do something heroic," said Clayton. "This man will kill you without flinching."

Stan shot back. "Listen. It's because of me we're all in this mess." He looked at the cabbie who, regaining consciousness, began rubbing his head. "Even this poor guy's an innocent victim." He squeezed his wife's hand again. "And I'm certainly not going to let Pick harm Maxine." He paused, then looked at the group. "I'm the only one who can bring an end to this."

"Don't you think you ought to tell us your plan, James, before you go executing it?" asked Clayton.

"Well, I can't just yet because I'm not quite sure what—"

"Stanford Kobe," Maxine said. "Don't go trying to be a hero."

He squeezed her hard then pulled away. "Maxine. I have to do this. It's the only way to get us all out of here alive. That's all that matters now."

"There's only one way we're all going to get out of here alive," she said, "and that's if Pick is distracted long enough for you guys to overpower Witherspoon."

"What do you have in mind?" Clayton asked.

"Pick wants his way with me. If I can get him alone, in the limo here, just for a few min—"

"No!" Stan shouted. "What are you saying? There's no way I'd allow that. No way I'd let him touch you—"

"Stan. I love you. Nothing will ever change that. Nothing."

The door to the car snapped open.

"All of you. Out! Now!" Witherspoon shouted, gesturing the instruction with the barrel of his handgun through the open door.

"What about the cabbie?" Clayton asked.

"Him, too. Pick wants all of you. Now."

Brian and Clayton helped the shaky cab driver, grabbing him under his arms and pulling him out of the limo. Stan and Maxine followed, Witherspoon shoving them from behind.

"There. Get over there." He pointed again with his gun.

A bright full moon peeked through the scattered clouds of the cool autumn evening, revealing a huge structure standing in the middle of a grassy mound where Witherspoon had pointed. The structure's base was formed by a massive limestone foundation about twenty feet square. One ancient-looking cannon sat at each of the four corners of this stone base whose slanted walls held large brass plates. Closer inspection of the panels would reveal the listing of thousands of names of deceased Confederate soldiers honored by the stark memorial under which they were buried.

As well, a line of small, white tombstones ran in a straight row on one side of the monument. Each represented the twelve Union soldiers who rested among their enemy brethren. These white headstones looked like pawns, protecting the figure of a soldier perched on the very top of a single pillar that rose from the base forty feet skyward.

"It's the Confederate Mound," Maxine whispered to her husband. "The one Barbara Reyes discovered."

Stan wished for a moment that he had never seen Barbara Reyes's notes. He thought about how finding out about this place was the impetus for devising his and Brian's plan to bring federal conspiracy charges against the former members of the Oakwood Rangers gang. He questioned himself, wondering what would have made him believe that he could go back in time and right the wrongs of the past. *All I've done is put all their lives in danger.*

As the five hostages walked toward the statue, Stan moved up alongside Clayton.

"This is it, isn't it?" Stan whispered. "The place where you heard them make their plans to kill Mister Fleischman and then cover it up."

Clayton nodded.

"It all stops here and now, Clayton. It ends tonight."

CHAPTER 45

As the five captives walked toward the Confederate Mound with Witherspoon pointing a gun at their backs, two men emerged from behind the huge, stone base of the monument. One was Pick. The other was a small stocky man in a Chicago policeman's uniform.

The policeman spoke first, breaking the eerie silence of the macabre scene. "You just couldn't let this die, couldja, kid?"

Epaulets on the shoulder of the man's uniform bore gold oak leaf. Gold oak leaves also adorned the top of the shiny, patent leather brim of his Chicago cop's dress hat. He didn't carry a weapon, but a Motorola police radio hung from his belt. Festooned on the right breast of his blue blazer were three rows of commendation ribbons, an ostensible representation of the man's many years of service in law enforcement. Over his left breast, he wore an engraved brass nameplate. It read: ABBATTI.

"Sal?" The name barely escaped Brian's mouth.

"Who the fuck joo expect? Maybe you thought you were gonna see your old man's ghost here?" Abbatti snapped.

"Sal Abbatti?" Stan's voice rose. "What's going on here?"

"And you. You just couldn't let the dead rest in peace. Couldja?" said Abbatti again, looking at Stan.

"What are you talking about?"

"Manny Fleischman. That's what I'm talking about."

"Rest in peace? Is that what you call it? Resting in peace?"

"It's been over thirty years, James," the police commander said. He then began to pace back and forth in front of the group, parallel to the base of the monument. Darkness engulfed them now as the moon dipped behind the cold-looking autumn clouds, back-lighting them. The air filled with a moist chill. He stopped his pacing in front of Brian and turned to the group. "When you called me, Brian, and told me about having Turner and DeSadier in your custody, I knew you'd start fuckin' snooping, especially when you told me your suspicions that Mister James Overstreet here got wind of who they were." Abbatti looked at Stan and sneered again at him. "Who could have ever guessed Stick Hanley's kid and you would cross paths in Arizona and start working together in law enforcement? I sure couldn't. What the fuck are the chances of that happening, I asked myself, a fuckin' million to one?"

"Ten fuckin' million to one," said Pick, eyeing Maxine up and down as he fingered his open switchblade.

"Shut the fuck up. If you had control of those two dogs Turner and DeSadier, they wouldn't be fuckin' incarcerated in a fuckin' Indian jail in fuckin' Arizona. And I wouldn't even have to be here to clean up this fuckin' mess."

"What do you mean, 'clean up'?" Stan asked.

"Just what I said: clean up."

A voice-bellowed from behind the group. "You ain't thinking of killing them all, are you, Sal?"

"And what the fuck do you suggest we do with them then?" Abbatti fired his answer back at Timbo Boscorelli as he approached the group huddled at the base of the monument.

"Timbo!" Brian cried.

"Detective Boscorelli?" gasped Stan. "You're in on this, too?" Stan paused for a moment, his mouth agape, then continued. "I thought you always hated Pick."

"I do hate the skinny little prick." Timbo turned to the silent Pick. "Don't I, Pick?"

Pick didn't take his eyes off Maxine and didn't answer the fat ex-cop.

Abbatti spoke up. "Pick here'll make it look like a mugging of tourists who got lost looking for the long-forgotten Confederate Mound. Except these stupid sightseers didn't know they were in the baddest part of town—the South Side of Chicago."

"Pick'll do no such thing. I give a shit about this nigger, Overstreet here, and his nigger-lovin' wife, but we ain't doing a thing to Stick Hanley's kid. No fuckin' way, Sal," Timbo shot back. "I ain't gonna be no part of killin' my ex-partner's kid. No way. No how."

"You forget you're in this shit as deep as the rest of us, Timbo," Abbatti corrected him. "You've been taking Pick's money, too."

"So that's it," Brian said, nodding his head. "Cops have been taking the guns off the streets of Chicago and having Pick here pawn them down in Mexico for cash and meth. Our task force couldn't figure out where these arms were coming from, why the flow never seemed to stop. But now it all makes sense. Bust the crooks in Chicago, confiscate their weapons, then sell them outside the country. All with the help of Chicago's finest. Dad would roll over in his grave!"

"Hey. Your dad was no saint, son," Abbatti said. "And he wasn't as sharp as everyone thought. Except you're sharper than your old man. Aren't you?" He got up close to Brian. "You see, if it wasn't for your father, Pick and his gang would have been found guilty of killing Manny Fleischman. But, lucky for all of them, your old man fucked up the investigation."

Brian remained silent as he stared down Abbatti, eye to eye.

"What are you talking about?" asked Stan.

Abbatti looked at Stan. "You know very well what I'm talking about, James. He never took you back to the scene of the crime before the trial. After the attack, he had the gang's escape route all ass backwards. He didn't listen to you *or* me. Neither did this fat fuck, Timbo." Abbatti nodded toward the big ex-detective. "Hanley and Boscorelli. The two hotshot detectives from Area 1. The dynamic fuckin' duo never presented the notes I took at the scene of the crime at trial. I was the first officer to respond." Abbatti turned to Brian now. "Your father looked at my notes and my sketch when he met me at the scene. I had suggested Fleischman's body might have been dragged by the killers. He dismissed my theory. Figured I was just a rookie and what the fuck would I know. Your old man didn't realize he fucked up until the judge brought everyone to the crime scene right during the middle of the trial. Turns out James here shows them how Fleischman was attacked north of the overpass, not south of it where we found his body.

Stick's testimony contradicted that of his eyewitness. No one spec-ulated the old man could have had enough strength left in him to drag himself nearly fifty yards, trying to get to the payphone." He turned back and looked at Stan once again. "Ain't that right, James?"

Cracking his knuckles, Stan didn't answer, but Brian didn't re-main silent.

"So you turn dirty, Sal, because your ego was bruised? What kind of excuse is that?"

"Shut up, Brian. What would you know? You were never a beat cop. I busted my ass to make detectives like your old man and Boscorelli here look good. I never got the glory the homicide cops did, never got the headlines. And what about narc guys? They skim cash and drugs on nearly every bust. I figured if I couldn't beat 'em, I'd join 'em. When this opportunity came along to work with Pick and make some cash, I figured what the fuck did I care if these guns ended up in Mexico. All I know is they weren't on the streets of Chicago anymore."

"You're pathetic," Brian told him.

"Enough of this banter. Pick," Abbatti ordered, "you and With-erspoon take Hanley and the cab driver and dump them some-where down in Indiana. Make sure you're not followed. Timbo and I will take care of James and the Mrs. here—the 'lost tourists from Arizona.'"

"No, Sal. It stops here. Right now," Timbo said, pulling his serv-ice revolver from under his coat.

Startled by Timbo's move, everyone turned their attention to him. As they did, Maxine bolted forward and karate kicked Pick in his groin with a full roundhouse move. He went down like a prize-fighter before getting the ten-count. Witherspoon cracked Max-ine on the back of her head with the butt of his gun. As she slumped to the ground, Stan rushed to her aid.

During the commotion, Clayton Thomas jumped on the fallen Pick and wrestled with him, trying to pry the knife out of his hand. Clayton and Pick grappled on the wet grass as the senator strug-gled to get the six-inch switchblade from the wiry Pick.

Witherspoon was raising his weapon to aim at the senator as

Brian jumped on his back, knocking him to the ground. As Witherspoon went down, a weapon discharged. Simultaneously, the wrestling on the ground ceased. Clayton lay underneath Pick, staring into the cold night air, a blank look in his glassy eyes. Pick pushed himself up off of Clayton, pulling his blade from the senator's belly as he did. Blood splashed like a park water fountain up to Pick's elbow.

"That'll teach that motherfucker! Now, you're next!" Now on his feet, Pick lunged at Stan, blade raised high above his head. Stan still knelt, cradling his unconscious wife.

Before Stan could react, two quick gunshots echoed against the granite base of the monument. Pick's body spun before it slumped over one of the headstones of the Union soldiers, the bloody switchblade still clenched in his hand.

Each bullet from the retired Chicago police officer's service revolver hit their mark squarely in the front of the ex-gangbanger's head.

Timbo holstered his weapon and dropped down over the senator. "Sal. Call an ambulance," he shouted as he applied pressure to the gash in Clayton's belly, "I can't stop the bleeding." Timbo shouted out again to Abbatti, "Sal, radio a bus to get in here quick!"

When no reply came from Abbatti, Timbo looked up and saw the police commander a few feet away, lying face down on the ground in a pool of his own blood.

CHAPTER 46

It had been two weeks since Stan Kobe returned from his first trip to Chicago after being placed into the witness protection program over thirty years ago. His plan to bring federal conspiracy charges never needed to be leveled against Monroe "Pick" Clarke since Clarke had died at the base of the Confederate Mound in Oak Woods Cemetery from two gunshot wounds inflicted by retired Chicago Police Detective Timothy Boscorelli. Boscorelli, it was later revealed, had been working undercover for the FBI, investigating a money laundering and border smuggling operation the federal agency had suspected was operating within Chicago's 3rd Ward and 21st Police District.

Tyrone Witherspoon, Pick's partner in crime for nearly thirty-five years, was charged with the murder of Prairie District Police Commander Sal Abbatti after an autopsy showed it was a bullet from Witherspoon's gun that killed the highly decorated veteran cop. Additionally, charges of aggravated assault, kidnapping, and a variety of other felony charges, were leveled against Witherspoon and Chicago 3rd Ward Alderman, Bertrand Rhodes. The two former Oakwood Rangers gang members were awaiting separate trials.

Shortly after, an announcement was made by the multiagency federal task force of the Arizona arrests of Pokie Turner and Bobby DeSadier. The two were charged with conspiring to transport contraband across the U.S. border. But they would not be brought to trial on those federal charges until the Gila Indian Reservation finished their own investigation against the pair. Gila Reservation Police Chief Jimmy Nejo was quoted as saying the following, during a Phoenix television news interview he had given:

"The investigation could take many, many more months to complete due to our backload here on the reservation, and due to our woefully understaffed resources for this type of legal matter. Until then, the two will remain indefinitely in our custody."

Salvatore Joseph Abbatti was buried with full police department honors, which brought representatives to his funeral services from over sixty law enforcement agencies, covering a three-state region. According to the news bulletin heard over Chicago's WGN News Radio the morning after his death, the on-scene reporter had told the listening audience the following in his live report:

> Commander Salvatore Abbatti, a thirty-year veteran of the Chicago Police Department, was killed in the line of duty during a failed mugging attempt on a group of unsuspecting, out-of-state tourists near the entrance of Oak Woods Cemetery near 67th and Ellis Avenue, where I am reporting from now. Details are sketchy, but it seems Commander Abbatti was riding in the limousine of Senator Clayton R. Thomas along with the senator. The limousine's driver, who wishes to remain anonymous, noticed two tourists—also wishing to remain anonymous—in distress. Evidently, both Abbatti and Thomas at that point exited the vehicle and intervened on behalf of the wayward tourists, who were leaving the cemetery after having visited there. Abbatti was shot once in the chest by one of the assailants, as yet still unidentified, at point-blank range and died at the scene. Senator Thomas suffered a severe knife wound and was rushed to Providence Hospital and remains there in critical but stable condition.
>
> Additionally, an as-yet-still-unidentified retired Chicago police officer, providing security for the

senator, was evidently trailing the senator's limousine in an unmarked car. It was this man who shot to death the other mugger, identified by Area 1 homicide detectives as Monroe "Pick" Clarke. Clarke, a former P. Stone Rangers gang member, most recently worked in a community liaison role for the 3rd Ward Democratic Committee. Some listeners may remember Clarke as one of five defendants who were found not guilty more than thirty years ago in the murder trial of Manny Fleischman. That trial made headlines back in the mid-seventies when Clarke and his gang were accused of attacking Fleischman, the last surviving member of the infamous nineteen-nineteen Chicago Black Sox team. Ironically, the deceased Fleischman is buried in Oak Woods Cemetery, not far from where Clarke met his fate.

This is Dean Richards reporting. Back to you in the studio.

As Stan Kobe sat in the cool morning sun that washed the backyard patio of his Scottsdale home, he sipped hot tea and read the newspaper. He felt reborn, as if his life was his again. He felt free for the first time in three decades. His recent visit to his hometown had redeemed the spirit he held so dear *travelin'* up and down the lakefront of Lake Michigan. Now, he was happy with who he was, with whom he had become—a husband, a father, a friend, a fighter for justice. That feeling of true happiness had been completely foreign to him for most of his life. Now, joy was the only word that could express how he felt.

The *Arizona Republic* had been featuring a special series on the federal and state governments' latest effort to crack down on the smuggling of guns across the U.S. border, detailing the arming of drug lords in the Mexican state of Sonora. As Stan read that day's final installment, the piece related the story of the capture of the largest shipment of methamphetamines and guns ever seized under an initiative coordinated by local Arizona law enforcement agencies and federal authorities under the guidance of the Department of Homeland Security.

The article quoted the Chair of the Senate Committee on Homeland Security and Governmental Affairs thusly:

> . . . and thanks to the coordinated efforts of a multiagency task force spearheaded by some of Arizona's finest law enforcers, we are stopping the flow of drugs, guns, and human contraband across our southern border.
>
> And, I would be remiss, I believe, if I didn't mention that I am, as I think all Americans should be, deeply indebted to the individual efforts of my fellow Homeland Security committee member from the great state of Illinois, Senator Clayton R. Thomas, who recently personally risked his own life by nearly single-handedly thwarting a mugging attempt on two tourists to his city where, sadly, a Chicago police officer was killed. We pray for Senator Thomas's own continued successful recovery and thank him for his indefatigable patriotism. It is this type of unselfish service in upholding the ideals of our country which makes me firmly believe will make him an outstanding candidate for the next president of the United States.

"What you readin', hon?" Maxine asked her husband, kissing him on the top of his head before she took a seat across from him.

Stan smiled back at her without looking up, contentment showering his face. "Oh, just looking at the sports page," he replied, folding the paper in two. "I see here where it looks like Paul Konerko signed a big contract extension with the Chicago White Sox. I just love to see a Scottsdale boy do good."

Maxine smiled. "Well, Konerko may be a 'Scottsdale boy' who's done good, but I've got a 'Scottsdale man' who's done even better."

Although still considered by Arizonans to be "Maricopa

County's Most Ruthless Prosecutor," the rejuvenated Stan Kobe much rather preferred the title given him in a headline two days earlier by the *Chicago Defender*. The Bronzeville-based newspaper, renowned as the first, major all-black newspaper in the country, had named him to its list of the top 100 outstanding black achievers in its 100th anniversary edition. A copy of the tabloid's front page lay on the desk in his home office, proclaiming in its headline:

JAMES OVERSTREET SELECTED
BRONZEVILLES'S #1 FAVORITE SON

AUTHOR'S NOTE

This is a work of fiction. All the characters and events portrayed in this book are fictitious, and any resemblance to real people or events is purely coincidental. Although a work of fiction, the framework for the murder in the story was loosely based upon a true crime, which happened in July 1979, along the lakefront in Chicago's Burnham Park. In that case, an elderly man, riding his bicycle, was attacked by a gang of four youths. The attack, which resulted in the death of the victim, was witnessed by a boy who later came forward and testified for the prosecution. A Cook County Juvenile Court trial ensued and the attackers were found not guilty. The eyewitness was placed into protective custody and never heard from again.

ACKNOWLEDGMENTS

Many people have helped me on my miraculous journey to publication and within the restraints of these pages all cannot possibly be thanked.

To my sixth-grade writing partner, the late Danny Dietrich, who showed me not to be afraid of using my imagination.

To my writing mentor, Deb Ledford, whose unselfish dedication to the craft, keen editing skills, industry insights, and unending patience was nothing short of inspiring.

Virginia Nosky taught me the craft of writing and how to move story forward. Other Scottsdale Writers' Group members Ron Barnes, Brenda Boychuk, Mary Burt, Keridwen Cornelius, Michael Greenwald, Loreen Hoover, Heidi Horchler, Leslie Kohler, Bill Levy, Seth Page, and the late Terry Charuhas—each contributed in their own special way.

Meeting retired Chicago Police Homicide Detective Andrew Abbott was one of many serendipitous events in my journey. His generous offer to consult on police procedures was a remarkably unselfish gesture as was his determination to prevent inaccuracies. A million thanks, Andy.

My children—Regina, Dominic, Della, and Anna—have been with me for every step of my creative journey. You inspired me more than you'll ever know. Thanks Brian Rahberger and Sean Kemp, too.

My grandson, Jordan Rahberger, gets special mention for submitting the key idea for the book's jacket design, expertly interpreted and executed by George Foster. Thanks, you two.

My dear friends, Terry Tinney Cipolletti and her husband,

Mike, provided input on the story's plot development. You two are the greatest. Thank you, too, Jane Vazzana.

The following people were priceless in their own specific way: Geri Whowell, Meghan Murphy, Phil and Nora Barnicle, Deb Horne, Naomi and Bob Bajda, Eileen and Rick Hoagland, Vicky Ottenfeld, Debbie and Chuck Taylor and the very special, Deb Simanski. Thanks goes out to Skip's Crew in Williams Bay, Wisconsin.

Libraries were invaluable in helping me create *Identity: Lost*. Paula Crossman, Arabian Library, Scottsdale, Arizona, gave outstanding professional help; to Nancy Krei and her friendly staff at The Village of Fontana (Wisconsin) Public Library; and to the entire research staff at the Lake Geneva (Wisconsin) Public Library. Please support your local library.

Other key people were Tammy Vavra at Arizona State University's School of Law; ASU's Gary Lowenthal, my point person as I developed the original legal structure of the novel; and Federal Public Defender Donna Elm, who unselfishly devoted many hours helping me keep the story legally on track as well as to assure its stark realism.

To Jim Nasella, my former high school English teacher, for sparking my desire to create.

To Mike Bobko, Tony Byrnes, Joe Danzl, Dyanne Greer, Kris Lehmann, Richard Siegel, John Tuchi, and Marilyn Lester for enthusiastic help and input. And to Ray Carl, too. Your loving support was a godsend as was support from Rees Candee.

Sam Barone unknowingly inspired me to believe an Italian kid who's never written fiction before could be good at it if he put his nose to the grindstone, listened to suggestions, and never gave up.

If it weren't for Patricia and Robert Gussin you would not be reading my words on the printed pages here today. Their belief in me has been one of the greatest gifts ever received. Thank you, Pat and Bob. Special thanks to editor, Susan Hayes.

Finally, three people have had a profound impact upon my life and my writing, first, Mike Cronin: your voice and passion for all things creative has been a life-long inspiration to me. Next, Bettina Chiarmonte Gosselin: you believed in my ability to write a story that would capture the uniqueness of our hometown, Chicago. Your enduring friendship is cherished and your consistent encouragement throughout the process will never be forgotten. *Molto grazie, signora.*

Finally, I now know the fullest meaning of the word muse. For forty years Karen Cronin Marco has been my lighthouse beacon, showing me the way, keeping me from crashing against the rocks. I fell in love with her the first day I saw her. She is without doubt the finest person I've ever met and knowing her has been the greatest privilege of my life. She is my best friend. A persevering life coach, this book is the culmination of her relentless belief in me and the good she has always seen in me that I never saw in myself. I will never be able to thank her enough.